GIRL NUMBER ONE

Jane Holland

THIMBLERIG BOOKS

First published in 2015 by THIMBLERIG BOOKS,
Holsworthy, England

ISBN-10: 1517410649
ISBN-13: 978-1517410643

For my brother Michael

Other Publications by Jane Holland

Fiction

KISSING THE PINK
MIRANDA

Poetry

BRIEF HISTORY OF A DISREPUTABLE WOMAN
BOUDICCA & CO
CAMPER VAN BLUES
THE WANDERER
ON WARWICK
FLASH BANG: NEW & SELECTED POEMS

Jane Holland also writes fiction as:

Beth Good
Victoria Lamb
Elizabeth Moss

ACKNOWLEDGEMENTS

My grateful thanks to Luigi and to Lesley, the first readers of my debut thriller, for their expert suggestions and enthusiasm, and to Steve, my husband, who has worked patiently with me through numerous painstaking drafts. Thanks also to those readers who have sought out this novel and will hopefully enjoy reading it as much as I enjoyed writing it.

Life, I have found, is like a novel, in that it does not always go according to plan. But we make of it what we can – and must – in order to keep going in the right direction, even where the path grows a little narrow.

PROLOGUE

I know Mummy's dead. But I have to check. You always have to check, right?

Kneeling beside the perfectly still body, I stare up through the trees, watching the flash of white trainers disappear.

I hear a crack of twigs as he makes his way higher up the slope. He's not really hurrying. There's no other sound except the nearby stream. Even the birds have stopped singing.

Maybe he's going to come back.

'Mum?'

She does not move when I touch her cheek. Her throat looks red and swollen. I guess that's where he grabbed her and squeezed. Squeezed until she stopped struggling. Her eyes are wide, staring up into the leafy branches that sway gently above us.

I should never have run away. Perhaps I could have done something. Perhaps I could have stopped him.

But Mummy yelled at me, 'Run, Ellie! Run and hide!'

Then he grabbed her.

I ran like he was coming after me too. I ran gasping and crying. Brambles scratched my face, tore at my clothes. Then I stopped, lost and defeated in the unfamiliar undergrowth, and loped slowly back towards the stream. Because where could I go without Mummy? What could I do on my own?

I'm old enough to understand what death is. I kneel beside her for a long time, leafy twigs pressing painfully into my knees. There's one bird still singing in the trees above us. Its hoarse repeated cry was like a warning before. Now it sounds like it's laughing at me. I don't look up.

I take her limp hand and squeeze it hard, waiting for her to wake up, to start breathing again, to smile at me and tell me everything will be all right. But it doesn't happen. It will never happen again.

'Mum?' I whisper, bending close to her face. 'Mummy?'

In a minute, I will drop her hand and run.

CHAPTER ONE

I remember what day it is even before the alarm on my phone goes off.

My eyes are still closed, my mind fighting its way back from the suffocating world of my nightmare. I wait for the alarm tone, aware that it's coming, the way you know a storm's on the horizon. The tiny hairs have risen on my skin, one arm angled stiffly above the pillow, the other dangling out of bed as though pointing to the floor. I'm frozen in that position, my body still partially asleep at some level. But my brain is alert and suffering.

It's like waking up on a birthday and immediately thinking, *today is going to be wonderful, today is going to be special.*

Only it's the reverse situation. Like a photographic negative. Today is going to be special alright. But it's not going to be wonderful. It is going to be bad. Very, very bad.

Something shifts me out of sleep. Memory clicks back into place, as it does every morning, and suddenly I'm properly awake, totally in the moment.

Ground zero.

I've spent years in therapy, I know what to do when all the colour bleeds from the world. I take a few deep breaths and run through what the doctor used to call my 'blessings'. The good things in life. This cottage, my job. My friends, the ones that have stuck with me and not fallen away since university. But I still feel the darkness beckoning. Not much, just a vague sensation of …

The alarm sounds.

Rolling over, I fumble for my phone, turn off the alarm, swing myself out of bed.

Deal with it, Eleanor.

Not bothering to look in the mirror, I drag a comb through my shoulder-length hair, then twist it up into a rough ponytail. No shower yet. That can come later, after my run. It's not like anyone will see me in the woods. Not at this hour.

7am.

I pick up my mobile, check it for new messages. A reminder from Jenny about end of term festivities. I hesitate over it, then flick past. I resent having to think about work when I'm not actually there, which makes marking books a nightmare.

A late reply from Tris to my text sent just before midnight. By which time I had downed several glasses of rum and coke, and was undressing for bed.

Planning to run through the woods tomorrow. As a salute to my mum.

His reply, sent at 1.45am, is terse. *Don't. Not a good idea.*

Chicken, I text back, then press Send.

Still nothing from Denzil about next weekend, which irritates me more than it should. We've dated a few times, in a non-committal way. It's not like we have any kind of special arrangement. We were so close in school though. I wonder if he finds me boring now that I'm a teacher and no longer lurching from one adolescent drama to the next.

Vaguely disappointed, I toss the mobile back onto the bed. The woods at Eastlyn are a notorious signal blind spot, so a phone is dead weight on a run there.

I wriggle into black Lycra shorts and a white tee-shirt

with a bold red Nike logo. Drag on my new pair of Mizuno trainers and lace them up. Open my bedroom door. The house is quiet. Hannah must have come home while I was sleeping and gone straight to bed.

A quick trip to the bathroom. Toilet and teeth. Hands still damp, I tiptoe past Hannah's room, then down the stairs, carefully avoiding the step that creaks. Since she started to work nights at the hospital, my early morning runs have become an issue and I'm keen not to get into an argument with her again.

Not today.

Out in the lane, the air feels sultry and shut-in, the sky drawn tight across the cottage roof. Migraine weather, Hannah calls it. The sun may be shining in our little part of the world but dark clouds from the moors are already on the edge of the valley, promising rain later.

I stretch out my hamstrings, then swing my arms up and down to warm up. Ten times forward, ten times back. Shrug my shoulders a few times, roll my head slowly round to the left, then back to the right.

I head off towards the village at a gentle warm-up pace, pretending not to consider which route to take even though there's nothing else in my head today.

About half a mile down the lane, the road runs past the gated entrance to what used to be our farm, once upon a time, but is now a partial ruin. Renovation work that was started years ago still lies unfinished, the roof flapping with poorly secured plastic. There's a thin black cat crouched on top of the old piggery, staring malevolently in my direction, ears flattened on its head.

I stride out, beginning to run.

The decision is made, I realise. I'm going through the woods today, not the village. I need to live for the future.

Mist is rising slowly in Tinker's Field, obscuring the legs of the black-and-white cows grazing there. Crossing the road that leads up to the village, I pause for a noisy diesel van hurtling down the hill at standard Cornish breakneck speed. WOODS VALLEY GARDEN CENTRE is written on the side in large green lettering.

The driver's window is open, music blaring out. Dick Laney is at the wheel, owner of the garden centre, bearded, middle-aged and compact. He's wearing work overalls, so I guess he's on a delivery.

He raises a hand to me. 'Morning, Eleanor.'

I nod. 'Morning.'

His son, Jago, is in the passenger seat. He was at the local school with me, though we were never close and have not seen each other for ages. He looks at me without smiling.

When the van has passed, I cross into the sunlit meadow and keep running. The grass half-obscuring the path to the woods has not been cut this year and is almost knee-high now. But I don't mind, threading my way through with pleasure, flicking the bright, rustling grasses on either side.

Running is a ritual, and one I've grown to love over the years. To be able to shut out everything else in your life for an hour and concentrate solely on your body, your technique, your stamina. That's the beauty of running. It purges the soul.

That's why even on a bad day, on the worst day imaginable, even a day like today, I still need to run.

There is someone else in the woods today.

I often get that feeling, to be fair. The sensation of being watched when I run or spied on through windows at the cottage. Like there's someone out there, keeping me under observation. It's just nerves, my therapist used to say; a lively imagination playing tricks on me.

Today feels different though. Like it's real, not imagined. Today my skin is prickling as soon as I vault the stile from the meadow, before I'm even ten feet into the woods. There's a physical edge to the sensation of being watched. Like it's three-dimensional.

At first I try to ignore the feeling, pumping air with my arms, checking that I'm striking the ground toe-first, not heel-first, the way you're supposed to.

I hear a crack of twigs behind me, and glance round, frowning. But the wooded slopes are empty.

The woods feel unthreatening here, still so close to the meadow and the main road into the village. On sunny days like these, light slips through gaps in the leaves, soft and dappled, to give the woods an almost magical air. I often catch a glimpse of fleeing brown rabbits on these morning runs, or the occasional grey squirrel watching me from halfway up a mossed trunk. Most days, I prefer to skirt the edge of the meadow rather than enter the woods. I often head up towards the moor and enjoy the wide-open vistas there instead. But today is special. And I've made up my mind, for better or worse.

The deeper I move into the wood, the more the air becomes curiously still, maybe even claustrophobic. There is no chukking of alarm from the birds today, no odd rustles in the undergrowth. Even the sound of the stream below seems muffled.

My mother used to love running in these woods. I don't remember much about her, and can only picture her face from having studied old photographs. But I know she loved running, and where, because my father used to mention it whenever I went out for a jog.

Not surprisingly, he always hated me going anywhere near these woods.

I can understand the pull of this place. The woods nestle secretively beneath the village church, curving round the hill like a dragon's tail, dark green in the sunlight. The trees stretch for several miles of shady paths, birds clattering among the leaves, and a noisy stream at the bottom. It's beautiful and peaceful, popular with walkers and runners alike, especially in the summer.

Another tiny cracking sound.

All in your imagination. Don't look to left or right. Head down and keep running.

My trainers are beginning to squelch in the mud. Last night's rainfall hasn't helped the dampness of the woodland paths. But I'm nearly at the dip. The dip is where the path divides, one descending narrowly to the stream, the other broader and more welcoming, rising into sunlight once it hits the road above.

I push on round the next bend, keeping out of the muddy morass in this shady part of the wood.

And slither to a halt.

There's a sign blocking the path ahead.

A large metal sign, legs sunk in mud, leaning slightly at an angle, bold yellow lettering on a red background.

PATH AHEAD CLOSED
FOLLOW DIVERSION

The white arrow beneath points downhill towards the stream. The path is narrow and very steep, and I can see from here that it's badly overgrown.

I study the metal sign again, my chest suddenly tight. It takes an effort to persuade my fists to loosen, my breathing to slow down. I look around, gauging the stillness of the woods, the solitude. This sign is unexpected, yes. But not even remotely suspicious. I'm doing it again; I'm over-reacting, letting the past win.

It's nothing.

The main path is closed, so I have to take the diversion. I start to run again. Not back the way I've come but down towards the stream. Taking the path I haven't taken in years. The path I still see in my nightmares.

The path that has always been waiting for me.

It's strange how the years have changed my perspective of the place. In my memory, trees crowded this narrow track, branches dipping overhead, leaning in to block my view, some of the trunks rotten and decayed, roots barely clinging to the soil. But the slopes are not as overgrown as they once were. Perhaps as a terrified six-year-old, the trees seemed closer-set, the undergrowth darker and more threatening.

Further along, the track begins to wander and deteriorate. This is more like the dangerous territory I remember, the lost ground where the worst could – and once did – happen. Here, the edges of the path blur into undergrowth. The earth banks are mossed, riddled with muddied hollows and the tracks of deer. Some of the trunks on the bank are scarred where deer have rubbed against them on their way down to the stream.

I am light-headed at the risk I am taking. The risk to my sanity. What would Dr Quick say?

Nothing in life is without risk.

I no longer see Dr Quick, of course. I decided some years ago that I had outgrown therapy and told her I didn't want any more sessions. To my surprise she did not push the issue. Perhaps she thought, as I did, that it was time to move on.

I glance up, startled by a rustling above me and to the right. Catch a flash of white between tree trunks.

There's someone else running on the heavily wooded slope above this path. It's the merest flicker through shadowy trees: a momentary glimpse into insanity, like a little white rabbit that appears for a second, then vanishes down a rabbit hole.

White trainers.

That's when I lower my gaze, and realise there is something on the path ahead of me.

Or someone.

'What the hell?' My heart is galloping and I can't seem to catch my breath. Panic swells like a balloon in my chest.

I struggle to clamp it down, to remember my breathing exercises. I know the signs of a panic attack and how to control them. I must be calm and logical, go through the drills Dr Quick taught me. But I can't seem to reach that state anymore. I'm past logic; I'm locked out of it and into nightmare.

I slow down, staring.

The assailant is described as tall and well-built, wearing brown leather gloves, dark tracksuit and white trainers.

That was the only description of my mother's killer we ever had. Because a six-year-old was the only one to see him.

CHAPTER TWO

I'm running again. Only this time it's for my life.

Tree branches slash my cheek, brambles tear at my legs with their sharp green thorns. Stumbling over uneven ground, I plunge to my knees, deep in a patch of tall, deep-green plants, their soft heads bowed around me. For a moment all I can hear is the loud rasp of my breath, the erratic thud of my heart.

I register pain. There's a smell of damp, musty leaves in my nostrils now. Something fresh with something rotting.

I clamber back up with stinging hands and legs. Fumble for a trunk to lean on while I catch my breath. Then I keep running.

Reaching the village of Eastlyn, the first person I see is the vicar. He's smoking a cigarette with a hunched air, his Jack Russell running about his feet near the back of the church.

Reverend Mortimer Clemo is in his early fifties, tall and loose-limbed. Innocuous enough, but I've never warmed to him, perhaps because I don't like churches. His once-dark hair is part silver now, razored round the nape of his neck. He's wearing black jeans today and the obligatory short-sleeved black shirt-front with white dog collar, plus a pair of muddied wellington boots. His last name, Clemo, is pronounced 'Kleemo' in one of those quirks of Cornish pronunciation. It's a common name in these parts.

Across the path from the church, I notice the back door to the vicarage has been wedged open with a garden gnome. One of the red-cheeked sort with a fishing rod and a plastic grin.

The vicar looks startled when I explode out of the undergrowth and come stumbling towards him across the grass verge as though straining for a finish line.

'Eleanor.' He glances past me as though expecting to see a pursuer. Or perhaps a running companion. 'On your own?'

Everyone knows everyone else in our village. Apart from the second-homers, that is, who are only there a few months in the summer anyway, and the few people who drift in and out of rented accommodation without wanting to get involved in village life. It was Reverend Clemo who officiated at my mother's funeral. Her quiet plot is a short distance up the hill in the cemetery – that's where they bury everyone now the old churchyard is full.

'Eleanor?' he repeats, looking me up and down, beginning to frown. 'Is something wrong?'

I can see what he's thinking. My flyaway brown hair, never inclined to do what I tell it, has come loose from its ponytail. My trainers are wet from running through the stream. One of my laces has come undone and is flapping behind me. I'm breathless and making a squelching sound with every step.

'I'm fine,' I lie, panting.

His Jack Russell trots over on stubby legs to sniff at my ankles. I bend to pat his head, and he dances around me with sharp staccato barks, eager and excited, perhaps sensing that something out of the ordinary has happened.

I push the hair back from my face with a shaking hand. That's when I notice the cuts. A crisscross of thin bleeding cuts on my hands and bare forearms, probably on my face too. I can feel my right cheek stinging.

Brambles.

I look down and my legs are red-raw with tiny white bumps. As soon as I see them, I'm aware of the pain. It feels as though I've been stung by hundreds of furious wasps.

Reverend Clemo has noticed the marks too. He studies my legs, then his dark narrowed gaze rises to my face, slowly enough to make me uncomfortable.

'Are you sure you're all right? Perhaps you should come into the vicarage and sit down for a while, catch your breath.' His frown deepens. 'It looks like you've had a nasty fall in the woods. Stung yourself. We have a first aid kit in the house. Let me call my wife.'

My mind flashes back to what I saw on the path.

'No,' I mumble through lips that feel oddly swollen. Did I sting my face too? 'Thanks, Rev, but I have to go. Sorry.'

I break into another ungainly run, heading past him and away from the church. I am making instinctively for Jenny Crofter's house, though I'm not sure why. Too far to get home quickly, I suppose. And her place has always felt like a safe house.

The vicar calls after me, 'Please, Eleanor, at least let me call someone to come and pick you up. You're not yourself.'

You're not yourself.

That makes me smile. I keep running and don't look back.

I haven't been myself for years.

I thud past the black-timbered kissing-gate that opens onto the path to the church door, then swing left onto the main road through the village. Nobody in view. But it's still early. Not even the school kids are out, waiting for the lumbering bus that will take them through half a dozen sleeping villages before it reaches the school. I remember the route well; I took the bus often enough as a girl.

My trainers sound loud on the tarmac.

Jenny Crofter's house is at the end of the row. She's about thirty but still lives with her parents in this whitewashed bungalow with its small unfenced garden and seven wooden steps up from the roadside.

I stumble up the steps and along the garden path, past an untidy bank of hutches, some standing on top of each other, filled with fat, lop-eared rabbits. Jenny's father breeds rabbits. He keeps a mating pair of ferrets too, apart from the rest; one silver-bellied sable ferret is standing against the wire on its hind legs, probably the male. The animal watches with narrowed eyes as I pant up to the front door and lean on the bell.

Jenny opens the door, a piece of half-eaten toast in her hand. She's a little shorter than me, about five foot six or seven, with dark-brown hair cut radically short and a lean, athletic figure. Typical PE teacher build, in other words. Her tracksuit is navy with a white stripe, functional-looking, not leisure wear in disguise, with a dark blue tee-shirt underneath.

She's wearing blue and white trainers, bog-standard Nike. There are traces of dried mud on both. The heavy industrial mud you get outdoors in this part of Cornwall, thick and cruddy; a hazard of running anywhere around the village. I expect my own Mizuno pair look even worse after today's little adventure in the woods.

Jenny is surprised to see me. She takes in my expression, then her eyes widen. Exactly the same way the vicar's did when he saw me. 'Eleanor? What's the matter, what's happened?'

'Going to be sick.' I clamp a hand over my mouth, and Jenny stands aside.

'Upstairs,' she orders me.

There's no time to look grateful. I run past her and straight up the stairs, where I nearly collide with her mother on the landing. Sue Crofter. She's just come out of one of the bedrooms, belting her worn dressing gown with a distracted air. Her thin dark hair hasn't been brushed yet and is still matted at the back from her pillow.

I can see past her shoulder into the bedroom. Inside, she's drawn back the curtains and daylight is streaming in across the double bed, crumpled and empty. Presumably her husband is already out at work.

'Sorry, Sue,' I mutter, darting past her into the bathroom.

I'm in such a hurry I don't even shut the bathroom door, just toss up the pale avocado toilet lid and drop to my knees.

Afterwards, I lean on the cold toilet rim for a few minutes, gasping and trying not to heave anymore.

'Eleanor?'

I open my eyes and see the wet wipe being held out to me. 'Thanks, Jenny.'

'That's okay.' She sounds sympathetic but wary too. 'Take your time. There's a bin next to the loo. For the wipe.'

I clean my face quickly and surreptitiously, then chuck the wet wipe in the designated bin. It's green, presumably to coordinate with the rest of the fittings. There's something wonderfully ordinary and a bit shabby about everything in Jenny's house. It's a narrow, old-fashioned bathroom with an avocado bath and toilet suite, and plain white tiles on the walls. The tired-looking bath mat is fern-green, matching the towels draped over the side of the bath and arranged neatly in a metal display unit under the window.

Everything is green, in fact, except for the shower curtain which is see-through plastic decorated with rows of yellow ducks. Waiting to be shot, I always think.

When I straighten up, Jenny is still there, blocking the doorway. 'I'll ring the school,' she announces, 'let Patricia know you're not well enough to work today.'

'Thanks.'

'And you can't walk home in that state. I'll run you back to the farm on my way to the school.'

'I'm happy to walk.'

'Nonsense.' Her mother is peering in. Jenny shuts the bathroom door and stands with her back against it, arms folded. 'What the hell's going on, Eleanor? This isn't a stomach bug, is it?'

'No.'

I bend over the sink to splash my face with cold water. I'm desperate to brush my teeth too but can't until I get home. I'd have to ask if I could borrow Jenny's toothbrush, and that would be too grim for words. I swill my mouth out with cold water instead, and try to tidy my hair in the mirror.

'Fuck, have you seen your legs?'

I look down. 'Yes.'

'Nettle stings?'

'Looks like it,' I agree.

'I'll get you some antiseptic cream.' She rummages in the cupboard and produces an old tube of antiseptic cream, not quite squeezed out. I apply it gingerly to both legs, hissing with pain. Jenny fusses about me, trying to help. 'Christ, you're covered in the bloody things. You must have fallen in a massive nettle patch.'

'I don't really remember.'

'Your wrists too. And your hands. Are these cuts?'

'Bramble thorns, I think.'

I wipe the excess cream off my sore palms, then wash them, and swill out my mouth again. The smell of the antiseptic cream is making me feel sick again.

'So?' Jenny hands me a thick green towel, staring at me. 'Come on, I want the truth. What in God's name has happened?'

I dry my face and hands meticulously, not looking at her. 'I went into the woods before breakfast.'

'Running?'

I nod. 'The usual path was closed. There was a sign up, with a diversion. So I had to take the lower path. You know, the overgrown one that goes down towards the stream?'

'Oh shit.'

She understands at once.

I bury my face in the soft green towel, though my skin is dry now. I listen to my breathing in the darkness, the judder of my heart. This would be a bad moment to go wrong. I run through it all again, like a checklist, make sure of my facts before I say anything more. What I saw, what I thought, what I did.

When I emerge from the towel, Jenny is still staring at me, her expression sympathetic.

I know that look. She thinks I've had an episode. A flashback or a nervous breakdown or something. And it does feel like that. Except for the details, the reality of it all. But how to tell my story without sounding crazy?

'There was a woman lying near the stream. Right across the path. She was ... '

I have to finish but I'm afraid of the word. Afraid of what it means.

She interrupts, frowning. 'Look – '

'Jenny, she was *dead*.'

CHAPTER THREE

After I finally ring the police, then endure a fraught three-minute phone conversation with a sleepy and disorientated Hannah, Jenny insists on driving me home.

'Come on,' she says, flinging open the passenger door for me. 'I know I'm running late now, but it's barely five minutes out of my way. And the school will understand.'

I don't argue.

I want to get back to the cottage quickly so I can grab some breakfast and try to make myself comfortable. There may even be time for a quick shower before the police arrive, if it's not too callous to be thinking about bodily hygiene at a time like this. Besides, I want to explain to Hannah exactly what happened in the woods, not just give her the gruesome highlights, which was all I could manage with Sue hanging round the kitchen during my phone call, earwigging like mad.

Then there's my dad to consider. He too will have to be told, though I don't relish the thought.

Not today.

As Jenny pulls sharply away from the kerb, I tighten my seat belt and hang onto the door as a precaution. Her driving has never been good. Jenny Crofter came to work at the secondary school when I was still there as a sixth former. When I came back to Cornwall and landed my first job as a newly qualified teacher at my old school, she offered me a daily lift into work in exchange for the occasional tankful of fuel. It did make sense, both of us living in the same village. But I value my life too much, so said, 'No thanks,' then bought a scooter to tide me over until I can afford my own car.

I do occasionally accept a lift from Jenny though, when it's unavoidable.

Like today.

Her driving seems more aggressive than ever. No doubt the news of a dead woman in the woods where Jenny likes to go running has not improved her mood. She accelerates when the road looks clear, then brakes wildly at every corner, throwing us either forward or sideways, or both at the same time. It's true though that visibility is never good here, especially in spring and summer when the steep banks are crowded with grasses and wild flowers, the Cornish hedgerows abundant with delicate pink campion, bluebells and the purple spikes of foxgloves. I never really noticed the hedgerows until I got interested in botany at university; now I can name most of the wild flowers along the verges.

Jenny glances at me sideways, which worries me. I wish she would keep her eyes on the road. 'How's Hannah?'

'She sounded a bit shaken on the phone, but I'm sure she'll get over it. Hannah's bombproof.'

'I mean, is she well? I haven't seen her in a while. Is she still working nights at the hospital?'

'Yes.' I study the road ahead. 'I don't know how she does it.'

'Discipline.'

I grin, knowing Hannah rather better than Jenny does. But then, I was at school with Hannah, and discipline has never been her strong point.

We live at East Cottage, in a tiny hamlet called Little Well, just over half a mile from the village of Eastlyn. It's a small cream-coloured cottage at the end of a single track lane, surrounded by fields. There are only five houses in the hamlet, including Eastlyn Farm where I used to live with my mother and father, though it's barely habitable now.

Behind our cottage, through the trees and up a rough slope, less than a mile as the crow flies, is Hill Farm where Tris and Connor live. We were never farmers ourselves, though while my mother was still alive, we kept a noisy rooster and a harem of chickens in the farmyard. Now there are only hundreds of rabbits popping their heads up in the back field every spring. But Tris and Connor are proper farmers. They jointly inherited the farm three months ago when their father died, and both decided to continue farming the land as he had always done. They keep sheep and goats, and somehow scrape a living from the poor, hilly moorland.

There's been a small settlement at Little Well since medieval times. I have no idea where the original 'well' is, but there's a stream that runs busily through the lower fields here, then curves round the valley bottom into the back of the woods. My father used to say that Cornish folk have always lived here because it's the first good grazing land west of Bodmin Moor.

Standing high on Rough Tor, looking down across vast empty acres of moorland, you could be forgiven for believing those really are the ghosts of long-dead travellers you can hear among the crags, as local legend suggests, not the sound of wind whistling over hollows and through narrow crevices in the rock.

But the moor can be beautiful too, in the right mood. I'm not unnerved by its bleakness; I love that I live close enough to touch the wilderness.

Our farmhouse originally belonged to my mother's Great-Aunt Teresa, who left it to my mother. My mother was pure Cornish, not like my father, who was born on the edge of Wolverhampton in the Midlands. But when Mum died, she left everything to Dad, so we stayed on at Eastlyn despite the memories.

It was hard on him though, after Mum died. He would drive past the woods every day when he took me to school, and glance across at the dark shroud of trees, his hands clenched on the wheel. Maybe he was thinking about the violent way she died, or remembering how the police carried her out of the woods in a body bag.

I did not see that part myself. But Hannah did, and described it to me in a whisper, both of us sitting in my bedroom at the farm.

It sounds gruesome, but for a long time I needed to know everything about my mother's murder. Every last detail. Knowing more about her death is a compulsion that still haunts me, like a jigsaw puzzle you know you can never finish because the last piece is missing. In those days, I kept newspaper cuttings in a book hidden under my mattress and used to study them for hours, going through that day in my mind.

My father said little in the months after she died, hunched like a sick hawk, staring at Mum's photograph, holding her clothes against his cheek. Every night he would cry himself to sleep or drink heavily until he fell asleep in front of the television. He was sick in those days, no good to me as a father. Though I don't blame him for that. I understood, and still share his pain.

Then one night, a few years back, I woke to find the air thick with smoke and my father unconscious in the living room. It took all my strength to drag him out of there. By the time the fire brigade arrived, the place was well alight. An accident, they said; my father had been drinking while watching television, and had fallen asleep with a cigarette in his hand.

The firemen saved the farm from complete destruction, but much of the ground floor was gutted and had to be rebuilt. Is still being rebuilt, in fact. Brick by brick. Slate by slate. And my father lives alone in a caravan on the property now, keeping himself warm at nights with a bottle of whisky.

When I came back from university and found East Cottage for rent, further up the lane, it seemed like the ideal situation; I could keep an eye on my father there without having to live with him.

We hurtle past the ruins of my family home and approach the turn to the cottage. Lush green hedgerow on either side of the narrow lane whips at the wing mirrors.

Jenny suddenly brakes violently. 'Bloody hell.'

A man has come stumbling out of the unseen fields next to the lane, muddy and unkempt. He skids down the overgrown bank of weeds and grasses, landing awkwardly on the tarmac a few feet from the bonnet of the Renault.

I recognise the man before he scrambles to his feet. Wide-eyed, grass in his hair, staring at us like a fugitive on the run.

'It's your dad,' Jenny says blankly.

CHAPTER FOUR

My father tries to smooth down his hair, unsuccessfully, and kicks a few strands of cow parsley off his boot before limping towards us. There's still grass poking out of his hair, and what looks like sticky weed caught on the shoulder of his jacket. Mud scuffs on his faded jeans and wellies make him look like a farmer come from herding cattle. But it's been a long time since he did a full day's work; he's lucky now if he gets offered work at all. His speciality used to be website design, and living out of a caravan with only mobile coverage is not ideal for that kind of job. The insurance money from the fire is long since spent, so I have no idea how he's managing to survive.

As he reaches the car, I wind down my window to speak to him. 'You look bloody awful, Dad. What's the matter?'

'I lost the dog,' he says shortly.

'You lost Churchill?'

'I couldn't sleep, so I took him out early for a walk. But he ran away.' He won't look me in the eye, bending to gaze past me at Jenny; I can smell alcohol on his breath. 'Hello there. I know you. You work with Eleanor at the school, don't you? Another PE teacher?'

She smiles politely. 'Yes,' she agrees. 'Jenny Crofter.'

'Jenny,' he says, nodding. 'That's it, yes. I knew I remembered you.'

'So where's Churchill now?' I ask, interrupting.

Churchill is a black Labrador, eight years old now and seriously overweight. Like most Labs, he may run about like a crazed puppy at times and loves nothing better than chasing round the farmyard after a ball, but he's basically lazy. The sort who sits down on the way back from a long walk and looks at you sideways, as if to say, 'I'm done. Can you go and get the car now?' So this tale of him running off strikes me as odd.

'I let him off the lead over at Tinker's Field and he bounded away, straight into the undergrowth,' my father explains. 'He ... he wouldn't come back, however hard I whistled. I followed him into the woods, but he was nowhere to be seen. So I came back the short way, past that old derelict hut by the river.'

I nod, wondering when I should tell him about the body I saw. And the police.

'I thought I heard barking inside the hut, so I forced my way in through the brambles,' he continues, holding out scratched hands and wrists, uncannily like my own, 'but of course there was no sign of Churchill. It must have been someone else's dog I could hear barking.' His speech is slightly slurred, and I wonder if he's had any sleep at all, his eyes are so bloodshot. 'I guess he'll come back on his own when he's ready, useless bloody dog.'

'Is your leg okay? You're limping.'

'I hurt my ankle, that's all. Nothing serious. Twisted it in some sodding rabbit hole.' Dad glances down at me in the passenger seat. 'Hold on, why are you heading back to the cottage? Shouldn't you be at work by now, Ellie?'

Jenny sees my hesitation and intervenes. 'I'm dropping Eleanor back at home, Mr Blackwood. She saw something in the woods when she was out running this morning.'

He doesn't understand. 'Saw something?' he repeats, smiling uncertainly. 'What do you mean?'

'A dead body,' I mumble.

My dad's smile is wiped away. His hands clench on the window frame, his face loses colour; he looks twenty years older in a few seconds. I remember that expression on his face. He wore it for weeks after having to identify my mother's body.

'*What?*'

I put my hand over his and squeeze, staring up at him. 'I'm sorry, Dad. But we can't stop to talk. The police are on their way. I expect they'll want to ask me some questions. Maybe take a statement from me. Perhaps I could come round later and talk to you then?'

My father stares, then takes a step back. His voice sounds strange. 'Today? You saw a body in the woods *today?*'

'I know how it sounds, but ….'

But he is already walking away, heading back along the lane to the farm. To the ruins covered in plastic sheeting that he calls home. The sun has come out again, illuminating the grey back of his head. It will not last though. Those ragged clouds are still massing on the edges of the valley, ready to darken the morning.

'Dad?' I call after him, but he does not answer.

Jenny looks at me. 'Is he going to be okay?'

'I have no idea.'

She sits with the engine running, staring after him. 'The look on his face … '

'There's nothing we can do. It was a shock.' I pause, feeling the irony behind that, then add, 'For both of us. A real shock. I'll go and see him later. Right now, I'm sorry but I need to get home.'

'Of course.'

'I appreciate it. I know this is making you late for work.'

Jenny puts the car into first and accelerates up the lane

towards the small cottage I share with Hannah.

God, what will Hannah be thinking? My phone call woke her up. She must be in a state, waiting for me to get back, to explain properly.

'I told you, Eleanor, the school will understand. I don't want you to worry about that, this is more important. And you must take all the time that you need.' Jenny sounds concerned but focused, already thinking ahead to damage control. 'I'll talk to Patricia myself as soon as I get there, straighten it all out for you.'

I look down at my hands. Like my legs, they're trembling. Shock, of course.

'Thanks, that's very kind of you.'

'What are friends for?'

I wonder how my father is taking the news about another body in the woods. I must go and see him later as I promised, make sure he's coping.

First though, I need to be sure I'm coping too. Because it's possible I'm not, and am not even aware of it.

Hannah is waiting for me in the doorway to East Cottage. It's been a dwelling-place for nearly a thousand years, probably one smoky room in medieval times, now extended to a living room and narrow kitchen downstairs, with a bathroom and two small bedrooms upstairs. A gurgling rivulet passes in front of the house on its way downhill, and years ago someone built a miniature stone bridge across the stream so we don't have to wet our feet getting to the front door.

'Are you okay?' Hannah looks pale, her fringe damp, eyes slightly bloodshot, precisely like someone who has not had enough sleep but has splashed her face to wake up in a hurry. 'Oh my God, your hands. And your legs too.'

'I'll survive.'

'But is it true?' She raises a hand in greeting to Jenny, who is backing up her Renault in our small turning area. 'I mean, I believe you. Absolutely I believe you. But it's so incredible, isn't it? To have found a body in the woods today, of all days ...'

Today, of all days.

I watch Jenny pull away. 'I should probably ring work. To be polite.'

'Eleanor?'

'Yes,' I agree, crossing the little stone bridge into the cottage. I'm dying for a cool shower. I glance at the table in the hall but the charging cradle is empty. 'It is incredible. Have you got the phone?'

Hannah holds out the phone automatically and I take it, beginning to look through the menu for the number of the cover supervisor. But even as it starts to ring, I'm interrupted by the familiar, unmistakeable roar of a quad bike.

Hurriedly I stop the call and go back outside just in time to see Tristan on his quad bike, swinging wildly out of the lane and towards the cottage.

His brother Connor crouches behind him in the trailer, clinging onto the sides of the metal box as he is jolted up and down on the uneven track. Completely illegal, of course, but nobody round here cares about that shit. Not even the police, who turn a blind eye most times to antics that would get you arrested up country.

Connor is two years older than Tris. Older and wiser, usually. This morning though both men look fierce. Like they've come prepared to fight.

I glance back at Hannah, who has come to stand in the doorway. 'Okay, what did you tell them?'

She looks guilty. 'Enough to get them round here.'

'Fuck's sake.'

'I need to get some sleep, I'm sorry. I'm dead on my feet. But I didn't want you left on your own today. Not with the police coming.'

Tris and Connor are not blood brothers. Tris was adopted. Nonetheless, they are almost never seen apart. Though that's begun to change now they run the farm together. Tris does not share his brother's fanatical work ethic, so I'm not entirely surprised to see him today. But I would have thought Connor had better things to do than come racing up here in response to Hannah's summons.

So much for my chance of a shower.

Tristan stalls the quad bike in the turning area, jumps off and runs towards us. He has not even shaved yet. There's a streak of oil on his cheek, and an oily rag sticking out of the back pocket of his soiled blue overalls.

'Jesus, Ellie.' Tris is out of breath, wiping dirty hands on his overalls in a way that tells me he's planning to hug me. 'Hannah told us what happened. You idiot, I told you not to tempt fate like that.'

I glare at him silently.

'Oh come here,' he says, relenting at once. 'You look like you need a hug.'

'No, really,' I mutter, but he pays no attention.

He throws his arms around me and embraces me tightly.

Tristan is twenty-four, my own age, dark-haired and built like a bear, though thankfully without all the fur. Unlike his older brother, who may be tall and dark too but is curiously hairless when he strips off at the beach or the pool. For years the three of us knocked about together at school, me and him and Connor. I even dated Connor a few times in sixth form, though it never worked out. At school I preferred my dates to be a little bit broken, and Connor could never compete with Denzil in that respect, whose love affair with narcotics is well-known.

These days I'm more interested in Tristan. But he still sees me as the sister he never had, and I'm not about to wreck things for either of us by going weak-kneed over his stubble.

Connor looks at me past his brother's shoulder. Like the other two, he's concerned. 'Shit, Eleanor, today of all days. You must be in pieces.'

Today of all days. It's becoming a common theme.

I glance back at Hannah and wonder exactly what was said on the phone between the three of them.

No wonder nobody believes me. Finding a body in the woods on the anniversary of my mother's death? Put like that, I wouldn't believe it either. But when the police bring the body out, that will put an end to all this uncomfortable subtext.

'It was awful at the time, but I'm getting over it now.' I smile wryly. 'More or less. To be honest, I'm still processing what happened.'

'No police yet?' Connor asks.

'They said they'd be here within half an hour. Then the circus will really kick off.'

Tris rubs my bare arms as though trying to warm them, looking into my face. He's had some difficult mood swings since his dad died, but I can identify with that. I meet his eyes, which are so dark they're almost black. He's a real Celt, I guess. But tall with it.

'You're so cold, Eleanor, you've had a shock. Hot sweet tea. That's what you need.'

'Or a large gin,' Hannah says frankly.

I make a face. 'Hold the gin. I don't think the police would understand. And I need to run cold water over my hands. They're stinging like crazy.'

We go into the cottage, into the narrow galley-style kitchen with an old gas oven and a microwave, white-washed walls, and rows of spotlights in the low, beamed ceiling. It only has one tiny window because it's the oldest part of the house, set into the bank by some fourteenth century builder. The white-washed walls are at least three foot thick.

'These walls will keep you cool in summer and warm in winter,' the estate agent said when we first looked round the rental property. So close to my dad's farm, it had been the obvious choice for me. Hannah had been harder to persuade; five miles from the nearest bus route, Little Well was not perfect for her job at our small local hospital. But passing her driving test had made the house-share possible.

I had not wanted to live alone when I came home after university, and could not bear to live with my father. Hannah is an easy person to live with. She has hidden depths, but I've always been secretly relieved that she keeps them to herself. I have enough trauma in my past for both of us.

I cool my stung hands under the cold tap for a few minutes, then Hannah fills the kettle and puts it on to boil. Silently, Tris moves a few magazines and dirty plates off the table to make room for us to sit down. I watch him, a little embarrassed. Hannah and I have never been great housekeepers.

Connor leans against the white-washed wall opposite, looking at me. His hair is damp; it looks like he jumped out of the shower to come over here with Tris. I feel guilty to be upsetting everyone's day, which is ludicrous, given what has happened.

'Talk to us, Ellie,' Connor urges me. 'We're all friends here. What did you see in the woods?'

'I thought Hannah told you?'

'She wasn't very clear.'

Hannah makes a face at him. 'I was half-asleep. Sorry.'

Frankly I would rather gnaw my own arm off than go through it again. But endless repetition is part of the game. 'I saw a woman's body.'

'Where?' Connor asks, staring.

'Down by the stream.' I watch steam begin to rise from the kettle. 'She was naked.'

Hannah looks horrified, as if being dead is not that appalling on its own, but being naked too is somehow unacceptable. 'Oh my God, she was *naked*? You didn't say that before.'

I stiffen, hearing the sound of a car out the front. The engine is quiet, ticking over as it idles outside the cottage.

No putting it off now.

Tris has heard the car too. He looks round. 'The police.' His dark gaze meets mine. 'What are you going to tell them?'

'The truth.'

CHAPTER FIVE

'Connor?' Tristan nods at the door.

'Right, yes, I'm on it.' Connor shoots me a reassuring look, then disappears through the hall and out the front door. I hear deep male voices in the lane. The police, trying to get in to talk to me, have come up against one of the Taylor brothers.

My protectors, I think drily.

Tris starts to make the tea, pouring hot water straight into the mugs, not bothering with the teapot.

'I wish I'd listened to you,' I tell him.

'Hmm?'

'Your text last night. Advising me not to go through the woods on my run.' I shake my head. 'I'm my own worst enemy sometimes.'

'I just thought it would upset you,' he says. 'Not that you'd find … '

'I know, it's okay.' I manage a wry smile. 'Who knew, right?'

Hannah looks at me sideways. 'Somebody knew.'

'That's for sure,' Tris agrees, his face solemn for once. He glances round at Hannah, nodding. 'It's one hell of a coincidence.'

I shiver. 'God, don't.'

'Sorry, just putting it out there.'

I nod, watching him work. It's odd that Tris is so big and broad, built like a rugby player, yet seems perfectly at home in a kitchen, his movements assured as he makes the tea. But like me, Tris got used to doing jobs round the house from an early age, helping out his brother Connor. Their mum left when they were still young, walked out after a family row and never came back. And their dad died of cancer three months ago, so now it's just them.

It must be lonely at Hill Farm, I think suddenly. Or an endless house party, depending on your point of view. Two good-looking men muddling by on their own.

You wouldn't know that they weren't related, not at first glance. But up close, you can see that their eyes are different – Connor's are much lighter, more like hazel – and Tristan is broader, more muscular.

Tris puts a mug of tea in front of me. 'So,' he asks quietly, 'this dead woman you saw, did you know her?'

I shake my head. 'Why?'

'No reason,' Tris says, and runs his thumb reassuringly across the top of my knuckles.

'You think I *should* have known her?'

His gaze comes back to mine, startled. 'No. Why would I?'

I decide not to answer that.

Connor returns with two police officers in tow, who shuffle in after him with no apparent sense of urgency. The narrow kitchen feels suddenly crowded. I study the two newcomers, but don't know either of them from the investigation into my mother's murder. The greying policeman looks to be in his fifties. The police woman is younger, smiling warmly, too busy checking out Tris to bother with me. She's in her late twenties and very blonde, her fringe straight and even.

'Detective Sergeant John Carrick,' the policeman is

introducing himself, taking out a black notebook and pen with an easy air, as though all this is going to be routine. Which maybe it is. 'And this is PC Helen Flynn. We're here to talk to Miss Eleanor Blackwood about a reported sighting of a body.'

'That's me,' I say, standing up.

'Pleased to meet you. No, don't get up. This won't take long.'

Detective Sergeant Carrick draws up a chair opposite me and Tris, making himself comfortable with the air of a man who has been at work for hours and has not had a break yet. I don't believe his smile.

'So you're Eleanor,' he says, studying me closely before glancing at the other three. 'And these are ... friends? Family?'

'Friends.'

Connor bends forward to shake the sergeant's hand. 'Connor Taylor,' he says coolly, 'and this is my brother Tristan.'

Hannah introduces herself shyly.

I may not know DS Carrick or the other police officer, but from the way he said, *So you're Eleanor*, I'm guessing they know about me.

Bloody marvellous.

DS Carrick looks at me from under heavy grey brows. 'I'm told you found something in the woods this morning, Eleanor. A woman's body.' He waits for me to nod before continuing, 'And it's eighteen years to the day since your mother was murdered in those woods.' Again, Carrick pauses, his eyes on my face. 'Is that right?'

Connor has been leaning against the wall again, arms folded as he listens. Now he straightens up, angry and protective. 'Excuse me, but how is that relevant?'

'I'm just verifying the date of Mrs Blackwood's murder.'

'Connor, it's fine,' I say, not wanting him to interfere. He means well but it will only make things worse. I meet the detective's gaze. 'Yes, that's right. It's the anniversary of her death today.'

'You were a witness to that murder?'

'Yes.'

'And what age were you at the time?'

'Six.' I stare at the wall above the kettle. The white gloss paint is still slightly damp from the steam. 'I was six years old.'

'Thank you. That's very helpful.'

Carrick takes another minute to scribble a few crabbed lines in his little black notepad. I wait for his next question, watching him. Tris is staring down over his shoulder at the open notepad. I wonder if he can see what the detective is writing.

Friends defensive. Hiding something? Witness a complete fruitcake with a compulsive need for attention.

The police sergeant frowns over his notepad, then looks up at me again. 'Perhaps you could talk us through everything that happened this morning. In particular, we need you to pinpoint the exact location of your find for us.'

'My *find?*'

'The body,' he says gently. 'Two of our officers are already down in the woods but the area is quite large, as I'm sure you'll appreciate. We have to know where to start looking.'

Hannah sits beside me, which is when I realise that I have not answered the police officer's question and everyone is looking at me. 'Do you need anything, Ellie? Some painkillers, maybe?'

My hands and legs are stinging, but I shake my head. The pain is useful. It gives me something to focus on. To distract me from the questions.

DS Carrick hesitates. 'I know it's difficult to get your thoughts together when you've had a shock. But perhaps if you were to describe exactly what you think you saw, and where you think you saw it.'

What you think you saw, and where you think you saw it.

He does not believe me either.

I'm feeling a bit chilly now in my running gear, bare-armed, bare-legged, everyone watching me like I'm an insect under a microscope.

The kitchen falls silent.

I cup my hands round the hot tea, and wearily launch into my story again. 'I went out for my run at about seven — '

'Wait, can I just check this? You went running in the woods?' DS Carrick asks, his eyes narrowed. 'Deliberately? On the anniversary of your mother's death?'

I glare at him resentfully. 'Yes.'

Connor seems to get it immediately. Or perhaps his brother told him on the way here. 'Like an act of defiance,' he explains to the sergeant. 'Two fingers to the past, and all that.'

I shoot him a grateful smile.

Tris is shaking his head disapprovingly. I remember his terse reply to my text. *Don't. Not a good idea.*

'Very well.' But Carrick sounds dubious. More scribbling in his black notepad. 'Go on.'

'It was still misty in places, but I could see it was going to be a sunny day. I took the lane down to the village, then cut across the fields into the back of the woods. There was nobody about, but I felt like someone was watching me.'

I take a sip of my tea. It tastes horrible. Tristan must have put half a cup of sugar in there. *For the shock.* 'I know that probably sounds stupid. But it was like one of my nightmares.'

DS Carrick looks at me sharply. 'Nightmares?'

'I suffer from bad dreams. Mostly about what happened to my mother.'

'Still? After all these years?'

I shrug, not bothering to reply to that. I could have said, *I'll never get over it.* But what would be the point?

'Can you try to describe what you saw in the woods,

Eleanor?' PC Flynn asks gently, coming to stand behind Tristan.

I stare into my mug of tea, considering that request. A flurry of images, some blurred, some horribly clear.

'I can try.'

I've stopped running now. It had to happen sometime. I take another few steps on the woodland path, then come to an abrupt halt. I can see it clearly now, the obstacle lying still under the rustle of leaves in the dappled sunshine. Only it's not a fallen tree trunk stripped of its bark, as I thought at first.

It's a woman.

A naked woman, lying across the woodland path as though she stripped off there and lay down for a nap. Except she's not asleep.

I creep forward, expecting at any moment to see the woman jump up and laugh at me for having fallen for her trick. But then I see how still and pale she is. Like a woman made of polished wood.

Her hair is tousled, with what appears to be grass caught in it, her right arm lying stiffly above her head at an angle, face turned away so I can't be sure how old she is nor even if I know her. Her skin is like white marble except for her throat, which is bruised. Dark and livid. That shocks me more than her nudity.

'Hello?'

I'm hit again with that terrifying sense of familiarity, of déja-vu. I stare at the woman, both of us motionless now, me holding my breath, her daring me to go further. We're statues in one of those playground games where if you move, you're out. Grandma's Footsteps. Not that she has much chance of losing this round; she has too great an advantage over the living.

She's slender, almost flat-chested. Her nipples look discoloured. Her legs are bent at the knee, slightly drawn up. She's twisted at the hips too, one of her bare feet smudged with dirt. The index finger on her outstretched hand is slightly crooked, pointing at the sky or maybe the stream, like that portrait of God's bulbous finger outstretched towards Man on the ceiling of the Sistine Chapel in Rome. Michelangelo Buonarroti. The Creation of Adam. I remember the first time I saw that painting, thinking how bored Adam looked, as if he would much rather be somewhere else. Like I would now.

She is younger than I thought. Early-to-mid twenties, my own age. Gently upturned nose, parted lips – bare, no lipstick – and her eyes closed, lashes startlingly dark against the paper-pale skin. Chestnut hair, worn long. Probably shoulder-length, though it's hard to tell, because it looks damp and slightly matted.

What I can see of her throat is horrific: blocks of mottled bruising, the marks almost overlapping at times, running like a rope-burn all the way from one side of her throat to the other. Two distinct shapes stand out on either side.

Thumb marks?

I take another step, and suddenly I see what had been hidden from me up until that moment.

A digit, marked in thick black pen on her forehead.

The number three.

The bottom curve of the 3 is flatter than the top curve and slightly wonky, as though the writer started too big and nearly ran into the woman's eyebrows. It looks like permanent marker.

There's another crack of twigs.

I hear a rustling high up on the wooded slopes above me. Like someone moving through the trees.

I glance up, my breath catching.

Out of the corner of my eye a dark figure shifts behind a trunk as my head turns. But when I stare, I see nothing but the haphazard trunks of trees, an empty slope, sunlight on the leaves.

I plunge through the shallow stream without bothering with the bridge and head away from the path, charging through the trees, making a hell of a noise. There's an old track somewhere ahead through all this undergrowth. Nature is trying to reclaim it, a strip of deteriorating tarmac seeded with grass and vast clumps of cow parsley, tinged white for May. But it's still there.

I find the track, struggle over the locked metal gate that bars the way, collapse on the other side in the long grass and weeds. I can smell dog shit somewhere nearby.

I lurch onto hands and knees, head hanging, then crawl to my feet. Stumble through weeds, sunlight and flies in my face. Somehow I keep running.

'That's the one I was telling you about,' they used to say behind my back. 'The one whose mum was murdered in front of her. When she was a little kid.'

I've had years to get used to this sick notoriety. All the whispers and stares they think I don't notice. The gossip I catch at the tail end of someone's conversation as I enter the staff room. The bloody ridiculous assumptions. That I'm going to be quiet and withdrawn, emotionally scarred, not fit to work with kids. If anything, the opposite has always been true. I can identify with their problems because I've been there myself, down in the dark.

'It was on the telly and in all the newspapers. They did one of those crime reconstructions, but never caught the murderer.'

That was one reason I came back to Cornwall after university. Not to lay my mother's ghost to rest, but because my old school was one of the few places where I could make a fresh start. When your past is already known, no one can blow your life wide open with some grim revelation.

'So the killer is still out there somewhere?'

I burst out of the track at the top of the hill. I haven't run so hard in years. My legs are shaking. There's the church ahead of me, I can see the squat bell tower above the trees, its clock face precisely three minutes fast.

The bell is tolling the hour.

CHAPTER SIX

Detective Sergeant John Carrick stops writing, checks through what he's written, nods once, then flips his notebook shut. I can tell nothing from his expression, which is still calm and professional.

He stands up and pushes his chair under the table. 'I'll have a quick chat with the officers in the woods, see how they're getting on. The signal's stronger outside. If you don't mind.' He jerks his head at PC Flynn to follow him outside. 'Thanks for the tea. Back in a tick.'

I know what that means; Carrick wants to talk about me to his colleagues behind my back.

Hannah disappeared while I was speaking to the police; I remember her muttering something about putting the water heater on, then slipping unobtrusively out of the kitchen door. But I know she's headed back to bed, still recovering from her night shift.

That's another thing I like about living with Hannah. She's unfazed by all this, totally focused on her own life, and I love her for it. There are plenty of people in my life to look concerned and take statements. What I need is someone who will just shrug and go back to bed, make me feel like all this insanity is somehow ordinary.

40

The police come back in. *They know something.* The detective sergeant charges in with arms swinging, looking for me. The police woman is fumbling with her phone, her expression grave.

'Are those the training shoes you were wearing earlier?' Carrick asks, studying my Mizuno trainers. They are still a little damp from where I splashed through the stream, toes tinged green from the undergrowth. 'In the woods?'

'Yes.'

Everyone looks at my trainers. I resist the urge to do up my right lace, which is trailing again.

With a bright smile, PC Flynn says, 'They look new.'

'That's because they *are* new,' I say, not smiling back at her. I can't stand being patronised. 'I only bought them recently, because my others were getting worn.' Then I add, by way of explanation, 'I teach PE. We get through a lot of trainers during the school year.'

'We need a photograph of the soles,' Carrick announces, then nods to the policewoman. 'Both feet, please.'

I don't move, mystified.

'Don't worry, this will only take a minute.' PC Flynn peers at her mobile phone screen as she fiddles with the settings, then adds, 'Probably be easiest if you take them off.'

I know this routine. *Good cop, bad cop.*

'I'd rather not.'

'Okay.' Her voice has hardened. The patronising smile has gone. 'Could you stand then, please, and hold your foot up behind you? Left foot first. Then we'll do the right.'

Connor is frowning. 'Why do you need a photograph of her trainers?'

'For elimination purposes,' the sergeant tells him flatly, and I can tell that is the most we will get out of them for now.

Last time I went through this, at the tender age of six,

my father was always there, one step ahead the whole way, his arm round my shoulder, protecting me from the police and the journalists, making sure I was not put under pressure, that the horrors of the past could be forgotten as easily as possible.

This time, I'm on my own. I'm not even sure my dad registered what I told him this morning, still locked in the misery of the past.

Today, of all days.

Tris moves his kitchen chair out of the way. 'Come on, Ellie,' he says, his smile cajoling, 'let's get this over with. You can lean on me.'

Not quite on my own, I concede.

I stand rigidly, holding onto Tristan's shoulder for balance, my left leg thrust back like a flamingo's, then the right leg, while the constable shuffles about behind me. She takes several shots of both soles of my Mizuno trainers, muttering under her breath about the dim lighting in the kitchen.

'Thanks, we'll be back later,' Detective Sergeant Carrick tells us as his constable finishes her work, 'when there's something to report.'

Connor shows the police to the front door of the cottage, then hurries back into the kitchen, looking furious. 'Unfeeling bastards. Anyone would think you were the bloody suspect, not the victim.'

'I'm a witness, not a victim,' I remind him.

'All the same.'

Connor is another one who's always been there for me. Hannah, Tris, Connor, Denzil, even my father until the night of the fire. And Jenny is a good friend now too. I have a network in place, and one of which even the exacting Dr Quick would approve. But perhaps it's time I shouldered the burden on my own for a while. I still need a shower, after all, and some time alone in my room sounds very welcome. I've never been one for crowds.

'Look,' I tell the Taylor brothers, 'you two have been

great, but this could take hours and I don't need anyone to babysit me. I need to shower and change my clothes. Besides, Hannah is in the house if I do need anything.'

Connor hesitates, then nods. 'Of course.' He nudges Tris. 'Come on, let's give the woman some space. We've got to shift the sheep down from the top field anyway.'

Tris, who has never done this before, looks at me with an uncertain expression. 'Are you sure, Ellie? Because we can stay if you want.'

'Go, both of you.'

Connor kisses me on the cheek and heads back outside to the quad bike, whistling an old Cornish tune. He's probably already thinking about his sheep.

Tris hovers in the kitchen doorway, still unwilling to leave me alone, bless him. 'But what happens now?'

My head is still in the green space of the woods, but I glance at the clock on the kitchen wall. It's one of those fake antique clocks with a large face and stiff black hands, the kind you might find in a Victorian railway station. One of Hannah's discoveries at the local garden centre. The time is a little after half past nine. I've been awake less than three hours.

'Now we wait until they find her.'

Much as I have always relied on my old friends to keep me sane, it's good to be on my own for a while. I ring the school and check with the cover supervisor that he does not need me to email any instructions for the lessons I'm missing. He doesn't, which is a relief. I chuck my sticky running gear in the bathroom wash basket, one of those tall wicker baskets with a lid that look like they're concealing a snake, then take a leisurely fifteen minutes to shower and wash my hair.

As the warm water runs over me, I close my eyes. The darkness comes back and I push it away with an effort. *Ten, nine, eight, seven …*

After the shower, I drag a bath towel from the shelf

and wrap it round myself, anchoring it above my breasts. When I pad through barefoot into the bedroom, everything is just as I left it this morning.

I pick up my phone from the crumpled bed. Several concerned voice messages from the school, a text from Connor – *We love you, even if you do see dead people. Call us anytime* – and a monthly notification about my bill, which I don't bother to open.

Still nothing from Denzil.

I root for matching bra and knickers in my drawer, then change into jeans and a strappy gold top. My weekend wear. It feels odd on a work day, but then I am hardly likely to be going into work today.

Carefully, I hang my work clothes back up in the wardrobe. A grey tracksuit with a pink V-necked polo shirt underneath: typical PE teacher fare. My damp Mizuno trainers are sitting on an old newspaper near the door. I study them a moment, then choose a fresh pair from the box under the bed. Nike, with a pink stripe. A little worn on the instep, but perfectly good for casual wear.

I towel-dry my hair for speed, then fix it up in a ponytail again. I don't bother with make-up. I rarely do these days, unless I'm going out for the night.

There are two vehicles parked in the turning area by the time I walk down the stairs after my shower: a black Vauxhall Corsa, tinted windscreen glinting in the sunlight, and a marked police transit van. A small group of men is standing beside the police van, some in uniform, their heads bent together, deep in conversation.

One of the men is Carrick. Another is my father.

I stand in the hallway a moment, staring at them through the glass panel, then open the front door. 'Hello?'

Dad stops speaking. I can't decipher the look on his face as he glances in my direction. Guilt? Suspicion?

The man in the light grey suit has turned as well, staring at me. His eyebrows rise slowly.

Suddenly I recognise him. *DI Powell.*

My stomach pitches, rolling horribly. It's like I've stepped straight back into the past, into a time when our world was falling apart around us and there was nothing to cling onto, no safety rope.

Just when I thought things could get no worse, a vision right out of my childhood nightmares has appeared to prove me wrong.

Detective Inspector Powell. Tall, white-haired now, easily in his sixties. I thought he would have retired by now. He was one of the officers who investigated the unsolved murder of Angela Blackwood eighteen years ago.

This would be a bad moment to throw up again.

'Dad, were you looking for me?' My palms are sweating; I wipe them on the back pockets of my jeans, trying for a calm tone. 'You should have come straight in. I was in the shower, but Hannah's around somewhere.'

Asleep, most probably. But I'm not thinking straight.

My father does not answer.

DI Powell steps away from the group. His gaze is cool but sympathetic as he assesses my face, my hair, my appearance. No doubt he remembers me as an hysterical six-year-old, sobbing her heart out and barely coherent enough to give a description of the man who had attacked her mummy. We had met a few times since that investigation, but the events of today seem to have left my head stranded in the past.

'Hello again, Ellie,' he says, holding out his hand.

The voice tugs at me. I remember the strong West Country twang to his accent, a slow drawl that makes him sound like he's only one or two generations away from ancestors who were farmers and tin miners. Far from parochial though, he had always seemed open to new approaches, especially the idea of hypnotherapy.

There is a faint smile on his face. A senior policeman attempting to be friendly, but vaguely regretful at the same time, aware of an unbridgeable gap between us. There's no warmth there. Only a hint of the same suspicion I saw on my father's face. It leaves me uncomfortable.

We shake hands. 'It's been a long time,' he remarks calmly. 'How have you been?'

'Okay up until today.'

'So your dad has been telling me. It sounds like you've had a tough morning.' He hesitates. 'Do you mind if I call you Ellie? Or would you prefer Eleanor?'

My throat is clogged up. 'I'm Eleanor now. Ellie was … a long time ago.'

Except for my close friends. This man is not a friend.

'Of course.'

My head is buzzing, but I force myself to smile and behave normally. It's what they expect. 'Come into the kitchen, please. I'll make coffee.'

'Not for me, thanks. But feel free to make one for yourself.'

We walk through to the kitchen, my father following behind the police officers without a word.

I can't wait any longer, impatient to hear their news. 'So, did you find the body?' I ask Carrick straight out. 'Did you find her?'

'No,' Carrick says bluntly.

I stare. 'What?'

DI Powell is shaking his head. There's that regretful smile again. The smile I remember. The smile that used to leave me feeling sick.

'I'm sorry to be the bearer of bad tidings, Eleanor. We looked where you told us to look. We looked everywhere. We scoured the woods, in fact, from the stream right up to the top car park. We even had the dogs out,' he says. 'But we didn't find a body.'

CHAPTER SEVEN

I think about my dead mother. The long investigation, the false leads, the unsolved murder. The newspaper cuttings I managed to salvage after the house fire and still keep in a box under my bed. There's a powerful sense of *déja-vu*. I look from the white-haired policeman to my father, who is still saying nothing, and then back again.

'But did you look exactly where I told DS Carrick?' I ask. 'Down near the stream, next to the little footbridge?'

'We looked beside the stream like you told us,' Carrick jumps in before Powell can reply. 'We didn't find anything.'

There is no sympathy in Carrick's face. His voice is sharp. I can tell what he thinks about all this. He thinks he has spent the morning on a fool's errand.

'As I was just telling your father, we searched the whole wood,' he continues coldly. 'Combed the undergrowth, searched up and down the banks. There was nothing there. Just your footprints in the mud on both sides of the stream. It was a bit of a mess down there, animal tracks and so on, but the tread of your trainers matched the prints we found exactly.'

'That's impossible,' I say, staring at Carrick. 'There

must have been other footprints on that path. How else –
?'

'We checked and double-checked, Miss Blackwood.'

Hannah slips quietly into the kitchen, still in her
pyjamas, and takes up a position near the fridge, watching
me with raised eyebrows through the pack of dark,
uniformed shoulders.

I shake my head, looking from Carrick to Powell.
Neither of the two detectives appear to be joking.

'I don't understand.'

'There was no Path Closed sign either,' Carrick adds,
getting out his police notebook and flicking through it.
'You mentioned a diversion sign in your statement this
morning. We got a council worker down there, and
someone from the Forestry Commission. There have been
no paths closed in the woods today. No paths closed *for
weeks*, was what they said.'

This makes no sense to me.

'But there was a diversion sign,' I tell them, trying to
stay patient, not to lose my temper. 'It was standing on the
bend where the lower and upper paths divide. If it's not
still there, someone must have moved it. Perhaps
deliberately.'

Carrick shakes his head. 'Not according to the man
from the Forestry Commission. And he's got no reason to
lie.'

Powell folds his arms across his chest, watching me.
One of the other police officers is looking away, smirking
behind my father's back.

They think I'm mad. Or a liar.

'I tell you, I saw a body down by the stream,' I say
doggedly. 'You can't give up. You have to go back to the
woods and look again. She can't just have vanished.'

'For God's sake, Eleanor, stop it,' my father bursts out,
glaring at me like he hates me. 'It's nearly two decades
since your mother died. When are you going to let it go?'

I turn, staring at him. 'Dad?'

'No, this needs to be said. I thought you were over it, I really did. You spent all those years in therapy, got through university, found a good job. But to have sent the police down there again in search of a non-existent body … ' He makes a convulsive noise in his throat. 'This is beyond attention-grabbing. This is sick.'

I don't know what to say in reply to that accusation. But I go through each word of his speech again in my head, weighing it carefully against what I know and what I saw.

When I glance around the room, I realise that nobody is looking at me anymore. They've moved on, discussing what should happen next. Powell starts flicking through a notebook. Carrick is talking about a visit to the police station. There's an edge of contempt in the sergeant's voice. He's suggesting to my father that I should make an admission of guilt at once, agreeing that it was a lie. Though 'mistaken' is the diplomatic word he uses after a stern look from DI Powell. A formal statement with a signature, withdrawing my previous claim. So the police can all go home and cross 'mad woman sees dead body' off their list of things to investigate.

Hannah tries to defend me – she's fantastic, I owe her for that – and my father snaps round at her, tells my friend to mind her own business.

Sick.

My rage clears for a moment. I force myself to say the words I've been trying to repress. 'I'm sorry, Dad, but I need you to leave.'

He stares. 'What?'

'This isn't your house, Dad, and I want to speak to the police alone. Could you leave, please?'

My father slicks back his hair in a nervous gesture, but does not move. 'I don't think you know what you're saying, Ellie.'

DI Powell looks sympathetic. His eyes meet mine frankly. 'No one is saying you've lied, Eleanor. But maybe you *thought* you saw a dead body. The light in those woods can play funny tricks on your eyes, especially ... Well, you must admit you're in a heightened emotional state right now.' When I protest, he raises a hand to stop me. 'Listen, we've had six officers down there this morning, hunting through the woods, checking everywhere. We found nothing. Nothing at all.'

I think of the woman's body. Her finger, pointing. The bubbling gurgle of the stream, so noisy I can barely hear myself think.

'So, this was all some kind of hallucination?' The sense of betrayal is so strong, it tastes like blood in my mouth.

DI Powell remains calm, but his expression is intent. 'I think your mother's death hit you hard, Eleanor. And your father tells me you haven't seen your psychiatrist for some years. Perhaps now would be a good idea to go back into therapy. Just until you're over this bump.'

'What bump?'

'Your father tells me you recently started work at your old school.' DI Powell looks at me with that vague smile again. Trying to appear understanding. Hands in his trouser pockets. 'A new job can be very stressful, and perhaps going back to the school has kicked up some old memories. Emotions you thought you'd got past. I remember when I first joined the force, it wasn't easy to adapt to the demands of the job. And I had nothing like your excuse.'

The inspector pauses, and his brow creases uneasily. 'Obviously we're not going to charge you with wasting police time. But we do need some assurances that you'll visit your doctor, get yourself sorted out with some therapy sessions.'

My gaze swings round the circle of concerned faces. 'You don't believe a word of my story. You think I've lost it.'

Even Hannah is looking uncertain now. 'It's not like that, Ellie. But perhaps you should sit down for a few minutes. Think things through properly.'

Et tu, Brute?

My head is buzzing and I can't seem to catch my breath. I feel like I'm going mad, which would suit their theory.

'Look, I saw a dead woman in the woods this morning,' I tell them flatly. 'I don't know what happened to her body afterwards, but I didn't imagine seeing her. And whoever she was, I owe it to that woman to keep telling you the truth. Shouting it from the rooftops, if necessary.'

PC Helen Flynn raises her eyebrows. 'Even if nobody *ever* believes you?'

'Especially then.'

CHAPTER EIGHT

I ignore Hannah's advice as well as the head teacher's, and am back at work two days after the anniversary of my mother's death. It would probably feel too soon to another person, but to me it feels about right. I hate kicking my heels at home anyway. Pressure like this makes me want to be active, to do things, make stuff happen. I can't bear sitting about an empty house and staring at the television screen with nothing to do but fret and remember.

'You should be taking longer at home after what you've been through,' Jenny tells me as we pull up in the car park, not bothering to hide her disapproval.

'Better here than at the cottage.'

'I suppose it's less lonely.'

'Especially when Hannah spends the greater part of every day *asleep*.'

'She's still on nights?'

I nod, averting my gaze as a swarm of noisy kids rush past from the bus bays and towards the side entrance. The school building in front of us is long and low, facing due east, a dozen large windows right in my eye line reflecting the sun.

Putting on a pair of sunglasses, I instantly feel safer,

more anonymous. Which is a complete illusion, of course. But it helps.

'So what did the police say?' she asks, negotiating into a narrow parking place near the playing fields.

'That I need psychiatric help.'

Jenny looks round at me, surprised. 'And do you agree with them?'

'Absolutely not.'

'That's the spirit.' She turns off the engine, then checks the mirror in her sun visor, quickly tidying her hair. 'I'm glad you accepted a lift from me this time, you know. I'm sure that scooter can't be very safe. And I'm sorry I didn't have time to come round yesterday evening. Family nonsense, you know. I've got a free period this afternoon if you still want a chat over coffee.'

'I'd appreciate it.' I rummage in my bag and study my timetable. 'I'm in the gym until the end of fourth period. That any good?'

'Sounds perfect. I'll come and find you after the bell.'

We walk into the school together, heading for the gym and changing rooms. Our territory, for what it's worth. In the corridors, it's obvious who has been reading the daily regional newspaper. A journalist rang yesterday to ask for my side of the story; I put the phone down on her. But I guess they went ahead and printed whatever they had from the police anyway. Some of the teachers glance at me in passing, their eyes curious. The younger kids stare openly, fascinated. Some of them point, then whisper behind my back. I start to wonder whether I should have taken the head's advice to stay home and 'keep a low profile' for a few days.

But why the hell should I? I have done nothing wrong. I told them the truth. I have no idea what happened after I left the woods, and no way of proving what I saw, but my dead woman was real. Too real and solid to have melted away, that's for certain.

We part company at the changing rooms.

'Told you it wouldn't be easy.' Jenny frowns at two Year 10 girls who are talking about me in loud, excitable squeaks; they giggle and run past as the bell rings. 'You ought to have stayed at the cottage until the excitement had died down. This kind of attention would drive me crazy.'

'Didn't you get the memo? I already *am* crazy.'

'Right, you should all know what you're meant to be doing. Has everyone got a partner and a mat?'

The kids shuffle about in crumpled shorts and polo shirts, some arguing over mats, others eyeing their opponents from crouched positions like they're about to reenact some martial arts movie.

'I don't have a partner, Miss,' one lad says plaintively, sticking his arm straight up in the air.

'You can partner me, Paul,' I say, then immediately wish I hadn't when I see his grin and the quick glance over his shoulder. I'm a target for these kids at the moment. One sniff of weakness and they will close in, thirsty for blood. But it's done now; I'll only look afraid if I back off now. And I don't do afraid.

'Find a mat, then,' I tell him curtly. 'Come on, hurry up. Everyone's waiting.'

I blow the whistle hanging round my neck, and Paul immediately grabs me by the sleeve. He may only be fifteen, a Year 10, but he's strong, just taller than me at about five foot nine, and well-built with it. On top of that, I know he doesn't like me. Actually, to be fair to Paul, he doesn't like any woman who can knock him to the floor and make him look like an idiot in front of his mates.

Normally, I show these kids how to put an attacker on the ground in about thirty seconds. But maybe what I saw in the woods has knocked me off balance, because either Paul is stronger than I expected or my usual grapple-and-throw needs some rehab work.

I struggle with him for a moment, trying and failing to

'locate my core' as Jenny likes to put it during staff training sessions. I'm a hair's breadth from losing control of the situation.

Then I see him smile. The lad's grip slackens almost imperceptibly. He's over-confident; thinks he's got me, that it's all over.

As he hesitates, hoping his mates are watching his moment of triumph, I hook my foot round his ankle, press my knee up under his left leg, then jerk him off balance.

Paul falls backwards, a look of comical dismay on his face. He lands heavily on his back in the middle of the blue mat. 'Shit.'

'Language, Paul.' I step back, breathing hard. 'Keep it clean or you'll be out of my class.'

'Sorry, Miss.' He drags himself up off the floor, tidies his rumpled shirt, then shoots me a look that promises revenge. His next words are muttered, for my ears only. '*Freak.*'

I stiffen, staring at him. 'I beg your pardon?'

'I didn't say nothing, Miss.' Surly now, Paul slicks back his hair and shuffles away, a pair of pink-striped underpants showing above the loose waistband of his shorts.

Chrissy, his girlfriend, is two or three mats behind us. The other kids are making a racket, laughing and struggling to throw each other to the floor. All the same I hear the whine of her voice cutting through the chaos in the gym. 'Why did you let her do that to you, Paul? Everyone knows she's mental.'

My temper is up near the top of the red line. I want to send them both out of class, slap a detention on them. But our time's nearly up, and besides, I'm on probation; the head teacher made that clear in her phone call last night. Patricia was blunt. 'First sign that you can't handle being back at work, and I'll insist you take a full week off. Is that clear?'

I blow the whistle to signal the end of the bout.

Nobody stops.

I blow the whistle twice again, then clap my hands, trying to get the kids' attention above the noise. 'That's enough for today, everyone,' I shout. 'Start packing it up.'

I hear someone mutter an expletive behind me, and turn, looking at Chrissy. She's a tall blonde, skinny with angular hips and waist-length hair always gathered up in a high ponytail that swings violently from side to side when she's walking. She's standing still now, with her hands low on her hips, pink hipster joggers loose on her narrow frame.

'What was that?' I ask her coldly.

'Nothing, Miss.' Chrissy is enjoying herself, raising her voice as she repeats her boyfriend's denial. Some of the other kids nearby have stopped messing about and are staring at us, fascinated. 'Maybe you're hearing things as well as seeing them.'

Paul is grinning now. He nods at his girlfriend in approval. Some of their cronies have gathered round as though hoping for a fight. It's like being surrounded by a pack of growling hyenas.

Chrissy ignores them, looking back at me with a cold smile. She turns fully towards me now, and I watch her hands come away from her hips, swing loose, curling into fists.

The girl's sizing me up for a punch, I realise. She thinks she can take me, teacher or not.

'Everyone knows, Miss,' she says. 'The whole school. Paul's uncle is in the police, remember? He told Paul the only reason they didn't charge you with wasting police time is because you're obviously mental. Wrong in the head.'

Her teeth are bared, perfectly straight and white, like someone in a toothpaste commercial. I imagine her brushing them exactly one hundred times before bed and one hundred times when she gets up in the morning.

My fists clench, adrenalin pumping round my body. I'm

ready for a fight too. It would be so good to get her in a clinch and bang her head on the floor. And I could do it, I could take her. I've been studying martial arts for years: judo, karate, taekwondo. It's tempting to show Chrissy what I can do.

Control is what I need right now though. I'm a teacher now, albeit newly qualified. If I can't control myself, how can I ever hope to control these kids?

I hear the bell ring for the end of the lesson but don't move, still staring at Chrissy. I breathe slowly through my nose, counting slowly down from ten. Dr Quick's favourite strategy for regaining self-control at a moment of crisis.

Another whistle blows, loud and shrill, and the gym falls silent.

'Right, everyone, that's it. Shake your partner's hand and get changed. Did nobody hear the bell?'

Jenny Crofter is in the doorway. She shouts over the noise of thirty or so kids still wrestling noisily with each other, 'Mats at the back there. Neat piles, please. And make sure you take all your bags with you. I don't want to see anything left behind in the gym.'

Students start to move reluctantly, dragging their blue mats with them, leaving a streaky dust trail over the floor.

Chrissy shrugs and turns away, leaving the mat for her partner to carry. Paul hurries after her, limping slightly as though he hurt himself when I threw him. Probably planning to make a complaint. 'The teacher hurt me.' I should never have partnered with him, it was a mistake to let these kids get under my skin.

Jenny glances at me. Her voice is bland. 'Ready for that coffee?'

'I'll be right with you.'

I bend to straighten the floor mats as students toss theirs on the stack and shuffle out of the gym. The mats are a dusty blue, the stack dangerously lopsided. As the last mat is slapped down on top, I see mockery in the boy's eyes.

'Thanks, Miss.'

Freak.

The door slams shut behind him. Jenny puts her hands on her hips and looks at me, head on one side. 'What the hell was that about?'

'I had the situation under control.'

'You were a long way from that, Eleanor.' She glances at her watch. 'We're both free now. Why don't you let me drive you home?'

'I'm fine.'

'Are you worried how it might look to take more time off? Because if Patricia gets to hear about what just happened, you could end up in far more serious trouble.'

'Come on, it wasn't that bad.'

She raises her eyebrows. 'Did I see you throw a student onto the mat?'

'That was a mistake,' I admit.

'Let's hope his parents don't get on the bloody phone about it. Because that could be difficult,' she says bluntly, 'given the events of this week.'

The events of this week.

I follow her out of the gym. She's over-exaggerating the importance of what happened with Paul and Chrissy. It was an awkward moment, I can't deny that, and Paul could make trouble for the school if his parents decide to get involved. But it was not as serious an error of judgement as she seems to think. I can hardly argue with her though. Jenny may be my friend but she's also my Head of Department.

'Let me take you home early,' she insists, and I see no point in refusing.

On the way back to Eastlyn, Jenny stops at a moorside garage for fuel. I study the newspapers displayed behind wire on the forecourt.

For fuck's sake.

I go in and buy a copy of the local paper. The front page headline screams, VICTIM'S DAUGHTER REPORTS MYSTERY BODY IN WOODS.

When Jenny gets back in, she glances across. 'Oh shit. I'd hoped you wouldn't see that.'

'I might as well read it. Everyone else will.'

She nods. 'There was a copy in the staff room at lunchtime. I threw it in the bin.'

'Did you read it first?'

When Jenny doesn't answer, I glance across at her. She shrugs, her face guilty. 'Sorry.'

'Don't worry about it.'

Carefully, watching the busy moor road, she pulls out of the garage. I see the owner watching us through the window. He had said nothing but served me with a sly half-smile on his face that had not needed much interpreting. It seems that I am once more a local celebrity. With all that entails for my privacy and peace of mind.

'Maybe a professional view would help,' she suggests, and I cut her off.

'I'm going back into therapy.'

Her smile is relieved. 'That's a great idea, Eleanor, that's exactly what you need. To talk things through with a person who can really help you.' She checks her mirror, then signals, turning down the narrow track that leads to Eastlyn. 'Is it someone you know?'

'Same therapist as before.'

'Excellent, I'm so glad.' Jenny hesitates, and the smile falters a little. 'I go running in the woods sometimes too. At weekends and during the school holidays.'

She's taking the back lanes to the village because the A30 is often nose-to-tail traffic this close to the weekend. Hedges flash past, damp and green. A brown tourist sign to the woods, our local attraction. Summer is not far away. Soon even these quiet lanes will be busy.

Jenny grips the wheel, staring ahead. The track runs

along the edge of the moor, thin and winding, the hedgerows tall and overgrown. Anything could be coming in the opposite direction, and at any speed.

'I know your history with the place,' she says at last, 'and I didn't want to upset you. The woods can be a wild place, especially off the main track. I know what it implies in the newspaper report. That you ... '

'Made it all up to get attention?'

Jenny nods, her expression thoughtful. 'I don't believe that though. I saw your face when you came to my house that morning, Eleanor. Whatever you thought you saw down there, it was real to you.'

CHAPTER NINE

To my surprise, Hannah is awake when I stroll into the kitchen. Still in her dressing gown, bleary-eyed and no make-up on yet, but awake. I suppose if she did not get up mid-afternoon, she would never have time to do anything but work and sleep. Night shifts are punishing, and I'm glad that I will probably never have to work one.

'How was work?' Hannah is lounging on her favourite chair in the corner, slippered feet up on the pine kitchen table.

'Don't ask.'

She raises her eyebrows. 'That bad?'

'I'm lucky I still have a job.'

I sit down with a cup of tea and scan the report in the local newspaper, and my last hope of anonymity disappears. Someone talked, all right. For hours, it looks like. And the report is not just about what I saw in the woods last week. They've been digging. There's an old colour photo of me as a child, probably from their archives, and an inset photo of my mother's face in grainy black and white, with the sensational caption, 'Angela Blackwood: murdered. Her killer is still at large.'

Hannah is watching me. 'I forgot to tell you, a reporter

and photographer showed up yesterday while you were still asleep. It was early; I think I'd just got in from work. I told them you'd gone to the school and they took off again. But they took some photos of the cottage. I think they may have stopped at your dad's too.'

'He won't have talked to them either. Dad hates reporters.'

I study the headline again. VICTIM'S DAUGHTER REPORTS MYSTERY BODY IN WOODS.

Victim's daughter. Nice touch.

I glance through the first few paragraphs, which focus on a garbled account of my statement to police. Some details are wrong, some have been embellished by a malicious fantasist masquerading as a journalist. But the rest of the story is ancient history. My ancient history, that is. They've pulled out everything in their archives. My mother's murder, the 'trauma' I suffered, my years in therapy, even a brief mention of an incident which took place when I was ten and had somehow forgotten about. The police had been called that time too. And I got a new therapist a few months later, a specialist in childhood trauma.

Dr Quick.

I hand the newspaper to Hannah. 'Bastards are making me out to be a complete nut job.'

'You shouldn't worry about it.' Hannah crumples up the newspaper without reading it, then throws it to the floor with a dramatic gesture. I'm surprised she doesn't jump up and trample on it too. 'They want to sell copies. But it's done now, and you can move on. These stories never last. By next week, no one will care.'

'Meanwhile, I sound deranged.'

She shakes her head. 'No one believes any of that crap.'

'The kids at school believe it. They think I'm certifiable. Most of the staff too.' I pause, reconsidering that. 'Except Jenny.'

'Is that going to be a problem? I thought the head

teacher was on your side.'

'I'm not sacked, if that's what you mean. But she wants me to take some more time off. And Jenny agrees with her.'

'Working nights is the worst decision I ever made. I never seem to get enough sleep, and my eyeballs feel like I've been rubbing them with wire wool. I could do with a few days off myself.'

'So take a holiday. You must be owed some leave. Spend it with me.' I sip my tea, which is strong and dark, only a dash of milk. Exactly the way I like it. 'We can go to the beach if the weather's good, maybe hit some clubs afterwards. Pretend we're students again.'

There's a quiet knock at the front door while Hannah's still laughing at that suggestion.

'Oh Christ, who the hell is that?' She gets up and peers suspiciously down the hallway. 'It had better not be another reporter. I'm not even dressed yet.'

'Ignore it.'

There's a sudden silence. 'Oh my God,' she says blankly.

'What? Who is it?'

Hannah looks round at me from the doorway, clearly bemused. 'It's Mortimer Clemo,' she whispers.

'The *vicar*?'

To my horror, I realise that I must have left the front door open. An open invitation to someone like him. I hear footsteps in the hall, then the Reverend Clemo's deep voice. 'I'm so sorry, am I intruding? Hannah, isn't it? Should I come back at a better time? I just wanted a little chat with Eleanor.'

Wearily, I nod at Hannah, who is still guarding the kitchen door. 'It's okay, let him in.'

She shrugs, then steps aside for the vicar. Never very good at hiding her disdain for religious people, she tells us, 'Look, I have to change for work, so if you'll excuse me …'

'Of course.' Clemo watches her go, then turns and smiles at me. He's using his church voice, deep and authoritative. 'Eleanor, Eleanor.' He opens his large hands wide, like he's forgiving me for something. 'What can I say? I heard your bad news on the village grapevine, I hope you don't mind. How are you?'

That seems to be the default question these days.

'I'm good.'

'You look a little pale though.' He pulls out a kitchen chair from under the table. 'Forgive me, do you mind if I sit? It's quite a walk from the village.'

I smell cigarette smoke on him, and wrinkle my nose. Denzil smokes occasionally too, but with him, it's almost sexy.

I try to be polite. 'Of course, please.'

'Thank you.' He seats himself on the creaking chair, a tall man, folding his legs underneath him. His white dog-collar is pinching him about the throat; too many cream teas at the vicarage, I think, then tell myself off for being uncharitable. He is still smiling, but more solemnly now. 'I had to come and see how you are, Eleanor. I feel guilty, you see.'

I look at him, my eyebrows raised.

'Because I was there that morning. Right by the woods. Perhaps I could have … ' He pauses in his explanation, looking at me helplessly. 'If I had known what was happening when we met in the village, if you had only confided in me, I could have gone down into the woods with you straightaway. To where you saw that unfortunate woman.'

I study him.

'You believe my story, then?'

'Well … ' Reverend Clemo makes a wordless rumbling noise in his throat, appearing to answer without really answering. It's probably a method he has developed over the years to allow him to avoid awkward questions. I imagine vicars get a lot of those. 'It's not a question of belief, as such. My interest is strictly in your welfare.'

'My spiritual welfare?'

'If you want to put it like that, then yes.'

There's a sudden creaking above our heads.

Clemo looks up at once, frowning sharply as though he thinks we have an intruder. Then his brow lightens with inspiration. 'Ah, Hannah. Getting ready for work.' He looks back at me, his smile a little too broad. 'Your friend takes good care of you, I can see that.'

'We try to be there for each other.'

'I understand.' He nods sympathetically, rocking back in his chair. 'You two are *very* close.'

It sounds like a statement, not a question. I puzzle over it for a moment, then say, 'We're not gay.'

Reverend Clemo pretends to look confused, a slight flush in his cheeks. 'I never suggested – '

'I'm not gay, at any rate. I don't know about Hannah. I've never asked her. But I doubt it.'

This is not quite true. I know for a fact that Hannah is a serial one-night-stander with men of a certain age, but I am not about to share that with the vicar. He's a man of a certain age himself, one of my dad's generation, and I don't think I could handle a complication like that. Not that it is even remotely likely.

A question suddenly occurs to me. 'Do you remember when my mother died, Reverend?'

The vicar looks taken aback by my directness, but answers without any obvious hesitation. 'Indeed I do, yes. It was a terrible business. Truly appalling. I hadn't been ordained then, of course. Hadn't got "The Call," as we say. But I remember seeing news of her murder on the television, and praying for you and your father.'

'You were living in the village then?'

'Oh no, I was … nearby. But not in the village itself. Though I had friends and family here. Such a shock for our little community.'

'Were you still in touch with her?'

'As a friend, yes. In fact, I danced at your parents' wedding.' Mortimer Clemo smiles at me sadly, his tone suddenly gentle, and I can see that he is deeply pleased to be of service to me now, having missed his opportunity eighteen years ago. 'I can only imagine the impact her brutal death must have had on your own life. That it is still having, I suspect.'

'Meaning what?'

Thoughtfully, the vicar steeples his long fingers together and leans his chin on them, looking at me.

'You should feel free to unburden yourself to me. To unburden your heart, if it will help. And you don't need to fear more exposure. Trust me, Eleanor, nothing you say will leave this room. The sanctity of the confessional, you know.' His voice drops. 'You are clearly going through something very difficult at the moment. Something that has destroyed your peace of mind. But it's nothing to be ashamed of.'

Nothing to be ashamed of.

The vicar might as well call me a liar and a hysterical woman, and have done with it. In an earlier century, I would probably have been hanged as a witch for what I saw in the woods, by men just like him.

Abruptly, I rise from my chair. 'Well, thanks for stopping by, Reverend. It was very kind of you. But what I need right now is to be alone.'

He hesitates, staring. 'Oh, I see.'

I open the kitchen door and stand waiting.

With obvious reluctance, the Reverend Clemo gets to his feet, tucks the pine chair back under the table, and agrees to be shepherded from the cottage. His head brushes the low beams on the way out. 'If you ever feel the need to talk – '

'I know where you are,' I finish for him politely. 'Thank you, vicar. Goodbye.'

A few minutes later, I happen to glance out of my

bedroom window as I'm changing out of my tracksuit, and I see Clemo again. He's standing in the shadow of the trees a little further down the lane. I can only see his shoes and trousers from that angle, but it's definitely him.

I freeze, wondering what on earth the vicar is still doing there, hiding in the bushes. Is Clemo watching the cottage?

There was such a strange look in his face when I showed him the door, as though my asking him to leave had made him angry. It unsettled me.

Then I spot thin tendrils of smoke snaking up through leafy branches towards the sky.

Get a grip.

I reach for my jeans and wriggle into them, ludicrously relieved and a bit embarrassed by my own paranoia.

The man is having a crafty smoke, that's all. Enjoying a secret cigarette on his way home because his wife won't let him smoke in the vicarage.

CHAPTER TEN

'When I finish counting back from ten, you will wake up feeling refreshed. There will be no more nightmares, no more daydreams, no more ... unfortunate episodes.'

The voice is familiar. A soft feminine tone, soothing and trustworthy, yet somehow sinister at the same time.

'Ten, nine, eight, seven ... '

I drift, hanging onto a last dim memory. My mother's face, smiling as I show her the bird's feather I've found. A strong black feather, slightly dusty from the ground. She takes it and holds it up to the light, then laughs, stroking it across my cheek.

'Six, five, four ... '

I look up into dappled sunlight and see her face change, the smile fading to a look of surprise. What has Mum seen behind me?

Hearing footsteps at my back, I begin to turn my head, curious, taking a little alarm at her expression.

'Three, two, one.'

Something clicks in my head. My mother disappears.

I struggle to get her back, to rebuild that half-forgotten face in my memory, suffering an almost intolerable sense of loss. Yet after only a few more seconds I can't even recall what I've lost.

My mind begins to empty and I find myself floating in the silence.

Light burns against my closed lids.

I am aware of a strong feeling of relief, as though I have been standing too long on a precipice and someone has drawn me back from the edge at last. The past begins to fade away, and reluctantly I let it go, allow myself to return to the present. Slowly I grope for my surroundings, hearing muffled voices in another room, a telephone ringing in the distance, traffic in the street below, the sounds of a busy town.

'Wake up, Eleanor.' The voice is insistent.

I open my eyes.

I'm lying on my back on a long, low couch. There's a large rectangular window facing me across the immaculately tidy office, the cream blinds only pulled down partway. Afternoon sun is pouring in below the slats, filling the office with golden light. I'm dazzled at first, squinting up at the woman bending over me. There's a momentary confusion, then I remember.

Not my mother. No longer the dream but reality. All the same, her face is familiar. Familiar and unsettling at the same time.

I study her face, my eyes adjusting to the light. Honey-brown hair, neatly cut in an easily manageable bob about an oval face, a trace of face powder and pink lipstick, tiny creases about her mouth and eyes.

Dr Quick.

'Welcome back.' She studies me closely, eyes narrowed on my face. 'How are you feeling, Eleanor? Any headache? Dizziness? Nausea?' When I shake my head to each of these questions, she straightens. 'Good, that's very good.'

I sit up groggily. 'What happened?'

My throat is dry, a bad taste on my tongue. I turn blindly, reaching for the glass of water she always used to place at my elbow during these hypnosis sessions. It's not there.

'Oh, sorry. Water?' The doctor leans forward and hands it to me. 'Give yourself a minute. Try not to hurry.'

I remember Dr Quick from my childhood as an uber-friendly doctor, habitually clad in a colourful wool cardigan, soft-voiced, always cracking little jokes to put me at my ease. Today she is sombre in dove-grey and black, the small red-jewelled brooch pinned to her blouse her only concession to colour.

'I'm fine.' I take a few sips, then replace the water glass carefully. I'm aware of a slight tremor in my hand. 'Did the hypnosis work? What did I say?'

'You don't remember?'

I shake my head, though I do remember vaguely. Snippets of dream-memory, flashing images, half-truths. Nothing I can quantify, and certainly nothing I can take to the police.

Her mouth tightens. She retreats to her desk, sitting in her black leather swivel chair, and looks down at her notes. 'That's a pity. I was hoping to be able to discover the root cause of your nightmares by probing your memories outside hypnosis. For instance, when we talked earlier, you mentioned a "shadow man" you see at night sometimes, standing at the foot of your bed.'

'Yes.'

'I asked you to identify it during the session, to give the "shadow man" a name of some kind. You didn't seem very cooperative. I'm still not sure what that signifies. But I would suggest it's some kind of hangover from the day of your mother's murder.'

I can't hold her gaze. Maybe the sun behind her head is too bright. I look down, study my hands in silence. That was the one thing I had hoped to achieve with this hypnosis therapy. Saying goodbye to the shadow man who still haunts me. Though Dr Quick also refers to it as 'childhood trauma manifesting as ritual superstition' which means little to me.

But then she's not the one who wakes up in the middle of the night to find a faceless shadow looming over her bed.

'So there's nothing new,' I state flatly.

'I'm afraid not. There was nothing you didn't already say in your original sessions, according to my notes. Except perhaps ...' Dr Quick hesitates a beat. 'Well, there was a single detail that seemed out of place.'

I look up, interested. 'Tell me.'

'First, you need to understand that what a person says under hypnosis is unlikely ever to be admissible in a court of law. But that does not mean it isn't factual, that it doesn't represent the truth as your subconscious sees it.'

'You mean I could have imagined it, even if it seems true to me? But it's still true as far as I'm concerned?'

'Precisely.'

I push myself up into a sitting position. 'Wonderful.'

'Basically, your subconscious may no longer make any distinction between what you remember and what you *think* you remember.' She smiles, the merest twitch of thin lips. 'So, do you still want to hear what you said?'

I swing my legs round and sit up properly on the couch. My mobile, switched to vibrate, is a hard bulge in the back pocket of my jeans. I was asked to turn it off completely before we started, but of course didn't. Though it would be pretty strange to experience a sudden vibrating sensation in my bottom during one of these sessions.

'Of course.'

'Then I'll read it through from the beginning. You can draw your own conclusions.'

She reads her notes on the session in her usual flat voice, almost robotic. There's nothing new, just as she said.

But towards the end, Dr Quick pauses and glances up at me. 'Then you said, "I recognised the white trainers, as he ran up the slope." That's something new.'

'I've always said he wore white trainers.'

'Not precisely those words though.' The doctor shuffles through the document file on her desk, then stops, picking up and studying an older transcript. 'Yes, here it is. You've always mentioned seeing his white trainers, certainly. But you never before said that you "recognised" them. Not once.'

'So I used a different word this time.' I shrug. 'How is that revealing?'

'Bear in mind that I'm a hypnosis therapist, not a detective,' Dr Quick tells me, leaning back in her chair. 'And perhaps it means nothing at all. But the word "recognised" would suggest that you had seen those particular white trainers before. That you *knew* the man wearing them, in fact.'

I need to see Denzil Tremain.

Denzil is uncomplicated, and not entirely into the idea of a relationship, which makes him perfect right now. If I confide in one of my close friends – Hannah maybe, or Tris, or Connor – I'm going to end up getting an emotional response, plus the kind of heartfelt advice that sounds great late at night but isn't worth very much when you find yourself alone again.

He understands because he's been there. He's got his own version of the shadow man. Only in his case, it's a real person. His father, who has been in and out of prison most of Denzil's life. So I'm unlikely to get much advice or sympathy from him. But I'll get an intelligent ear, and sometimes talking out a problem can make you see a clear solution where you were blind to it before.

Denzil has a weekend job at the Woods Valley Garden Centre. It doesn't pay much. But with his history, he's lucky to have any kind of gainful employment at all. He has tattoos and piercings, like thousands of other people in Cornwall, but where most flaunt a rose or a skull on one arm, Denzil has both arms covered in designs, and much of his back. His ears have multiple piercings, and last year his nose and lip were both pierced too, with a delicate chain running from one to the other. And his father's in prison for aggravated assault at the moment. Nobody seems to know when he'll get out.

None of that stops me from liking him. I first made friends with him shortly after my mother was killed. We were at the same school, and his dad had just been sent to prison for burglary. People pointed us both out in the playground and hassled us outside school. Even at primary school, we had a common understanding that life was shit, and if you wanted to survive it, you had to toughen up.

Saturday morning, I head for the garden centre to see Denzil, and find him lugging immense sacks of manure from a trolley onto the display pallets.

Denzil straightens in surprise, wiping a dirt-covered hand across his face and leaving a black streak on his cheek. He's got huge tawny hair like a lion, naturally curly. 'Ellie? What are you doing here?'

'I've been calling and texting you for days, but no reply.'

He looks guilty, not meeting my gaze. 'I did mean to call you but my phone's been turned off. I ... lost the charger cable. Sorry, you know how it is.'

I don't believe him but say nothing. I understand how it feels not to want to communicate.

Jago leans out of the office. The boss's son, thick-set like his father, and trying to grow a beard by the stubbly look of his chin. Another one who went to school with me. The place is crawling with them, which isn't surprising when you consider that our school is the only one for miles.

'Hey, Ellie,' Jago says in his whining voice. 'Saw that story in the newspaper about you. Shocking stuff. You must have been furious.'

His knowing smile makes my skin crawl. I look him in the eye and say, '*Story* being the operative word.'

'Come again?'

'She means it was a load of shit,' Denzil says drily, and heaves another bag of manure onto the pallet. 'Like this lot.'

Jago stares. 'You watch your language. Or you'll be out of a job. Talking of which, you'd better hurry up with that. You've got another two trolleys to unload.'

Denzil tosses the last sack of manure onto the pallet, then straightens again, wiping his hands unhurriedly on his black apron. Like me, he has always had a problem with authority.

'I haven't taken my break yet.'

'So?'

'I want to take it now.'

Jago looks from him to me, his small eyes unpleasant. 'Like that, is it?' But when Denzil stands looking at him, his face impassive, Jago shrugs. 'Take your break, then. But not a minute longer than fifteen.'

Denzil unties his apron and drapes it over the empty trolley. 'Come on,' he says to me. 'I know somewhere we can talk in private.'

Jago watches us go. 'No smoking anywhere on the site, remember,' he says, and jabs his finger towards the sign by the office door that reads in plastic gold lettering, PLEASE, NO SMOKING.

'Jago hasn't changed much since school,' I remark to Denzil as soon as we're out of earshot. 'Sorry if I've caused trouble by coming here. It sounds like he's looking for an excuse to sack you.'

'Don't worry about him. Jago's only the monkey. His dad's still in charge, and Dick knows I'm a good worker.' Denzil winks at me. 'When I bother to show up, that is.'

I smile. 'Idiot.'

CHAPTER ELEVEN

There's a small staff-only area behind the shed displays. The ground is partly paved, partly gravelled, with weeds poking out between paving stones. It's hot and sunny today. There are some damaged stone benches set to one side, and a pot filled with soil where people have ground out sneaky cigarettes. Denzil kneels beside one of the scroll-ended benches, reaches carefully down behind it, and pulls out a sealed pouch of tobacco. Concealed inside is a pack of extra-thin rolling paper and a lighter.

He sits on the bench and gestures me to join him. The stone is warm from the sun, surprisingly comfortable. 'Ciggie?'

'I've given up.'

'Quitter.' He lays the tobacco pouch open on his lap and expertly starts to roll himself a cigarette. 'I'm sorry I didn't return your calls.'

'I thought you didn't know I'd called.'

'Well ...' He does not elaborate on that, but licks the sticky crease of the paper, then rolls it over, sealing the thin cigarette. 'You're no fool, Ellie. You know I don't like to feel tied down.'

'I wasn't offering.'

'Understood. I'm glad you came to see me, anyway. How are you?'

'Not brilliant.'

Briefly, I fill him in on what has happened. The woods, the dead body, the number three on her forehead. Being Denzil, he does not push the issue or ask further questions, but simply grunts again. That's another reason why I like him so much. There's never any hassle with Denzil and no need for long-winded explanations.

He lights his roll-up, blows a soft smoke-ring into the air, and then asks casually, 'Up for a night out, then? Something to take your mind off all that shit?'

'Where?'

'Newquay. There's a beach barbecue tonight. Some of my surfer friends are going. Then we could hit the clubs, go dancing.'

'All of them?'

He grins. 'We don't have to if you don't fancy that scene. We could float the coast instead. See what else is happening.'

'Sounds good to me.'

'Pick you up at six, then. At the cottage.'

'I'll be there.'

Denzil takes another drag on his roll-up, then offers it to me.

'I told you, no thanks.'

He blows out the smoke, looking at me through narrowed eyes, then bends his head to kiss me.

His lips are warm, his skin rough and stubbly. I hook a hand round the back of his neck, pull him closer. His tongue plays lazily against mine, exploring my mouth. He tastes of smoke but I find that sexy, just like I find his casual attitude to dating attractive. Denzil is elusive, yes, but at least that means he's never going to trap me into a long-term commitment.

I close my eyes, enjoying the hot sunshine on my back as we kiss. His hand gently caresses my breast, and I wonder what tonight's date will be like.

We are interrupted a few minutes later by loud, abrasive coughing. An old man in a flat cap is browsing through the shed selection, and has seen us kissing. Frowning, the old man stops to stare at us through the narrow gap between a wooden pagoda and a tool store, then wags his finger as though we have been caught misbehaving.

'Christ,' I say, startled.

I think at first that I know him from the village, but when I study him more carefully, I don't. The old man must be at least seventy-five, maybe older. His hair is white and he's wearing a thick woollen scarf pulled up to his chin, though it's quite warm today. He's tall but stooping in an exaggerated way, as though he needs a stick for walking but has forgotten to bring it with him. And he has huge bushy eyebrows under his flat cap; they look unlikely and theatrical, like they've been stuck on with glue.

'Nosy old sod,' Denzil mutters, drawing back. Reluctantly, he drops his roll-up into the pot of earth, then stands up. 'Break's over though. Thanks for coming to see me.'

'Six o'clock,' I remind him, a little embarrassed, tidying my clothes.

He nods, and trudges off past the sheds, presumably to fetch another trolley load of manure for the display pallets.

I leave him and the old man in the sunshine, and wander back through the garden centre aisles and past the office. It's empty, neither Jago nor his dad anywhere to be seen. Probably on the shop floor, dealing with customers. The garden centre is always busy on Saturdays at this time of year, people buying new tools and young plants for summer bedding. I notice several shoppers looking at me sideways, then whispering to each other. I can imagine what they're saying.

And maybe they're right. Maybe I am stark staring mad. Because they never did find the dead woman. So if she existed, what happened to her? Dead people do not get up and walk about on their own. Either she was only pretending to be dead, or somebody moved her body after I had left. Both of which are far-fetched scenarios, at best.

I have to concede that it's possible I imagined her. But that is not going to stop me trying to discover the truth.

About to leave, my gaze falls on a framed colour photograph on the wall of the office. It's new. Or rather, the photograph is old, but the frame looks brand-new and I have no memory of seeing it there before.

I lean close to the glass of the office window. It appears to be a school photograph from several decades ago. The school kids are gathered outdoors around a huge and lavishly decorated Christmas tree, their haircuts and uniforms old-fashioned, their shirt lapels narrow and pointed. It must have been taken in the seventies, by the look of it.

I glance around, but Jago is nowhere in sight. I slip through the office door, which is ajar, and stand in front of the framed photograph.

It's the girl to the left that interests me. I know that face. And her eyes, so familiar. There's a boy beside her, taller, his arm around her shoulder. It's a possessive gesture. I frown, not recognising him. His eyes are narrowed, he has lanky shoulder-length hair, and he's smiling. Somehow I don't believe that smile though. It gives me the creeps.

'I found that a few weeks ago in an old chest up at my house,' a deep male voice says. 'It's a good photo of her.'

I turn, startled.

It's the owner of the garden centre, Dick Laney. I didn't hear him come into the office. How long has he been standing there in the doorway, watching me?

'Hello, Mr Laney. I'm sorry. I shouldn't be in here, I know.'

He smiles, coming closer. 'Call me Dick. And it's no problem, Eleanor, no problem at all,' he insists. 'You go on now, take a good look. Only natural you should want to look at a picture of your mother.'

'I've never seen this before. How did you get hold of it?'

'It's mine. My dad took it, so he'd have a record of the Christmas tree.' He studies the photograph, standing shoulder-to-shoulder with me. 'This place was only a small outfit back then, but he sold Christmas trees to most of the village. That was the biggest tree he had in stock that year, so he donated it to the school. We made the decorations ourselves in class. Blue Peter stuff, you know, all tin foil and glue and sparkly nonsense. Not bad though.'

Realization hits me and I turn to stare at him. 'You were at school with my mum.'

'That's right. I was in the year above.'

I look again at the smiling boy with his arm around my mum's shoulder. Who was he? Her boyfriend at the time?

I glance from the photograph to Dick Laney, and then back again. 'Is that *you* standing next to my mother?'

'That it is.'

'So you were going out with her in school?'

He hesitates. 'We were just friends.'

I look again at the photograph, my mother's wary expression, the smile on Dick Laney's face, his arm looped arrogantly about her shoulders, and am not sure I believe him.

'Well, the tree decorations look good,' I tell him, trying to inject some enthusiasm into my voice, 'even if they were homemade. Very professional.'

I study my mum's expression while pretending to look more closely at the Christmas tree and its tin foil decorations. She is smiling too but the smile does not reach her eyes. Then my attention is caught by another face, half-hidden in the crowd of other kids thronging beneath the Christmas tree. A boy with dark hair and dark eyes. He's not looking at the camera like everyone else, but staring across at my mother and Dick Laney. Brooding, like a child whose toy has been snatched away.

I've seen that same expression on someone else's face, and recently too, I'm sure of it. But whose?

'Mr Laney, who is this?' I ask curiously, tapping the glass that protects the photograph.

The office telephone begins to ring, loud and insistent.

'Excuse me, I have to answer this.' Dick Laney turns away and picks up the phone. 'Good morning, Woods Valley Garden Centre, how may I help you?' He hesitates, frowning. 'Yes, we sell a wide range of garden ornaments. Gnomes too.' As he listens to the customer, his gaze slowly returns to the photograph on the wall. 'Five-thirty close on a Saturday. That's not a problem, sir.'

He puts the phone down on the charging cradle.

'Sorry to be interrupting your work like this,' I say quickly, worried he may ask me to leave without answering my question. 'I promise I'll be out of your way in a minute. But who is this boy?'

Dick Laney picks up a pen and taps it on the desk, frowning across at the framed photograph. 'Which … which one?'

I show him again.

He steps closer as though to check, but I get the feeling he already knows exactly who I mean and is stalling. 'That looks like Mortimer Clemo.'

I stare, not sure I heard him properly. 'The *vicar*?'

'He weren't no vicar then.' There's a sharp tone to his voice that wasn't there before. Anger? Contempt? He tosses the pen back onto the desk. 'Morty was always *odd* at school, I suppose. But I don't think he got God until much later on.' He laughs, and for the first time I see Dick Laney's resemblance to his son in that sneering look. 'Probably couldn't hold down a proper job, and realised the church was his only chance to earn a decent wage.'

'I didn't know he went to school with my mum.'

'Ah, there's a fair few of us about.' He glances impatiently at the door. 'Sorry, but I've got work to do.'

'Of course.'

Before leaving the office, I take a final look at Mortimer Clemo in the old photograph, his tight expression as he stands there in his duffel coat, watching Angela Blackwood.

So both Dick Laney and the vicar went to school with my mother. I'm not sure what to make of that new information. Though, as Dick said, quite a number of the middle-aged people in the village would have been at school at the same time too, and not all of them come from upcountry.

But how close was she to Mortimer Clemo?

Heading towards the exit from the garden centre, I realise the old man in the flat cap is watching me again. He's standing in the hosepipe display area, right behind one of the largest reels, peering through the gap at me. His cap is pulled down to hide his face but he's staring at me from under those ludicrous bushy eyebrows. Staring as though he knows me.

There's only one explanation for that.

I glare at him. The old man backs away, almost falling over a display of spades in his hurry. I watch until he's shuffled round the corner towards the bedding plants display area, then head out into the sunshine.

That bloody newspaper report.

CHAPTER TWELVE

Denzil was right. I feel much better sitting in his battered jeep with my bare feet on the dashboard, listening to music as we swing across the moor on our way to the north coast. The sun is shining, and I'm wearing my hair down at last, and a short dress for dancing.

I realise Denzil is staring at my bare legs. 'Eyes on the road, please.'

He laughs, but looks back at the road obediently enough. 'I love the anklet. Very sexy.'

'Thanks.'

'Did you bring your bikini?'

I stare at him in dismay. 'I didn't know we'd be swimming.'

He shrugs big shoulders. He's changed his clothes since work, wearing cut-off denim shorts and an old white tee-shirt with a black leather waistcoat, hanging open. His deejay gear. It's a very sexy look, but not what I was expecting to see tonight.

'Beach barbecue. There'll be surfers there. Maybe some lifeguards off-duty, kicking back for a few hours once the sun's gone down. Most of us go in the water at some point.' His sideways grin is wicked. 'You can always strip it all off. Go skinny-dipping.'

'In your dreams.'

He laughs again, and shakes his head. His tawny curls bounce. 'I know which way the wind blows.'

'Oh yeah?'

Denzil looks at me more seriously. 'Look, before there are any misunderstandings, let's get one thing straight. I'm helping you out tonight as a friend, Ellie. I'm not taking you to Newquay so I can get you into bed.'

I stare at him, taken aback by his bluntness. 'Okay.'

'The last thing you need right now is someone else screwing with your head. I figured you could do with a night out, that's all. So shake it loose, whatever's bothering you, and let's have a good time.'

I'm secretly disappointed but he's probably right. I'm still not sure what the question is, but sex is unlikely to be the answer.

'Thanks, I appreciate it.'

He hesitates. 'But?'

'But nothing, really. Things on my mind, you know.' I lean my head back against the seat, enjoying the wind in my hair. Yes, he's definitely right. I do need to shake it loose, this feeling of dread and *déja-vu*. 'I'm seeing a specialist again.'

'What kind of specialist?'

I hesitate, not sure if I want to say it out loud. But this is Denzil. I know it won't go any further. 'A hypnotist. To help me calm down and maybe remember what happened.'

'Hypnotherapy?' Denzil slows down for a tight bend in the lane, staring ahead. 'Hold on, didn't they try that before?'

'When I was younger, yes, and I kept getting in trouble with the police. It might work better now.' Briefly, I explain about Dr Quick. 'She regresses me to the day of my mother's murder, and records everything I say under hypnosis. She does that repeatedly.'

'Why?'

'I think she hopes that by asking different questions each time, she may be able to drag up new information from my subconscious. Or at least get my head to process my emotions properly, so I can forget what happened that day and move on with my life.' I feel uncomfortable, talking about it. 'Dr Quick thinks I'm stuck in the past, emotionally speaking. That I need *closure*, as the Americans put it.'

'But you don't like going to see her?' Denzil sounds curt, as if he does not approve. 'So don't go. Refuse the treatments.'

'I don't have a choice, Denzil.'

'Everyone has a choice.'

'I don't have anything. Except a psychosis.'

'Says who?'

I close my eyes, seeing their faces. 'The doctor. The police. My father. Hannah, probably. Everyone, in other words.'

'For what it's worth, I don't think you're crazy.'

'Thanks,' I say again.

'No more than I am, anyway.'

I laugh, hearing the cynical note in his voice. 'That's me off the hook, then. I'm so relieved.'

The dance music changes to a moody tune I don't recognise: wistful, haunting, with a female vocalist who sounds American. When I open my eyes, Denzil is mouthing the words as he drives, not looking at me. He seems lost in his own world.

I fold my arms across my chest and stare at the wild moorland ahead of us, a patchy brownish-green of grass and heather strewn with whitened boulders. It's so barren and wind-swept on the moor that nothing much seems to grow; even the native ponies look stunted and thin-ribbed. It's a hard life up here. The wild ponies are hunted and driven across the moors once their numbers grow too high, so they can be trapped and culled if no one agrees to purchase them. Like they're vermin. It's a disgrace. But I don't know what the solution is.

I wonder what Denzil is thinking. Perhaps he secretly believes I'm mad too, seeing dead bodies that aren't there. But then why would he encourage me to turn down hypnosis?

He draws up at a narrow crossroads, tall hedgerows blocking our view in every direction, then roars across the junction, changing gear noisily.

'Look,' Denzil says, 'however bad this gets, don't forget you're not under suspicion of any crime here. You were a child when your mum died, and I agree you had no choices back then. Neither of us had choices over what they did to us as kids. But if you don't want this doctor messing with your head, with your memories of your mother, for God's sake, then you should tell her – and the police – where to stick it.'

The hedgerows have fallen away to long expanses of flat rock and sparse moorland. The land stretches for miles on either side of the road, no fences, no houses, just the occasional dirt track leading into wilderness. It's lonely up here on the moors, even when the tourist season is in full swing. There are so many places to hide once you leave the road. There are wooded slopes and crags, and lakes and treacherous marshlands. You could go walking and disappear up here, fall down and die in a ditch, and no one would find your body for days. Maybe even weeks or months.

'I will. Next time.'

'Good for you. You've got to stand up for yourself. Don't let the bastards push you around.'

'I don't let anyone push me around. I was only a kid the first time round, or I would have said no then. I may say no now, I haven't decided yet.'

'Remind me what happened before?'

'I went round the bend a bit when I was about ten. Ran away from home, did some stupid stuff. The police got involved, forced my dad to take me for therapy. Do you remember?'

'Not so much, sorry.' He shrugs. 'I was probably in trouble myself back then. Too busy fighting my own demons to notice yours.'

Denzil had a difficult childhood too, got arrested a few times as a kid for minor offences. That's probably why I find it so easy to talk to him. He knows how bad the fallout can become when the world tilts the wrong way on its axis, even for a few minutes.

'The police recommended Dr Quick,' I explain. 'She was just starting out in her practice. She thought hypnosis would help stop the nightmares.'

He looks at me. 'Nightmares?'

'It's stupid, really. Forget it. I don't like talking about it.'

'Try me,' he insists.

I'm embarrassed by this trip down memory lane. It's the last thing I wanted when I agreed to go out with him. But maybe talking it through with Denzil will help me get the past straight in my own head.

'I used to wake up in the night and think someone was watching me. Standing over my bed, or by the window. But whenever I put the light on, there was never anyone there.'

He nods as if he understands. 'So did the hypnosis work?'

'For a while, yes. I stopped having the nightmares.' I do not mention that they have returned in the past few months. I don't want him to think I'm unbalanced. 'But looking back, I think those sessions were as much for the police as me. They wanted me to describe the killer. The doctor used to ask me what he looked like, what he was wearing – '

'*What?*'

Suddenly intent, Denzil reaches out and snaps off the music. He's so serious, I've never seen him look like that before.

'You were able to remember under hypnosis who

murdered your mother?' he demands, staring at me like he's never seen me before. 'You mean, you know who the killer is?'

I shake my head. 'My therapist usually regresses me to the morning of my mother's murder to see if we can uncover anything new. But I only ever remember seeing the killer from the back. Oh, and a pair of white trainers. Never any new details. Nothing that the police didn't already know from the description I gave at the time.'

I choose not to mention what the doctor said, that I had used the word "recognised" this time, talking about the killer's white trainers. It's a new and private fact, something I want to keep to myself a while longer.

Denzil says nothing, but I suspect he's disappointed. He looks back at the road.

'The police weren't thrilled by our lack of success,' I continue, 'as you can imagine. They were hoping I'd be able to identify the killer. But I probably never saw his face.'

'What makes you say that?'

'If I'd seen the killer's face, I would have said so at the time. Told the police, and done a photo fit so they could catch him. I was only six, yes, and I was terrified. But that's not something you easily forget. The face of the man who murdered your mother.'

'I can imagine.'

'I hate being hypnotised. It takes away your control, your privacy. There's nowhere to hide. But I can't deny that it calms me down. I stopped behaving like an idiot after I had those first sessions, and started focusing on my work instead. So I guess it's useful in that respect.'

'And now the police think another few sessions with a hypnotist will sort your head out again? Because of what happened in the woods?'

'Something like that.'

The jeep is open-topped. The air feels chilly this high up, despite the sunshine. I slump in my seat, my hair whipping in my eyes as we accelerate across the moors.

Denzil glances at me, then strokes a few strands away from my face. 'Hey, babe, don't cry. You ever need a bolt hole, you know how to get hold of me.'

'Thanks,' I tell him. 'Always assuming you can remember where your charger is.'

He grins. 'Always assuming that, yes.'

CHAPTER THIRTEEN

By the time we reach the beach resort of Newquay, the sun is much lower in the sky and the air is distinctly cooler. But there's still another hour or two of daylight left, and people are still wandering about in beach shorts and flip-flops.

The seaside town is crowded, even though the school holidays haven't started. Denzil drives slowly through the narrow streets, occasionally sounding his horn or waving at a friend on the pavement or in a shop doorway. People grin when they see who it is, and a few young men shuffle over to grasp his hand and chat for a few minutes while we hold up traffic.

Denzil introduces me casually as, 'Eleanor, a friend of mine,' then we drive on, getting closer to the beach.

He's turned down the CD player but music is pounding out of the bars along the main street, so I'm still tapping my foot. The setting sun is in my eyes as we turn downhill, blinding me. It's a resort town but most of the tourist shops are only just closing up, owners dragging signs inside and lowering metal grills over their windows.

We reach the beach front. The air is fresh and salty, and I can smell fish and chips from one of the cliff top bars above us. Heads turn as the car slows, people staring at

Denzil. There's a barbecue already set up a short way between the cliffs and the outgoing tide, I can see it smoking furiously. I squint into golden light; there's a group of teenagers messing about on the sands, silhouetted against the setting sun, chasing each other and shrieking with laughter.

I check my lipstick in the pull-down mirror. I'm probably a bit old for the beach scene. I just hope none of the sixth formers from school hang out here at the weekends. That would be embarrassing.

Denzil finds a spot to park. 'Come on, we'll stay a couple of hours, then move on to the club where I'm gigging.' His gaze is appreciative as I hop out of the jeep. 'You look gorgeous, by the way. I love that dress.'

I focus on what he just said. 'You're deejaying tonight?'

He looks at me blankly. 'Didn't I tell you? I got a call after we spoke at the garden centre. A friend of mine is sick tonight, so I'm standing in for him. You don't mind, do you?'

I usually love to watch Denzil doing his deejay thing with the decks. But part of me is still feeling a bit fragile, so I don't like the idea of being left on my own for hours while he's working.

'When will you finish?'

'No idea,' he murmurs, and slips an arm about my waist, pulling me close. I let him, half-seduced by the sheer charisma of the man, though he annoys the hell out of me at the same time. He nuzzles into my hair. 'You'll be fine. With your legs, everyone will want to dance with you. Mmm, I love that perfume too. What is it?'

'Something I got for Christmas.'

'From Hannah?'

'Connor, actually.'

He raises his eyebrows as we start walking. 'Connor. Should I be jealous?'

'I thought this was just a pity date.'

He sucks in his breath, then grins appreciatively. 'Ouch,

little cat. Yeah, I'm not in the market for anything long-term. So if you and Connor are an item ... '

'We're not.'

'Whatever you say, gorgeous.' He shrugs, but tightens his arm round my waist. 'Still, just because I'm not after the whole meal, that doesn't mean I don't want a taste.'

I throw back my head. 'Oh my God, corny.'

'Was it?'

'Horribly.'

He laughs too. 'Sorry.'

We're crossing the sands towards his friends. The blokes look okay, standing about the makeshift barbecue with beers, most in scruffy jeans and shorts. The girls look like supermodels, tall and skinny in tiny shorts and bikini tops, their hair long and impossibly straight. None of them are older than twenty, by my estimate. One of them turns and stares at me, hands on hips, her make-up immaculate, face frozen in an expression of disbelief.

I feel uncomfortable at once and disentangle myself from his arm. 'Who's that?'

Denzil makes an irritated noise under his breath. 'It's nobody. Relax, enjoy the party. You'll be fine.'

An ex-girlfriend, I guess. I accept a can of beer – warm, unfortunately, but still drinkable – and sit on a rock near the barbecue, carefully not looking in her direction. Someone turns the music up. I drag my phone out of my bag. Two missed calls, three texts. Two from Hannah, one from Tris.

I read the two texts from Hannah first.

The police rang. Wouldn't leave a message. Hx

Text number two is simpler:

PS. Tris just called, looking for you. Hope it was okay to tell him.

I frown, perplexed, and thumb back to the main menu. The text from Tris himself is even more troubling.

Hannah says you are in Newquay tonight? Connor wanted to go clubbing so we're both here too. If you're going to Tempest, maybe we could hook up. T.

What is he playing at? Tris has barely looked at me for months, he and Connor have been so focused on keeping the farm together since their dad died. Now suddenly he's interested in meeting up with me at a club? I want to read something into that, but dare not.

Denzil is right. I don't need any more complications right now. And Tris would be a massive complication.

'Denzil?'

He's talking to the blonde who glared at me, but turns at my call, cigarette in hand, looking vaguely guilty. 'Yeah, what's up?'

'Are we going to Tempest tonight?'

He nods. 'That's the club where I'm gigging. Why?'

'I might meet some friends there, that's all.'

'Cool, good idea.' He turns back to the blonde, who is still staring at me through narrowed blue eyes, and continues with what he was saying.

I feel a bit embarrassed by his brush-off, then tell myself to get over it. What was I expecting? I like Denzil, and I'm interested in him sexually, but we're not dating. Besides, we didn't come here together as boyfriend-girlfriend. Like he told me earlier, he sees this night out as a favour for a friend. Not a date. Whatever might happen at the end of it.

I text Tris back, *Maybe see you at Tempest*, then turn off my phone. I don't want to appear needy.

Jumping down from my rock, I decide to work the party. Better than sitting on my own for the next hour. I get into a conversation about films with one of Denzil's friends; he's a little younger than me, not bad-looking, with a shaved head. Some of the others come over later with a bowl of hot spicy sausages from the barbecue and we all help ourselves. After a few beers, I start to relax, and even agree to dance with one of the guys. It's not turning out to be such a bad night. At least none of them seem to know anything about the body in the woods.

It's nearly nine o'clock by the time we leave the beach party and move on to the club where Denzil is working that night. He's the guest deejay, which means I get in for free.

'Remember,' Denzil says in my ear as he shows me to a much-coveted seat near his deejay platform, 'you're here to shake it loose. So enjoy yourself tonight, understand?'

'I'll try.'

He sends over a tall, orange-red house cocktail with an umbrella and sparkler, then proceeds to ignore me for the next hour. But I don't really care. I'm out of the house and anonymous, that's what matters.

Sometimes I get up to dance, leaving my cocktail unattended at my seat, sometimes I keep my eyes on Denzil on his high platform. It's not a bad way to spend an evening. New drinks arrive at intervals, and Denzil waves a hand as the bartender points him out, winking across at me.

I watch women drooling over him, all of them beautiful and exquisitely made-up, wearing tiny outfits in green and pink neon, armed with clubbers' pom-poms and glow-sticks, and I can see why he has hang-ups about dating. As a deejay, Denzil is constantly surrounded by all these gorgeous, adoring women; why would he want to tie himself down to one girlfriend when he could have a different lover every night?

Halfway through the evening, I weave to the ladies through a heaving pack of dancers, the beat thumping through every bone and nerve, unsteady on my feet, pleasantly drunk.

I see a familiar dark head ahead of me. 'Tris?'

But there's too much noise, he can't hear me. The heaving crowd shifts and merges, and he vanishes.

'Tris?'

The strobe comes on. Everything goes weird. Heads moving, arms whirling, lights flashing, and none of the faces familiar. I start to feel sick. Stumbling, I turn back towards the ladies' toilets, then catch another tantalising glimpse of Tris under the central mirror ball. I stop, swaying slightly, and scan the dancers for his face. Again, there's no sign of him in the crowd. One minute he's there, the next he's gone. It's almost like Tris is playing a game with me, and I'm losing.

I turn, staring all around, confused and frowning. Where the hell did he go?

'Hey, looking for me?'

I spin round at the voice in my ear, over-balancing. Tris catches me by the shoulders, looking surprised. 'You drunk?'

'Cocktails, that's all.'

'Where's Denzil?'

I point out Denzil on his high platform, tending to the decks with his headphones on. 'He thinks I should let my hair down, forget about the … the body.'

'Hang on.' Tris pulls out his phone, which is lit up with an incoming call. He puts it to his ear, then nods. 'Yeah, okay. Five minutes, out the front.' He ends the call, looking at me soberly. Like only Tris can do in the middle of a packed night club. 'That was Connor. He wants to go home.'

'But we only just hooked up.'

'You know Connor, he's a law unto himself. And he hates Newquay. I don't know why he insisted on us going out tonight. I've been dancing, but he's barely moved from the bar all evening, miserable sod.'

Still missing his dad, probably. I say nothing. Everyone deals with grief in their own way.

'Well, I'd better go and find him,' he says, then bends to kiss my cheek. His voice is husky in my ear. 'Take care of yourself.'

When Tris turns away, I grab his elbow. 'Stay for one dance,' I tell him, shouting to be heard above the music.

He raises his eyebrows. 'With you?'

'Why not?'

'In your state?'

'I told you, I'm not drunk. Just … tipsy. I can manage a dance.'

He half-grins, just a twitch of his mouth. 'I can't, sorry. Connor's waiting outside and I don't want him to drive off without me. I've got no transport. It's a long way over the moors.'

'Denzil will drive you home.'

He looks angry suddenly. 'What, you, me and Denzil in his jeep? I'm sure that'll be cosy.'

I shake my head. 'We're not dating.'

'You must think I'm stupid.'

'Maybe you are,' I mutter, not meaning for him to hear, but he gets the point anyway.

'So I'm Public Enemy Number One now? What exactly am I supposed to have done? Or is this the drink talking?'

'Nothing, forget it.'

He bends close, his eyes meeting mine. I try not to look at his mouth. But the rest is even more alluring. His chin is rough with stubble, his shirt unbuttoned just below the neck, some of his chest on show. 'Look, Ellie, why not come home with me and Connor? I'm worried about you. This place won't close for hours and Denzil can't be trusted to get you home safely. He can't be trusted, full stop.'

'I don't need you to worry about me. I don't need anyone.' My mouth is dry, and my head is starting to spin. Too many cocktails. 'Anyway, Denzil's not like that. You've got him all wrong. He would never abandon me.'

Tris glances down at his phone again. The screen is lit up with a new incoming call. He cancels it without answering, then pushes the phone down inside the front pocket of his jeans.

'You want to take your chances with Denzil, that's fine. But don't say I didn't warn you.'

'Whatever. See you around.'

'Goodbye, Ellie.'

Tris leans forward and kisses me roughly on the mouth, holding my face with both hands. Then he turns away and the crowd swallows him.

I regret it at once.

'Tris?'

I take a few steps after him and the room starts to spin horribly. I stop, then stumble on stubbornly, unsure of my direction. Time moves slowly. A while later, I find myself sagging against the wall near the women's toilets, drawing a few amused glances from girls queuing in the doorway.

Staring across the dance floor, I see dozens of dark heads that could be Tris. But none of them are Tris, of course, because he's gone. Gone home across the moors with Connor beside him. I could weep, or smash something. I remember his hands holding my face as he kissed me. I can still feel the imprint of his fingers on each cheek.

The music hammers at me like a rebuke.

I can't seem to breathe, this club is so hot and stuffy. Suddenly I feel sick again, my skin clammy, and grope my way along the wall towards the toilets.

Did somebody spike that last cocktail?

It's nearly three o'clock in the morning before Denzil supports me outside into the cool air. The club is on the coast road near the cliffs, and I sway there in the darkness while he's fiddling about with the jeep. The sea is crashing against rocks far below, a rhythmic boom-slap-crash.

I've been sitting in a corner for hours, refusing any more cocktails and wishing I had stuck to soft drinks. My head still hurts but at least I no longer feel sick.

Denzil wraps his jacket round my shoulders. He lights a cigarette and offers me a drag.

'No thanks,' I say, then add accusingly, 'You spiked my drink.'

He laughs and shakes his head, helping me climb into

the front seat of the jeep. 'No, you're just drunk.'

The black sky is spinning above us. Diamonds and more tiny diamonds, round in a circle. I try not to look.

'I only had a few drinks.' That's what I mean to say, but it comes out wrong, I know it. My tongue feels numb, and I can't seem to keep my eyes open. He's leaning across me, putting my seat belt on for me. 'What's wrong with me?'

'Don't try to talk. I'll drop you home.' Denzil climbs into the jeep beside me. My dress has ridden up, my exposed thigh pale under the overhead street lights. 'You're completely out of it, aren't you? Do you know how many offers I had to turn down tonight because I was taking you back home after the gig?'

'Sorry,' I mumble.

'And you're gorgeous too.' He hesitates, then smooths back my hair. 'And maybe not too drunk.'

I should have realised he would try this. Perhaps that's why he spiked my cocktails. To make sure I would not fight him. His mouth is firm and demanding. His hand is warm, moving suggestively on my thigh, and I fumble to push him away.

'It's okay, I don't want anything you're not willing to give,' he whispers against my mouth, then kisses down my throat.

I push at his chest. 'No, I don't … I can't do this, sorry.'

To my relief, Denzil does not force the issue. He pulls away, shrugging, and only then do I see the small white card tucked under the windscreen wiper.

I point at it. 'What's that?'

Denzil frowns and reaches round the windscreen for the card. There's silence as he reads it, then he shrugs and hands it to me. 'Looks like it's for you, Ellie.' He watches me turn over the card. There's a note of frustration in his voice. 'You gave some dude your anklet? While I was working?'

'What?'

My eyes can't focus at first. But the message rouses my brain from its drunken stupor. It's been cut from a larger piece of card, and not very expertly. One edge is ragged, the other less than straight. One side of the card is blank. On the other is a handwritten note in black marker pen, clumsy letters but clear enough to take in at a glance.

Suddenly I understand there's more than one person who could have spiked my drink tonight.

You're my Number One. Thanks for the anklet.

CHAPTER FOURTEEN

I stare down at the card in my hands, not quite understanding the message, then read it through again slowly. Force myself to concentrate, despite the alcohol in my system.

Number One.

I think of the dead woman in the woods. The number three written in what looked like black marker pen on her forehead.

Thanks for the anklet.

I glance down automatically but my ankle is bare. The little gold chain I was wearing earlier in the evening has vanished. Did the anklet fall off when I was on the beach? Or in the club?

I have been dancing tonight, and climbing on rocks, and getting drunk. And all the while this person was watching me. Composing this note in his head.

'Did you ... ' I stare at Denzil. 'Is this from you? Did you write this? And the number on her forehead?'

'Don't be stupid.'

I am starting to panic. There was nothing in the newspaper about the number written on the dead woman's forehead. So whoever wrote this note knows about it. That is only a very small number of people, I realise.

And one of them is the killer.

Denzil takes the note from between my slack fingers and clicks open his lighter, setting fire to the edge of the card.

'No.' I try to reach for it, horrified, but he holds it up in the air.

'It was left on my car, I get to decide what happens to it. And I can see that it's upsetting you.'

'It's evidence.'

'Of what?' Denzil shakes his tawny head, looking serious for once. 'It's only evidence that there's some bastard out there who gets his kicks out of frightening women. Don't worry, I'll get you home safe.' He tosses the burning card out of the window, then starts the engine and pulls away from the kerb. 'You've got to be careful who you talk to at these clubs.'

I begin to say, 'I didn't talk to anyone ... ' Then stop, slowly going back over the evening – or what I can remember of it.

So I'm Public Enemy Number One now?

Tris.

I talked to Tris.

The drive across the moors from the coast has never seemed so long nor so tiring. I doze off several times, then jerk awake, instantly aware of the man next to me, the danger I could be in if I'm wrong. Denzil drops me in the turning area outside the cottage. He's exhausted, like me, and not very talkative.

'See you around,' he mutters.

The car roars away in the darkness, and I stand listening to the engine until I can't hear it anymore.

I pull my phone from my bag and light up the screen. It's nearly four in the morning. I check the signal strength. One bar. Enough to send a text.

Meet me Sunday 2pm at the church. Wear running gear.

I text it to Tris, then turn off the phone. It's probably a stupid thing to have done. I should go straight to the police, tell them about the note. But I have to know the truth. And the only way is to ask.

There is a sudden rustling noise from the hedgerow behind me.

Sometimes deer cross the lane here, plunging from heavy woodlands into open fields, probably in search of water. Or foxes. There is a large male fox in this area, we often spot it padding silently past at dusk, red bushy tail held out straight. It could even be a badger. There's a large holt dug into the sandy bank behind the cottage.

Then I hear something more frightening.

Breathing.

You can hold your breath when standing still, but it's a lot harder when moving. Someone nearby is breathing and moving at the same time, getting closer and closer. My ears track the sound and I turn abruptly to my right, holding my own breath.

The breathing continues another second, then stops too.

Like an echo.

I catch a movement behind the hedgerow opposite the cottage, and fix my gaze there, staring harder. There's a shadowy shape, darker than the night surrounding it. It shifts half an inch to the right as I watch; a distinct movement, not my drunken imagination. Human, not animal. Someone is standing a few feet away behind the hedgerow. Someone roughly the same height and build as the shadow that comes to the end of my bed some nights, watching me through the darkness.

Shadow man.

I feel the familiar swell of panic in my chest, and it makes me so angry. Why should anyone get away with frightening another person like this? If it's a person behind that hedge, they ought to be ashamed of themselves. And if it's a phantom of my sick imagination, then it can bloody well piss off.

There's a long knotty stick near the door; we use it for unclogging the rivulet that runs past the cottage when it gets blocked up with leaves and silt, which it frequently does.

I make a grab for the stick, and then lunge at the hedgerow like a crazed Samurai.

'Take that,' I yell at the shadows, repeatedly smashing the sturdy pole against the hedgerow. Great puffs of green and white fly up into the darkness and drift back down around me like rain, ragged shreds of hawthorn blossom and nettle heads and cow parsley. The whole structure creaks ominously. 'Do you hear me? You can stick this in your pipe and smoke it. Go on, get out of here, leave me alone ...'

'Eleanor?'

Someone is standing in the cottage doorway, directing the white beam of a torch towards me. The outside light is broken, has been for months, so we keep a torch on a low table by the front door. With relief, I recognise the voice.

I toss the stick aside, clatter across the stone bridge in my heels, and throw my arms around my housemate.

'Hannah, oh my God.'

She snaps off the torch, and draws me comfortably inside the cottage. 'Good grief, Ellie. What the hell did that poor hedge ever do to you? Are you on drugs?'

I laugh wildly, then kick off my heels. 'No.'

'Pity.' She puts the torch back on the hall table. 'I could do with a pick-me-up.'

I lean unsteadily against the wall in the hallway, rubbing my right foot. 'I didn't know you were in. I thought you were working tonight.'

'Not Saturday night. I was trying to catch up on my beauty sleep, but hey, what do you know? It turns out my body thinks it's daytime, so I decided I might as well get up and watch a film until dawn.' She smiles ironically.

'Then maybe I'll be able to fall asleep.'

'Can I sit up with you for a bit?'

'Sure, that would be great.' Hannah pauses, looking thoughtful. 'By the way, I heard what sounded like a mouse in the walls earlier.'

'Ugh.'

'It was upstairs near your bedroom. I hate the idea of putting down traps or poison. Do you think we should get a cat instead? It might scare the mice away.'

'Absolutely.'

'Good.' Hannah smiles, and her whole face changes, becoming almost beatific. 'One of the women I work with at the hospital, Sally, has a tabby cat who's just had a litter of kittens. I hope you don't think this was high-handed of me, but I spoke to Sally on the phone earlier, and she says we can have one of the kittens for free once they're six weeks old.'

'That sounds perfect.'

'Great. I'm going to make some cocoa. You interested?'

'Sure, if you're making some. Thanks.'

Hannah shuffles into the kitchen to make cocoa, looking like Mrs Tiggywinkle in her fluffy dressing-gown and slippers.

Once the door to the cottage is safely locked and bolted, I stand with my back flat to the frame, then peer round out of the glass. I stare at the lane and turning area for several minutes but can see nothing in the darkness. Not even the hedge.

I remember Denzil outside the club, burning the note. *It's only evidence there's some bastard out there who gets his kicks out of frightening women.*

It's working.

CHAPTER FIFTEEN

I decide to drop by my dad's place on my way out to meet Tris. It's a little after one o'clock in the afternoon, and I'm dressed for running. I hesitated over what to wear, but in the end picked out exactly what I was wearing last time I was in the woods. Black Lycra shorts, white tee-shirt with red Nike logo, my Mizuno trainers. That may be a mistake; I don't know. I'm acting purely on instinct now.

I tried to do the 'right thing' last time. And look where it got me. Now I'm under suspicion from the police, and back in hypnotherapy. I even had a brisk letter yesterday from the head teacher, reiterating what had been agreed about my taking more time off, and mentioning that Paul Cannell's parents had been in touch about an 'incident' during our lesson on self-defence.

I jog slowly down through the yard to the caravan where my dad lives. Plastic sheeting flaps uneasily over the ruined walls and roof of the farm. I remember the night of the fire, my father's drunken confusion, the fast blue and white strobing of the fire engines and ambulances that had packed into this yard.

One cigarette. Such a small thing to have caused such long-lasting devastation. Though of course much more than one cigarette lay behind the wreck of our lives.

Dad opens up after my third knock, still in the crumpled shirt and jeans he had worn last night, I suspect. When my mother was still alive, he had always been impeccably dressed. Suit and tie, his shirts ironed, leather shoes polished. He has bare feet today, and badly needs a shower.

'Ellie,' he says, frowning at me through the half-open door. He's growing a beard and moustache again. I suppose it's easier than shaving. 'What are you doing here?'

'Checking how you are. I'm worried about you, Dad.'

'I'm your father. I can take care of myself.'

Churchill appears behind him, wagging his tail at the sound of my voice. 'He needs to go out,' my dad says, and opens the door wider to let the dog jump down. Churchill stays for a quick fuss from me, then trots away across the farmyard to do his business.

'Can we chat for a minute?' I come up the steps into the caravan, and my dad hesitates, then reluctantly moves aside to let me in.

The place is a mess, and stinks of stale smoke and alcohol. The bin has spilled over and there's rubbish on the floor beside it, mostly crushed beer cans and empty whisky bottles. The beige carpet itself is filthy and needs to be shampooed; my trainers stick to its tacky surface. The sink is stacked high with dirty plates and pans, and there are flies crawling on them. As I approach the sink, the flies lift and slowly circle.

'Christ,' I say.

He watches me angrily. 'You never change, do you? Don't think I don't know why you're renting that cottage, Ellie. To keep an eye on me. When you're the one who needs to be locked up.'

'Thanks,' I say drily.

'We lost your mother, but you weren't content with that.' He looks almost sick, his cheeks hollow, dark bruises under his eyes from lack of sleep. 'Years of that nonsense about shadow men, and people watching you through the windows, so we had to keep the curtains closed as soon as it got dark. And the tricks you pulled at school. Do you have any idea what I went through, especially when it looked like I would lose you too? The months of therapy, and never knowing if you'd be brought home in the back of a police car … '

'I'm sorry about that, I really am.'

My father shakes his head, leaning back against the plate-stacked sink, his arms folded. 'What's the point in apologising? I thought you'd sorted your head out at last. But now it's starting all over again.'

'I was just a kid then,' I say, struggling to hold onto my temper, 'and yes, I needed therapy for a while, and probably made your life hell. But this new thing is real, I didn't make it up. I saw a dead woman in the woods, exactly where Mum was killed, maybe even deliberately posed to look like her. And I need to convince the police that I'm not crazy or lying to get attention.'

He makes a disbelieving noise. Like a snort.

I hesitate. 'Will you help me or not?'

'I can't help you, Ellie. You're beyond help.' He indicates the mess around us. 'See all this? You and your obsessions have reduced me to this. If I hadn't been using all my strength to keep you out of care, I might have kept my job. I might never have started drinking. The house fire wouldn't have happened.'

I hate the accusation in his voice.

'Now you want my help convincing the police you're not crazy. Well, sorry to be blunt, but I think you are.' He straightens up, pointing to the caravan door. 'You threw me out the other day, remember? Now it's my turn to throw you out.'

'There was a note,' I say, not moving.

'What do you mean?'

I tell him about the note on Denzil's windscreen, and for a few minutes he seems to calm down and listen.

'Where is this note?' he asks, frowning.

'Denzil burnt it.'

My dad sneers. 'How very convenient.'

'The note was real, we both saw it. You can ask Denzil if you don't believe me. I'll give you his number. The note proves I'm not making any of this up.'

'All it proves is that you are a manipulative little bitch,' he tells me coldly. 'You probably wrote that note yourself and planted it on his windscreen to get attention.'

I stare at him, shocked. Not simply by what he said, but the way he said it. I don't recall my father ever swearing at me before now.

'That's not true,' I insist, 'and you know it. Why are you being such a bastard? Is it because you're drunk?'

He slaps me round the face. I do not see the blow coming and stagger backwards in surprise.

My hand whips up though and I slap him in return. Pure instinctive response. When I lower my arm, there's the livid imprint of my hand on his cheek, and a thin bleeding cut under one eye where one of my fingernails must have caught him.

He stares at me, his mouth open, breathing hard. 'Get out,' he manages to say. 'Get out and don't come back.'

I stumble out of the caravan, my palm aching from where I slapped him, only to falter at the bottom of the steps. 'Wait,' I say, looking back at him.

He is closing the door. 'Goodbye, Eleanor.'

'There's more,' I say quickly through the door crack. I can see my father staring back at me, one bloodshot eye rolled in my direction, his mouth trembling. 'I think someone might be watching me and Hannah. Up at the cottage.'

'For God's sake, this business is driving me out of my mind. Don't you see that? Can't you, of all people, understand that?'

He shuts the door. I hear a key turn in the lock, then the sound of him stumbling back to the crumpled sheets of his bunk.

'Dad, are you okay?' I wait a minute, listening. 'I'm sorry I hit you. But you hit me first.'

There is no reply.

Churchill appears, still wagging his tail. I stare at him blindly. The dog whines, then lies down at the base of the caravan steps in the shade.

My father has never hit me before. Angrily, I put a hand to my cheek. It feels tender and slightly swollen.

He's right though. It's not beyond the realm of possibility that I slipped out of the club while Denzil was deejaying, wrote that note myself, stuck it on his windscreen, and am simply too far gone in my psychosis to remember a single minute of it.

The sun dips momentarily behind a cloud. I look around the yard. There are weeds sprouting from the cracked concrete, dandelions with bright yellow heads, dusty nettles and tufts of grass. Beyond the caravan, the fields stretch away into the distance, climbing inexorably towards the steep, brown-grey outcrops of rock that mark the start of Bodmin Moor.

I remember long summer days here as a child, my mother stretching up to hang washing on the line, the chickens pecking at the dirt as they wandered freely about the yard.

Then came the day that changed our lives.

'Hello, Eleanor,' the lady says, getting up from behind her big wooden desk. She speaks softly and slowly, as though I'm a little kid, which I'm not. 'How very nice to meet you at last. I've heard so much about you from your Daddy.'

The lady comes round to stand in front of me. She is wearing a flowery blue skirt down to her knees and a white shirt with flounces on her collar. Her shoes are black and shiny. I think she looks very smart and a little bit stern, like our head teacher.

'I am a doctor,' she tells me, 'and my name is Isabel Quick. Do you know why your Daddy has brought you to visit me?'

I raise my eyebrows. Everyone knows what a doctor does. 'Because I keep getting into trouble, and the police think there must be something wrong with me.'

The doctor smiles as though I've said something funny. She shakes her head, then looks up at my dad. 'Not quite, Eleanor. Do you mind if I call you Eleanor?'

'Most people call me Ellie.'

'Then I shall too.'

She's got a nice enough smile, I decide, but I don't much like her office. It reminds me of hospital rooms, the walls white and clean, important-looking notices on the board behind her desk. The doctor has a glass vase of flowers on her desk: pink and yellow flowers, very pretty. I can smell them even from my seat on the other side of her desk.

Dr Quick sees me looking at the vase. She slips one pink flower out from the rest and hands it to me. 'They're called freesias. My favourite flowers. Smell nice, don't they?'

The smell is strong but very sweet. And I do like flowers. My mum used to keep flowers like this in a round blue vase on the kitchen table. I don't remember much about my mum but what I do remember makes my tummy ache. The smell of her perfume, and the flowers she kept on the pine dresser; the pretty clothes she wore; her smile, that was for me alone.

Dad never brings flowers into the house.

I say nothing but grip the flower stalk tightly, breathing in its sweet perfume as the pink petals tickle my nose.

I feel tears pricking behind my eyes and fight them, embarrassed. I don't like crying. I try never to cry in front of other people.

'I'm not the kind of doctor who looks after you when you have a physical sickness, Ellie. I'm a very special kind of doctor. A doctor of the mind.' She crouches in front of me so her eyes can look directly into mine. It's not a very comfortable thing, but I try not to look away. 'I'm a hypnotist. Do you know what that means?'

I shake my head.

'It means I'm going to ask you to look inside your head. Deep inside your oldest memories. But it may take some time. You might have to visit me quite a few times before it starts to work.' She smiles.

'It's not always easy to remember things, is it?'

I'm in trouble with the police for what I did, that's the truth, or we would not be here. I don't remember everything I did wrong, those days are all confused in my head. But I know the police insisted on this visit. They think it will keep me out of trouble in the future.

That doesn't mean I have to take it seriously though. I'll play along with the doctor, that's all. Maybe Dad will not be so angry with me then.

The doctor checks her watch. 'Right, I think we should start. First I'm going to let you get nice and comfy on this couch, so you can fall asleep. Then I'm going to ask you some questions.'

'How can I answer questions if I'm asleep?'

My tone is rude, deliberately so. But the doctor keeps smiling. She puts a hand on my shoulder. 'You let me worry about that. Lie down now and get comfortable.'

She helps me lie back on the long seat. There's a cushion for my head; it's softer than the scratchy grey material of the seat. I stare up at the white ceiling, wondering what's coming next. She slips off my outdoor shoes, tucking them beneath the seat.

I'm a little bit worried now, but I'm not going to let her see that. I look round at Dad, who winks.

'Do what the doctor tells you, angel,' he whispers, then bends and kisses me on the forehead. 'I'll be right here if you need me. Everything's going to be okay.'

The doctor sits beside me on the seat. 'Look at me, Ellie,' she says firmly. 'I want you to listen very carefully to my voice.'

Great, I think, another lecture. I prepare myself to be bored.

She talks to me for a while in her soft voice, then starts to move her finger back and forth a little distance from my eyes, asking me to watch it very carefully as it goes back and forth, back and forth, back and forth, swinging like a pendulum on one of those old Victorian clocks. I try not to watch her finger, or to listen to what the doctor is saying, but it's impossible not to. Something about my eyelids starts feeling heavy. Dr Quick tells me this is going to happen, and I wonder how she knows.

Her finger keeps moving back and forth, growing pink and blurry. Her words become a vague murmuring in the background as I drift away into some shadowy place.

They want me to fall asleep.

So I struggle to stay awake, to defy them, to keep watching and listening, but I can't. I can't …

CHAPTER SIXTEEN

I meet Tris at Eastlyn Church a few minutes after two o'clock. It's clear from his expression that he's been there a while, waiting. But I wanted to take a run round the village before we met up, make sure there are people about, people who could hear me if I scream. Ridiculous, perhaps. But I'm very much aware that I'm on my own now. Hannah is still fast asleep, my dad is having his own private breakdown in the caravan, and Connor is probably out with the sheep on the edge of the moor. Nobody will be coming to rescue me if all this goes wrong.

The weekly church service is at eleven-thirty on a Sunday morning, so not many people are about in the churchyard. There's an old woman in a black hat, laying flowers on an overgrown gravestone that looks almost as old as her. A man in overalls is sweeping out the church porch; another is in the Victorian portion of the graveyard, cutting the grass between graves with a strimmer. The whine of the strimmer bounces off stone as I walk up to the church door from the kissing-gate.

The man with the broom glances at me oddly, then shuffles inside the church and half-closes the door.

Tris is waiting for me in the shade of an old yew hedge.

He comes towards me, staring. 'What happened to your face?'

I put a hand to my cheek, embarrassed. I haven't had a chance to look in a mirror. 'Is it so bad?'

'Did Denzil do that?'

It's my turn to stare. 'Of course not.'

'I wouldn't put anything past Tremain.' He touches my cheek with long, cool fingers. 'So who hit you?'

'I told you, nobody.'

I don't like having to lie to him. But then I have no idea if he's been lying to me. However angry I may feel about my father raising a hand to me, it's family business. Nothing to do with Tris. Besides, I hit him straight back. So as far as I'm concerned, it's finished.

'Liar,' he says softly.

I start to walk away, uncomfortable now. 'I slipped in the bath this morning. Banged my face on the wall.'

He shrugs, giving up and turns to follow me. We take the twisting path that leads behind the church, past the vicarage, and eventually into the woods. 'Okay, so why did you ask me to meet you here? What are we doing?'

'Going for a run in the woods.'

He stops, sounding shocked. '*What?*'

'It's time I went back to where I saw the body. I need to figure out what happened. How she disappeared.'

Tris is shaking his head. He grabs at my arm when I keep walking. 'No, no, that's a really bad idea. Seriously, Ellie, you don't want to do that.'

'Give me a good reason not to.'

He stares, then seems to gather his thoughts. 'It could be the last straw for you.'

I raise my eyebrows. 'Explain.'

'Fuck.' He runs a hand through his hair. 'Okay, don't get upset about this, but you've been … well, *unstable* ever since it happened. When I saw you in the club last night I was really worried, you seemed so wired. Like you're deliberately on the look-out for trouble now, aiming to self-destruct.'

I can't believe what I'm hearing. 'Why, because I went on a date with Denzil Tremain?'

'Because to go into those woods could knock you back years in therapy terms.' He meets my eyes. 'I'm serious, Ellie. I don't think you're ready for this, and I don't want to see you in any more pain.'

We're standing behind the red brick wall of the vicarage. The back gate into the garden is closed today. I catch a brief movement out of the corner of my eye, the twitch of a curtain, and glance upwards. It's the Reverend Clemo, staring down at us from an upper window. He looks intent, frowning from under heavy brows. As soon as the vicar realises I've seen him, he drops the curtain.

Tris follows my gaze. 'What is it?'

'Nothing.'

I keep walking, heading for the entrance to the woods. I remember how I burst out here that morning, covered in nettle stings and thorn cuts, and found the Reverend Clemo smoking, his Jack Russell dancing about his feet. That strange look on his face. It could have been guilt. Or am I just imagining things?

'You coming?' I ask, looking back at Tris.

'I can't talk you out of this?'

I shake my head.

'Then I can hardly let you go down there alone,' he says.

My body has cooled down considerably since I met him at the church. I stretch out my calves and hamstrings, using the same basic lunges and warm-up exercises I teach the kids at school. Tris shrugs, then copies me, dragging his right foot up behind and holding the stretch while he counts under his breath.

I hate my brain. It keeps thinking even when I want to shut it out and concentrate on my body. But something's nagging at me and I can't ignore it. Reverend Clemo was at school with my mother. Like Dick Laney too. And it was clear from that photograph in Laney's office that he had resented anyone else getting close to my mother.

She must have been quite a catch for the local boys, I realise. But then my mother was beautiful. And kind too. Too kind to push Dick Laney away when he put his arm around her.

'Sure you want to do this, Ellie?'

Something about the way he uses my pet name jerks at my heart. I finish stretching out my hamstrings and straighten up, looking at him sideways.

Apart from the mud-covered trainers, Tris Taylor looks exceptionally good in his running gear. Strong and lithe. Damn him. All that hill-climbing and fence-mending on the farm has given him muscular thighs, a narrow waist, and a tight backside. No, not bad at all.

'Absolutely,' I say, lying again. The truth is not always useful, I am beginning to discover, and on this particular occasion, a lie will serve me better. 'How about you? Cold feet?'

'What?'

He's been staring down the track into the woods, but turns now to look at me, looking distracted. He's pale, and his gaze keeps wavering, sliding away from me to those dark spaces between trees. It's as though he's looking for something in particular. Or someone.

'Penny for your thoughts?'

'Sorry,' he says, as though suddenly realising what I said. 'It's not you. I had a row with Connor this morning.'

'Seriously? I thought you two never argued.'

'It was over something so stupid. Connor borrowed my trainers to take the dog out early, and got them covered in mud. He does it all the bloody time. I told him, why can't you ruin your own shoes? Then I asked him to clean them.' He shakes his head, scraping at the dried mud on one trainer with his other foot. 'Connor threw them back at me, told me to clean them myself.'

'Brothers.'

He grins. 'Oh, we love each other really. You know what it's like with families.'

I look at him speculatively. If his parents hadn't adopted Tris, Connor would have been an only child. And later, when their mum left, he would have been an only child in a single parent family. Like me.

'Not really. I've been protected from the horror of siblings. It can get lonely though, being an only child.'

'Poor kid.' Tris puts an arm round my shoulders, making a sad face. 'Poor, lonely, no-mates Eleanor.'

'That's me.'

'Well, I still love you. Even if no one else does.'

I look away, remembering the creepy note left tucked under the jeep's windscreen wipers last night.

You're my Number One.

I was insanely suspicious about Tris last night. My head was muddled with drink, my nerves on edge. Looking at him in the daylight, it feels impossible that Tristan Taylor could ever have written that note. At least, that's my gut instinct.

But my gut instinct has been known to be wrong.

'Look, Eleanor,' he tells me quietly, 'I have no problem with doing this. But I am genuinely worried about what kind of impact it could have on you.'

So we're back to Eleanor, I think. Not Ellie anymore. 'You don't need to be worried.'

'Really? You were acting pretty weird last night. Now you want to go back into the woods and risk falling apart again.' He studies me, his expression brooding. 'We're good friends, and I don't want to be rude, but what if this sets you off again?'

'You make me sound like a dysfunctional siren.'

'Not a bad description.'

I recall my father calling me a manipulative little bitch only an hour ago, and find it hard to smile.

'Thanks,' I say lightly.

'You're welcome.'

We're good friends.

I suddenly realise I'm supplying a silent *just* before that *good*, and hating it. I bend to fumble with my laces, needlessly untying then relacing them in a loose double bow.

I glance round at him, my tone deliberately offhand. 'Shall we get going, then? If the obligatory lecture is over?'

His mouth tightens but he shrugs. 'Might as well. You lead.'

'We can run two abreast most of the way, actually.'

'Sounds fun.'

I pull a face at his lewd expression. He and Connor both love the dirty puns, but they never seem to push beyond that. Typical male banter, Hannah calls it, and claims she's heard far worse at the hospital, especially on the night shift.

We jog down the sunlit track into the woods. I decided that reversing my route might be a good idea, help me see things in a different light. So we're entering the woods behind the church, on the narrow overgrown track I used to reach the village after seeing the body. We slow to skirt the nettle patch, then walk single file for a while because the dirt track is so narrow and steep. That's where I take the lead, and Tris falls in behind me.

'Stay close,' I tell him.

I hear water rushing and gurgling as we descend towards the stream. My body is warming up now, but my palms feel cold and clammy. The horribly familiar sound of the stream brings back memories of the day when I stood among these same trees, a scared six-year-old, and closed my eyes, listening …

I slow as the path widens out, then come to a halt fifty-odd feet shy of the stream, not entirely sure of my next move. Behind me Tris stops too. I hear his light breathing, and it reminds me of the shadow behind the hedgerow. The sound of a man breathing a few feet away in the darkness. It could have been him. He's the right height and build. But then so is Connor, and so is my father, and the Reverend Clemo, and just about any male of six foot and above.

I stand, not speaking, listening to the sounds of the woods. Above us, an unseen bird calls out a shrill warning: *Humans! Humans! Humans in the woods!*

Tris breaks the silence between us. 'I have to say, I was surprised to see you on your feet after last night, let alone running.'

'Four o'clock in the morning is a record even for me,' I admit.

'Denzil needs a punch in the head.'

I look round in surprise at the barely concealed tension in his voice. 'Why? I told you, he got me home safe.'

I don't mention my glimpse of the shadow man outside the cottage. I'm unsure whether it was real or imagined, and am still ashamed of the way I reacted last night. The primal fear that had me running into Hannah's arms like a terrified kid, waking up a few hours later after a bad dream, sunlight in my eyes, exhausted but unable to sleep.

So much for my expertise as a martial arts teacher. That had been my big selling point when I first started interviewing for teaching jobs in Physical Education, that I could teach the students anything from karate and judo through to elements of aikido and Krav Maga. Yet faced with the possibility that my childhood bogey-man was back, those much-vaunted defences had crumbled like they were made of tinfoil.

'Safe is always a relative term with you though.' Tris looks even paler down here in the dim light of the woods; his skin is almost translucent under the tree canopy. 'There's only one reason a couple stays out until four in the morning. And it's not so you can go stargazing on the moors.'

'Oh my God, I wasn't wrong last night. You really are jealous.'

'No.' He shakes his head vehemently. 'Christ, no. You can date anyone else you like, I don't give a shit. But Denzil Tremain is the wrong choice for you.'

'Reasons?'

'First off, everyone knows he does drugs. Deals them too, Connor says. And he deliberately got you drunk last night. I could see that as soon as I talked to you at the club.'

'Stop exaggerating. I only had three or four drinks, for God's sake.'

'What was in them?'

'I don't know.' I shrug it off, not wanting this conversation. 'They were cocktails.'

'Right, Denzil's special drain cleaner mix. He might even have dropped a couple of Ruffies in there and you wouldn't have known anything about it until it was too late.'

'Denzil isn't like that,' I say, though I don't believe it.

'Convince me.'

I may have a blind spot where Denzil is concerned, but I know what Ruffies are, and he would never use the date rape drug. 'I don't need to. It's none of your business. But take it from me,' I tell him directly, 'Denzil doesn't need to drug women to get them into bed with him.'

'Fine.' He looks past me at the rushing stream, his face distracted. 'Are you going to see him again?'

'Denzil's a good friend. Of course I'll see him again.'

I turn away, finishing the conversation, and continue down the slope to the brink of the stream. It's true that I've made some errors of judgement where Denzil is concerned. But they are my errors, and not up for discussion.

The stream is at its broadest here in the bottom of the wood, water constantly tumbling over stones, its busy gurgle louder now, no longer the low level hiss that seems to permeate the woods on a still day. The path becomes uneven at this point, thick with ruts, the track widening into a muddy clearing. The water's not deep but is maybe five or six feet across, I would guess, measuring it with my eye. There's a wooden bridge a little further ahead, a simple structure for walkers who don't want to get their feet wet.

Tris comes to stand at my side. 'So we're here. At the stream. Where did you see the body?'

I stand there, looking right into untidy undergrowth, then left to the bridge. Everything is as I remember, except that the earth is less muddied than it was that day and the path is empty. I remember the stillness though. That's missing today. Birds are chirruping all around us, and somewhere above us in the main body of the wood I can hear a party of walkers. The high voices of children, laughing and calling to each other through the trees.

'I came round the bend over there,' I tell him, and point to the exact place on the opposite bank. 'From a distance, it looked like a fallen tree was lying across the path. The mind tries to make sense of things, I suppose. I wasn't expecting to see a naked woman, so I saw a fallen tree instead.'

'Shall we?'

I hesitate, then nod. We walk a little further along the track in silence, then cross the bridge one after the other.

There's a dark, gleaming pool below, perhaps waist-deep, the air bright with flies above the water. I hesitate, staring along the stream to where it disappears into green shadows round the next bend, and try to quell the sickness in my stomach.

I need to confront Tris about the club last night, and the disturbing message on Denzil's windscreen. I'm not one hundred percent convinced he left it there, but the more he condemns Denzil's character, the more I feel he has a motive for trying to frighten me. Maybe it was initially intended as a lads' prank, a collaboration between him and Connor. Maybe one of the brothers saw my anklet fall off on the dance floor, and the other wrote the note to spook me. I should just come straight out with it, ask Tris if he wrote it. It could be completely innocent, and nothing to do with the dead woman.

Something is holding me back though, playing on my nerves, my hair-trigger imagination, and that sense of uneasiness is intensifying the closer we get to the spot of my mother's murder. Last night, this had seemed like the perfect place to speak to Tris alone. If he does not admit the truth here, he's unlikely to do so anywhere else. But have I walked myself straight into a trap?

Tris leads me to the muddied edge of the stream, and we look back at the opposite bank where we had been standing moments before.

'So?'

'The woods were very quiet, not like today. It was still early, maybe half past seven, maybe a little later. I slowed down, and considered going back to the main path. But I'd already come that far. So I kept going, and walked straight towards her.'

'You knew something wasn't right?'

'I was already nervous. I didn't want to take this path. This is where ... where it happened before.'

'Where your mother was killed?'

'Yes.'

He pauses, then looks around. 'This exact spot?'

I nod.

'Shit, I'm sorry.'

We both stare down into the water, standing shoulder to shoulder. Our reflection is vague and shadowy, moving constantly with the current. The trees behind our heads ripple on the water.

'So what happened then?'

I look back, and it's as if the whole thing is happening in front of me. I see the body on the path. The eerie way the light and shadows played on her skin. The number three on her forehead.

You're my Number One.

That's a threat, a promise. A warning not to be complacent. The killer has a step-by-step plan and he's following it. He's in control.

Thanks for the anklet.

That's him telling me how clever and powerful and resourceful he is. How he can get to me at any time. Take whatever he wants from me. My life, potentially.

I remember Denzil setting fire to the note, then throwing it out of the jeep. The only piece of solid evidence that could prove I'm not imagining any of this. It could have gone to forensics. Did he destroy the note deliberately?

It's an unsettling question. I trust Denzil, always have done. But there are doubts in my head now. I remind myself that I heard him drive away last night, so he could not have been the man watching me from behind the hedgerow. Still, he could have stopped the car a little further down the lane, then got out and run back through the field. He would have been out of breath by the time he arrived back at the cottage, of course. But I did hear odd rustling noises from the hedgerow, and then what sounded like somebody breathing ...

He deliberately got you drunk last night.

'Ellie?' Tris prompts me.

I nod, saying, 'Once I got closer, I could see it was a woman. She was naked. Maybe playing some kind of sick joke on me, I thought at first. She looked asleep from a few feet away. Then it became obvious to me that she wasn't breathing. I stood there looking down at her, and I thought ...'

'Yes?'

I hesitate, seeing it again in my head, the horrible jarring misfit between the beauty of the woods and the corpse on the path. 'I don't know what I thought, actually. I stared for a minute or two, then something seemed to take me over.'

'*Something?*'

'Sheer panic,' I admit, embarrassed. 'It felt like I was six years old again and my mother was screaming at me to run. So I did exactly that. Only I didn't take the bridge, then follow the path up to the car park, where I might have found help quicker.'

'Why not?'

'I'm not sure. It's been bothering me.'

'Which way did you go?'

'I ran through the water over there,' I say, pointing along the stream to where there are a few unevenly-spaced stepping-stones, 'then ran up the steep track we came down today. Heading for the back of the church. It's barely a path in places, and hell to climb going the other way. Yet that's the same way I ran when I was six.'

I remember soft earth giving way under my trainers halfway up the slope, the violent lurch as I fell among nettles. 'Maybe that's why it felt like the right thing to do.'

Tris turns in a slow circle, studying the ground. 'To cross the bridge, you would have needed to go past the body. It was probably easier to run sideways and through the stream.'

'Easier?'

'Less traumatic. You didn't want to look at her that closely.'

I'm diverted by this explanation.

I turn too, scanning the narrow bridge, the path where the dead body lay that morning, then my chosen escape route through the stream.

He's right.

'Of course. I didn't think of that.'

He smiles grimly. 'Your brain again, making decisions for you without telling you why.'

'Stupid brain.'

Tris takes my hand, squeezing it gently. His fingers are warm and comforting. It's hard not to trust him. This is Tris, after all, and I've known him for years. But I can't seem to shake the memory of that note last night. *Thanks for the anklet.*

I look down at the muddy ground beside the stream. This is where I saw her body. And it's clear the police searched this area thoroughly. I can see the marks of booted feet passing to and fro for the past week, a morass of footprints and bike wheel tracks, the dried ruts leading down to the mushier ground beside the stream itself. How many people have walked through there since I saw her, contaminating any trace of evidence there might have been?

But then maybe I didn't see her at all. Maybe the whole thing was a figment of my warped imagination, seeing a dead woman in this exact spot because of the anniversary. Because my head isn't right. That's what everyone else thinks, after all. I ought to give it careful consideration, not brush it aside.

You probably wrote the note yourself and planted it on his windscreen.

I could actually be mad. Do mad people ever know? Or are they always too far gone by the time it gets to that stage?

The water is running brightly in the sunshine, under the bridge and into dappled woodlands. The birds are singing now, no longer shrieking. The place is idyllic.

Tris has followed me. 'So you saw the body here? Right where I'm standing?'

I study the place. 'Yes, about here. I think her hand was almost in the water. As though she was pointing at the stream. But I can't be one hundred percent sure.'

'Show me,' he says calmly. 'Be the dead woman for a minute. Lie down and pose your body exactly the way you remember seeing hers.'

'*What?*'

'Come on, it's fine. There's no one here to see you.'

'It feels disrespectful.'

He locks his gaze with mine. 'What, disrespectful towards a woman who, according to the police, doesn't even exist? Look, it's obvious you brought me down here for a reason, Ellie. I still don't know what that is. But we're not going to get any nearer the truth if you keep thinking with your heart instead of your head.'

Everything he is saying makes sense. It's time to stop reacting and start engaging. I find the right spot in the morass of footprints beside the stream, then lower myself slowly to the ground, palms and knees squelching in the mud. I'm going to look such a mess after this. Slowly, I rotate my position, letting my hip down first, then my shoulder, trying to remember …

Tris stands a few feet away, glancing about, his face unreadable. I'm very aware that I may not be able to trust him, this man who is as close to me as any brother. They say it's the quiet ones you have to watch. Interpreting that literally, I keep an eye on Tris until my shoulders are both flat on the ground, then my head goes back and I'm staring up at the trees and the sky beyond, patches of blue glimpsed between the leafy green canopy of branches.

It's a disorientating position. I feel oddly detached, like I'm dead too and watching myself, looking down on my body from above.

'Is that exactly the spot where you saw her?'

I wriggle backwards another inch or two, moving my legs into what feels like the right position. 'More or less.'

I can hear the stream near my head, so noisy, it's almost deafening. It reminds me of something else I have to do. I stretch one arm above my head as though pointing towards the water, as I remember the dead woman seemed to be doing. The water is so close to my fingers, it feels as though I'm touching it.

'She was pointing to the stream,' I say. 'At least, her hand was. I guess the killer deliberately positioned her like that.'

Even through my clothes the dirt track is chilly and startlingly hard against my back. The woman was left here naked. Exposed and on show. I don't like to think about that possibility, it makes my skin crawl. I gaze up into sunlit trees, feeling exposed too.

Tris crouches down, frowning past me. I tilt my head, staring up at him. His profile is framed by greenery, and so close, I can see every inch of his skin, his dark eyes and hair. I look at his mouth, then wish I hadn't.

'I know how he did it,' he says abruptly.

CHAPTER SEVENTEEN

'Sorry?'

Tris looks down at me, zero humour in his eyes for once. Again, I feel that shiver of unease and try to repress it. 'Our killer. I know how he managed to carry the dead body here, then take it away again after you'd gone. All without leaving any footprints for the police to find, and no scent for the dogs.'

'How?'

He points past my head at the rushing water. 'He came through the stream.'

'Through the stream?' I repeat.

I lean up on my elbow and stare over my shoulder. The water gurgles innocently a few feet behind me, bright in the sunlight.

'Think about it. You leave no tracks if you walk through water.'

'But the depth – '

'Waders, maybe. Dark clothing or camouflage gear, with thigh-high waders … Yes, I think he carried the body away through the stream after you saw her.'

I consider the stream, try to imagine the scenario, some

man staggering away through the stream in the early morning light, a dead body slung over his shoulder. It makes sense as a quick getaway route for a murderer intent on hiding his victim before the police can arrive. But had he arrived the same way too?

I had always assumed the woman had died here in the woods, maybe strangled after an argument. Tris is making me see things differently.

'So he killed her somewhere else?'

'It seems the most likely explanation. If he *had* killed her here, there would have been some sign of a struggle.'

'Crushed plants, footprints in the mud, maybe tracks from something heavy having been dragged through the undergrowth …'

'Exactly. But we know there can't have been anything like that, because the police combed this area and came back with nothing to report.'

'So?'

A strand of hair has fallen in my eyes; Tris strokes it away, rather like Denzil did last night, looking down at me. Our faces are only inches apart. Suddenly I'm uncomfortable again, but not for the same reason as before. What made me agree to go out with Denzil? He's good-looking, and he understands the unholy mess that is me, but there's no way I find him even half as interesting as Tris.

'So,' he repeats, not breaking my gaze, 'it was not an accident that you saw her. The murderer placed the dead body here deliberately. He planned the whole thing like a military operation.'

I blink, not wanting to face that possibility. It was way too creepy. 'Let's say you're right. Why would anyone do that? If he didn't kill her here, why go to all the trouble of carrying the body here?'

'Display?'

'An exhibition of his work?'

'And a demonstration of what he can do. Showing off.

Like a cat bringing a dead mouse to the back door. *See, this is what I'm capable of.*'

I frown, not entirely following his reasoning.

'Then why move the body before the police can find it? Surely if he was showing off, he'd want as many people to see her as possible. Only one witness. That's a bit sad.'

'You still don't get it, do you? He was showing off to *you*, Eleanor. He placed her body here like a display for you to see it because you are his only audience.' He leans closer, so close we might almost be kissing. I dare not move, staring up at him in a kind of mesmerised shock. 'You, Eleanor Blackwood, are the only person he wants to see his work. Nobody else.'

Our eyes meet and lock in the stillness. Behind us the stream rushes on regardless of our conversation, cheerful in the dappled sunlight. My skin has goosepimples, I can feel the tiny hairs prickling all along my arms. I would almost rather discover I was mad than be told someone has targeted me for this sick charade. Someone who knows me and my history. Who can predict my moves so accurately.

'Are you kidding?'

'A little bit, yes,' he admits. 'But you have to admit, it's strange.'

My heart is beating uncomfortably fast. He almost had me convinced then that I was the one who had inspired a killer.

I scrabble to my feet, ignoring the hand he holds out to help me. 'You, my friend, are the one who's strange.' I brush the dirt off my palms. 'So what now?'

'Now we walk down the stream, see exactly where he went after he picked up the body again.'

I stare. 'You really believe he came through the water?'

'It's the only possibility that makes sense. If I were the killer, that's how I'd do it. Throw any dogs off the scent by staying in the water all the way, or as far as I could.' He bends and squints up and down the stream, first in one direction and then the other. 'But which way did he come?'

I point further into the woods. 'That way comes down from the main car park for the woods and café. It's quite a hike uphill, but not so bad coming down. The stream runs beneath the car park. Maybe he had her body in the boot of his car. He parked up near the stream, popped the boot, dragged her out and down the bank ...'

He shakes his head, interrupting. 'Too public.'

'It was early.'

'Even so, there are still people around in the main car park at that time. Before he got sick, my dad used to walk the dog in that part of the woods some mornings, as early as seven o'clock. And the body was naked, remember? That's not something you'd miss if you were out walking your dog. A man dragging a naked woman into the stream is hardly a regular event round here.' He grins. 'At least, I hope not. Though maybe for the Denzils of this world ...'

'Watch it.'

'Sorry.' His smile grows crooked. 'True love, is it?'

He has me off-balance and I don't like the sensation. 'Let's stick to murder, shall we? Not my love life.'

Tris turns slowly on his heel. 'Okay, he didn't come from the car park end of the woods. Or it's less likely. So he must have come from the village side, from Eastlyn itself.'

'Seems likely.'

'Maybe.' He stares down at the water, his expression preoccupied. 'What borders the woods that way?'

'The lower road through the village.'

'Except it's narrow most of the way. There are no laybys, no passing-places, nowhere to stop a car without arousing attention. Not very promising for someone looking to dump a body.'

'There's the old water company station before the road bridge,' I say. 'It's gated off and padlocked, but if you pulled your car deep enough into the bushes beside the gate, you wouldn't be seen from the road.'

'I know where you mean. And there's a path that leads through the meadow opposite into the back of the woods.'

'That's the path I take when I go running, except I don't usually go through the woods anymore. I head uphill instead, and skirt the woods.'

'So a parked car definitely wouldn't be seen from the road there?'

'Pretty sure,' I say. 'Hannah likes to park there sometimes, so she can take a walk in the woods without having to pay the exorbitant charges up in the main car park.'

'So if the killer climbed into the water with her at that point,' he says, 'he would be able to walk all the way into the woods under cover. That part of the stream is completely shaded from view by all the trees and bushes.'

'Wait, what about the Path Closed sign? He must have planted that on the upper path to make me come down this way.'

'Good point. So he put the sign up first, maybe came into the wood normally, maybe posing as a jogger, then run back to his car. He could have brought the sign with him.' Tris frowns. 'No, that doesn't make sense. Too easily seen again.'

I join in with this game. Guessing what our unknown killer might have done. It's macabre but could be useful. Assuming there *was* a body in the first place.

'Perhaps he brought the diversion sign into the woods during the night,' I suggest, 'or even a few days beforehand, then hid it in the undergrowth. There are dozens of places he could have left it without anyone noticing.'

Tris nods, looking thoughtful. 'Yes, good idea. He sets up the diversion sign, jogs back to his car, pulls on the waders, gets the body out of the boot ... Then carries her downstream and displays the body here for you to find.' He looks down at the muddied ground as though seeing the body exactly as I did, then raises his head, scanning the woods around us. 'Maybe he hides in the bushes further upstream so he can watch your reaction. Then, as soon as you've gone, he scoops up the body again and carries it back to his car.'

Which all suggests it must be someone who knows me and my daily routines. Someone close enough to be able to second-guess my reactions. To correctly assess my mood that morning and be sure I would take the path through the woods, despite my fear.

I keep coming back to that unnerving thought.

Someone I know locally may be a killer who wants me to see his handiwork. But who?

'You okay?' he asks.

'Sure.'

'We should follow the stream down, check exactly where it goes.'

I look dubiously at the water. 'Not having any waders to hand, I'd rather not get my trainers wet. But I'm up for walking along the bank, if that's okay with you.'

We walk in silence along the bank for a while, watching the busy water rushing over shale and around stones, dazzling with light, flies spinning and dancing in clouds above its surface. There is no one else in this part of the wood, though laughter and shrieks from kids on one of the upper paths drift across through the trees. It's a lonely spot, perfect for a crime scene.

'No way the killer could be a *she*, I suppose?' I ask.

'Carrying a dead body all that way?'

'You seem so certain it's a man. I'm wondering why, that's all. It's not like women never kill each other.'

'Sexism aside, you said her neck was red and swollen, probably from where she'd been strangled. And she'd been stripped naked. Do you think a woman did that? Yes, a woman could strangle another woman, and even strip her too. But to carry a body out here, then take it away again? People are heavy when they're dead. I know that from having to move dead sheep. Lifting a dead sheep is totally different from trying to shift one that's still alive.'

'Maybe she used a wheelbarrow.'

'That left no tracks?'

I say nothing, looking away.

'I'm sorry,' he says a minute later, watching my face. 'I'm not trying to cut off possibilities or be sexist. But I don't see how this could be down to anyone but a man.'

Which brings me back to my closest friends. There's at least one person who knew I was going to run this way on that morning, and that's Tris himself. With a jolt, I remember our exchange of texts beforehand.

Planning to run through the woods tomorrow. As a salute to my mum.

Don't. Not a good idea.

Chicken.

But if it was Tris, he would hardly be helping me like this. The thought steadies me. I have to trust someone in this business. Not least because I can't trust myself.

We walk for another five minutes, picking a path through increasingly heavy undergrowth. Then the painful wall of brambles and nettles becomes impossible for us.

Tris looks at me. 'Come on, this is getting us nowhere.' He nods me towards an old mossed tree stump. 'Hop up there and you can jump on my back. I'll give you a piggyback ride.'

'Sorry?'

'We have to get down into the water, it's the only way to keep tracking the stream back to wherever he came from.' He grins at my dumbfounded expression. 'You don't want to get your feet wet, so I'll carry you. It's fine, I'm strong enough.'

It's easy to jump up onto his back, but it feels weird to have Tris gripping my legs, and to hold onto his head and shoulders for balance, riding him down the rough, muddy bank like he's an elephant.

Tris lurches into the stream at full tilt, stumbling across

the uneven rocks. I feel the cool splash of water. He staggers another few steps, and for a second I think he's going to fall.

'Fuck.'

Steadying himself with an effort, Tris laughs. 'Stop making a fuss, woman. I'm the one that's soaking here.'

'You're insane.'

'That makes two of us, then.' He squeezes my ankle in the silence that follows; a kind of apology for the lame joke. 'I'd guess we're about five minutes' walk from the road. You comfortable enough up there?'

I don't answer at first. I'm remembering what he said about the killer carrying the dead woman through the stream, and that only a man would be able to do it. What did he say?

It's fine, I'm strong enough.

'Yeah, I'm good.' I lean forward over his shoulders, shifting awkwardly. 'Let's do this.'

At first the going is fairly easy, Tris stepping from slippery stone to stone, their edges bearded with green weed, or splashing across wet shale in the shallows nearest the bank. It's warm, perched on his shoulders, the sun striking through the trees here where the canopy is thin above us. I listen to his breathing, steady rather than laboured, and am impressed by his strength. I'm not exactly a featherweight.

We've moving against the flow of the current, and the water is growing deeper. I see tiny shoals of fish flicking past us in the shadows. There must be a pool ahead, perhaps around the next bend. Dragonflies skim across the surface of the water, jewelled wings moving so fast they're a blur.

It's really quite beautiful here.

Round the next bend, Tris comes to an abrupt halt, both of us staring at the unexpected obstacle in our path.

'Shit,' he mutters. 'I didn't think of that.'

The stream has been fenced off with a wire fence,

higher than a man and dipping several feet into the deep-flowing water. An ancient greening sign, tacked onto the wire fence by all four corners at one time but now hanging by one edge, says: PRIVATE PROPERTY. DO NOT ENTER.

The fence extends onto the bank, though it's clear that people have climbed over it in the past, treading it down until the fence is bowed. Even so, a man carrying a heavy weight would not find it easy to climb over. And he would have to scale the bank first, and risk leaving prints in the loose soil there.

Tris carries me to the bank and lets me hop down.

'Sorry,' he says. 'This seemed like a good idea back at the bridge. But he can't have come this way. Looks like I got soaked for nothing.'

I don't answer. I'm too busy studying the ground between the bank and the wire fence. The muddy soil looks unusually soft and loose there, considering it's covered in a huge tangle of brambles, where you might expect the earth underneath to be tough and compacted, a mass of roots. Only some of the brambles look oddly wilted. At this time of year they are usually fresh and bursting with bright green leaf buds, or tiny white flowers ready to be pollinated. The beginnings of berries. But the brambles nearest me look old, like last season's growth, all the flower heads drooping.

'What is it?' Tris asks, watching me.

For answer, I push my foot into soft dirt under the brambles. It gives easily, leaving an impression of my trainer sole behind.

I stare, and cannot breathe properly. This soil has been freshly dug. And recently.

'Ellie?'

'I don't think you got soaked for nothing,' I manage to say. 'How are you at digging?'

CHAPTER EIGHTEEN

We have no spades, no implements for digging. So I forage in the debris along the bank until I find a suitably-shaped fallen tree branch amongst all the leaves and dirt. Tris puts his foot on it at the mid-point, snapping it in half with a loud crack that sends birds clattering away in the trees above us. Reluctantly, he hands me one half of the broken branch, then uses his own half to dig over the loose soil.

We take one end of the bramble patch each. I'm nearer the stream, he's nearer the wire fence. The brambles are covering most of the soil at my end, so I have to beat back the thorny tangle of branches before I can even start digging.

'I'm not sure we should be doing this,' he says, poking at the soil as if he would rather be anywhere else in the world. Which is a feeling I'm beginning to share. It's not an enviable job, digging for a corpse in a lonely wood.

I heave at the brambles, feeling a bit over-heated and wishing I had chosen to wear a vest top.

'Why?'

'If there's anything here, we could be destroying evidence. Trampling all over the place. I mean, there might be footprints all round this area.'

'You were the one who said he came by the stream so there wouldn't be any footprints.'

'Agreed, but he must have climbed up the bank if he buried a body here. He must have stood ...' Tris looks down, waving the branch vaguely at the ground, 'somewhere about here. I'm probably standing in the exact same spot.'

'We can't go to the police with a suspect patch of soil. They already think I'm disturbed. What if there's nothing under here?'

'So let them find out.'

'No, I have to be sure this time or I risk being charged with wasting police time.'

'Fair enough.'

He digs in silence after that, and I do the same at my end, probing under the brambles with my ineffectual tool. A few scoops of soil are loosened with every poke and dig, but it's slow progress. And I understand his reluctance, because I feel it too.

This place is so quiet and still, a long way from even the narrowest of the tracks that crisscross these woods. The stream runs deeper here, so it's less noisy, a smooth glide of water through the wire mesh of the fence that separates the public woods from someone's private land. The birds flew away when Tris broke the branch, so there's no longer any cheerful birdsong from above. And the skin on the back of my neck is prickling, like we're being watched.

I stretch my back, hot and tired. There's no one in sight. Just hundreds of trunks and leafy branches, standing in staggered rows up and down the gentle undulations of the woods.

But when I look away, I catch a tiny shiver of movement out of the corner of my eye. As if someone has ducked behind a tree. Someone who had been standing perfectly still a second before when I was looking. Acting like a tree in a forest.

I force myself not to look again. As though to look again would confirm me as a nutter. Or let whoever is watching us know that I'm on to them.

There's no one there. *No one there at all.*

I've cleared about a foot down when my branch-spade hits something under the next layer of stony soil.

I hesitate.

Probably another stone.

But at the back of my mind I'm panicking, because it didn't make the hard clunking sound that the stones have been making. It was a soft-hard contact. Like something organic. Like flesh.

I poke my branch back into the soil.

'Shit.'

Tris is next to me in seconds. 'What is it?' He sounds as on edge as I feel. 'Did you find something?'

I swallow and nod, pointing with my branch to the spot where something pale and dirty is protruding through the soil. It could be a trick of the light, but there's a kind of greenish tinge to it which makes me want to vomit.

'I think it's a … a hand.'

Tris stares over my shoulder, then slowly presses his own branch into the shallow indentation left by my digging. He gives a start when a little more soil runs away, uncovering more of the hand.

'Christ.'

It's definitely a knuckle, the finger bent back like it was clawing at its own grave. I can see the tiny whorls on the skin, ingrained with dirt, but white under that. And sickeningly real.

'That's it, we've got to call the police.' Tris drops his branch, fumbles for his mobile instead. Stares at the screen with a blank expression. 'No signal. You're kidding me. Okay, think, think. Where's the nearest phone we can use?'

'The vicarage,' I say automatically.

'Right.' He grabs my hand and jerks me to my feet.

'Come on, we'll go back down the stream, then run up to the church, same way we came down. Fifteen minutes, tops.'

I shake my head, refusing to move. 'I'm not going anywhere.'

He meets my eyes then. His face is almost as white as the hand in the makeshift grave below us.

'Eleanor, please.'

'You think I'm going to risk the killer moving her again while we're away, fetching the police? No thanks, I'm not playing that game.'

He looks confused. 'Game?'

I tug my hand free. 'You make the call. I'll stay and watch the grave. She's not going anywhere this time, and neither am I.'

'I'm telling you, it's not safe. This grave has only recently been dug. What if the killer's still here, in the woods, watching us?' Tris pauses. 'Hasn't that occurred to you?'

'Then he'll be ecstatic. Because this is precisely what he wants, isn't it? Some serious attention at last.'

He frowns. 'What are you talking about?'

I tell him about the note on Denzil's car. *You're my Number One.* Then my scare in the lane after Denzil dropped me off.

Tris looks furious by the time I'm finished with my explanation. 'I don't believe it. Why didn't you tell me at once? Or the bloody police? Why keep a note like that to yourself?'

Then his eyes widen. He stares at me fixedly, as if everything has clicked into place for him. I can see him struggling not to lose his composure.

'You think I'm the killer.'

'It did cross my mind. But that's not important right now. Go ring the police, Tris. I'll be fine here.'

I see him struggle, still staring at me. Then he makes the decision, an angry flash in his eyes.

A moment later, he's gone.

I hear his continuing progress long after he's out of sight, echoes bouncing off the trees at first, then fading rapidly to silence.

Everything in the wood looks calm and still. There's no one among the rows of trunks. The water glides past in the dappled green shade of the tree canopy above me, empty and innocent.

I turn and force myself to look down at her exposed knuckle. I think of the woman's face, hidden beneath layers of dirt, and wonder what her name is. I'm standing next to a dead woman whose dead body has been dumped in a shallow grave, and I don't have a clue who she is or even why she was killed.

Dropping to my knees, I knock the soil away. Slowly, a pale hand emerges. Long fingers and short stubby nails, like she used to bite them. There's a mark on the back of her hand. I can't quite bring myself to touch her skin, but use a leaf to gently brush the last of the soil from her hand.

I thought it was a tattoo, but it's too faint, one side missing like it wasn't done properly. A stamp of some kind. A faint red triangle with a circle in the middle?

It reminds me of the ink stamp you get on the back of your hand when going into a night club, to say you've paid.

I frown, looking from the back of her hand along her wrist. The skin is pale but there's bruising on it, all the way round. It looks like she's had her wrists tied at some point.

I push the brambles aside with my feet. Clear the grave so it can be dug out properly. I know I'm probably destroying evidence, as Tris warned me not to, but if the killer is even half as clever as I think, there won't be any forensic evidence to destroy. Soon the police will descend again with their specialist tools and their sniffer dogs. I imagine they'll set up a forensic tent here. They'll take photographs before moving her, messing her about, touching her impersonally.

But right now it's just the two of us in the sunny

woodlands. And I'm going to do what needs to be done.

Once the brambles are cleared at what I judge to be the 'head end,' I drop to my knees and dig with my bare hands. Carefully and gently, tiny scrapings, not wanting to disturb her. I'm aware all the time of the very real possibility that the killer is out there somewhere. Maybe watching me from behind the trees. But I pay no attention. He has no place here. It's just me and her now.

A hint of something pale in the soil catches my eye, and I pause, then scrape more slowly. Strands of hair.

I stop.

The silence is suddenly deafening. My skin prickles and I feel cold. It's almost as if I can hear him behind me, breathing quietly, watching me, only a few feet away ...

How long has Tris been gone? I seem to have lost all sense of time. I glance at my watch, but it makes no sense to me. My brain has stopped working.

I dig again, two-handed, my fingers pushing deeper into the soil, nails crusty black now, packed with dirt. I find her face by touch, the high forehead, bony and hard. The eye sockets below. I avoid them, feeling nauseous, and dig lower, scraping soil away to expose her face, one dirty patch of skin after another.

Her face comes clear and I stare, hardly able to breathe.

You're my Number One.

I hear Tris from a great distance, crashing through the undergrowth and calling my name. I guess it won't be long before the police arrive. For the second time.

I stumble to my feet and vomit into the stream.

My stomach heaves again, but there's no more. Hurriedly I wash my face in the clear moving water, then my hands. The soil under my nails refuses to be washed away though, and my knuckles are still dirty when I stand up to meet Tris. Just like hers.

'They're coming,' Tris tells me when he finally reaches me, bending over and panting, out of breath. There's a fine sheen of perspiration on his face, like he ran the whole way without stopping. 'The vicar wasn't there, but his wife was. I called the police, told them we'd found her body, and where. They're sending a car out.'

'A body,' I mutter. 'We've found *a* body.'

He looks a question at me, and I point down at the shallow grave.

Still breathing hard, he looks down at her in silence for a moment. Then says, 'I thought you said she had a number three on her forehead?'

We both look down at the number on the dead woman's forehead. Faded now, dirtied by the soil, but still legible, written clumsily in black permanent marker.

'Yes.'

'Any chance you made a mistake?'

'No.'

'Okay, perhaps the number was changed.'

I say nothing.

'But you said the woman had dark hair,' Tris continues, frowning. 'I remember the statement you gave to the police.'

I nod.

'I don't understand,' he says at last.

'Neither do I. Yet there it is, right in front of us.' I stare down at the dead woman's face, glancing from the number on her forehead to the dirty blonde hair above it, and hear myself saying the impossible. 'Different number, different hair colour. This is not the same woman.'

CHAPTER NINETEEN

I don't know the two police officers who are first to arrive in the woods. They descend the track from the church heavily, trying to avoid slipping on loose soil and stones, then stand a moment, glancing up and down through the dappled shade.

Tris cups both hands to his mouth and calls, 'Over here,' then waves. Like we're meeting them for a barbecue or something.

They approach without any sense of urgency, barely looking at us. One is swatting away flies on the back of his neck. They introduce themselves briefly. Both constables, Cornish accents, unsmiling. I sense some low-level irritation too. Have we disturbed a quiet Sunday afternoon in some sunny layby off the A30?

One of the constables takes a quick look in the grave, prods the exposed hand with the toe of one boot, then turns to stare at us. Perhaps he had assumed it was a hoax.

'Bloody hell,' his colleague says, looking over his shoulder. He walks back up the slope a little way, probably for better reception, then gets on his radio.

The other officer asks us a few more questions, conscientiously writing everything down in his notebook.

Including my name. Which he does not appear to recognise.

When he has finished taking notes, the constable nods at us calmly, as though people find dead bodies in the woods every day. He says, 'Best to stay here until the detective inspector arrives. Either of you hurt or in shock?'

'We're fine, thanks,' I say for both of us.

He takes a long, thoughtful look at my face. I suppose there is still a mark there where my father hit me. 'You sure?'

'Positive.'

Tris has fallen silent. He is staring at the shallow grave a few feet away. Despite the exercise of running up to the village and back, his face is still pale.

I ask, 'Do you mind if we move a bit further away from the body?'

The constable looks at me dubiously, but agrees. 'Don't stray too far though. The DI will probably want to speak to you in person.'

'I'm sure he will,' I say drily.

But the officer has turned away, and is writing in his notebook again. *Something suspicious about these two …*

We wander slowly along the damp bank until we're roughly a hundred feet upstream of the two police officers. Tris finds a mossy old stump to sit on, staring down into the stream. I look back, watching as the two constables confer. After a lengthy conversation, the one who spoke to us disappears back up the track towards the village, leaving the other one to stand guard over our find. Like buried treasure. *Mouldering* buried treasure.

'Macabre,' I mutter.

'Sorry?'

'The way my mind works.' I shrug. 'Never mind, I was talking to myself. But one thing about this certainly surprises me.'

'And what's that?'

'I expected all this to feel different. For me to feel

different. After all, I've been proved right. There *was* a body in the woods.'

'But not the same body,' Tris interrupts me.

'No, but at least we can be sure I'm not going mad. Well, probably not. Or no madder than I was before all this started. But whoever she is, that poor bloody woman's existence – or lack of it – proves that s*omebody* killed *somebody else*. None of this has been my imagination.'

'I wish it was, though.'

'What's the matter?'

I look at him searchingly. He's one of the few friends I have left, and I need to look out for him.

I also feel bad for suspecting him of being the killer. Having seen the way he reacted to unearthing that dead body, I can't believe him capable of having put her there. Unless he's a Jekyll and Hyde killer, the sort who can block off one entire half of their personality in order to commit atrocious crimes, while the other half is blissfully aware that they are a total psycho.

'Is the shock catching up on you?' I ask. 'Don't feel bad if it is. I felt a bit sick too, looking down at her lying there.'

'It's not that. The problem is … ' He stops.

'What?'

Tris glances across at the lone police constable, hands clasped behind his back, no doubt waiting for the forensics team to descend. But the man's too far away to hear what we're saying, and anyway we're both speaking quietly. Too quietly to be heard above the rushing noise of the stream beside us.

'I'm worried about you, actually,' he says frankly. 'You're too calm. After everything you've been through, to find a body like this … I'm no expert in psychology, but shouldn't you be running about screaming, or having a nervous breakdown?'

I meet his open gaze. He's lying, I'm sure of it. He was going to say something completely different, but then thought better of it.

There's no point demanding the truth. He would simply deny it. I wonder if he's suspicious about my find. It's true that we found her grave rather easily, almost as though the killer had done a poor job of concealing it on purpose. Perhaps Tris thinks I already knew where the dead woman was buried, and he's protecting me by keeping his suspicions to himself.

Neither of those possibilities make me feel very good.

'Maybe I'm saving that up until later.'

He manages a half-grin. 'I look forward to it. Especially the screaming and running about.'

'I do a good impersonation of a chicken with its head cut off. It's all good though.' I glance back at the grave, and abruptly change my mind. 'Or it was until now. Shit.'

Tris turns to follow my stare, then gets up and fumbles for my hand. He squeezes it hard. 'All good, remember?' he says, for my ears only. 'Don't let him wind you up.'

My old nemesis is trudging through the trees towards us, kicking aside brambles and leaf detritus as he walks. Detective Inspector Powell. Like the two constables, he too does not look amused by this interruption to his Sunday afternoon. To my surprise, he's in faded jeans and what looks like a yellow tee-shirt with a sun design under a light blue jacket. Almost hippyish. The large black wellington boots look totally mismatched with the rest of his outfit, like he's been dragged away from a relaxing day off with his family to come and dig up a corpse. Which I'm guessing is precisely what has happened.

Behind him I see several other police men and women coming down the slope, and what look like plain clothes officers following slowly, some carrying metal boxes and other heavy equipment.

Forensics.

Powell comes to a halt in front of us. He nods at Tris, then looks at me broodingly. 'So you couldn't leave it alone.'

'I told you there was a body.'

'So I understand. I'll take a look at that in a minute.' He glances across at the shady patch of soil by the stream, the one uniformed police officer standing guard over it. 'You just stumbled across it, I'm told. While out on a Sunday walk.'

I nod, mutely.

'Which is an idea I find hard to believe. Not exactly a relaxing spot for you, these woods.'

I shrug.

'Hurt yourself?' DI Powell is looking at my cheek.

I shrug again.

Clearly frustrated by my silence, his gaze interrogates Tris. 'I don't think I know you. Boyfriend?'

'Friend,' I say sharply, not letting Tris speak for himself. 'His name is Tristan Taylor.'

The inspector looks back at me, eyebrows raised. 'You still have friends, then?'

'I have hidden qualities.'

'I'm sure you do, Eleanor.'

'So what's next?'

'Nothing too demanding. You'll need to give a formal statement, of course. Back at the station.' He looks at Tris. 'You too.'

Tris says nothing, merely looks back at the inspector. The two of them lock gazes and say nothing. Like two male stags locking horns in the woods.

First the inspector thought I was a liar. Then he thought I was mad and needed psychiatric help. Now he seems to suspect me of having planted a dead body in the woods just so I can be proved right. Which is precisely what I thought Tris was trying to suggest, but coming from the inspector it feels a thousand times more offensive.

Perhaps it's an urge to make him give me respect that makes me blurt out, 'It's not the same woman, you know.'

'*What?*'

'She's someone completely different. I never saw that

woman before in my life.'

A shout interrupts us. 'Inspector?'

Reluctantly, Powell tears his bewildered gaze from me. 'What is it?' he demands, his voice deep and impatient. One of his team is signalling him from the graveside, a woman in white forensic overalls and hood. 'Okay, yeah, I'll be right over.'

Most of the other police have reached the shallow grave and are setting up their equipment around its narrow perimeter. One man in a leather jacket and jeans is kneeling in the dirt, pushing back the lid on a large case of expensive photographic equipment. The photographer, presumably. Two of the others are already erecting a white tent above the half-dug grave, as if to shield her from onlookers.

Powell summons one of the police constables who were first there. 'This your call-in, Timms?'

'Yes, sir.'

'These two make any calls since you arrived? Speak to anyone?'

'No sir,' the policeman says, looking perplexed. 'Only to each other. There's no signal in these woods, anyway. We even had a job getting the radio to work.'

'Look after them, would you? I want a full statement from both of these witnesses, to be taken *separately*,' he says, emphasising that last point. 'And at the station. Not here.'

'Yes, sir.'

Powell looks back at me, still frowning. 'I'll talk to you later, Eleanor. At the station.'

'I can't wait.'

I look up at a familiar cry: there's the black hunched figure of a crow perched on a high branch above us. It caws again, glossy throat convulsing, then swoops away through the leafy canopy of trees.

In the old days, some Cornish witches kept a crow as a familiar, others a midnight-black cat. I've been to the

Museum of Witchcraft at Boscastle on the north coast, seen all their spooky exhibits, the weird mandrake roots and feather totems. I enjoy reading about that time too, sixteenth and seventeenth century England and the witch hunts. But until now I never found any of those superstitions particularly frightening. They're not real, just strange old stories. Folk tales and legends strung together to scare people in the dark.

Sitting in a wood though, a few feet away from the half-buried body of a murdered woman, it's difficult not to wonder if there is such a thing as true evil.

'Arrange for a car to take them to the station,' Powell tells the constable. 'As soon as possible.'

'Right you are, sir.'

'And no reporters, you understand? Cordon this whole area off. I don't want anyone in this part of the woods who isn't directly related to this inquiry.'

'Yes, sir.'

I watch the detective inspector head over to the grave, sidestepping the team already working there in order to get a proper look at the victim. Powell stops, staring down at the loose patch of soil without speaking while the plain clothes police officer talks to him rapidly.

I remember what the inspector is looking at, and shudder. That could be me in that shallow grave. Or Hannah. I don't know the dead woman, but that's how personal this feels.

PC Timms glances at us, then fumbles with his radio. All we hear is static. 'Bloody signal.' He hesitates. 'Wait here. Don't talk to anyone. You understand?'

Tris looks furious. 'So, are we suspects? Are we being charged with finding a dead body? Because last time I checked, that wasn't a crime.'

'Calm down,' the constable says wearily. 'Nobody's accusing either of you of anything. The inspector wants a statement from you both, that's all, and it's better if you don't talk to anyone else until you've given that. Now stay here. I'll be back in a jiffy.'

He hurries away towards the base of the slope, where it seems the signal on his police radio is stronger. He speaks into the radio, head bent, presumably arranging a car for us to the station. Powell is talking to the woman in white overalls. Both of them look very serious, as they should. Perhaps if they had not assumed I was round the bend when I first saw a dead body here in the woods, this new victim would have been found sooner. Or might not have been here at all. Because it feels like the killer is playing games with us. With me, more specifically.

When the white forensics tent closes round the grave, shutting the team out of sight, I pretend to throw stones into the stream, but I'm covertly studying Tris, which surprises me. It seems I'm monitoring his response as much as my own. Do I still think one of my own friends is guilty, that Tris of all people is somehow connected to this?

Perhaps, perhaps not. It's infuriating, but I can't make up my mind. Whatever the truth, he does seem to be behaving oddly today. And not just because we found a body together.

The constable comes back, looking relieved. 'Right, job done. There's a car waiting for you up top. It'll take you to the station where a police officer will sit down with you and take a formal statement. Come on, I'll walk with you.'

'Thanks.' I glance at Tris, but he does not appear to be listening. 'Tris?'

He's staring at something on the damp soil between us. A crow's feather is lying there, black and dusty.

When I was a kid, I always thought of my mum whenever I saw a crow's feather on the ground. Perhaps because there was a crow above us in the trees that day, making that odd cawing noise in the backs of his throat, more like a jeering laugh than birdsong.

'Tris?' I say again.

'Sorry?'

'Time to go.'

'Right. Yeah, okay.'

Tris runs a hand through his hair, then smiles at me. But behind the smile is that blank, unreadable look again, like he's concealing something. From me. From the police. From everyone.

'Sorry,' he says again, 'I was miles away.'

I smile back at him, trying not to let my anxiety show. *Please, not Tris. Don't let it be Tris.*

CHAPTER TWENTY

Once he has a signal, Tris phones his brother on the way, keeping details to a clipped minimum on the advice of the police driver. Always protective of his younger brother, Connor meets us about twenty minutes later at the police station. We've only been there a few minutes when he walks in. He's wearing his old, olive-green, waterproof jacket with the patches at the elbows, the left pocket slightly ripped. Wellington boots, covered in dried mud. Probably been out in the top pasture most of the afternoon where they're mending and replacing fences while the weather is fine. His dark hair is untidy; he's smoothing it down as they buzz him through the door into the waiting area.

'Hey,' Connor says, and hugs me.

Tris looks mildly irritated to see his brother. 'Christ, you didn't have to come all the way down here. I told you, I've got this. It's just a witness statement.'

Connor ignores him. 'You'll need a lift home afterwards. Both of you. I brought the car.'

'Thanks, but I could be here for ages,' I tell him calmly. 'DI Powell wants to speak to me after I've given them a statement. And he's still down in the woods. Take Tris home when he's finished, don't worry about me. One of the officers will give me a lift back. Or I could give Hannah a call, see if she's free.' I check the time on the wall clock in the waiting area. 'She's not at work until six.'

He looks at me. 'So there *was* a body.'

I decide not to tell him it's not the same woman. 'It appears so.'

'You must feel vindicated.'

I make a face. 'I feel a bit sick actually. It wasn't a pretty sight.'

'Jesus, come here.' Connor gives me another hug. I can smell sheep on his old jacket. It may sound gross, but I'm comforted by the farmy, homely smell. 'We can hang on until you're finished here. You don't need to trouble Hannah.'

One of the police officers comes out, a burly man with reddish hair and unlikely sideburns like some Victorian copper. 'Sir,' he says politely to Tris, 'they're ready for you now. Interview Room Two. It's this way, if you could follow me?'

Connor says brusquely, 'I'll be out here when you're done, Tris. Okay?'

'I told you, don't wait around for me.'

'You're my brother. I'm going to fucking wait even if this takes all night. You got that?'

Tris looks frustrated, then glances at me, his face grim. It's obvious there's something else on his mind, but he shrugs and follows the officer through the swing doors without saying anything else.

Connor drops into one of the plastic seats along the wall of the waiting area. It squeaks under him protestingly. 'This is so fucked-up.'

'Tell me about it.'

He buries his head in his hands, sucks a deep breath in through his nose, then looks up at the white panelled ceiling. He's looking tired too, I realise, as though leaving the club early last night had not meant he got much more sleep than I did.

'Sorry,' he says, looking at me sideways as I sit next to him. 'I'm not being much of a friend here. You must have had a horrible shock, Ellie. How are you coping?'

'So-so.'

'That doesn't sound too good.'

'I'll survive.'

'Good to hear.' He squeezes my knee briefly. 'You've not had an easy run of it. But your luck can only change for the better.'

We sit together in silence for a while, our shoulders touching. I fret about Tris, and can feel his brother doing the same. Tris has not been himself since his dad died. I know better than most how long and bloody the bereavement process can be, and perhaps I'm expecting too much too soon, but that gaunt look in his face as he followed the police officer to the interview room has left me with a chill feeling in my heart.

Something's nagging at me again. But my mind keeps slipping away from the answer every time it swings round to face me, jumping over it, like a scratch on a CD.

I remember passing the vicarage this afternoon, Mortimer Clemo staring out of the window at us. I can't help feeling that the body in the grave was left there for me to find, just like the dead woman lying across the path. But why? Am I being punished for some past mistake or sin? Is this karma? I'm not dragging a fictional God into this, but I do believe in justice, whether natural or man-made. And this is beginning to feel like revenge of some kind. But revenge for what?

'I hear you went out for a long walk with the dog this morning,' I say, trying to distract both of us from our morbid thoughts. 'Trying to keep fit?'

Connor laughs, and relaxes in his chair. 'I've got a long way to go before I can compete with you, but yes, I thought it might be a good idea not to let any of this muscle,' he says, slapping his stomach, which is impressively flat, 'turn to flab through lack of use. The farm takes every waking moment of the day. I haven't been to the gym in months.'

'According to Tris, hauling sheep around counts as exercise.'

He grins, but it's lopsided. 'Actually, I could do with fewer dead sheep. It's already bloody expensive just keeping the farm going without losing livestock too.'

'Is that a thing? Like, frequent?'

'At the moment, yes. That's why I was out this morning. I didn't tell Tris this, he hates bad news, but Dick Laney rang early to say he'd seen another dead ewe on our western boundary. Looks like she lay down and couldn't get up again. Sheep do that sometimes. Get stuck on their backs, like beetles.'

'How awful.'

He grimaces. 'That's sheep farming for you. Death and shit. And sod all money. It's small wonder so many farmers shoot themselves.'

The swing doors clatter open. DI Powell is standing there, looking directly at me, a bunch of official-looking manila folders in his hand. He seems flustered, like he's been hurrying, his silvering hair in disarray. He has changed his clothes though, which may account for it. The hippy look has gone, and in its place is a dark, sombre suit and polished shoes.

'Ah, Eleanor,' he says briskly, nodding to me. 'Shall we talk?'

'I haven't given my statement yet.'

'That's fine, we'll get to that in due course.'

Connor stands up at the same time as I do. His voice is very deep and angry. 'Just hang on a minute. This isn't right, Inspector. My brother is a witness. Not a suspect.'

Powell tucks a pencil behind his ear, and gives Connor a quick, assessing look, as though worried there's going to be trouble. 'And you are … ?'

'Connor Taylor. You've got my brother Tristan in one

of your interview rooms.'

'We need to take a statement from him, Mr Taylor, that's all. Standard procedure in a murder enquiry. Your brother is not under suspicion.'

'Murder?'

The inspector hesitates, glancing down at his folders. There's a flash of irritable impatience in his face; perhaps an awareness that he's been indiscreet.

'Obviously nothing's official yet,' he says. 'We need to hear back from the pathologist first. You know how it is. Small steps. But I'm sure as soon as we're satisfied with your brother's statement, he'll be free to go.'

Connor takes a step forward, his voice low but aggressive. 'I bet you're feeling stupid now though.'

DI Powell raises his brows. 'I beg your pardon?'

'You didn't believe a word Ellie told you. Now *she's* found the body in the woods that you couldn't find. You and your merry men.'

'Thanks for your input. But if you could hold off on your speculations until we've established the facts here – '

'Oh, I'm sure you'd like that, Inspector. You'll be wanting to keep your incompetence as quiet as possible.'

There's an awkward silence, then DI Powell gestures me to follow him. 'Miss Blackwood?'

Connor isn't finished yet though. 'Hold on. Should I be arranging for a solicitor for my brother?'

'That's up to your brother, Mr Taylor, not you. But I'm sure if he needs legal counsel, the duty officer will ensure he receives it.' Powell nods to me, seeming to dismiss Connor from his thoughts. 'Shall we go through? Sorry to rush you but I've got a meeting in an hour.'

As I follow the inspector through the swing doors, I give Connor an apologetic smile. 'I'm sure Tris will be fine. Try not to worry. I'll call you later, yeah?'

'Yeah, later.'

The interview room is clean and looks to have been newly

decorated. The walls are so white they seem freshly painted, almost dazzling, and the window blinds are dust-free. The floor is carpeted in a bland mushroom colour, no marks showing, the drag of the pile indicating that someone hoovered there in the past twenty-four hours. Walking in there gives me the impression of a place run like clockwork, possibly overseen by a control freak with a rubber glove fetish. Hannah and I could do with someone like that at the cottage.

The whole building is new though, a recent high-profile build stuck on a hillside overlooking the town. So maybe it's that squeaky-clean feel you get with a new house, like nothing's bedded in yet. One of Connor's friends bought a semi-detached on a new housing estate in Truro last autumn, and it was like this when we dropped by during a night out, that odd 'new build' smell, something between disinfectant and fixative.

A police constable is already standing in the room, hands behind his back, face impassive, as though he's always been there, part of the fixtures. He looks at me, then away. Like I'm contagious.

'Thank you for coming in, Eleanor. Please take a seat.' The inspector shrugs out of his jacket and slings it about the back of his chair. 'Let's make ourselves comfortable. Would you like a coffee? Maybe a cup of tea?'

I sit down at the interview table. 'Thanks, tea would be good.'

He is carefully laying out the manila and plastic see-through folders he's brought in with him. 'Sorry for the delay, we'll start in a couple of minutes.' He glances up at the constable, and then nods. Like it's a pre-arranged signal between the two of them. 'Two teas, constable.'

The constable nods back solemnly. 'Sir.'

It's not a signal, I tell myself firmly. That's just the stirrings of paranoia speaking. I force myself to smile at the constable as he leaves the room. 'Thank you.'

He does not smile back.

Now it's just the two of us. I place my hands on the table, then remove them to my lap because my palms are sweaty and I don't want the inspector to notice. Last time I did anything like this my father was in the room because I was a child. Now I'm an adult and alone.

Though if my dad was here now, he would probably shout or throw up on the inspector's highly polished shoes. So I tell myself it's a good thing that I'm on my own.

I am worried about what Connor said outside though. Do I need the duty solicitor? Should I demand a lawyer along with the obligatory cup of tea? Surely I am only here as a witness, like Tris, and not under suspicion myself?

It's ridiculous but I can't seem to shake this feeling of unease.

The interview room is functional, not particularly welcoming. There are grey blinds at the window, blocking the late sunlight, a bare noticeboard displaying nothing but a No Smoking notice, and this table with four chairs set about it.

The door opens, and I glance round. It's PC Helen Flynn, the woman officer who came to the cottage when I saw the first body.

'Ah, PC Flynn, there you are.' DI Powell gestures her to sit down beside him. 'We're just waiting on some cups of tea. Are you having one?'

'No thank you, sir,' she says, her manner very correct, seating herself straight-backed in the seat opposite mine. My eyes meet hers. Hers are coldly professional. There will be no help from that quarter.

The constable returns with two plastic cups of tea, and places one in front of me, and one in front of his superior officer. The name on his uniform sleeve says Hanney. My tea does not look very appetizing, a greyish brown swirl with flecks of white. Powdered creamer? Or off-milk?

'Sugar?' the constable asks quietly, pushing a plastic spoon and small paper sachet towards me.

I shake my head.

It's like a dinner party without the dinner. I wonder if paper hats will be handed round next.

Powell brings a notebook out of his pocket and lays it in front of him, then arranges it neatly alongside the manila folders, making sure everything is properly aligned.

Obsessive Compulsive, much?

PC Flynn prepares the statement sheets. She asks for my full details. I answer in a monotone, feeling like a criminal. I am half disappointed not to find a mirrored wall in the room behind which psychologists are lurking unseen, waiting for me to make some fatal slip. To reveal my guilt. My secret psychosis. They'll be waiting a long time for that to happen, I think grimly, and lay my hands flat on the table, looking straight across at Detective Inspector Powell. Sod the sweaty palms.

'Am I under arrest?'

Powell shakes his head, smiling. 'Of course not. Mr Taylor is mistaken. Like I said, we need a simple statement about your discovery of the body today. To get the facts straight.'

'Perhaps I should get a lawyer.'

'That's up to you, of course.' DI Powell shrugs as though it makes no difference to him whether I ask for a lawyer or not. But I can hear the impatience in his voice. He leans back in his chair, his smile forced. 'No one's saying you've done anything wrong though, Eleanor. And it's a Sunday. You would probably have to wait several hours for a lawyer to arrive, and I suspect you'd rather just get this over with.'

I can see the sense in that. 'Okay,' I agree, perhaps recklessly. But he is right; I do want to get this over with. 'What do you need to know?'

Powell looks relieved. 'I'll ask you a few questions, and you must answer them as accurately as possible, and we'll start to piece together a statement from there. PC Flynn here will take notes to keep us on the right track, and make sure nothing gets missed. Is that okay with you?'

I shrug. 'I guess.'

PC Flynn gives me a cool look, then sits waiting, pen poised above the lined sheet of paper. I begin to dislike her intensely.

He smiles. 'So let's start at the beginning, Eleanor. Why were you in the woods this morning?'

The table surface is tacky. I shift my palms, unsticking them. 'It was a nice day, and I felt like a relaxing run.'

'With Tristan Taylor?' When I nod, his eyes narrow thoughtfully on my face. 'Is Tristan your boyfriend? I know you said you were "just friends" when we were in the woods. But maybe you didn't want to be too specific in front of him. I know how delicate these things can be.' He hesitates, his smile persuasive. Then gives me another nudge. 'Especially if you've only just started seeing each other.'

'I don't have a boyfriend.'

Not entirely accurate, but a strategic response. If I say no, he will ask if I have a boyfriend. I will then be forced to say yes, and he will then ask his name. Denzil is known to the police, and if they should discover that we have history, they'd jump on that at once. He would look like a golden ticket to the police. Once his name came up, they would never believe Denzil has nothing to do with this.

Besides, I would not characterize Denzil Tremain as a boyfriend. Especially after the way he treated me last night. And as for Tris, it's complicated. From my side, not his. Unfortunately.

'No boyfriend,' I insist when the inspector stares, and draw my clammy hands out of sight under the table. 'Like I said, Tris is a friend. A good friend.'

'So you went for a walk in the woods with your good friend, for a spot of weekend relaxation?'

I nod, looking him in the eyes.

His face hardens. 'And then you decided to head off the main path and follow the stream instead. Near where you saw a dead body last week. Doesn't that strike you as rather odd behaviour for a peaceful Sunday walk?'

'I thought it might help me get over it. If I could see the place again, get things straight in my head.'

Powell considers me for a moment. Then shrugs, nodding. 'Okay.' He opens the notebook in front of him, and consults its spidery writing with a frown. 'Now, according to the officer who questioned you at the scene, you walked along the stream from the bridge, and found a patch of loose soil that looked like someone had been digging there recently.'

'That's about it, yes.'

'Whose idea was it to go that way in the first place?'

'Tristan's.'

'And what did Tristan think about this "loose soil"? Was he keen on digging it up? Was that his idea too?'

'I don't think so, no.' I can still feel that gritty soil under my nails from where I cleared her face, even though I washed my hands thoroughly in the ladies when I got to the station, soap and hot water. 'It was mine. My idea.'

PC Flynn has been scribbling all this time, looking at me occasionally while writing down what's being said. DI Powell leans across and whispers something in her ear, then sits upright again, his gaze returning to my face.

'So it was you who wanted to dig up the ground? Is that what you're saying?'

I nod, feeling uncooperative.

But he presses me, asking, 'Why?'

'Isn't it obvious?'

'Indulge me, Eleanor. For the record.'

'I don't know exactly.' I shrug, trying to verbalize the thing. 'It was a hunch. Like police work. Detectives get hunches too, don't they?'

'When we're lucky.'

'I had that kind of feeling about it. A suspicion. The soil looked freshly dug and I couldn't see a reason for that. So I decided we should dig there. We didn't have spades, so we used what was to hand.'

'And what was Tristan doing during all this? Did he dig too?'

'Of course.'

'I suppose he thought it was a good idea as well.'

'No, in fact he didn't. He tried to stop me, said we should wait for the police. He said we could be destroying evidence.'

I see the note on Denzil's windscreen again, the way he burnt it so aggressively and drove away. I should tell the police about the note, it could be important. But the inspector would not understand the delicate nature of things, how my sanity is balanced on a knife edge, nor can I explain my uncertainty over that note, or what happened to it. If I tell Powell about the note, he will want to question Denzil, and I don't want this man trampling all over my private life.

'Tris was the one who wanted to call you at once,' I decide to add, 'but I wouldn't let him. So if anyone's to blame, it's me. Not Tristan.'

His gaze flickers over my face, then drops lower. It is as though he can see my hands through the table, twisting restlessly out of sight. I try to keep still, to look calm and normal and sane. But this whole business is hitting me on so many levels at once, I can feel it triggering every defence mechanism I've ever had. I struggle to remember my mantras, to control my breathing, and keep smiling.

'You said in the woods that you'd never seen that woman before.' He is suspicious, his eyes narrowed. He knows I am withholding information. 'Which is strange, given the circumstances.'

'That's right, she was a completely different woman.' Carefully I describe what the first woman looked like, and compare it to the one I saw in the shallow grave. 'I know it sounds weird but that's the truth. I don't understand it either.'

'It is almost unconceivable that she is not the same

woman,' Powell agrees calmly, and plays with the pencil on the table, watching me. 'Unless the woods are peppered with dead bodies. Any chance you might have made a mistake in your initial description?'

'No.'

'You were in a state of shock, Eleanor. And the woods were very misty that morning, you said so yourself. Perhaps you didn't look as closely as you thought.'

'It was a different woman.'

The inspector smiles. 'Okay, let's put that possibility aside for now and focus on the *facts*.'

He doesn't believe me. DI Powell did not believe me when I reported the first body. Now he accepts that I was not imagining things, but does not believe that there could be two dead women out there, neither of them yet identified. That's one step too far for him.

I say, 'It's just as well they've proved beyond a shadow of a doubt that the world isn't flat, or we'd be in serious trouble.'

Powell gives me an old-fashioned look.

Someone knocks on the interview room door and Powell barks, 'Come in,' then listens impatiently as a young police officer enters the room and bends to his ear, whispering urgently.

I catch the words, 'woods' and 'body' – but nothing else.

When the door closes behind the police officer, Powell gives me one of his unrevealing half-smiles, the kind that briefly plucks his lips upwards for a second, then drops them again like smiling hurts him.

'Right, we've made a useful start on your statement.' He stands up, grabbing his jacket off the back of his chair. 'I'll have to leave you, I'm afraid. I'm needed urgently elsewhere. But PC Flynn will help you draw up a full statement. Once you're happy with it, you can sign it and you'll be free to go.'

There's something about his flat expression that leaves

me cold after his departure, like there's a sudden draught in the room.

PC Flynn smiles at me, rearranges the various papers in front of her, then clicks the top of her ballpoint pen a few times. I can tell it's an irritating habit of hers.

'Don't worry,' she says. 'This won't take much longer, I promise.'

Despite her promise, it's another hour before I get away from the police station. Too late to expect Hannah to come out and pick me up. She'll probably be on her way to work by now. PC Flynn ushers me out into the brightly-lit lobby, says goodbye in a consolatory way, presses a Victim Support leaflet into my hand, then disappears back inside without another word. The heavy door locks automatically behind her and it's over.

The place is not empty. People are slumped in plastic chairs or reading the noticeboard. A few turn to stare as I ask the sergeant on the desk to call a taxi for me. I have no money and will have to run into the cottage for my purse once we get there. But walking is out of the question, it's a good five miles to the village through treacherous country lanes, and I'll be damned if I'm going to ask the police to give me a lift home.

I head for the exit, and stop dead in the doorway as Connor appears from the direction of the visitor car park, coming in just as I am leaving.

I stare. 'Connor?'

Connor looks at me blankly, like I am the last person he expected to see there. He's looking tired and strained, and is carrying a small plastic bag. 'Hey, Ellie,' he says, not meeting my gaze. 'You on your way home? What's going on?'

'I could ask you the same thing. The police took ages taking a statement from me. I thought we'd never get away. Tris must have finished hours ago, surely. Why are you back again?'

'Tris is still here,' he says grimly. 'I had to go home again for an hour. To check on the livestock and grab some things for Tris.' Connor holds up the plastic bag. His voice is uneven. 'Toothbrush, toothpaste, and so on.'

'*Toothbrush?*'

'Didn't I say? They've arrested him on suspicion of murder.'

CHAPTER TWENTY-ONE

I sleep badly that night, waking several times with the old absurd fear that someone is standing by the window, watching me sleep. *Shadow man, shadow man.* Where will it all end?

I cannot stand another day of inaction though, and ring Jenny first thing. 'I'm going insane here,' I say, which is probably not the best to say under the circumstances. But I trust Jenny not to take it the wrong way. 'I need to come back to work.'

I explain about the body we found, then about Tris's arrest. I keep the details to the bare minimum. Before I left the station, PC Flynn warned me not to talk to anyone about the particulars of the case, even if the newspapers should get in touch. Not that I need that warning. I have a long history of hating reporters; I'm not about to feed them. But knowing what to say to close friends like Jenny and Hannah is less clear-cut.

Jenny is shocked and falls silent for a moment, then says, 'Well, under the circumstances, I can't see any reason why you shouldn't come back to work. But it's not my decision, of course. I'm only head of department. I can recommend you come back, but for the official go-ahead, you'll have to speak to Patricia.'

'She's my next call.'

Jenny hesitates. 'Poor Tris. He didn't do it, of course.'

A few days ago, I would have agreed without the need for thought. I would have said, 'No way in the universe did he do it.' But today is different. Today I am less sure of everything.

'Yeah, it took me by surprise too.'

'Well, keep in touch. I'm heading into work in a few minutes. I'll hope to see you there.' She pauses. 'It will be good to have you back.'

'It will be good to be back, believe me. Fingers crossed Patricia doesn't find an excuse to keep me at home. Like she's worried I might start finding bodies buried under the playing fields.'

She laughs. 'What, the skeletons of teachers past?'

'Something like that. Speak to you later.'

'Good luck.'

I end the call, then dial the head teacher's office. She's not in yet, unsurprisingly. It's just her answering service. I leave a brief message on her service, again avoiding any specifics, then put down the phone and fix myself a healthy breakfast of oats and fresh, chopped apples with dates. It seems Hannah has been shopping, which means I owe her money. She's in bed though, recovering from her night shift, so after I've eaten, I write a quick note of thanks on the memo board in the kitchen. Then the phone rings.

It's the head teacher, Patricia, calling me back. 'So you're off the hook,' she says bluntly, her voice a hoarse bark like a sergeant-major's.

'No more crazy lady,' I agree, perhaps a little too flippantly. The sugar rush from the fruit must have gone to my head. I force myself to sound more sober and measured during the explanation that follows, avoiding all mention of the fact that we could not agree on the provenance of the body. 'To sum up, the police have apologised. I no longer have the need for therapy hanging over my head. And I'd very much like to come back to work.'

Patricia thinks it over for a moment, then says slowly, 'Very well, yes. But bear in mind that this latest development may not be public knowledge yet. Until it is, you will have to run the gauntlet of some hostility from the student body.'

'Understood.'

'Also, if there are any more unfortunate incidents with the students, I may have to reconsider this decision.'

'Of course. I'll be extra careful. Thank you very much, I appreciate it.'

'Don't make me regret this, Eleanor.'

I end the call, and perform a little victory dance around the kitchen. I am going back to work. And I did not even have to grovel.

The shadow of Tris's arrest still lies over me though, like a stain on my heart. I do not know what to make of it. It has to be a mistake. Doesn't it?

Sure enough, the kids begin to stare and whisper again as soon as I park my scooter in the staff car park. I check in with Patricia as agreed, change into my work gear, then stride out across the playing fields in my grey tracksuit and trainers. I'm wearing the Mizunos again, each training shoe conscientiously scraped clean of mud and back in service. Rather like me. But I am better able to ignore the stares of the kids this time, armed with the newfound confidence that I am not mad, and find myself slipping back into the demands of school with ease. Though it's hardly a full timetable now. The weather is turning hot and sticky, a proper Cornish summer, and I have more free periods than at the start of term.

Some of the kids are at home, or in the library, revising for their exams. Others have finished and left school for good. perhaps planning on an apprenticeship or A Levels at one of the sixth form colleges. There are not too many options in this part of Cornwall for education post-GCSE, but the kids seem to cope. I suppose they don't have much choice now higher education has been made compulsory up to the age of eighteen. I can't recall feeling restricted at that age though, and I attended the same school, so perhaps it's about perspective. You can't miss what you have never had.

Jenny Crofter and I meet up in the PE equipment store room at the end of the school day. To count balls, which is a more serious business than it might sound. Kids love footballs and basketballs and cricket balls, any kind of ball really, and will take every opportunity to steal them. So we have to do a stock take every few weeks, to keep on top of the situation.

Jenny is still shocked about the police arresting Tris. I can't blame her. 'But of course Tristan didn't kill that woman. How could he have done? And why? Hand me that clipboard, would you?'

I reach for the clipboard. 'Exactly. There's no motive.'

'It sounds to me like the police are desperate to arrest anyone, and as quickly as possible. To make tourists think the police know what's going on, that it's still safe to walk in the woods. And for some reason, they chose Tristan.' She checks the clipboard. 'How many basketballs?'

I tell her, and she writes the number down. 'Any loss since last time?' I ask.

'No, all present and correct.'

'I can understand why they feel the need to arrest someone,' I say. 'A murder puts people off visiting the woods. Locals too, not just tourists. It's bad for the pub and the woods' café and the garden centre. Bad for business all round.'

'Everyone in the village is talking about it.' Jenny stretches up to take down the large cardboard box that contains cricket balls, only ever used during the summer term. 'When my mother saw the police cars arriving, she went along to have a look. They'd taped off the area, and the police were keeping people back, but word started going round the village almost immediately that they'd found a body down there. She asked me not to go running anywhere near the woods until they catch the killer.'

'And she's right. It's not safe.'

'You hear about this horrific stuff on the news. But you never imagine it happening where you live. Practically right on our doorstep, for God's sake. Here, hold this.'

I accept the clipboard back again, and watch her count the cricket balls with quick efficiency. 'I wonder if they've brought the body out yet.'

'They brought her out late yesterday evening. Probably waited for darkness so the reporters would have less of a look-in.'

'Did you see anything?'

She nods, then shuts her eyes. 'Shit, I lost count.'

'Sorry, my fault.'

'No, it's okay. I think they're all there anyway.' She puts the lid back on the cardboard box and returns it to the shelf. 'I was taking a walk through the village and saw the commotion, so I went back for a look. They'd put her in a body bag, you couldn't see anything. It was dark too. But there were still people there, watching the whole thing.'

'Reporters?'

'Reporters, yes. But other people as well. There was quite a crowd outside the vicarage, some of them in slippers and sipping cocoa, it was crazy. Dick Laney was there, sitting in his van with his son. They're an odd pair, those two. Mr and Mrs Parks from behind the village hall. Seth and Vi from the pub. And your friend with the tattoos.'

What a circus this is turning into. And Tris is the unlikely star act now. I think back, remembering his expression as he looked down at that pale, dirty face protruding through the soil. Tris had been shocked, horrified, appalled, all the same perfectly natural emotions

I was feeling. Yet there had been something else in his face too.

Recognition?

Belatedly, I realise what Jenny said. 'My friend with the tattoos? Do you mean Denzil Tremain?'

'That's the one. He turned up in his jeep just as they were bringing her out. Didn't park though, sat there like Dick Laney with his engine running.'

'Good God,' I say blankly.

'Could you count the footballs? There should be twenty-five. I'll count netballs, then we're done here.'

I turn to count the footballs, my mind preoccupied. 'Twenty-four. But we could have missed one out on the field. I'll check the perimeter fence before I go home.'

'That would be great, thanks. The budget won't stretch to all these replacements.'

'Did you speak to Denzil?' I ask.

'God, no. He's not my sort, is he? Besides, he didn't stay long. As soon as the body was brought up from the woods, the police went over and moved him on. I expect they didn't like the look of his tatts. Clipboard, please.'

'He does have quite a few tattoos,' I admit, handing over the clipboard. 'The one on his back is amazing. A phoenix, spreading its wings.'

Suddenly, I remember the tattoo-like mark on the dead woman's hand. Like a night club stamp. The kind of place where Denzil works when he's deejaying along the coastal resorts.

'I don't suppose you saw which way he went?'

She notes down the final count, then signs the sheet at the bottom as head of department. 'Actually, yes. He did a three-point-turn in the road outside my house, then headed back the way he came. Though I only noticed because his jeep makes such a godawful noise. Why do you ask?'

'I thought he might have been coming to see me.'

'Maybe he changed his mind and went to the pub

instead. The Green Man was packed all evening. Everyone wanting to gossip about the murder over a pint, I expect.'

'Or was frightened off. He's not keen on the police.'

We leave the stock room and I wait while she locks the door. A sudden violent crash behind my back makes me jump. I turn, startled, my heart racing, ready for action. But it's nothing. Two Year 10 lads have burst out of the dressing rooms, both skinny-looking boys with spots and dishevelled hair, shouting and shoving each other on their way out to the field for after-school cricket practice.

'Bloody kids,' I mutter, sagging against the wall of the corridor.

Jenny frowns and calls after them, 'Calm down, you two. How many times do you have to be told? No running in the corridors.'

'Yes, Miss,' both lads call back, slowing to an unrepentant trot. The other kids trooped out to the field ten minutes ago, so these two are clearly late. 'Sorry, Miss.'

We look at each other with tired resignation at the sound of the two boys belting for the field as soon as they're round the corner.

'Children,' Jenny says, rolling her eyes. 'Can't live with them, can't kill them. Remind me never to become a mother. I don't know how all these parents do it. I swear, I wouldn't last an hour with a screaming baby.'

I laugh. 'You'll change your mind one day.'

'What, when I meet the right person?'

I tease her. 'Stranger things have happened.'

'Not in Eastlyn.'

'There's always Connor Taylor. He's still unattached. And he's very hard-working.'

'Connor? He's too young for me. What is he? Twenty-six? Older? I've probably got at least four years on him. Maybe five.'

'Five years isn't so much. It's not even a box set of Buffy. That show ran for seven seasons.'

She shakes her head. 'And you think you're not crazy.'

We walk down towards the staff room where I've left my jacket and bag. The corridors are deserted. This is the time I like best. End of the day, hardly any kids about, only die-hard staff, the ones with no families to go home to, and all the classrooms peaceful and empty.

Through the floor-to-ceiling plate glass windows in the bridge corridor I see Harry Tenzer out on the field in his blue shorts and polo shirt, a short, athletic man, blowing his whistle for all he's worth as a pack of Year 9 and 10 kids fight over the football. I try to calculate his age. Somewhere shy of forty, I guess. And conveniently divorced.

'You could date someone here at the school,' I suggest, nodding towards the football field.

She glances towards Henry, then smiles to herself like I've said something funny.

'What?' I ask, puzzled.

Jenny hesitates, then says, 'I'm gay.'

'Oh.'

She tucks the clipboard under her arm. A defensive gesture. 'And I already have a girlfriend, though it's true we don't see much of each other. Too bloody busy all the time. So you don't need to match-make.'

'I'm sorry, I had no idea.'

'No reason you should. I keep it very quiet. Schools, you know. A tough environment if you're even remotely different.'

I smile drily. 'Tell me about it.'

'And being head of department has brought even more pressure. More public scrutiny.' She pauses a beat. 'You won't mention it to anyone else, will you? I'm not entirely in the closet, of course. That is, my close family knows. But nobody at work ... Until today.'

'I'm honoured that you've told me,' I say, 'and I would never dream of breaking a confidence.'

'Thanks, Eleanor.'

I consider telling her about the shadow man, sharing my own secret burden. But then stop myself in time. It's one thing to share a few details of your personal life with a trusted work colleague, and quite another to admit to checking under the bed every time you go to sleep.

In the staff room, there's a tabloid newspaper left folded open on the table to the centre spread. The lurid story of the body's discovery has even made the nationals. There's a photograph of my mother again, and one of the woods, looking idyllic. I wonder how long it will be before the press track me down at the cottage. Or find my father.

The thought makes me sick and angry.

Jenny glances at it, then shuts the newspaper and drops it into the wastepaper bin. She shudders. 'That poor woman. Killed, then dumped in the woods. It feels so … casual. So dismissive. Who would do such a terrible thing?'

'A murderer.'

She misses my dry tone, perhaps still thinking about what we discussed at lunch time. 'But you think she isn't the same woman you saw before?'

'According to the police she is.'

'The police think you're wrong about that?' Jenny is annoyed for me. 'I don't think they're doing enough, frankly. There are so many empty properties out there. They should be searching them, doing a proper sweep of the valley. This killer is obviously operating out of somewhere remote.'

'I'm sure they'll get round to searching them all eventually.'

Jenny nods. 'Well, I'm off now. I want to do some training tonight. I'm thinking of entering a triathlon in September. First I need to bulk up muscle though, and work on my stamina.'

'I'm sure you'll be great.'

'Thank you.' Her smile is self-conscious. 'I can give you a lift home if you want.'

'I'm heading into town. Got a doctor's appointment.'

'Sure you don't want a lift? I could drop you at the doctor's.'

'Thanks, but I came on my scooter today. See?' I pick up my red helmet from the table. 'And if you ask me, the vicar did it.'

She stares, astonished. 'Reverend Clemo? What, with the length of lead piping in the conservatory?'

'Why not?' I shrug. 'To my mind, he's no more ludicrous a suspect than Tristan Taylor.'

'Eleanor, can you hear me?'

I nod.

'That's great.'

I let myself drift for a moment, enjoying the peace and quiet. But the voice intrudes, brings me back to that shadowy place where I have to look into the past.

'And you've been doing really well at remembering, so well done. But today will be a little different, so I need you to concentrate even harder. Today I want you to remember what happened before you went into the woods with your mum.' The voice is familiar, but impersonal; I trust it implicitly but I don't like it. 'So try to relax and think back to the day before. Can you remember what you are doing?'

'I'm at school.'

'Okay. And what did you do after school finishes?'

I know that I need to remember but it's difficult. The memories are cloudy, that afternoon mingled now with a thousand other afternoons just like it. We would have done whatever we always did, day after day, until the morning she was taken from us ...

I pick over the blurry memories, carefully peeling the days apart until I reach the one I want. I am six years old again. I go to the village school and play with my friends in the playground after school. Patter-cake patter-cake baker's man. Skipping games. I can manage five skips in with the double rope. Most afternoons Mum comes to pick me up after school. Sometimes it's Dad in his van. When the weather is fine, we walk home together through the lanes, holding hands, while I tell her about my day, the pictures I have drawn, the new things I am learning. Sometimes it rains and Mum drives us back in her car. I sit in the back, staring up at the trees and sky. She likes to listen to the radio while she is driving.

'She gets a phone call.'

'At home?'

'In the car. On her mobile.'

I cock my head to one side, remembering that afternoon, the sound of the phone ringing. Mum frowns, reaching for her phone on the passenger seat

'She pulls in by the bridge to take the call.'

'Who's on the phone?'

'A man, I think.' I try to listen into their conversation, but the actual words escape me. It's too long ago and I wasn't really paying attention. I can hear a deep voice.'

'Does she say his name?'

'No.'

'What are they talking about?'

'I don't know.' I am finding it hard to breathe. 'But Mum's upset. She says ... She says no. Keeps saying no. Forget it, and no.'

'Then what?'

'She finishes the call, throws the phone in her bag.' I am worried. I can sense that something is wrong. I watch my mum as she looks in the mirror, glances back at me over her shoulder, says something reassuring, then signals to pull back onto the road. 'It's muddy by the bridge. The wheels spin and she gets angry. Says a rude word.'

'Does your mum often swear?'

'Never.'

Mum brushes back her hair. She is driving too fast. The trees whizz past. Is she crying?

'It's okay, you're safe here. Take a nice deep breath. That's it. And another.' She pauses a beat. 'Don't forget, you're only an observer of these events. Nothing that happened in the past can hurt you now.'

I try to follow her instructions. I know she's right but everything feels so real, so powerful, it takes my breath away.

'Listen to me, Eleanor,' she says. 'I need you to stay calm.'

My chest is hurting. I use her voice as an anchor, so cool and steady, keeping part of myself in the present while my spirit is soaring in the past.

'What do you remember next?'

'I'm at home in my bedroom. It's late but Dad's not there. He's … gone to a meeting in Truro.'

'Are you alone?'

'Yes, but I can hear voices.'

'Where?'

I describe how I creep to the top of the stairs to listen, crouching down to peer through the banisters. There are voices in the kitchen. It's Mum, arguing with a man. She sounds upset again. My tummy hurts and I want to rush down and protect her, but I'm scared. The man is so angry, raising his voice.

'Tell me what happens next, Eleanor.'

I hear the sound of the back door slamming. Then silence. I run down the stairs and push through the kitchen door. The lights are still on. There are two coffee mugs on the table, and one chair lying on the floor like it was just knocked over. The room is empty.

'She's outside with him, I can see them in the dark.'

Her voice is calm, but there's something urgent there too. It disturbs me. 'What does the man look like? Describe him to us.'

I press my face against the glass of the back door. I can see Mum clearly, her head is lit up by the light falling through the kitchen window. But the man is further away.

I stare, trying to make him out. But his features slip away and blur, and staring so hard through the past makes me feel sick. Small and sick and empty.

'He's just a shadow,' I whisper, shaking my head in denial. 'A shadow man in the dark.'

CHAPTER TWENTY-TWO

After my unsettling session with Dr Quick, I ride slowly home on my scooter and try to push its new information to the back of my head. My 'memories' in these sessions, if that is what they truly are, and when I remember them at all, do not make any sense to me. But the doctor thinks it may take several more hypnotherapy sessions before the odd things I'm seeing and hearing begin to come together into a coherent pattern.

I take the road through the village on my way home, though it's the long way round. The roads are dry and the scooter is easy to handle, even on the tight bends coming down the hill towards the church. It's still warm, the late afternoon sun on my back as I ride slowly past the vicarage.

There's a police car outside the vicarage, sun glare bouncing off its rear window. The gate is open and so is the front door to the vicarage. It's hard not to be curious about what's going on in there. Perhaps someone has been stealing the vicar's gnomes, I think. Or sneaking into his garden at night and moving the little fellows into suggestive poses.

Just after the vicarage, I glance along the back path into

the woods. There are several police cars still tucked onto the grass verge there, and the track past the graveyard has been cordoned off with a Police Line Do Not Cross tape.

I halt the scooter and let it idle, watching a young policeman in a white short-sleeved shirt load equipment into the open boot of one of the police cars. One of the items is a heavy-looking metallic case and he's sweating; I guess he must have carried it all the way up that steep slope.

The old green school bus is just leaving as I carry on slowly down into the main part of the village. It takes almost an hour for the bus to make the full round of stops, dawdling through all the tiny villages and hamlets beneath the moors. A few local kids clamber down, blinking at the sunshine, then the bus pulls away in a little puff of exhaust fumes, heading up the hill to its next scheduled stop, the next village about three miles on through winding lanes.

I turn and look back at the police car, still parked at the side of the road near the vicarage.

The vicar has come out and is talking to the policeman through the car window. He's wearing his dog collar today. He looks formal and untouchable, on official business. I expect he's furious about all this. It can't be very good for the reputation of the church, having police permanently stationed outside his vicarage. Though a murder always sends people to church, they say. Guilty conscience, I guess. Or there but for the grace of God ...

As I watch, the Reverend Clemo straightens and looks over in my direction. He's still talking to the unseen police officer in the car. He seems to lift his arm.

Is he pointing at me?

A cloud passes across the sun. The top of the village turns dark and sullen, lying in shadow, and suddenly it's a different place. It's uncanny the way weather can change the look of this valley in a matter of seconds. But that's what comes from being so close to the high moors; the weather systems are unpredictable and fast-changing, winds sweeping in and shifting us from bright sunshine to driving rain in the space of a few minutes.

I remember the early mist rising as I plunged into the woods that day, sunshine falling dappled through the tree canopy. The crack of twigs from somewhere above me, that creepy sensation of being watched. And when I burst out of the bushes behind the church that morning, the Reverend Clemo had been standing there, startled but not surprised, smoking his cigarette.

Almost as though he had been *waiting* for me.

There's a note pushed under the door when I get back to the cottage. I recognise the handwriting before I even see the final initial.

Come and see me. We need to talk. C.

Hannah's car is gone, so I assume she has either gone to work for the night or is out with one of her other friends. She likes to take off occasionally without saying anything, always a bit of a free spirit. And I expect she's been shaken by recent events and is probably in need of a break from this place. Beautiful as our little cottage may be, it's also very isolated. Not the most comfortable place to be with a murderer creeping about the place.

I leave Connor's note on the kitchen table. Upstairs, I change into denim shorts and a yellow sun top, smooth on some sun cream, and head out across the fields.

I'm not in the mood to take the scooter out again, and besides, this weather is fantastic. I need to feel the sun on my face and shoulders, and to get hot and sweaty, to enjoy the fresh air and countryside before wet weather sets in again. Because however sunny it becomes in Cornwall, I know the mist and rain are never far away, waiting to sweep in from the sea or the high moors ...

It's just over a mile cross-country from our cottage to the farm where Connor and Tristan live, slightly further by road. I walk it comfortably in about fifteen minutes, stopping several times to navigate the stream which passes the path at various points in the valley bottom. I try to leap from stone to stone without getting my feet wet, but it's not easy and I dunk my foot in the cold water more than once.

Eventually I find myself within sight of the farmhouse. There are sheep grazing between me and the house who raise their heads as I follow the footpath round the edge of the field, staring with slanted, demonic eyes. A few sheep bleat at me balefully, others continue cropping the grasses without much interest. They belong to Connor's new herd, their woolly backsides spray-painted with a distinctive green mark. Like the signature tag of a graffiti artist. Some of them have tiny counterparts on wobbly legs. Ewes with newborn lambs to look after, I realise, and keep as far from them as possible.

I check my phone in case Tris has been released. I've been texting him all day. *Thinking of you. Let me know when they let you out.* But there's no reply to my numerous texts yet. There's no signal either though, so even if he has texted me back, I won't be able to pick up any messages until I get home.

I look up suddenly, hearing a high song in the blue. There's a tiny black dot above me. I squint up into the sunlight for a moment, then smile. A skylark. Too high to be anything else.

Hill Farm is a ramshackle collection of buildings clustered around one central farmhouse. They have no money to keep up with repairs, so there are gaps in the roof where slates blew off last winter and were never replaced, and a few broken windows fixed up with black tape or hardboard. When their father died a few months back, he left the farm jointly to both brothers, treating Tris no differently just because he was adopted. But of course sheep-farming is not easy, and he probably knew it would take two men to keep the farm afloat. They've already lost sheep to bad weather and illness, animals they haven't been able to afford to replace. Meanwhile the bills keep coming in every month. So the farm barely makes enough to pay off the remortgage their father took out on it a few years back, simply in order to keep going.

I know Tristan was hoping he could get away from the place after he finished school. Go to university and get a proper job, one that did not involve getting up at dawn or struggling through rain and mud every winter. But his father had made him feel too guilty to leave, and now the old man was gone, his departure would probably mean selling the farm, because Connor could not possibly run it on his own.

So far they don't seem to have argued about it, but I know that day can't be far off. Tris has become more and more restless since his father died, and though he claims it has nothing to do with any wish to escape, I know something is eating at him. Something that has left him pale and withdrawn, and with a haunted look in his eyes.

I jump over the wall into the farmyard. The house is standing silent and empty. The back door, usually left wide open during the day for the dog to trot in and out, is shut and locked. There's a shiny new padlock on the garage door, but otherwise the place looks unbearably rundown. On the far side of the farmyard are a few mangy-looking hens, pecking in a depressed fashion at the dirt. But their sheepdog is nowhere in evidence, the car is gone, and the mud-spattered quad bike is parked under a lean-to next to an ancient dog kennel.

I knock at the back door, loudly, thumping with my fist against the soil-flecked wood. Nothing is clean here, not even the door.

No reply.

I knock again. 'Connor? It's Ellie.' I pause a beat, head down, thinking. 'Tris? Are you in there?'

I go to one of the narrow kitchen windows, rub a small port-hole in the grime, and stare inside. There's no one moving inside. I take a few steps back, staring about the place. I should have called Connor before setting out, of course. His note seemed so urgent though, I assumed he would be here when I arrived.

But perhaps Tris has been released, and Connor has driven over to the police station to collect him. That would explain his absence.

I scramble up the rough bank of earth behind the house and look out over what they call the Long Field. It's a peaceful scene. Short grass and clumps of young thistles ripple in the breeze, stretching gently uphill to a line of trees in the distance. When their father was still alive, the land nearest to the house was always dotted with white sheep. This field contains nothing but wild rabbits, judging by the white tail-flashes as they scattered across the grass at my approach.

I wonder how many sheep they've lost this year. Too many, by the look of it.

It's a lonely place, out on the fringe of the village. Not another house in sight from where I'm standing. And so quiet. Only barren moorland stretches beyond the next hillside, and there's nothing much after that until you reach the yard of grey brick and cobblestones that is Jamaica Inn at the steep village of Bolventor. You can't even hear the busy A30 from here, a black ribbon winding over Bodmin Moor only a few miles to the north-east.

I stare out across the rippling fields again. Whenever the wind drops, the air becomes oddly hushed, like in a church or library; a voice might carry for miles out here on a still day. But there's something just on the edge of my hearing. A new sound above the rustle of trees, above the soft baas of far-off sheep, and the distant barking of a dog in the wooded valley below.

I scramble down from the bank of earth, ready to admit defeat. Connor is not here and I have wasted my time coming out to the farm.

Then I realise what I've been hearing. The sound of an engine in the distance, growing louder now as it negotiates the abrupt turns, dips and slopes of the narrow lane between here and the village.

It could be anyone. Anyone with a diesel engine, that is, who has business this far out on the edge of the moors. Not Connor; his car runs on petrol. The postman, then? It's too late for the post, but maybe a special delivery?

But it's not the postman. A familiar white delivery van bumps into the yard less than a minute later, Woods Valley Garden Centre in bold green lettering on the side.

Dick Laney is at the wheel, looking surprised to see me. No sign of Jago. He's probably back at the garden centre, playing the boss while his dad's out. I fold my arms, suddenly cold despite the sunshine. *Like someone's walking over my grave.* Such an odd expression, I've always thought. Today it feels unpleasantly apt.

I recall the framed school photograph I saw in the office at the garden centre, Dick Laney's arm round my mother's shoulders. That odd look in her eyes. I still can't put my finger on what it means. But why did Dick choose to put up that photo now? He must have had it lying around for years, yet I've never seen it before.

I'm abruptly aware of the remoteness of Hill Farm, and realise I left no word with anyone where I was going. Though Connor's note is still on the kitchen table. Would that be enough of a clue for Hannah if I were to go missing?

Dick pulls up in the yard with his window open, Radio Cornwall blaring. I recognise the jingle as he turns the engine off. He leans a tanned and tattooed forearm on the window frame, shirt sleeves rolled up, and stares out at me.

'Well, this is a turn-up for the books.' His voice is level, but I can tell from his expression that he's not in a good mood. 'What are you doing all the way out here?'

CHAPTER TWENTY-THREE

'I'm visiting Connor and Tris.'

'Tris?' His eyes narrow, looking searchingly from me to the empty farmhouse. 'Thought that boy was in the nick. On suspicion of murder.'

'Tris hasn't done anything wrong,' I say sharply, and take a step towards him. 'The police wanted to ask him some more questions, that's all.'

Dick Laney shrugs, looking unconvinced. 'Whatever you say. Is Connor in, then?'

'Nobody's in.'

'That's a pity. I've got a delivery for him from the garden centre.' Dick jerks his head towards the back of the van. 'But I suppose it won't matter if he's out. I'll leave it outside the garage as usual.'

He turns off the radio and gets out of the van, his frizzy hair wilder than ever. Now the radio is silent, the farmyard feels quieter and lonelier than ever before. Again that sense of unease prickles down my spine, and I begin to wish I had indeed called Connor before setting out. Then I would not be here on my own with Dick Laney.

'Help me with it, would you?' he asks in that thick Cornish accent, not looking at me.

It's only thanks to my dad that I don't sound the same as him and Jago, I suppose. His family came from the Midlands, so I grew up with a flatter accent than the rest of my friends. 'Never quite proper Cornish,' Hannah calls it.

'It's not heavy,' he adds, 'just awkward to lift on my own. I prefer to get Jago to come with me on a two-man delivery job. But there weren't no one else to shut up shop for us. So I'm on my lonesome today.'

He throws open the back doors of the van, then looks back round at me with a slow, crooked smile as though well aware I dislike feeling so vulnerable. 'Well? You going to help me or not? I thought you feminists didn't mind getting your hands dirty?'

I meet his eyes, then nod. 'Of course I'll help.'

With a consciously nonchalant expression, I step round to the back of his van, and hope a spanner to the side of the head isn't waiting for me.

I immediately see the reason for that knowing smile. Besides his tool box and a pair of soiled gardening gloves, there's nothing inside but a vast roll of thick wire fencing. I don't know what I expected. Duct tape, perhaps, or a length of rope. The kind of thing you find in most serial killers' vans.

Dick nods towards the garage door, locked with its shiny new padlock. 'We're heading over there with it. Can you take that end?'

I don't have much choice. 'No problem.'

Together we wrestle the unwieldy roll of wire fencing out of the van and carry it across the yard, depositing it on the cracked concrete in front of the garage.

Dick nods, wiping his hands on his jeans. 'Ah, thanks, that'll do nicely. I told Connor I'd be delivering it after work today, so I expect he'll be back soon enough.'

'But what does Connor want all this fencing for?' I ask, perplexed.

'He said something about a vegetable plot over at the

old mill. Wants to keep them thieving rabbits out, I should imagine. He had a few sacks of sand and topsoil delivered a few weeks back too.'

'The old mill?'

Dick Laney scratches his sweating forehead. 'Not much left of it now, I would suppose. It was a tumbledown ruin last time I saw it. Must be fifty years at least since anyone worked the mill wheel.' He waves vaguely across the open fields behind the house. 'There's a footpath down past those trees. It was sold with the farm here when his dad bought it, a job lot. I expect he's trying to make a go of the land, get some profit from the old place. Maybe do it up and resell to some filthy-rich Londoner for a second home. That's the way to make money round here. You should tell your dad to do the same. No point him hanging on at Eastlyn Farm if he isn't going to finish those renovations.'

I look at him with distaste. 'I'll let him know.'

'Ah, you do that.'

I look across the fields at the gnarled trees he pointed out. Could there be a path there? I remember some talk of an old mill in the village, but never realised it was this far along the stream.

He looks at me, his crooked smile back, one gold tooth showing. It's the face he uses at the garden centre when he's trying to be friendly to a wealthy customer. 'It's a long walk back in this hot sun. I'll give you a lift in the van, if you like?'

My skin crawls at the thought of being alone in the van with him. 'No thanks,' I say quickly, 'I'll take the footpath back the way I came. It's only a fifteen minute walk, and I like the sunshine.'

Dick shrugs. 'Suit yourself. Causes cancer though. Nasty death, that.' He looks at me oddly. 'Pete Taylor died of cancer. They say he weighed less than a sack of potatoes at the end.'

Pete Taylor. He must mean Connor and Tris's dad. I'm not sure that I ever knew his first name.

Without another word, he climbs into the van, backs it up with Radio Cornwall blasting out at top volume again, and a moment later he's gone, leaving a cloud of dust behind as he accelerates out of the yard.

My fingernails are digging into my palms. I relax them slowly, surprised by myself. Strange reaction. Dick Laney can be creepy, but he's not exactly dangerous. I doubt he's done much more exercise than lugging sacks about for the past ten years. I could take him in a minute. Seconds, even. No contest.

I wait until I can't hear the van engine anymore, then tread round to the back of the garage.

He said something about a vegetable plot over at the old mill. Wants to keep them thieving rabbits out, I should imagine.

Connor and Tris are born defrosters. They don't eat fresh vegetables; they open a can or throw a ready meal in the microwave. The idea of Connor on a health kick, breaking his back to grow his own veg, makes me grin. No way, no way in hell.

I clamber through overgrown brambles to peer through the back panes of glass, which are filthy. Through the darkened window I can see old sacks on the concrete floor, some still fat, others empty. Chicken manure? Topsoil? Dick Laney mentioned delivering a few sacks of that recently. The garage interior is surprisingly clear of junk, though the wall shelves and the workbench are both in disarray, pots and debris tumbled everywhere. A broken-looking lawnmower stands next to two old bikes, both rusting, one with the chain hanging off.

No spades. No sign of gardening equipment: seeds, labels, garden twine, potting compost, bamboo stakes. But maybe Connor's storing it all down at the old mill. That would make better sense than lugging it back and forth every time he wants to do some gardening down there. Trouble is, I don't know what I am looking for, nor even why.

But there is something about the garage door that

makes me curious.

I walk all the way round the garage around, picking a path gingerly through patches of young nettles, and stare at the padlock.

It's brand-new. A shiny new padlock on an ancient door. With nothing of much value inside, from what I can see. And thieves are hardly queuing up to break into isolated rundown farmhouses out here on the edge of the moor. So why would Connor and Tris suddenly decide the place needs to be locked up?

The house stands silent behind me. Nobody at home. No one to answer my suddenly urgent questions.

I climb up the earth bank at the back of the house again and stand there, listening.

Nothing.

I balance along the earth bank until I am standing directly below the part of the kitchen that juts out – the old fireplace, I expect – and use the window ledge to lever myself up. Standing on tiptoe, I reach up and grab the bathroom window ledge above, then swing myself onto the flat roof to the right of the kitchen. After months of demonstrating techniques on the bars in the school gym, it's the work of a moment.

The flat roof is made of corrugated plastic, filthy and covered in patches of moss where the guttering above leaks. It judders as I begin to crawl forwards, creaking violently under my weight. I freeze on hands and knees, holding my breath. The laundry room is directly below me, and for a terrifying moment I imagine myself crashing through onto the concrete below.

I close my eyes and tell myself not to be so stupid. Tris's bedroom window is almost within reach, just a few more feet to crawl.

Slowly, I crawl across the creaking and protesting corrugated roof until I reach the window ledge to Tris's bedroom. To my relief, the old sash window is not locked and opens easily enough when I pull down. I struggle over the top and into his bedroom, knocking something off the window ledge inside and landing on the floor with a painful thump.

I clamber to my feet and hurry to the door. I open it slightly, listening. But the interior of the house is dark and silent.

No one is at home.

If anyone deserves to be arrested, it's me. For breaking and entering. Well, not breaking. But certainly entering. It's Tris's house though, and I'm not here to steal anything. Except secrets.

Despite their constant jokes about the state of our cottage, I discover that Tris and Connor are not great housekeepers either. Tris's room is an horrendous mess. I came up here quite a few times as a teenager, to hang out and play board games with him and Connor, but it was far tidier then. He's totally let it go since those days. The bed's unmade, his crumpled sheet half pulled away from the mattress, duvet unbuttoned and slipping out of its plain black cover. One of his pillows is lying on the stained carpet, as are most of his clothes. A lone sock dangles from a dusty bookshelf. There are some old posters on the wall, peeling off: hardcore rock groups from when we were kids, most now disbanded. The wardrobe door is open and there's nothing inside but an old pair of black trousers. Everything else has been hung up on the floor.

I look around, vaguely disappointed. What was I hoping to find? Some kind of clue that would tell me if he's guilty or not? There's nothing here but dirty clothes and old socks.

I should not be here. And yet I am.

I catch a reflection of myself in the rectangular mirror set into the back of the wardrobe door. Shoulder-length brown hair hanging loose about my face – I released my ponytail when I got home from work – and big eyes. A determined expression.

Did I really come all this way, climb into my friend's bedroom, tiptoe through his empty house, to go home meekly without any answers?

I cross to the door again. It creaks as I go through it. The landing is unlit, the stairs gloomy.

I creep along the landing and peer into the next bedroom along. It's Connor's room. I have never been in there but it's obvious. There's his olive-green, waterproof jacket draped over the back of a chair, and I recognise the shoes kicked off in a corner. His room is neater than his brother's, but only marginally. A question of degree. No rock posters, but some old maps of Eastlyn on the wall, and one Ordinance Survey map of Bodmin Moor, with campsites circled. He and Tris used to go camping alone on the moor when they were younger, sometimes for several days. I suppose their father must have trusted Connor to take care of Tris, because they could both only have been teenagers at the time.

I try the third door, but it's a room full of junk. A bed pushed against the wall and piled with bags and boxes. Their parents' bedroom. Though their mother walked out when they were both quite young, and their father was gone now too. So this is just dead space. A store room for things they don't want but can't bring themselves to throw away.

There's a photograph on the wall. Framed, the glass dusty. It's of a man and woman, arms around each other, smiling at the camera, sitting on a car bonnet outside a handsome building in sunny weather. Their parents in happier days, clearly. I don't recognise the place. But I feel uneasy.

I look at their father, then move on to study the woman's smile. Is it my imagination or does she look unhappy behind that fixed smile?

It feels a little unnerving to be standing in a dead man's room looking at his personal items, so I go out again and close the door with a quiet click. The only other room on this floor is the bathroom, so I head downstairs.

The stairs creak.

Again, this proves unnerving in an otherwise silent house.

The hall and living room are not immaculate, stacks of newspapers and junk mail lying about, unfinished meals congealed on plates, beer cans on the floor, but they are still tidier than upstairs. I wonder if I ought to offer to come round with cleaning wipes and a bin bag.

The kitchen is grim. I back out with my lip curling.

There's a door under the stairs.

A cellar?

I try the handle tentatively. It's locked. I bend to check the make. I look about nearby for a matching key, but there isn't one, so I head back into the kitchen and force myself to open the drawers. I find a few old car keys, and a vast, black, wrought-iron key that looks like it would open the Addam's family vault. But nothing that would fit a Yale lock.

I give up and head back into the living room. That's when I notice the door. It looked like a simple wood panel before, half hidden behind a tall, wooden room divider. I slip behind the screen and try the door. It opens easily enough into a small office of some kind: there's a tired-looking desk with an old-fashioned table lamp, and a four shelf bookcase, and a gun cabinet.

I cross the room and check the gun cabinet. But it's locked, and through the glass front I can see the lone shotgun inside is secured with a chain in the approved manner. I know they have a valid licence for it too. Nothing suspect there.

When I turn, I'm faced with a row of square, glass-covered box frames hung at precise intervals on the wall opposite. Each frame contains a selection of butterflies, pinned to the felt backing, their tiny labels meticulously written out in black ink and placed inside next to each butterfly.

I step closer to read one of the labels. *Vanessa Atalanta, or Red Admiral.*

The frames are dusty, like the glass-covered photograph upstairs, and look like they've been there for decades. I'm guessing their father was the butterfly enthusiast. On the narrow table below the frames are three dead creatures, stuffed and preserved. A fox with glass eyes, a magpie, and a weasel with bared teeth, mounted on metal stands. Taxidermy. I have a dim and unpleasant memory of my dad taking me to a museum of stuffed animals at Jamaica Inn. I found it horrific, though Dad seemed to enjoy it and even visited it again several times before the museum closed down.

I eye their rigid forms with misgiving, then stiffen at the unmistakeable sound of a vehicle approaching the farmhouse.

Time to get out.

I head straight for the window in the living room. But it's painted shut and I can't loosen it. The front door is too risky. And the back door is probably the way they will come in. I stand in the gloomy hallway like a ghost, thinking and listening hard. Two car doors slam outside, one slightly after the other. Then I hear familiar male voices in the yard.

The Taylor brothers are back.

I take the stairs two at a time, not caring how much noise I am making this time, and dive into Tris's untidy bedroom.

The back door is being unlocked. I can hear barking now. Connor must have taken the dog with him to pick up Tris.

I pick my way to his bedroom window over discarded socks and underwear. I need to climb out and get myself home as fast as possible. There will be no easy way to explain my presence if they find me here. And I could end up being the one in trouble with the police.

I overbalance on something hidden under the clothes

on the floor, and lurch sideways, grabbing onto the bed frame. There's a bag under the clothes. An old blue rucksack that I recognise as belonging to Tris. With something poking out of it.

It's a photograph.

Crouching, I draw it out of the rucksack and stare down in disbelief at one of our own family snapshots. A holiday photo of me and my parents on a sandy beach, taken while my mum was still alive. Only a short while before she was murdered, in fact, so I would have been six at the time. My face is beaming, my hand tucked in my mum's, my little red bucket and spade lying on the sand beside us. It's a photo I know intimately, one of the old family snaps in the keepsake box under my bed.

I turn the photo over, and feel like someone has just thumped me hard in the chest, almost stopping my heart.

Angela, Ellie and me. Polzeath.

My dad's handwriting.

This is not an extra print.

It's exactly the same photo I have at home. Or rather, *had* at home. Because it's been stolen from me.

Abruptly I remember one night not long ago when I woke up and thought someone was in my bedroom, standing over my bed. When I got up and groped along the wall for the light switch, I found the room empty, but my keepsake box out in the middle of the floor, the lid off.

The shadow man.

I stare at the photo, my heart plunging into the pit of my stomach. I have always assumed it was my disturbed imagination, that man-shaped shadow standing by the window. But perhaps it is a real person, climbing in through my unlocked window at night and watching me while I sleep.

Tris?

I can't bear the thought, yet here's the evidence of this stolen photograph. He's the right build too, for my shadow man. And I did see him at the night club in

Newquay. Maybe he often goes there at the weekends to dance and hang out. Maybe he met the dead woman there, lured her away, and …

I slip the photograph into my bra, rather than risk a crease by folding it into the tight rear pocket of my denim shorts.

Then I freeze, listening. There are voices in the kitchen below, raised in anger. The two brothers are arguing.

'You're not Dad, Connor. You can't tell me what to do.'

'Dad's dead, remember? And he left me in charge. So stop arguing the toss and do what I bloody well tell you.'

'Why should I? You're not even my *real* brother.'

'You ungrateful little shit.' Connor sounds furious, and I'm not surprised. 'I'm telling you to be careful with Eleanor. No, don't you walk away from me, I mean it.' His voice deepens. 'She's not right in the head. Never has been. A woman like her can only land you in trouble. And I mean serious trouble.'

'Don't talk rubbish.'

'Oh right, I see. So you didn't just spend a night in the police cells because of Eleanor Blackwood?'

Tris raises his voice. He sounds like he's ready to thump his brother. 'You are bang out of order. You know my arrest was total bullshit. It was just for the tourists, to make the area look safe again for walkers and ramblers. Why do you think they let me go so quickly? Because that lawyer showed them up as idiots.'

There's a long silence below. Then Connor says in a hoarse voice, 'Have you forgotten what Dad told me before he died?'

'I haven't forgotten.'

'Dad didn't think you knew how much he loved you, Tris. He made me promise to take care of you. And that's what I'm going to do.'

I climb onto the window ledge as quietly as possible and ease first one leg, then the other, over the top of the sash window, standing on the narrow window ledge below. At least with all the noise they're making, they are less likely to hear someone sneaking out of an upstairs window.

I hear Connor swearing below, his voice muffled, then a thud of feet on the stairs. Tris, heading for his bedroom in a rage.

'Shit,' I mutter.

Tris is about to find his window open. And the mad girl outside, hanging onto his window frame by her fingertips.

There's no time to worry about breaking the corrugated roof below. I let go and drop the last few feet, landing in an unsteady crouch. It cracks ominously under my weight but I can't take it slow this time. I balance hurriedly to the edge, making one hell of a noise, then swing down, this time straight into brambles at the back of the house.

Landing awkwardly, a white-hot bolt of pain shoots up my ankle. I stifle a cry of pain and lean against the house wall, eyes closed, waiting for my racing heart to settle. For all I know, Tris is looking out of his window above me, wondering why it's open. But that's a risk I'll have to take.

I count backwards from ten, then test my ankle. It hurts, but not so badly that I can't walk. Not too much damage done, thankfully. I can't afford yet more time off work.

I limp up the hill at the back of the farmhouse, hoping I'm out of sight of the windows. Nearing the top of the steep field, I look back, sweaty and panting in the late afternoon sun. There's no one following me. No sign of anyone, in fact. The valley lies beneath me like a patchwork quilt, a higgledy-piggledy network of fields and sprawling hedgerows and farm buildings, the untidy cluster of houses that make up the village invisible from here, nestled in a dip beside the woods.

I wriggle the old photograph out of my bra, turn it over and study the handwriting again.

Eleanor, Angela and me. Polzeath.

It does look like my dad's untidy, slanted handwriting. Especially the big loop of the *P* on Polzeath. But to be absolutely sure it's my own copy of the photograph, I'll have to check in my keepsake box at home.

She's not right in the head. Never has been.

Is that what he wanted to talk to me about? To warn me off his brother?

Climbing the stile at the top of the field, the back of my neck prickles like someone is watching me.

I look round, narrowing my eyes. High above I can hear the skylark again, a distant dot enjoying the last of the day's sunshine. The shadows stretch long and stark all the way back to the farmhouse. But there's no one moving in them.

CHAPTER TWENTY-FOUR

I scramble through an old deer gap in the hedge a few hundred yards from home, and find a car marked with a familiar stripe and the words in blue, *Devon Cornwall Police*, parked outside the cottage. There's a young officer leaning against the bonnet, checking his smartphone. I remember him from the woods, He's got a faintly stubbly chin and looks about the same age as Connor.

As I approach, he straightens up and nods. He's wearing a black earpiece linked by a curly wire to his radio, and even at this distance I can hear a thin crackle of voices.

'Miss Blackwood? DI Powell would like a word.'

'Where is he?'

The officer looks embarrassed.

'Here I am, Eleanor.'

I turn, surprised, at a rustling from the sunlit field behind me where the hedgerow was damaged by my violent attack with the stick. Suddenly, the hedge shakes, and DI Powell emerges through a gap. He has a few petals of white hawthorn blossom caught in his hair, and a long, drooping grass stalk between his lips. He's in wellington boots again, and looks like a country yokel from a previous century.

'Sorry,' DI Powell says, striding off the grassy verge to greet me, 'I was just … investigating.'

'Investigating in a field?'

He smiles vaguely and shakes his head. The hawthorn petals drift to earth. 'Looking around, getting a feel for the place. I'm glad I caught you though. Shall we go inside?'

'I'm really bushed. I'm back at work now, and it's been a long day. If you've got something to say, perhaps you could just tell me out here?'

He looks at me thoughtfully, then shrugs. 'Eleanor, I need you to do something for me.'

'Do what?'

'I need you to look at the body again.'

I recoil instinctively, remembering at once. Her dead face flashes up at me as though from the end of a tunnel, her skin pale, faintly green in the gloom. 'Oh, no. Sorry. I couldn't possibly.'

'I thought that would be your reaction. And obviously I can't force you to do this. But it is important or I wouldn't ask.'

'But why? I told you everything I know at the station.'

He nods. 'And I'm very grateful for that. But we need to be one hundred percent certain she's not the woman you saw the first time.'

Temper flares inside me. 'You think I'm lying, don't you?'

'Not lying, no,' DI Powell says, and clasps his hands behind his back. He cocks his head to one side, regarding me steadily. I get the impression he's itching to strangle me. 'It can be a traumatic experience, coming across a dead body like that. We need to be sure you didn't muddle it in your head. Which would be perfectly natural for someone in your situation.'

'Someone in my situation?'

He means, *unbalanced.*

'I need to be sure, before I authorise a full-scale search of the area, that a second body exists. These searches can be very expensive. Hours of manpower, whole communities involved, dogs, helicopters … '

'I get the picture,' I say.

'So here's my thought. If you could take another quick peek at the woman you found in the woods, in more controlled surroundings, perhaps you'll be better placed to remember if she's anything like the first body you saw.'

'She isn't,' I say wearily, 'and I'm certain about that. There's the number, for a start. The number on her forehead.'

'That could have been changed, between when you first saw her and when you uncovered her grave.'

I remember Tris saying more or less the same thing. I shake my head. 'I don't need to see her again to tell you she looked nothing like the first woman.'

His smile looks like it's stuck in place. 'Humour me, Eleanor. We just want to jog your memory. And if you need counselling afterwards, we can arrange that too.'

I fumble for my house key in the pocket of my shorts. 'I don't want to go. But perhaps I should if it will help you find the other woman. Have you identified the body yet?'

DI Powell hesitates, watching me unlock the front door to the cottage. 'Yes,' he admits.

'So who is she?'

'I can't tell you her name. We haven't managed to notify her next of kin yet. But I can tell you what our victim did for a living. She was a surf instructor, working out of Newquay.'

'A local, then?'

Powell nods. 'Reported missing a few weeks back. The hotel staff said she spent her days on the surfing beaches along the north coast – Widemouth and Polzeath, mostly, judging by the parking tickets we found in her hire car – and her nights in the clubs. She liked to dance as well as surf, went to all the beach barbecues.'

He pauses, looking at me closely. 'A bit of a party animal by all accounts. Maybe you knew her.'

I open the cottage door but do not go inside. I don't like the idea of inviting the police in the cottage again. It's our private space and it's been invaded too much lately.

'Yes, I still go clubbing sometimes, though less than when I was in uni. There are clubs all the way along the coast. Hard to avoid them when you're out in a group. But that doesn't mean she was a party animal, or that I knew her.'

He smiles. 'You wouldn't make a bad detective.'

I raise my eyebrows, waiting.

'Right now, we need to focus on who she knew locally. Presumably someone from the village, since her body was left here. She might have met her killer on the coast, maybe gone surfing or clubbing with them. He could be someone who knows you too, given the way you seem to have been targeted.' Powell looks straight at me, his gaze suddenly piercing. 'Know any keen surfers, Eleanor?'

She liked to dance as well as surf, went to all the beach barbecues. A bit of a party animal by all accounts.

There are thousands of surfers like that hanging around Newquay and the surrounding area in the summer. I've met dozens myself that would answer her description. And he was right. I might even have met the victim at some point in the past, and not recalled her face when I saw it. Maybe at one of those night-time beach barbecues where people are just faces looming up out of the darkness, the fire reflected in their eyes. Without a name, I'm not sure where all this gets us.

The inspector is looking at me expectantly. I think of Denzil Tremain. But there's no way I'm dumping one of my friends in this. Not without one hell of a good reason.

'Hundreds,' I tell him, then turn away into the cool of the cottage. 'Give me a few minutes to change, Detective Inspector Powell. I'll come and look at the body.'

In the mortuary, the body is lying under a white sheet on a stainless steel table. Exactly like a corpse in one of those television shows where the dead come back to life, slowly sitting up on the table while the white sheet slides to the floor. Not a very comforting thought. I slow my breathing, wait for the light to stop flickering above the metal table. I can do this. I just need to get a grip on my emotions.

I think of the stuffed animals I saw in the farmhouse. The sleek weasel with glass eyes and bared teeth. That's all a dead body is, I tell myself. The physical form of a person without their essence. The husk without the spirit.

DI Powell is talking in a low voice to one of the mortuary technicians, a blond young man in a white lab coat, who looks incongruously cheerful considering the macabre nature of his job.

I'm sweating, my palms clammy. I try not to stare at the body shape under the sheet while I wait, wondering what the delay is. Something about the next of kin and a telephone call, from what I catch in their muttered conversation.

'Ready, Eleanor?'

PC Helen Flynn puts her arm around my shoulder. Her tone is professional but sympathetic. I expect she has to deal with this situation quite frequently: grieving relatives, shocked witnesses, people who can't deal with the reality of death.

I'm not a relative though. I did not even know the dead woman. I look down at her hand clasping my upper arm and the police officer releases me, moving back slightly.

DI Powell is behind me. His footsteps echo on the hard floor. 'We can wait a few minutes if you're not.'

'I'm ready.'

'Good.'

DI Powell comes to stand at the top of the table, looking straight at me, then pulls back the white sheet.

I was wrong. I am not ready.

I draw in a sharp breath and take an instinctive step backwards, staring. Then check myself, aware of the inspector still watching my face.

She looks very different from the woman I remember from the woods. They've removed all the soil, you would never think she'd been left in that shallow grave. Someone's even combed out her blonde hair so that it lies smooth and clean on her shoulders.

The number two is still there on her forehead, but fainter under the overhead lights than it looked in the woods.

She has a thin build and looks fit, so she was probably like me, physically active most days, constantly burning off calories. DI Powell said she was a surfer. And I can see that she was used to the outdoor life, her cheeks hollow and freckled, her face more tanned than the shoulder and upper arm exposed by the raised sheet. But no doubt she habitually wore a wetsuit.

She looks unreal, like a waxwork. Or a mannequin.

I take a step closer, peering at something that's caught my eye. Her throat shows the same signs of dark bruising with a thin central line that I saw on the other woman.

'So she was strangled too?'

Powell's eyes narrow on my face. '*Too*?'

'The other woman, the first body I found,' I say. 'She had been strangled as well. Don't you remember?'

'I didn't see her body,' he reminds me drily.

'But I gave you a statement.'

He glances at PC Flynn, and she nods, disappearing. The heavy door bangs behind her, shockingly loud in this quiet place.

DI Powell lets the sheet settle on the woman's chest. He looks at me. 'You're absolutely sure this isn't the same woman you saw before?'

'I'm sure.'

'You definitely couldn't have made a mistake? No one would blame you if you had. Finding a dead body can be very upsetting in the best of circumstances, and given your personal history … '

'I'm sure,' I say again.

'Take your time, Eleanor. Have a good look at her.' He waits. 'You say her throat shows the same bruising as the other woman. But isn't it more likely that she *is* the first victim?'

'Not a chance.'

'And you're basing that assumption on … *what*, exactly?'

Slowly, I count to ten in my head. He waits in silence, hands in his trouser pockets, head on one side, watching me.

'It's not a hunch. It's a fact based on simple observation. For starters, this woman is blonde, not a brunette.'

'But you could have been mistaken first time round.' He looks at me solemnly. 'You were panicked. You were on your own. It was the anniversary of your mother's murder. I doubt you were thinking that clearly at the time. Let alone taking note of the victim's hair colour.'

'Let's say that's true, but she's also Number Two, not Number Three,' I point out, then look away from the body. 'Can we have this conversation somewhere else?'

'Does it upset you to look at her?'

'Pretty much.'

His gaze does not leave my face. 'Yet you seemed perfectly cool when I saw you down in the woods, immediately after you found her. How do you explain that?'

'I was in shock.'

'You had dirt under your fingernails.'

'I'd been digging.'

'That is what surprises me most,' DI Powell says, and then pauses a beat, as if the idea has only just occurred to him. Which I don't believe. He strikes me as a man who thinks things through very carefully before acting, who likes to plan out most conversations before he has them. 'I mean, why dig there in the first place? In that exact spot, when you had the whole woods to choose from. It's almost as though you knew she was there.'

'I knew there was probably a dead body still somewhere in the woods,' I agree, 'because you lot had stopped looking for her.'

'I'm sorry about that. We had our reasons.'

'You mean the police decided I'd hallucinated the whole thing so you didn't bother looking any further.'

'We looked,' he assures me. 'We even looked in the same area where this woman was buried. There was nothing there that day, according to my officers. No loose soil.'

I frown, taking that in. 'You're saying this woman wasn't buried there when you searched the woods the first time?'

'That's correct.'

Respectfully, with careful precision, DI Powell lifts a corner of the white sheet and drapes it over the dead woman's face again. Her body discreetly disappears, just as it did under the soil. But I'm still aware of it lying there between us. Like a silent accusation.

'Preliminary results indicate that she died about a week ago,' he adds slowly, as though reluctant to share too much information with a member of the public.

I feel queasy. The unpleasant smell is beginning to get to me.

'Can we get out of here?'

DI Powell indicates the door behind me and we go outside. In the corridor he waits in silence, hands back in his trouser pockets, while I lean my forehead against the cool wall, breathing slowly in and out, trying not to throw up.

Me and dead bodies. We can't seem to stop meeting. But we don't get on.

'Better?' he asks.

'I want to go home.' I look up and down the corridor. Everywhere looks the same in this place. I can't remember now which way leads to the exit. 'Where's the way out?'

'I'll arrange for someone to drive you home.'

'Thanks.'

He walks ahead of me down the corridor. 'So you simply went back into the woods to look for her on your own?'

'With Tris.'

'With Tristan, sorry.'

'Not to look for her. I had a hunch, that's all.'

'I thought you said it wasn't a hunch.'

'I said knowing she's a different woman isn't a hunch. But going back into the woods … It was something I needed to do. For my own peace of mind.'

'And Tristan was there as back-up? Was it his idea to go into the woods?'

'I already told you, no. It was my idea.'

'And your idea to go digging in that particular spot.'

'The soil was loose there. It looked freshly dug. That made me suspicious.'

'So why not call the police?'

I stop and look at him directly. 'Why do you think, Inspector? Calling the police didn't work out so well for me last time.'

'Fair enough.'

'I suppose I wanted to be sure you hadn't missed anything. That's about as far as our premeditation went though. We didn't take any spades, there was nothing planned about it. Even when we started digging, we didn't really expect … '

'To find a body?'

I nod, and duck through the door he is holding open for me.

'Especially not a *different* body?' he murmurs.

'Dead right.'

He looks at me, brows raised, but says nothing.

We head out into the station waiting area, which is surprisingly quiet this evening, only one middle-aged woman sitting in a corner with a faux snakeskin handbag on her lap. I wait by the glass doors while Powell speaks to one of the officers behind the front desk. It's getting dark outside. The sky even looks a little threatening to the north of the town. I wonder if the weather is going to break at last and bring us rain.

I think about the next few days at work, and the various track and field activities we have planned in the run-up to Sports' Day. It will not be much fun if we get a downpour.

I try not to think about Tris, and the stolen photograph I found in his bedroom. I'm not going to mention it to Powell. Two things there: first, I would have to admit I got it by entering his house illegally, and second, I want a chance to confront Tris about the photo on his own. Whatever he's done, he's still my friend and I want to believe in him. However bloody stupid that may turn out to be.

'Right,' Powell says, coming to join me at the door, 'my sergeant will drive you back to Eastlyn. He's just getting his coat.'

'I appreciate it.'

'One last thing before you go, Eleanor,' DI Powell says, pulling a see-through plastic evidence bag out of his jacket pocket. There's something in the bag. Something small and golden and shiny. He holds it out to me. 'Have you ever seen this before?'

I take the bag and stare at it. My heart jerks in shock. 'Where … where did you get this?'

His gaze changes, becomes intent. 'So you do recognise it?'

I nod, my voice coming from a great distance. 'It's mine. Or it could be mine. My gold anklet. I thought I'd lost it.'

'Where? When?'

I turn the bag over in my hand, examining the chain

more closely. Of course, there must be hundreds of plain gold anklets in the world. Though this one looks identical to mine, I have to admit. Right now to the bent clasp, which is probably how it fell off my ankle in the first place.

The bag has been tagged with a label. Numbers and letters, some kind of identity code. I struggle against a sense of unreality.

'Newquay. Last Saturday night. I went clubbing there with … '

'With whom?' the inspector prompts me when I hesitate, his tone urgent. 'A man? Sorry, I really need a name from you. Just so we can exclude him from our enquiries.'

'Denzil,' I say reluctantly. 'I was with Denzil Tremain.'

'Thank you.'

DI Powell slips the evidence bag back into his inside jacket pocket, looking grimly satisfied.

'Wait,' I say as he turns away, 'aren't you going to tell me where you found that?'

Powell glances round cautiously, but the middle-aged woman has got up and is talking to the desk sergeant through the glass. There is no one to overhear us.

'This information has to remain completely confidential,' he says.

'Understood.'

'It was found on the victim,' he admits. 'The woman in the grave. She was wearing it round her ankle. No fingerprints, no DNA on it except hers. So we can assume it was wiped clean beforehand. Given that this anklet was all she was wearing, it must be significant, it must hold some kind of symbolic importance for the killer.'

'What are you saying?'

'I think it's a message. A message for you, Eleanor.'

I stare at him. A message?

I feel cold inside. *No fingerprints, no DNA.* I see again Denzil setting fire to the handwritten note on the windscreen, and dropping it to the ground. *You're my*

Number One. Thanks for the anklet.

'Inspector,' I say, 'there's something I haven't told you. Something important.

CHAPTER TWENTY-FIVE

I grab my leather jacket and helmet from the school staff room, then fish my phone out of my rucksack. Nothing from Tris. Nothing from Hannah. Nothing from Denzil.

Though the latter is hardly a surprise. DI Powell rang this morning to tell me Denzil had been arrested.

I have been feeling guilty all day. I cannot believe Denzil has anything to do with this, anymore than I can believe Tris is involved. But of course the police are desperately looking for a scapegoat to reassure local voters, and Denzil Tremain, with his long history of social problems and minor arrests, must fit their criteria very nicely.

They let Tris go. They will let Denzil go soon too. They will ask him about the note on the windscreen, and the anklet, and his relationship with me, and then they will let him go. There will be no evidence against him, I'm sure of it.

I study the clock on the staff room wall. Just over an hour until my next hypnotherapy session. I could do some shopping for tonight's dinner, or go for a coffee somewhere comfortable. There's a sharp wind blowing today, and the sky is cloudy. Not good weather for a walk through the park as I had originally planned.

I tell myself not to do it, but ignore that warning and tap the letters into the empty text box with deliberate recklessness.

Need to speak to you asap.

As soon as I send the message, I wish I could unsend it. I have not spoken to Tris since the police took him in for questioning. And I'm still smarting from Connor's damning portrayal of my character. I know he wants to protect Tris from getting in trouble with the police again, which probably does entail staying away from me, but does he have to suggest to his brother that I'm not right in the head?

A few minutes later though, I feel a buzz in my jacket pocket. Too late to back out now, I think, glancing down at the text on the screen.

Where are you? Call me.

I hesitate, listening again to that nagging internal critic, then ring his mobile anyway. He answers almost immediately. 'Eleanor? What's up? I thought you were at work today.'

'The head gave me the afternoon off. For another hynotherapy session.'

A short silence, then, 'You okay?'

'Not so much.'

Shut up, Eleanor.

'I thought you had been let off the hook for those sessions. They found the body, they know you're not having a relapse.'

'I chose to keep going of my own accord,' I tell him, but warily, not quite sure how much I should trust him. 'I used to hate hypnosis when I was a kid, but I find it oddly relaxing now.'

'Seriously?'

'Yes, seriously,' I insist, stalling on what I really want to say.

'So where are you now? Still at work?' He does not

sound much like a man who has been warned off seeing me. 'We can come to you. It sounds like you could do with some company. It won't take long, I'm already in town with Connor.'

'Doing what?'

He sounds awkward. 'Shopping, believe it or not.'

'I *don't* believe it.'

'Seriously, it's true. We both needed new wellington boots, and Connor wants to drop by the vet and buy some eye medicine for one of our sheep.'

'What an exciting life you two lead.'

'Hang on a tick.' The phone is muffled for a few seconds. I get the impression Connor is talking to him. *Is that the mad girl? Tell her to get lost. Only do it subtly so she does not have a clue we're trying to distance ourselves from her.* Then Tris comes back on the line, sounding friendly but a little stressed. 'Okay, I'll meet you on my own. Connor's got to shoot off before the vet closes. But I can always take the bus home.'

This is probably unwise. If I meet Tris now, and confront him about the photograph, I could end up going into my hypnosis session with my head messed up. But isn't that why I rang him? So we could talk?

We can't ignore each other forever, despite what's happened, even after his arrest and the stolen holiday snap I found in his room. There may be an innocent explanation for both those things.

Besides, we're still friends and that has to mean something. Or am I naïve to believe that?

I make the decision. 'I'll be heading your way soon. Towards town from the school. Meet me in the Turk's Head.'

'A secret assignation. I like it. How long?'

'About fifteen minutes?'

I see Tris before he sees me. I'm leaning beside the jukebox in the Turk's Head, watching passers-by while I sip at a tasteless half-pint of cola stacked with ice chips. I feel more like having a large glass of chilled white wine, but I'm on my scooter, and I still have my hypnotherapy session to get through first. It would hardly impress the good doctor for me to turn up tipsy.

There's a sharp wind, and Tris comes up the steep slope of the High Street towards the Turk's Head with his head down, hands in his pockets. His shoulders are hunched in his black jacket, collar turned up against the cold.

He does not look much like a killer. And presumably the police agree, because they released him without charge.

I walked past a rehearsal of the Shakespeare play, 'Macbeth,' in the main hall earlier today. The kids were doing some kind of modern version, I guess, rigged out in camouflage. I stopped in the doorway to listen for a few minutes. It made me think about all those bloody murders in the play, and the duplicitous nature of killers. 'There's no art to find the mind's construction in the face,' the old king says just before he is stabbed to death by Macbeth, who is supposed to be his host and his friend.

Whoever is killing these women may be exactly like that. A friend, perhaps even a colleague here at the school, someone I know and ought to trust. Whoever it is, he must be hoping he can drive me mad with these tricks and messages, by wrong-footing me and making the police doubt my judgement.

Why, though? I keep coming back to motive, and there doesn't seem to be one.

Still, does a serial killer need a motive? Aren't they just driven to kill and can't help themselves? I'm not sure of my logic or my information, and that worries me. I need to sit down in front of my laptop and educate myself about serial killers. Otherwise I run the risk of being surprised by this one. Because I'm beginning to think a serial killer is precisely what we have here, however much DI Powell may try to deny it. Two women, two bodies, two distinct murders. And two consecutive numbers on their foreheads. If not a serial killer, then a wannabe. A killer with pretensions of greatness.

Tris pushes the pub door open and glances about for me. I raise a hand and he smiles, then stops a foot away, as though afraid to hug me. Something flickers in his face. 'It's good to see you, Eleanor. How are you doing?'

'I'm not dead yet. That's a plus.'

His smile turns wry. 'Yeah, same here.'

I look at him. 'Shopping with Connor is that bad, huh?'

'You have no idea.'

He's right. I try to imagine Connor being all motherly, dragging his brother round the shops, and fail.

I find a table by the window while he wanders to the bar for a pint. I think about the photograph I found in his bedroom with my dad's handwriting on the back. It was definitely missing from my keepsake bed under the bed.

So how did Tris get hold of that photo? More importantly perhaps, *why* did he take it?

I could ask him outright, and am tempted. But then I would have to admit that I've been in his bedroom.

'I'm sorry the police kept you in for questioning,' I say when he comes back with his pint.

He shrugs, saying nothing. But his expression is uneasy.

'If it's any consolation, they arrested Denzil today,' I tell him.

He looks at me directly then, startled. 'Why?'

'They think he might be involved, I guess.'

'That's crazy.'

I'm surprised. 'I thought you didn't like Denzil.'

'I don't. But he's not a killer.'

'I agree. It's not that clear-cut though. The police think … ' I make a face and play with a beer mat, spinning it round and round. I dislike not feeling able to be straight with Tris. 'They found something on the dead woman. Something that belongs to me.'

'What kind of thing?'

I hesitate, remembering DI Powell's warning. *Completely confidential.* And Tris may still be one of their suspects, for all I know.

'I'm not allowed to say, sorry. But it's something I lost when I was out with Denzil last week. You remember, when we bumped into each other at Newquay.'

He nods, not replying, but there's that wary flicker in his face again. Like he's hiding something.

'Tris, what is it?' I ask urgently. 'If you know something, you have to tell me. Or tell the police. I won't hold it against you.'

'I don't know anything, Eleanor. What I know would fit inside a match box. Less than that, even.'

'I was in your room when you came home from the police station,' I blurt out, unable to rein in the guilt any longer. 'I found a photo there, a photo of me and my mum on the beach at Polzeath. It had my dad's handwriting on the back.'

He is staring at me, his eyes wide with shock.

'You … you stole it from my bedroom, didn't you?' I continue, pressing him. 'From the box under my bed?'

'You broke into my *bedroom*? I thought there was something odd when I got back. The window was open and – '

'I'm sorry I broke into your house. It was wrong, I agree. I'm a very bad person, okay? But that's not important right now. What about the photo of my mum?'

'Jesus Christ. You think I'm the one, don't you? Even though the police questioned me for hours, then let me go because there was no evidence at all, none whatsoever, you still think I killed that woman we found.'

I think of the shadow man standing by my bedroom window. That dark menacing figure, his face unseen. Could it really have been Tris, come to steal photos from my keepsake box?

'Well?' he demands.

'I don't know,' I say. 'I don't know anything anymore.

But you *did* have that photograph in your room, and it was strange how you seemed to know exactly where to look for that body.'

'I did *what*?' He shakes his head. 'No way, Eleanor. I was just following your lead. You were the one who said, let's dig here. I already went through all that with the police a hundred times or more. Don't try and unload your baggage on me.'

'All right, so where did it come from? The photo?'

He hesitates. 'I found it.'

'Oh, come on …'

'I swear to God. I found it.'

'Where?'

He drinks about a third of his lager, then replaces the glass carefully on his beer mat. 'I was out with the dog about ten days ago. And I found the photo just lying there on the ground. Near the old mill.'

The old mill again.

'But I've never even been down that way. How could one of my old photographs have got there unless someone stole it?'

'I agree,' he says calmly. 'Only it wasn't me who stole it.'

'So why didn't you tell me about it immediately? Why not give me a call and say, hey, Ellie, you'll never guess what I've just found while I was out walking the dog?'

When he does not reply, I stare at him accusingly. 'You must have known it belonged to me, Tris. That nobody else could have a photo like that. It has my dad's writing on the back, for God's sake. My name. My mum's name. So why not tell me you found it?'

His face is shuttered, unreadable. 'I had my reasons.'

'Which were?'

'Not yet, okay? Not yet. Trust me on this.' He necks the remainder of his lager in one long, inelegant swallow, then wipes the corners of his mouth on the back of his hand. 'I'm not ready. My head's not straight. But I'm glad you got your photo back.'

'Thanks.'

'Just don't ever break into my bedroom again.'

'Ditto.'

'Or, if you do,' he says, folding his arms across his chest and leaning back in his seat to glare at me, 'make the bloody bed before you leave next time.'

I should be furious with him, and more suspicious than ever, but for some reason I'm not. Maybe because I know – or at least I sense – that we're still friends. Still the best of friends.

'Your room was a total fucking tip,' I agree. 'I'm not joking, you need to get in there with some air freshener.'

'Better come round with your pinny on then, and tidy up.'

Is that a tease or a serious invitation?

I should be offended but I'm not. Instead I'm imagining myself in his darkened bedroom, the two of us alone together. I look down at the ice chips melting in my drink, and wish I could have some alcohol. But my appointment is in less than ten minutes now.

'Maybe I will,' I say, 'one day.'

We're sitting very close now. He reminds me even more of a grizzly bear, squeezed into this narrow seat under the window, his body too broad and muscular for the space. His long legs stretch out to one side of the table, muscular in tight jeans. His eyes seem very dark, locked on mine now and refusing to look away.

'You've known me forever,' he says softly.

I nod, not trusting myself to speak.

'I know it looks bad, with the photo you found, and me being arrested. But you know I had nothing to do with any of it.'

'Do I?'

His eyes close briefly. 'Jesus.'

'I'm sorry, really I am. But I don't know who to trust anymore.' I need to break the spell his voice is putting on me, and the only way I can do that is with blunt honesty. 'And I'm scared. That thing of mine the police found … They said it was a message for me from the killer.'

Tris has opened his eyes and is staring at me intently. 'What kind of message?'

'They don't know what it means. But whoever is behind these killings, it seems obvious that he can get to me if he likes. That he *knows* me personally.'

Someone has selected a song on the jukebox that reminds me of long hot Cornish summers when we were teenagers, still in school. One of those mellow lyric numbers. I surprise myself by remembering all the words to the chorus. What was I, fifteen, when it came out? Something like that.

I see him listening, glancing sideways at the jukebox like it means something to him too.

'Good memories,' I say.

He nods slowly, then swears under his breath. There's a tormented look in his face when he turns his gaze back to me. 'Eleanor.'

I wait, watching him.

Only he doesn't finish. Out on the High Street a police car rushes past to some incident, sirens blaring, blue lights revolving rapidly.

We both look round to watch it pass. The song on the jukebox finishes and another takes its place, more disco than ballad. In the aftermath Tris seems to change his mind about whatever he was going to say. He pushes aside his empty pint glass, and then gets up from the table.

'Come on, time's up. You're going to be late for your appointment if we sit here any longer.'

Reluctantly I grab my bike helmet and follow him outside the pub. The wind is still sharp, nipping at us.

He is staring across the road at the local newspaper board outside the newsagent. BODY FOUND IN WOODS.

I shrug deeper into my leather jacket, trying not to

over-think this. 'Will you come in with me?'

CHAPTER TWENTY-SIX

'Take your time.' The voice is softer this time, less demanding. 'Can you tell us where you are, Eleanor? Look around. Can you describe your surroundings?'

I tell her that I'm standing next to Mummy in the woods. She's dropped my hand. I'm staring up at the leaves, so bright with the sunlight falling sharp and hot through them. There are birds up there, unseen among the leaves. I'm breathing gently, listening to their high sweet song ...

'Is anyone else there? Anyone else in the woods?'

I'm wearing my new red wellington boots today. They're so smart. Look, do you like them?

'They're lovely. But I want you to look around, Eleanor.' A pause. I stay where I am, blinking in the sunlight. 'Are you looking around? Good girl, well done. Now tell me, are you and Mummy alone in the wood? Or is someone else with you?'

I smile up at Mummy, but she's not looking at me anymore. She's staring at something behind me. Her face changes. I don't look back, but I know there's someone there. Someone coming through the trees. I can hear the crack of twigs underfoot.

'Look round, Eleanor.' The voice is urgent now. 'Look behind you. Who else is there with your Mummy?'

I don't want to look. I don't like it anymore. I kick the dirt with my wellingtons.

'Is it a man? Can you describe him?'

I can't look. Mummy makes me run. Keep going, keep running. I run one way, then another. I'm not sure where to go. I fall over and get dirt on my hands.

I don't like this game, Mummy. I want to go home. I start to cry. But I can't hear her voice anymore.

Mummy? Mummy?

'Go back, Eleanor.' A long pause. 'You go back, don't you?'

Yes, I go back to see if I can find Mummy.

'And you see someone. A man.'

I can't find Mummy at first. Then I see her lying on the path. There's a man bending over her.

'Can you describe him? He's wearing a pair of white trainers.'

Yes, white trainers. I see them up above me afterwards. Flashing through the trees. Like he's running.

'But now, can you see his face? Maybe he straightens up and looks round at you.'

He doesn't see me. I stay behind the tree until he's gone. I only look out once, then never again. There's a bird croaking on one of the branches above me, like a warning not to move.

'But you see him when you look round the tree? I know it's hard but I need you to concentrate on the man, Eleanor. Can you describe his face?'

My hands are dirty. Nasty and dirty. There's a cut from a bramble, and it's bleeding. I'm going to get in trouble.

'No one's angry with you, Eleanor. You're safe here with us. Now take it very slowly. Have you seen this man before? Do you know who he is?' The voice pauses. 'If you can't describe him, maybe you can tell us his name?'

I struggle against the questions, deeply afraid. A phone rings, shrill and intrusive. To my relief the sunlit trees begin to fade, tilt into the past, sliding away …

'Shit.'

I know that voice but it jars with the dream I've just left. I'm awake again now but horribly disorientated. My head is aching. Where am I? My eyes open on the familiar dull surroundings of Dr Quick's office, the blinds shut against grey daylight.

'I'm sorry, Dr Quick.' Tris is speaking, his voice deep and apologetic. 'I set the alarm on my phone to remind me of the time when the bus leaves. I forgot to turn it off.'

Dr Quick ignores him. She is leaning over me, her smile concerned. 'Eleanor, are you okay?'

When I nod, she helps me sit up against the cushions, then hands me the obligatory glass of water. 'Small sips, remember. A rather rude awakening, I'm afraid. How's your head?'

'Aching,' I admit.

'Dizzy? Nauseous?'

I shake my head, then hand back the water. 'I'm fine. Thanks.'

Tris looks from me to the doctor. 'Are you able to … Is it possible to start again?'

Dr Quick glances at the clock. 'Not now. A pity, I thought we were really making progress this time.'

She goes back to her desk under the window, smoothing out her dove-grey skirt before sitting down. Studying her desk diary, she flicks over the pages for a moment. She crosses something out, then looks over at me, brows arched.

'Shall we meet again next week, Eleanor?' she asks. 'Same day, same time?'

'Did I remember something different?'

'I'm afraid we didn't get quite far enough today to be sure. But maybe next time we'll be able to break new territory.'

She writes my name down in the book, then lays down the pen and meets my eyes, her expression serious but sympathetic.

'It's important not to rush these things, Eleanor. Whatever it is that you don't want to remember, it must be buried very deep in your subconscious. It'll only come out when it's ready,' she says calmly, 'you can't try to force it.'

I nod.

'But maybe next time,' she adds, 'you should come on your own?'

Tris says, 'Sorry,' again.

I swing my legs round and stand up. Tris is there at once, his hand steadying me. I look at him ironically.

'Thank you, Dr Quick. See you next week.'

I didn't like her when we had those sessions before. Maybe I was too young to appreciate her peculiar skills, but the sessions felt so intrusive as well, I almost hated her for getting inside my head like this. Now though I'm ready to go back into therapy, to see what my subconscious can dredge up about my mother's death. Even if I don't like what we discover.

The truth of what happened that day has become too important to me.

Outside, the clouds have set in for the evening and it's started spitting with rain. I'm going to get soaked on the way home. We walk briskly back down to the Turk's Head where I left the scooter parked in a bike bay.

'I'm sorry about the phone,' he says again, waiting while I find my bike keys.

'I told you, it's okay. I'm only sorry I can't offer you a lift home in this weather.'

'The bus will be fine. Or I could ring Connor, see if he'll come out. We could always go for a drink.' He smiles wryly. 'We hardly ever go to the pub together anymore. The farm eats all our time, and our money too. It's not been easy these past few months. I'm sorry if we've both seemed a bit distracted. I really do want to help with all this,' he says deeply, and puts a hand on my arm. His touch feels warm and comforting, and it's hard not to give in to my temptation to confide in him properly. 'If there's anything you need, you only have to ask.'

'There is something,' I say quickly, before he can

change his mind. 'I only ever remember what happens in the hypnosis sessions as though in a mist, the vagueness of my memory drives me mad. And Dr Quick doesn't share everything with me, she's very careful not to lead me in any particular direction if she can avoid it.'

'You were listening to what I said today though. Was there anything that sounded new this time? Anything important?'

He frowns. 'You said … there might have been someone else in the woods that day. Someone else with your mother. A man.'

'A man?'

I struggle to remember for myself. It's so frustratingly unclear. Like a dream, only half-remembered, not quite real. And just as fast to fade from my memory.

'You didn't see his face though.' Tris grimaces. 'That's when my phone rang.'

'Well, it can't be helped. Like she said, we'll probably get it next time.' The rain is getting heavier now. 'Look, I'd better go.'

Tris lifts his collar up against the rain. 'Yeah, I'll see you at the weekend, maybe.' He turns away, then stops as though hit by a sudden thought. 'Oh, I almost forgot. Connor saw in the newspaper that there's going to be a memorial service at the village church on Saturday. For that woman we found.'

I think of the Reverend Clemo at once. 'Really? Whose idea was that?'

'Not sure. Anyway, I wondered if you wanted to go. With me.'

'You want to go to the memorial service with me?'

'It's fine if you'd rather go on your own.'

'No,' I protest, and wince to hear myself stammering in reply, 'I'd like to go with you. I mean, yes. That's a good idea. We should both go. Together.'

Tris nods, and strides away under the rain.

I stand there, watching until he is out of sight, bike

helmet forgotten in my hand, my hair getting wet.

There might have been someone else in the woods that day. A man with my mother. But who? And why can't I remember?

CHAPTER TWENTY-SEVEN

Sarah McGellan is the dead woman's name, I discover. Not from the police but from the national newspapers. I find a few reports online and read them attentively, but details are still sparing. Certainly there's little information there that I did not already know. She liked surfing, she was a popular young woman, nobody has a bad word to say about her. Which is so often the case when a life has been taken violently.

The killer is described as 'unidentified' and still 'at large,' and the public are warned to be vigilant and careful when visiting the woods.

The police released Denzil after only twelve hours, much to my relief. DS Carrick dropped by the house to let me know. Denzil has not been in touch with me since then though. I expect he is furious. And he has every right to be. But I could hardly lie about the anklet.

Sarah McGellan's memorial service is organised for Saturday morning at Eastlyn Church at eleven o'clock. Having been mentioned in one of the regional newspapers, and on BBC Radio Cornwall, it is expected there will be quite a large turn-out, so we decide to get there early.

The vicar has already telephoned Hannah about the

service, I discover, apparently determined to invite the whole village. Only for reasons of her own, Hannah chose not to pass that information on to me. But it seems she is happy to go with me and Tris, so I get a lift to the church in her car.

We queue outside the church along with dozens of other villagers and mourners, everyone in black, very sombre and formal. Even Tris and Connor are wearing clean shirts and black ties; I see them ahead of us in the queue, shuffling into church side by side, and try not to stare. They both look good in formal wear.

Hannah sees me looking at them, and nudges me. 'What's up with Connor and Tris? They haven't been round much lately.'

I don't tell her the truth, that Connor has decided I'm mad and he needs to keep his little brother away from me. Instead I smile wanly, and say, 'They're very busy at the farm. Still lambing, I think.'

'Mmm, I love lamb.'

'Hannah!'

'What?' She tries to look innocent. 'It's tasty, is that my fault?'

'Poor little things.'

'Whenever I see lambs in a field, I want to shout, "Mint sauce," over the fence at them. But people would stare, wouldn't they?'

'Yes,' I agree. 'Because you're a heartless fiend.'

'I'm a pragmatist. If the Great British Public didn't eat so much lamb, most of those sheep probably wouldn't exist at all. We only have so much demand for woolly jumpers.'

I glance at the gravestones on either side as she talks, and repress a shudder as I remember why we are here. My mother isn't buried here, of course. These are all old graves, most of them Victorian or eighteenth century. Her grave is a short walk up the hill in the new village cemetery, a quiet plot near a row of silver birches.

227

I'll walk up there and visit her after the service, I decide.

They seat us in the reserved seating at the front of the church, as though we're family, which surprises and touches me.

I hesitate, then place my small wreath in front of the altar alongside the others. Pretty white rosebuds and yellow freesias woven together in a green wreath by the local florist. They smell gorgeous, which I feel is important.

My handwritten note says simply, *'I'm sorry. EB.'*

As soon as I sit down, Tris appears. He glances at Hannah. 'Hello,' he says to us both. 'Can I join you? Do you mind?'

'I thought you were with Connor.'

A shadow passes over his face. 'Connor wants to sit at the back. I'm surprised he came. Last night he said he would be staying at the farm.'

It's obvious he's had some kind of argument with his brother. The front pew is already full, but Hannah makes room by squashing up to the woman next to her, who flashes her an irritated look.

'Come on,' Hannah tells him cheerfully, 'you can squeeze in between me and Eleanor.'

Tris sits down next to me on the unforgiving wooden pew. Our thighs press hard together, and our eyes meet. Instantly I imagine the two of us in bed together, and it's hard to breathe after that.

'Hello, Ellie,' he says to me quietly.

'Hello.'

'I wasn't sure if you would come.'

'I found her. It felt like the right thing to do.'

'Me too.' He pauses a beat. 'I thought we were going to come here together.'

'We're sitting together now, aren't we?'

'You know what I mean.'

It's hot in the church, and the temperature is only going

to rise the more people cram in through the doors. Avoiding his gaze, I run a finger round the back of my collar, feeling uncomfortable and restless in the sticky heat.

'Do I?'

'You know you do. Now stop teasing.' Tris is watching me, his dark eyes intent. He whispers in my ear, 'Perhaps we could go back to your place afterwards. Talk properly, without all these people around.'

I look round at him. I can't seem to stop staring at his neck, the line of his jaw, his broad shoulder pressed against mine. 'Yeah,' I mutter, aching for him but not yet ready to commit to whatever that might bring later. 'Perhaps we could.'

Trying to shake that heavy, languid feeling that is so wildly inappropriate in a church, I turn my head, recognising the thick Cornish voice booming in the doorway. The vicar is greeting someone, pointing out a half-empty pew towards the back. He doesn't sound very friendly.

The newcomer is Dick Laney.

The vicar straightens, glancing towards the front of the church. I don't look away quickly enough, and for a moment our eyes meet. He stares, his mouth tightening. Then he moves on, shaking hands with an elderly parishioner.

'Where's Jenny?' Hannah asks, also craning her neck to see who is here.

I scan the faces again, but don't see Jenny among the villagers behind us. I see her parents though, and her gregarious friends who run the pub, Seth and Vi, sitting together a few rows back on the left.

'I'm not sure,' I admit, turning back to face the front. 'Jenny told me yesterday that she was coming to the memorial service. Out of respect, you know. But I know there was a two-hour triathlon training session at the athletics club this morning, so maybe she decided to do that instead. I saw a poster for it on the noticeboard.'

Hannah's glasses have slipped down her nose. She pushes them back up, staring at me. 'Jenny's thinking about doing a triathlon?'

'Apparently so.'

'Wow.' She pinches one of her thighs. 'You two are so sporty. I need to do more exercise too. I haven't been surfing for ages. Perhaps we could drive out to Widemouth Bay together one day, take the surf boards, catch some rollers.'

'That would be fun,' I agree. 'Like old times.'

'It's this admin job at the hospital that does it. I'm either stuck behind a desk or doing paperwork over lunch in the café. I know I'm not overweight, but my legs are getting decidedly flabby.'

'You are *not* flabby,' I tell her scathingly.

'How would you describe me, then?'

I look up her up and down. 'You are comfortable and sedate.'

'Sedate?' she repeats, mildly scandalised. 'What, like the queen?'

'Exactly like the queen.'

Tris is reading through the Order of Service. There's a paragraph about the dead woman, written by her family. He reads it out to me in a whisper while I run another quick glance over the rest of the congregation.

The church seems to be filling up rapidly now. Mostly villagers, but some of the faces are unknown to me. I study the people in the pews near the front. Several groups look like surfers, dressed respectfully enough in black today but with tattoos and piercings, or with exotic beading in their hair. Friends of the deceased? The surfing community in North Cornwall is very close-knit, even out of season, and I know some surfers come back year after year to the same beaches.

There's a buzz of hushed voices as someone carries a last minute flower arrangement down the aisle and sets it down next to the altar: white fluting lilies and tall green foliage. There are even a few professional-looking cameras at the back, and someone setting up arc lights.

Dick Laney sees me and raises a hand in greeting.

I look away.

'Ellie?' Tris must have felt me shudder. 'What's the matter?'

'Nothing.'

I turn and face the altar, sick with apprehension. Are those national television cameras? I don't think I'll be able to stay calm once the media work out the possible connection between my mum's death and Sarah McGellan's murder. Which they almost certainly will. It's only a matter of time.

Tris squeezes my hand silently, and I flash him an appreciative smile. It's good to have him with me today. I can't ignore the stolen photograph, and the stamp on the dead woman's hand, and seeing Tris at the night club before that note appeared. So many arrows pointing at his head. And piercing my heart at the same time. I can't carry on suspecting him. It's wearing me out to keep Tris at arms' length when everything inside me is dying to let him in.

The vicar addresses the congregation, and everyone hushes to listen to him.

I stare up at the large wooden cross while he's speaking. Then the stained glass windows around us. Jesus with a lamb in his arms, fending off a wolf. *I Am The Good Shepherd*, it proclaims. Sunlight glows through the stained glass segments, warm and cheerful, making the whole scene brighter, the reds and blues more intense.

Her body is not here, of course, Presumably it's still in the police mortuary while the investigation is ongoing. I guess at some point it will be released to the family so she can be buried.

Someone has set a large, blown-up photograph of the surfer at the front. Her name is underneath on a vast wreath, spelled out in white and yellow flowers.

SARAH MCGELLAN.

After my first glance at her photograph, I try not to look again. But I can't get her face out of my head. Not the happy, windswept face smiling back at us from the photograph, which looks like it was taken at Widemouth Bay around low tide, the horseshoe-shaped beach behind her ablaze with sunlight. No, what I can see is the dead face in the dirt, soil in her hair, one pale hand protruding from a makeshift grave.

I close my eyes, but she's still there in the dark of my head. Brooding, watching me. It's almost as though she's accusing me of something.

'You okay?' Tris whispers.

I manage a smile for him.

I found you, I tell the dark presence inside my head. *Don't be angry. I saved you from lying undiscovered for months.*

But Sarah McGellan neither answers me nor disappears. Her accusation is like a weight on my shoulders for the rest of the service, making me slump in my seat. There are prayers and hymns, then more talking. Kids she taught to surf get up and say a poem for her. I find myself crying uselessly.

Then the unlikely opening chords of a Bon Jovi number fill the church. Her favourite music, according to one of the other surfers. He's a sandy-haired Australian in his thirties who climbs up behind the lectern to talk about Sarah. I remember seeing him once or twice around Newquay, one of those surfers from abroad who come to Cornwall on holiday and never leave. In a shaking voice, he shares what Sarah was like as a person – outgoing, friendly, a talented surfer, and generous with her time as an instructor – and describes how he first met her. He's in tears by the time he finishes.

The Australian surfer looks pointedly at me as he gets down from the lectern. For the first time I wonder what people are saying about me. That I am to blame for her death?

Without being narcissistic about it, the most gruesome things that have happened in this village do seem to revolve around me. But that doesn't mean I caused any of it. Or that I'm the murderer.

Again I am struck by the feeling that this is some kind of witch hunt. That this must have happened in the past to women like me. People got sick or died, then some scared villager pointed the finger at a woman living suspiciously on her own. Next thing her neighbours were hanging her from the nearest tree.

We stream outside into thin, windy sunshine once the service is over. The atmosphere seems lighter. People are talking more loudly, kids are running about, and some of the surfers are even laughing amongst themselves. Only the sandy-haired man is still crying.

I turn my face to the sunlight and push Sarah McGellan's image out of my mind. *I'm not to blame*, I tell her. *I'm sorry about what happened to you, but it's not my fault you died.*

DI Powell is giving a statement to journalists on a patch of neatly-mown grass near the church gate. There are daisies under his large black shoes, polished to a high shine.

I say to Hannah, 'I'm going up to visit Mum's grave.'

'Want me to come with you?'

'No, I'll be fine. Thanks.'

She kisses me on the cheek, then glances slyly at Tris, who is standing beside me. 'I'll see you later then. I'm on another night, by the way. But this is my last one. Back to the day shift for a fortnight next week. I can't bloody wait.'

The sun is very hot, and I begin to wish I had worn sunglasses, like the inspector. I move under the shadow of a churchyard elm, leaning against the rough trunk. Tris comes to join me and I smile at him, remembering how close we were sitting in church, the heat of his body against mine.

'Hey,' I say softly.

'Hey you too.' He strokes a finger down the sleeve of my black blouse, his touch making me shiver. 'I thought you were going up to the cemetery.'

'In a few minutes.'

'I don't think Connor will miss me. Not in the mood he's in. I can walk up with you.'

'I'd like that. First I need to speak to DI Powell, assuming he'll agree to it.'

Tris has been openly admiring my figure, but something flickers in his face at that, and he raises his gaze to my face. 'What about?'

'I want to know if he's got any further with the investigation. It's driving me mad, not knowing who the killer is, or when he might kill again. Especially given that he seems to see me as a target.'

'No one will lay a finger on you while I'm with you.'

I tease him. 'No one?'

His smile is delicious and slow-burning. 'Well, maybe one person.'

Again I have trouble breathing, and force myself to stay calm. But I know my cheeks are probably flushed, my eyes bright with desire. This is crazy. He's high on my list of suspects. But I can't help being attracted to him. To pretend I don't have the serious hots for this man would be worse than crazy. It would be total self-delusion.

'Where is Connor, by the way?'

'I expect he went back to the farm.' Tris checks his phone for messages. The screen is blank. 'He'll get in touch if he needs me.'

I look across to where DI Powell is giving his outdoor statement to the press. It's impossible not to feel intimidated by the flash of cameras, the throng of journalists pushing and shouting questions at the inspector. The reporters were being held back before the service, cordoned off at the top of the hill by a police line, out of respect for those coming to mourn Sarah McGellan.

Now though the street outside Eastlyn Church is packed with cars and vans, some with famous logos on the side and satellite dishes on top. It's not only local newspapers that are taking an interest in this murder hunt, but national television companies too. The story is starting to spread beyond Cornwall.

I look away, feeling sick. When will these hordes of journalists find my address and catch up with me? I can't seem to shake those memories from my childhood of journalists hanging round the primary school gate for weeks afterwards, cameras stuck in my face at the funeral, our phone forever ringing with offers of a newspaper exclusive. My father turned them all down, of course. 'Vultures,' he would say, slamming down the phone. But now, with the state of the farm to consider, and the way he's been drinking, he might be tempted to sell his story. For what it's worth, that is, eighteen years after the event.

The inspector finishes his statement to the press. After their final questions, most of the journalists pack up and shuffle away, photographers carrying equipment back to their vans. DI Powell takes off his dark sunglasses, coming towards us as though he too has been waiting to speak to us.

'Eleanor,' he says, though I note how his gaze flicks sideways to Tris. 'A moving service, I thought. Especially when the kids read out that poem.'

I wonder again about the night Tris was kept in for questioning. We've never discussed it, but I guess it's not an experience Tris is likely to have forgotten.

'Sarah McGellan was obviously very well-liked and respected,' the inspector adds, 'especially in the Cornish surfing community. Her family are devastated.'

'I'm not surprised,' I say.

DI Powell pockets his sunglasses, regarding me steadily. 'And how are you, Eleanor?'

'She wants to know if you're any nearer catching the man who did this,' Tris asks before I can open my mouth.

'Now, Mr Taylor, I know you're upset about the length of time my officers took to question you, but you have to be reasonable. This is a very serious murder enquiry. I can't discuss the particulars of any ongoing investigations.'

DI Powell does not look fazed by this sudden attack. I guess he is used to dealing with difficult members of the public. Including former detainees.

But Tris is not satisfied. 'What about Denzil?' he asks, pressing the inspector.

'I'm personally satisfied that Denzil Tremain has no connection with the murder of Sarah McGellan.'

'Ditto,' I say.

'But he must have known her.' Tris surprises me by persisting with his attack. 'Denzil knows all the local surfers. He spends most of his time on the coast, on the beaches or in the clubs. I expect he knew her intimately. Sarah McGellan was a surf instructor, after all.' He pauses significantly. 'And his father's always in prison.'

'We had no reason to hold Mr Tremain any longer.'

'So do you plan to make any other arrests?' Tris demands loudly. There are still mourners talking quietly in a group by the church door. Heads are beginning to turn. 'I don't like the idea that Eleanor could be at risk, that whoever murdered Sarah McGellan is still wandering about free.'

'We are currently following various lines of inquiry. None of them connected to Mr Tremain. I can understand your concern, Mr Taylor. But there's really no need to worry.' The inspector manages a thin smile for my benefit, though I can see he's annoyed. 'I have officers out there right now, Eleanor, making door-to-door enquiries. As soon as we know anything new, we'll be in touch.'

'Thanks,' I say, and squeeze Tris's hand, hoping he gets the message that I want him to leave it alone now. 'I look forward to it. You've been very helpful.'

Reverend Clemo walks slowly past with several elderly villagers, their heads down, talking to him earnestly. But he stops when he sees the inspector, stiffening a little as though he had not expected to see him there.

'Excuse me, ladies,' he says to the parishioners, and waits patiently for them to walk on before he turns and nods to the inspector. 'Detective Inspector Powell,' he says in welcome, using that authoritative church voice again. 'A sad day.'

Powell steps forward to shake the vicar's hand, holding his grip just a second longer than you'd expect. Like they're both members of the local branch of the Masons.

'Indeed, Reverend,' Powell agrees, using his police voice in return. Brisk and incisive. 'I thought the service was very moving though. And useful for the community. Good of you and the parish team to put it together at such short notice.'

'Not all, not at all. My pleasure, inspector.' Clemo pauses, looking first at me, then at Tris. His smile is unconvincing. I get the impression he would prefer not to acknowledge us at all. 'Well, I'm glad you could all come. And what a glorious day it's turning out to be.' His long robes flap about his ankles, right on cue. 'Apart from this infernal wind.'

'Maybe we could have a word while I'm in the village, sir,' the inspector suggests, smiling.

'Ah, not today. I do apologise. Maybe next week sometime?'

DI Powell raises his brows. It's clear he's not used to having his offers of a 'word' rejected. 'No police interviews on the Sabbath, Reverend?' he enquires.

'Nothing so dogmatic, inspector. I simply need to offer some assistance to my wife for tomorrow's garden party at the vicarage. An annual event, Detective Inspector, to mark the start of the summer season. Stalls with refreshments and bric-a-brac and church souvenirs. You know the sort of thing, I'm sure. But it does seem to require rather a lot of … ' The vicar waves his hand vaguely, not finishing. 'Well, if you would excuse me. Very good to see you all.'

DI Powell turns to watch Reverend Clemo's departing back, his expression speculative. Again, I wonder why the vicar seems to dislike me so much. It can't simply be because I turned him away from the house when he started getting too religious on me the other week. That must happen to him all the time. No, it's more likely that, in common with the older and more conservative residents of the village, Reverend Clemo believes I'm to blame for the things that have happened round here lately. Like I'm a magnet for evil.

Which could be true, I consider drily, given my history to date.

'Eleanor, on second thoughts, I would like to talk to you again,' Powell says, turning his attention back to me. He glances at Tris. 'Would you excuse us for a minute?'

I nod to him, and Tris sighs, but turns away, looking resigned. 'I'll wait for you outside the gate,' he says over his shoulder.

'See you right there,' I agree.

Once we are alone, DI Powell studies me thoughtfully. 'I think bringing you in again for another chat could be very productive, Eleanor.' A few strands of silvering hair are blown into his eyes by a gust of wind; he flicks them back into place with an impatient hand. 'I don't want to alarm you unduly, but you do appear to be the lynchpin of this investigation. Which makes me wonder if there's something we failed to uncover in our earlier interviews. Some small detail which may seem insignificant to you, but which could provide my team with a breakthrough. I often find it's the smallest details that make the biggest difference when you're trying to piece together a puzzle like this.'

'So why the change of heart? You seemed to think before that I couldn't help you any further.'

'This anklet ... I thought it was a message at first. A warning, perhaps. Or a boast. Like our killer is saying to you, *Look, I can take your things and dress my victims up in them.*'

DI Powell pauses, frowning in concentration as he continues to pursue that idea. 'Or maybe he's deliberately trying to make his victims *look* more like you. As though he wants to turn them into a new version of you by stripping them naked and making them wear something he's actually seen *you* wearing.'

CHAPTER TWENTY-EIGHT

I grimace. 'Oh my God, don't. That's too creepy for words.'

He looks round at me, startled, as though he has only just realised he is talking so frankly to another possible murder victim. 'Sorry, so sorry. Please ignore me, Eleanor. That was very wrong of me. I was thinking out loud.'

'Okay, I'll try to blank out that whole mental image,' I say, shaking my head in disbelief. 'But now you're not sure about the significance of the anklet?'

'Well,' he says more cautiously, 'it just occurred to me that it may have been a souvenir. Rather than a message.'

I'm taken aback. 'A souvenir? Of what?'

'That depends on his mindset, and also the degree to which he is close to you. It could be a souvenir of having spoken to you in person, or maybe having danced with you the night your anklet went missing. Right now it's hard to be definite about anything, the forensic evidence is so thin. That's why I'd like another opportunity to sit down and talk to you at length.'

'You said, *victims*. Plural. So you believe me now, about the other woman I saw in the woods?'

He shrugs. 'I'm keeping my options open.'

'If I'm right though, does that make me his next target?'

'From what we know so far, there's a good chance Sarah McGellan was picked out at random. She was unlucky. Which would indicate that although you should continue being careful and making sure someone knows where you are at all times, you probably aren't in any immediate danger. But I can put an officer outside your door at night, if you feel unsafe – '

DI Powell is interrupted by an angry shout from the church gate.

It's Denzil.

He looks wild, his tawny hair dishevelled. He's wearing an orange surfing vest with a blue wave design, his powerful arms and shoulders covered in sprawling tattoos. He launches towards me, stumbling as though he's been drinking, his eyes fixed on my face.

'Ellie, I need to talk to you.'

Denzil checks momentarily at the sight of the inspector, then keeps walking as though propelled by the strength of his emotions, the anger in his whole body deepening with every step.

'Was it you, Ellie?' he demands, staring at me. 'Did you grass me up to the filth? Do you really think I'm a murderer?'

'Denzil, please,' I say urgently, and he stops in front of us, his face tense, hands swinging loose at his sides like he's longing to do violence with them. 'This isn't helping.'

DI Powell is on his mobile, a step away, his level gaze on Denzil. It's obvious what's going to happen. At least the journalists seem to have gone. That would have been a nightmare come true, to have the media swarming all over this confrontation.

'Go home, Denzil,' I plead with him. 'Go home and sober up, please. The police don't think it was you either. You don't need to do this.'

'But who gave them my name?' He glares at Tris, who's

suddenly appeared out of nowhere, standing behind me as though ready to whisk me away at the first hint of violence. 'Was it you, Taylor? I know you can't stand me, it's in your face. But it's not my fault she prefers me.'

Tris narrows his eyes but says nothing.

DI Powell puts a hand on Denzil's arm. 'Why don't you come with me, sit in my car for a few minutes? We can talk.'

Denzil gives a roar and pushes him away. 'Get lost, copper.'

'Calm down,' I tell him urgently. 'You're going to get yourself arrested again.'

Suddenly Denzil turns on me, flushed with anger and breathing hard, and I crouch, ready to defend myself. He's going to be surprised if he takes me on, I think.

'As for you, Eleanor Blackwood – '

Denzil gets no further. Tris steps in, trips him up with one neat move, then pushes him to the ground, twisting one of his arms behind his back, pressing a knee into the small of his back. End of situation.

I straighten, impressed. It is exactly the move I would have used myself if Denzil had laid a finger on me.

'Give it up, Denzil,' Tris tells him, then steps back as a police officer comes running up the path. 'Yeah, don't worry. He's all yours.'

The constable wrestles Denzil to his feet. He looks like a caged lion, tawny hair springing everywhere. All the fight has gone out of him. His face crumples as he stares back over his shoulder at me. 'I'm sorry,' he mouths, then lets himself be dragged away.

DI Powell smooths down his hair and looks at me, clearly concerned. 'You okay, Eleanor?'

'Never better. He got nowhere near me.' I frown as the inspector turns away. 'Wait. You're not going to arrest him again, are you? Denzil hasn't done anything wrong. He's just upset because he thinks I betrayed him.'

The inspector looks back at me wryly. 'Drunk and

disorderly. Assault on a police officer. Public affray. Resisting arrest. Need I go on?'

'But you don't *have* to arrest him. You can choose to give him a warning instead.'

Powell hesitates. 'That's true, yes.'

I glance at Tris, who is a few feet away, still looking flushed and angry as he watches Denzil being manhandled into a police van. I say, 'If I agree to come in for another interview, will you let him go?'

'This isn't a barter system,' Powell says, his tone sardonic.

'I don't have to talk to you again if I don't want to.'

He looks at me closely, then sighs. 'Okay. No arrest. No charges. But perhaps a verbal warning. Does that satisfy you?'

I smile. 'Thanks,' I say, then hold out my hand to Tris. 'Come on, let's go and visit my mother's grave.'

The road outside the church is quiet now, and to my relief, the journalists appear to have vanished *en masse*, just as they arrived. I can see Denzil sitting in the back of the police van, head down, talking to one of the officers. He seems much calmer now.

We set off up the hill side by side. The overflow cemetery is only a three minute walk from the church, but the hill's steep so it always takes longer going up than coming down.

'What did the inspector want?'

'To frighten me. I have a feeling he thinks I know something I haven't shared with the police.'

Tris narrows his eyes against the sun, squinting back over his shoulder like he wants to check we're not being followed.

'And do you?'

I grin. 'Plenty.'

'Did you tell him about the photograph?'

'No.'

He looks at me then, suddenly intent. 'Why not?'

'No need for them to know. They'll only insist on a search of the cottage, make me see if anything else is missing. I couldn't stand that, the invasion of my privacy. Besides, I hate the way Powell is obsessed with me being some kind of target for this guy. I know I've got to be careful. I'm not an idiot. And yes, it scares the shit out of me to think whoever murdered Sarah McGellan might be watching me too, waiting for his chance.'

'He'd have to come through me first.'

'My hero.' I squeeze his hand, my grip lingering a few seconds longer than necessary. I haven't forgotten the way he looked at me in church. But now is not the time. 'But part of me is also thinking, fuck it, bring him on. Let him try his best shot. I'm ready for him.'

Tris shakes his head. 'Good grief. Keep going to the therapy sessions. You need them.'

I laugh, starting to relax now we're out of sight of the police. It may be ridiculous but I still feel guilty when DI Powell is around. Like I'm making it all up. Though the discovery of Sarah McGellan's body has at least made that an impossibility.

We round the bend in full sunshine and arrive at the newer cemetery, built because the old churchyard was overflowing, with no room for new graves. There's a sign on the chest-high metal gate: the usual small print about municipal sites; the council taking no responsibility, etc. It protests as we push it open.

'Hinges need oiling,' Tris comments, glancing back as the gate squeaks shut behind us.

I often wish Mum was buried in the old churchyard. It feels quieter and more peaceful there, sheltered by the church walls and overshadowed by dark, ancient yew trees. The strong Cornish winds blow straight off the moor and over the old graves, some of their headstones half-sunk into grass or eroded by the centuries so the names of the dead are no longer readable. But today I welcome the bright, breezy look of the modern plot. It's sunny here among the clean white and marbled gravestones, a few bouquets of flowers arranged in stainless steel pots on the newest graves, ribboned clusters nodding in the breeze, even a little blue teddy bear left on the baby's grave that I can never pass without wanting to cry.

We climb silently up through the sloping plot, round the grassy bend behind the trees, to where my mother lies buried.

Tris stops dead at the corner. 'Eleanor.'

I look at him, still hanging on his arm. 'What now?' I tease him, amused by his expression. 'Ready to confess it was you all along?'

He meets my eyes. 'Eleanor,' he repeats hoarsely, then points towards my mother's grave.

CHAPTER TWENTY-NINE

There's a woman, stretched out on her back, lying across my mother's grave.

I know at once that she's dead, and not least because I've seen her before, lying in the woods in the exact spot where the woman under that grave was strangled.

It's Number Three.

That morning she looked awkward, positioned in a ghoulish way to catch the eye, legs drawn up slightly, one arm above her head, her index finger pointing mysteriously down at the stream. Now it looks as though she lay down to sleep – and never woke up.

I stop in front of her and force myself to look at her properly this time, no flinching.

The body is partially wrapped in what looks like old sacking, but she appears to be naked beneath it. The rotting, yellowish material has fallen away in places, displaying her right shoulder and a little of her breast, plus part of her belly and thigh. Her skin underneath is dirty white with a yellowish tinge, like the sacking itself. The long, limp chestnut hair lies in clumped strands about her face and bare shoulders. She has a high forehead, a neatly upturned nose, pale lips. Too pale.

Her throat is horribly mottled though: livid white patches, then dark bruising in that only too familiar rope-burn pattern I remember from last time.

She was strangled.

For a second I'm back in those lonely woods, staring down at her body from above. Like standing above my mother's dead body. *Run, Ellie, run!* My breathing begins to quicken, my pulse hammering unpleasantly. Tiny flashes of memory flicker behind my eyes, leaving me sick and off-balance. A shadow moving behind trees in the woods. Someone watching from above. The sound of birds, calling out a warning.

The icy touch of *déja-vu* is like cold water down my spine. With an inevitable after-taste of madness.

Someone has touched up the number three in black marker pen since last time. It looks fresh but slightly smudged too. There's a faint ghost-line round the two curves of the three, I realise, as though whoever rewrote it had not quite removed all traces of the original number first, and just missed tracing it perfectly.

Tris has come to stand behind me. 'Is this the woman you saw first?'

I nod silently.

'Number Three,' he says. 'And we already found Number Two buried in the woods.' He pauses a beat. 'It's a kind of countdown. But who's Number One?'

I decide not to answer that.

There are tiny white crystals on her eyelids and slightly parted lips, as though she had breathed her last in the snowy Antarctic. That's new. I reach out and touch her one of the arms folded across her chest, not in any macabre way but to test a theory.

She's cold.

Not just chilly, as you would expect. Super-cold.

'I think she's been kept in a freezer.' I stare at the pale eyelids, the whiter-than-white cheeks. 'So he could preserve her body.'

'Until now,' Tris mutters, crouching beside me. He looks unsteady, his gaze locked on the woman's face.

I glance about at the sunlit trees, the quiet rows of headstones. 'Well, it's a good place for a dead body. It's just usually they're inside the graves, not on top of them.'

He looks at me sideways, and I hear myself apologize. 'Sorry, you're right. Not funny.' I study the dead woman again, frowning. 'Seriously though, why here?'

He hesitates. 'To make sure she's found quickly?'

'Too obvious.'

'For the shock value, then. Like you said, you expect graves here but not dead bodies. Then you come round the corner, and … *boom*.'

'That's closer to the truth, I think. It's like Sarah McGellan's body. That was about display too. But also a demonstration.'

'Of what?'

'Power. It's like he's saying, *this is what you're up against. If I can do this, I can do anything.*'

ANGELA BLACKWOOD, the headstone reads starkly, then my mother's dates of birth and death. So final, nothing you can argue with. Gold letters and numerals etched deep into black-flecked granite. LOVING WIFE TO BEN, MOTHER TO ELEANOR. He wanted me to see this, to show me how personal it is. That's why he left her here. To make a point. TAKEN TOO SOON. MUCH MISSED.

I look at the line of young silver birches dancing in the breeze, slim-trunked, still ringed with tags from their planting, that separate this higher part of the plot from the rest. The grass banks around us are neat and even, recently mown. I turn my head, looking around, ninety degrees. At our backs is thick hedgerow and fields beyond that, rough stony grassland stretching into woods where the ground gets too steep and wild to be farmed. It's a peaceful part of the churchyard, but a lonely one too.

'Whoever the killer is, he knows me. Maybe knew my mother too.' I look back at the headstone. 'He wanted me to be the one to find her. To get the full effect. But how could he be sure no one else would find her first and spoil his surprise? I used to put fresh flowers on her grave every Sunday, but I stopped after university.'

'Maybe it was guesswork. A sheer gamble. Maybe he had a hunch you'd be at the memorial service for Sarah McGellan today, so took a chance on the likelihood of you walking up to visit your mum's grave.'

I nod, feeling vaguely guilty. How long has it been since I last brought flowers for Mum's grave? I had intended to buy a nice bunch of flowers and bring them up here on the anniversary of her death. But of course everything had gone wrong that day, starting with the discovery of a dead body in the woods.

'So he's a gambler. Or was leaving me a message, knowing she would be found sooner or later. Whatever the reason, he chose this place, *this grave*, deliberately.'

'So disrespectful though. A slap in the face.'

'This is a killer we're talking about, Tris. I don't think he's concerned about social etiquette. Though I agree it's personal this time, and most definitely aimed at me.' I study the body, impressed by my own calm. It's almost unnatural. Perhaps I should be working in a mortuary, not physical education. 'Not an insult though. She's too carefully arranged for that. And her body's partially covered. If he'd wanted to be really offensive … '

A sudden thought strikes me. 'We must tell DI Powell,' I say quickly, 'before he leaves for the station.'

'I'll run down and see if I can catch him.' Tris straightens, then hesitates. He puts a hand on my shoulder. 'Sure you'll be alright on your own?'

'I'm not taking my eyes off her again. Last time I did that, she disappeared and nobody believed I'd even seen her. I owe it to this woman to stay put this time.'

Tris squeezes my shoulder. 'I'll be right back.'

As soon as he's out of sight, I realise that I may have made a mistake. The silver birches are moving uneasily in the breeze, the dancing flutter of their green leaves a distraction as I scan the rest of the plot, looking for movement, anything out of place. Worse still, as the breeze strengthens, the thick hedgerow of beech and hawthorn starts making a scraping sound like a bad violinist. Or a gate with a squeaky hinge. I listen to the eerie sound, kneeling beside the dead body. The sun has gone in and it's suddenly cool up here on the exposed hillside.

The loose sacking flaps back at a sudden gust, revealing her right breast. Something glitters on her nipple. Make-up? Fine sand?

I should probably drag the old sacking back into place, cover her up. Her body is naked underneath it, after all, and it doesn't seem right to leave her exposed like this.

I stand up, rubbing a hand over my eyes, and turn round, looking away from her body.

It's the wrong thing to do. He was waiting for me to do that. Gambling on it, in fact.

I gasp and jerk back like I've been electrocuted. I don't believe it. I stare at the overgrown thicket of beech and hawthorn some fifteen or twenty feet away, a boundary hedge between the cemetery plot and the field beyond, and realise I have not imagined that sensation of being watched.

There's a face among the leaves.

I don't move, staring.

The eyes move, a definite pale flicker among the vivid green leaves.

Someone is watching me from behind the hedge.

'Eleanor?'

I spin violently at the sound of my name. Footsteps thud heavily across the grass plot. I see legs first, black suit trousers and polished shoes, flickering fast through the row of silver birches in full leaf. Like one of those

Victorian cinematic toys, one frame at a time, the light flashing as the images revolve. Then someone comes running round the corner of the trees, holding down his tie to stop it flapping about.

It's Detective Inspector Powell, followed by one of his younger officers. His head turns from side to side, checking the site, looking for me.

I call his name. He sees me, raises a hand, then looks past me at my mother's grave.

Powell slows at the sight of the dead body covered in sacking, his expression incredulous and horrified. 'Oh God, not another one.'

My thoughts entirely.

I look away, pointing at the gloomy hedgerow still shivering and creaking behind me. My finger finds the exact spot where I saw the face. Except I can no longer see that pale flicker of eyes through the leaves.

'What is it?' Powell asks, following my pointing finger.

'I thought I saw ... '

At that moment, the sun comes out again, lighting up this side of the cemetery. There's nobody there now. The hedgerow is dark green ivy and beech trees decked in glossy new leaves. Light-coloured buds on the narrow, interwoven branches. Late hawthorn blossom gleaming in the sun, a cluster of spiny twigs creaking as they scrape harmlessly against each other. No face though. No watching killer.

I want to tell him about the face among the leaves, but I'm uncertain now. This man already thinks I'm crazy.

'What did you see, Eleanor?'

He asks the question but he's on the phone at the same time, not looking at me or the hedgerow marking the boundary of the cemetery plot.

'Damn signal,' he mutters, then nods at the young police officer, who's halted on the grass and is staring ashen-faced at the dead body. 'Get on the radio, would you?' Powell tells him, impatient but not unkind. 'Let them know down at Headquarters that we need forensics up here with their kit. Plus any other bodies that can be spared, the whole works. And don't let anyone just wander in before they can arrive and secure the site. This is a murder scene now. Quick about it, constable.'

I walk away a few yards, then sit down on one of the newer headstones, keeping my back to my mum's grave.

The headstone is square across the top, a block of hard white stone that cuts into the back of my thighs. My heart is racing, my chest tight, and I have to fight off waves of nausea. I know the symptoms of a panic attack and concentrate on my breathing, on staying deliberately blank.

Did I imagine that face? Those eyes, watching me through the leaves? Maybe there was no one there. Maybe it was my imagination the whole time.

I glance over my shoulder at the dead woman. DI Powell is bending over her, careful not to disturb the body.

I bury my face in my hands, breathing deep and slow.

'What did you see, Eleanor?'

I look up to find Powell standing right in front of me. How much time has passed?

'I saw someone among the bushes there, watching me. But it could have been a trick of the light.'

'Maybe.' He scrutinises the hedge, then looks back at me. 'You don't have to wait, Eleanor. We'll take it from here. But I'd like you to go straight home and stay there for the time being. Agreed?'

'Am I a suspect?'

'No, but I've just heard there's been another woman reported missing.' His voice deepens, and he meets my gaze steadily. I can tell from his face that he's genuinely worried. We go back too many years for him to hide it from me. 'I don't want you disappearing too. Got it?'

I nod.

He turns away to make a quick call on his phone, then comes back. 'One of my officers will run you home. I'll be in touch later. We'll need another statement.'

Tris appears at a run round the corner of the silver birches, breathing heavily. He sees me and Powell, and skids to a halt on the grass, then continues more slowly up the slope towards us.

I notice he's careful not to look at the dead body.

'Good, you found her,' Tris says to the inspector, who looks at him hard. Powell still suspects him of being involved, I realise.

'Where were you?' I ask.

'I stopped at the vicarage to tell Reverend Clemo. I thought he should know there's a body up here. Only he wasn't at home. His wife's not sure where he is, she's trying to reach him on his mobile.' Tris looks from me to the inspector. 'Why, has something else happened?'

I draw breath to tell him about the face in the trees, then stop and realise I can't tell him. Not this.

I don't trust him enough. Not anymore.

The realization is terrifying.

I try to figure out the maths behind my suspicion. Tris probably had just enough time to tell that young policeman where I was, then double back along the road, climb over the low wall beside the gate and slip into the field that way. It would have taken him only a few minutes to sneak round behind the hedgerow and watch me at the graveside. Though why would he do that? There's something I'm not seeing. Something important.

The sun disappears behind a cloud. I shiver again, though the breeze is not that cold. I hear the sound of a car coming briskly up the hill from the church. My ride home, probably.

'Nothing,' I say. 'Let's get out of here.'

The smell of baking assails us as we enter the cottage. Hannah has not left for work yet. She is bustling about the kitchen in a cherry-red apron covered in flour when we walk in, her hands powdery, a white smudge on her cheek.

She stares in blank disbelief when Tris explains what's happened.

'Another one? In the *cemetery*?'

I gaze out of the kitchen window while Tris tries to explain. The lovely sunshine has vanished and the sky is cloudy now, glowering down at us. It feels like it's going to pour with rain at any minute. There's a kind of prickling sixth sense you get about weather when you grow up so near the moor, where the weather can shift abruptly between rain and sunshine, sometimes managing both at the same time.

'What exactly are you making here, Hannah?' I turn to look at the floury mess on the kitchen table.

'Rock cakes.'

'They smell nice,' I tell her, glancing at the butter-smeared recipe book propped up against the scales.

'Hands off. They're for the vicarage garden party.'

I'm surprised, and stare at her. 'I didn't know you were involved with that.'

Hannah shrugs. There are specks of flour even on the lenses of her glasses, I realise. It must be like seeing the world through a snow storm. 'Mrs Clemo came round the other day. It's for a good cause. The shelter in town for battered women may have to close. Spending cuts, you know.' She wipes her floury hands on a dishcloth. 'They asked for donations of cakes, but I can't bake anything worth eating except for rock cakes. So I promised them two dozen.'

I see Tris out of the corner of my eye, waiting silently by the door, his impatience palpable. 'So, you're working tonight?' I ask Hannah, keeping my tone innocent.

'On my way out as soon as these little beauties in the oven are done. It's my second batch,' she explains, and whisks a cloth off a baking tray to exhibit a dozen perfect-looking rock cakes.

'They look amazing,' I say truthfully.

Hannah smiles, then gazes from me to Tris. At last the

penny drops. I see a faint flush come into her cheeks. 'It won't be long now,' she says, checking the wall clock in some confusion. 'Ten minutes max. Then I'll be out of your way.'

'No hurry,' I say lightly, and nod Tris to follow me out of the kitchen. 'Have a good shift, Hannah. See you in the morning.'

My black leather shoes are pinching. I kick them off in the hall and scoop up the phone handset in passing, just in case I get a call on the landline later from DI Powell. I don't fancy the idea of having to stop and run downstairs for the phone when I might be more interestingly occupied.

Tris crooks an eyebrow as we tramp upstairs. '*Rock* cakes?' he says under his breath. 'They don't sound very promising.'

'Don't be rude. Can you bake a cake?'

'I've never tried,' he admits.

'Well, then.'

'I can make a loaf of bread though.'

I glance at him, impressed. 'White bread?'

'Wholemeal.'

'Better and better.' I kick open my bedroom door. He's been in there before, of course, many times. But not recently. And not when we're both in a horny mood. 'Tired?'

'No.'

'Me neither.'

The bed is a mess. Nothing on the scale of his bedroom, though. 'Sorry, hang on.' I throw my phone charger to one side, chuck my black and white-striped tracksuit bottoms into the wardrobe, and shake out the duvet.

There's a sudden rushing noise outside, like a heavy vehicle passing. But it's not traffic, it's rain. Sudden, heavy, thunderous rain.

I straighten, listening.

Tris is standing by the window. Right where the shadow man stands in my nightmares. I stay beside the bed and look at him for a moment in silence, studying his profile. The sky behind him is almost black. To the far right I can see the edge of the lane that leads to the village, and beyond it the dark swelling crests of trees across the valley. The beginnings of the woods.

I've always thought of the woods as a separate world, a secret territory hidden away from the bustle of village life, the passing tractors, the cyclists stopping to admire the church tower, the neighbours mowing their lawns in summer or chatting over fences. The woods are a place where dark things happen, where I'm never quite safe. Though I've challenged that fantasy a thousand times, running along the woodland paths unaccompanied, refusing to let the past devour me.

But today, when I saw that dead body lying across my mother's grave, I knew the two worlds had finally collided. The world of the village and the world of the woods had smashed into each other at that instant with a terrible, silent explosion. It was as though the underworld had opened its dark gates, and someone had carried the dead woman through them and straight up into the land of the living.

For me to find.

CHAPTER THIRTY

'Eleanor?'

I don't realise he's moved until Tris reaches out and strokes my cheek with a finger, breaking the spell of the underworld. The caress is so unexpected, I almost flinch and catch myself just in time.

'You still think I've got something to do with these murders,' he says broodingly, 'don't you?'

Silently, I shake my head. But we've been friends a long time and he can read me better than that.

'I hate that you suspect me.'

'Sorry,' I whisper.

His gaze searches my face. 'No, you're not. It gives you a perfect excuse to keep me at arms' length.'

'Is that what I'm doing?'

Deliberately, I reach out and place a hand on his chest.

Tris catches his breath. I feel his chest rise with the sudden influx of air into his lungs. His eyes widen, the dark pupils dilating. The classic sign of sexual desire. Then he leans forward and I close my eyes instinctively, not quite believing he intends to kiss me, and am shocked when our lips meet.

It's not like that time when he kissed me in the club at

Newquay. That was an abrupt, unhappy, three-second embrace, a rejection of tenderness. This is a slow, tentative exploration for both of us, and I sense he's ready to draw back if I show even the slightest hesitation. But I don't. The gentle pressure deepens until we're kissing open-mouthed, his tongue sliding against mine.

I know he is strong. This is a man who works out by lifting sheep over his shoulders and carrying them across three fields. His body is built for strength and stamina, with his broad chest and muscular thighs, the effortless power of his biceps. But I had not realized until this moment how graceful Tristan is.

Midway through the kiss he slips an arm about my waist, as though to draw me closer, but instead wrong-foots me, supporting my weight over the crook of his arm, and lowers me to the bed.

I wrestle with his shirt buttons, and he focuses on mine, a look of fierce concentration on his face. Then his bare chest is under my fingers, strong and dark-haired. I stroke him, and then gasp when he drags my shirt off my shoulders, reaches round the back to unclasp my bra and release my breasts, and lowers his head to my nipple.

'Yes,' I say hoarsely.

I arch my back, enjoying his ministrations, then decide to take the initiative. In one smooth movement, I roll over to straddle him. I hug his hips tight with both knees, smiling as I keep him pinned down and bend to taste his nipples too, just as he tasted mine. He makes an incoherent sound in the back of his throat.

'What?' I tease him, flicking his nipple with my tongue. God, he tastes good. 'You like this? You want more?'

He bites his lower lip. I see a bead of blood there. 'Lower,' he says, daring me to take it further.

The hint of danger excites me. He could be a killer. And I'm about to have sex with him. I'm not scared though. Adrenalin has already kicked in, pumping heat and energy around my body like a shot of neat Russian vodka.

Plus, there's this odd, familiarity-versus-alien territory thing going on with us. I know this man so well, his face, his hands, his laugh, his quick, sharp breaths as I kiss his throat. But I don't know him at all really, because he is also this secret Tris, the man I don't know about, the one who keeps stolen photographs of me in his room ...

He jerks me across him, trying to get back on top, and I retaliate at once, flexing my muscles to resist him. We wrestle for a moment, sweaty and breathless, then end up on the floor with a thud, face-to-face, our legs tangled together, our arms about each other.

'Ouch,' he says, grimacing.

'Sorry. But I prefer being on top.'

'So do I.'

'Looks like we have a problem, then.'

'Not necessarily.' He kisses my throat. 'We'll just keep changing ends. Like a tennis match.'

I laugh.

'Come here,' he says breathlessly, and tugs me towards him. 'I need to fuck you.'

'Ditto.' I take his mouth, my kiss deep and urgent. He groans, and his hands find my skirt, drag it up, reach beneath, stroking me.

My head feels like it is going to explode. 'Baby, yes.'

It takes us a few frustrating moments to get his trousers unzipped and off his body; he has to help me, kicking his trousers away with growing impatience. To my excitement, he is extremely well-equipped, though this is not surprising, given his powerful build. Oh God, I keep thinking, touching him with my mouth open. Oh God, oh God.

'Condom,' he mutters.

'Don't you have one?'

He stares at me. 'At a memorial service?'

I shift onto hands and knees, and turn, scrabbling in the top drawer of my bedside cabinet. To my relief, the packet is still there, pushed right to the back. I haven't exactly been enjoying a great sex life since university.

'Here.'

Tris sits on the edge of the unmade bed, flushed and intent. I peel off my black skirt and thong, then kneel beside him. We kiss frantically, collapsing against the pillows. I'm half out of my mind with need before he's inside me.

The rain keeps falling hard, a dark curtain beating against my window in grim counterpoint to our rhythm. I think about Sarah McGellan's memorial service, the wreaths and lilies below her photograph, how the proximity of death seems to make us crave sex more keenly.

I clutch at his broad shoulders, wrap my legs greedily about his hips, pressing down on his buttocks, dragging him closer. The bed creaks noisily, shifting back and forth on the old floorboards, and I find myself hoping that Hannah has left for work by now, that she's not staring wide-eyed at the kitchen ceiling.

Then he kisses me, his naked body large and strong, thrusting hard against me, and I lose all coherent thought.

We make love twice more over the next few hours, hungry to taste more of each other's flesh, and are lying together sated and exhausted in the semi-darkness of a late dusk when the landline handset rings. Its screen lights up, illuminating the room with an eerie green light, as it buzzes on top of the bedside cabinet.

Not quite awake, I stretch an arm out of bed to retrieve the phone, and then grope for the right button to answer the call.

'Hello?'

It's DI Powell. He sounds urgent. 'Eleanor? I've been trying to reach your mobile for ages. I've left messages ...'

Tris is lying next to me in bed, listening. I see the gleam of his eyes in the dark. 'What?' I sit up against the pillows, frowning. It takes a few seconds for the inspector's words to sink in. 'My mobile's still in my bag downstairs. I'm in my bedroom, I didn't hear it ringing. Is this about the witness statement?'

'Sorry, were you sleeping? Did I wake you? Look, we can take your statement tomorrow, Eleanor. That's not important right now. I just wanted to make sure you were safe at home and everything was okay.'

There's something in his tone. Like he's withholding information.

'Why? What's happened?'

'Nothing you can help us with. You get a good night's sleep, okay? I'm going to send over an officer to sit outside your cottage overnight, if that's agreeable.'

'It's fine,' I say, though I am immediately uneasy about the idea of being watched in my own home. 'What about the woman in the cemetery? Do we know who she is yet?' I try not to think of her as victim Number Three, though the number on her forehead is hard to forget.

'We've spoken to her next of kin, so I suppose I can tell you her name. It turns out she was on our list of missing persons. From Bodmin, so quite local. Dawn Trevian.' He pauses. 'Does that name ring a bell?'

'Sorry, no.'

He sounds disappointed. 'Well, it was worth asking. I'll send that police car round straightaway.'

'I thought you said it would be a last resort, sending an officer to watch the house.'

The inspector hesitates, and I hear hesitation in his voice again. 'We may be getting there, I'm afraid. This new missing person report ... It's not looking good. Another local woman. Though I don't want you to worry about it. In most cases of missing persons, there's a perfectly simple explanation. She'll probably turn up tomorrow and be embarrassed about all the fuss.'

Some sixth sense prickles at me. I stare into the glimmering darkness uneasily. I remember being surprised not to see Jenny at the memorial service, though her parents were there and she had told me herself that she would make the effort.

Beside me, Tris struggles up onto one elbow. He leans across me to check the LED display on my digital clock. I glance that way too, automatically. It's just after ten o'clock. His hand brushes my breast, and I meet his gaze.

'Is it Jenny Crofter?' I ask.

DI Powell does not bother to deny it. 'How did you know?'

'A hunch.'

'Another one of your hunches.' He sighs, sounding deflated. 'Yes, I'm afraid so, it's Jenny Crofter. She went out early yesterday evening but didn't come home again, and didn't call to explain why. Which is highly unusual behaviour, according to her parents.'

I remember what Jenny told me about her girlfriend, that they rarely get a chance to be together. 'Maybe she went to a friend's house for the night.'

'Eleanor, I know Jenny is a good friend of yours as well as a colleague. But I think you need to prepare yourself for the worst.'

'What do you mean?'

'Her Renault was found in the upper car park at Eastlyn Woods late this morning. The ticket on her windscreen showed she had paid for an hour's parking yesterday afternoon, at just before five o'clock.'

'She went for a run in the woods,' I whisper.

'It looks like it, yes.'

CHAPTER THIRTY-ONE

Once Tris has gone home to the farm, which he insists on doing when he hears a police car may be heading our way, I take a long, cool shower and put on a pair of white cotton pyjamas, then head downstairs again barefoot. I peer out through the front door, and see the blurry shape of a car in the turning area, lights off, a darker shadow in the driver's seat. My guardian officer for the night, presumably.

I would have preferred Tris to stay the night. His warm body lying next to mine in bed would have been a greater comfort than this anonymous sentinel at my door. But I suppose he did not like the idea of being seen creeping away from my cottage at first light, and I can hardly blame him.

It's nearly midnight but my fatigue has dropped away in another wave of adrenalin. My head is processing what has happened, but not to any useful end, chugging noisily round and round the same territory, like a circular train track. I sit in the kitchen under the glare of the ceiling spot lights, nursing a mug of tea until it goes cold between my hands.

Why on earth would Jenny have gone running in

Eastlyn Woods so soon after our gruesome discovery there? She knew better than most how dangerous it could be.

I am bewildered that she would even have made such a stupid decision in the first place. Then I am angry. I push my cold tea away in disgust. What the hell had Jenny been thinking? Hadn't she listened to a word I said? And all those lurid, sensationalist stories in the national papers about a strangler preying on women in Cornwall … Had those warnings failed to register on her blinkered, athletics-mad brain, the brain of a woman who was intent on getting to a peak of fitness so she could take part in a triathlon, so she could push herself to the limit?

My eye falls on the white edge of a piece of paper across the kitchen. Something propped up behind the large black pepper pot.

Connor's note.

I stare at it blankly for a moment, then get up to retrieve it.

Come and see me. We need to talk. C.

I turn it over in my hand, thinking. Hannah must have tidied it away. Connor had wanted to talk to me, but when I went over to the farm, he had gone out to fetch Tris home from the police station. Then I had broken into the farm, and fled out the window when they got back, and since then I had not seen had a chance to speak to Connor. He was always busy with the farm, of course. He took his responsibilities there very seriously, more so than Tris. But he must have wanted to speak to me alone at some point.

Perhaps he had only wanted to warn me off seeing Tris. That was never going to happen though, especially now that we had slept together. But he was probably still worried about where our friendship might be headed. And our joint discovery of another dead body won't have helped him feel more at ease with it.

I fish for my mobile in my bag. Seven missed calls. Five

of them from DI Powell. Two from Connor, one only an hour ago. I would have been in the shower when he called.

I text him. *Sorry I missed your call. Too late, or do you still want to talk?*

I rinse out my mug and set it to dry on the draining board, tidy away a few things from yesterday's breakfast that I had forgotten about, and glance idly through the cupboard labelled ELLIE. I have not been shopping much lately, and the food cupboards are pretty bare. My stomach rumbles, and I realise that I haven't eaten for well over twelve hours. Tins of soup and beans, some old sesame seed crackers, a packet of jelly. There's not much to tempt me except Hannah's latest batch of rock cakes, left to cool on the side and covered with a dishcloth to prevent them from going stale.

I lift the edge of the cloth and breathe in the delicious cakey aroma, then reluctantly drop it again and force myself to nibble on a sesame seed cracker instead. She will go mad if she comes home to find I've eaten even one of her cakes for the garden party fundraiser. Though perhaps if I were to leave some money for the charity in its place …

My mobile buzzes. I walk over and look down at the screen.

Sorry, just off to bed. How about tomorrow? Lunch at The Green Man, 12pm. Just you and me.

I reply, *See you there.*

In the silence that follows, I finish eating my cracker and stand there, weighing the mobile in my hand. Should I call Tris? It's nearly one in the morning now, but he might still be awake. I could wish him good night.

Only he hasn't called me, has he? Not even a quick text message to say, 'Goodnight,' or 'Sweet dreams,' or even, 'Thinking of you.'

That may mean nothing, of course. It may mean I wore the big man out with hours of rampant, energetic sex, and an exhausted Tris has turned his phone off and crawled into bed. But it could also mean he's sitting there right now, a cold beer in his hand and his brother Connor by his side, in the untidy living room of their farmhouse, the two inseparable Taylor brothers, scrolling through my text messages and laughing over how easy it was to get the mad girl into bed.

I flick back to Connor's message and study it a moment before turning off the phone for the night. *Just you and me.*

I sleep late that morning, my body heavy and relaxed after a long and emotional day. By the time I have washed, dressed, and hurried downstairs, it is gone half past eleven and soon I'll be running late for my lunch date with Connor.

There's no time for breakfast, so I down a glass of tap water instead and brush my bed-hair in front of the glass door of the microwave. I am not bothering with make-up. I rarely do, I hate the way it makes my skin feel clogged up. I find a lipstick in my bag though and apply it carefully, then blot my lips with kitchen paper.

'You'll do,' I tell my blurred reflection. It's only Connor, after all.

I wonder if Connor knows about me and Tris yet. He might be jealous, after all. I know he used to hold a torch for me when we were in school, and we have dated a few times, though our relationship never got beyond kisses and cuddles. I suppose I always preferred Tris, deep down, and perhaps his brother could sense that even before I was aware of it myself.

Before leaving, I run back upstairs to look in on Hannah, who is still awake and watching television in her bedroom. She must have showered while I was asleep because her hair looks damp. She picks up the remote when I come in, and mutes the telly.

'How are you?' she asks, looking up at me with obvious concern. 'I saw the police car outside when I got home from work. I have to say, it freaked me out a bit. I thought something had happened to you.'

'Sorry, my fault. I should have called to warn you. The inspector thinks I may be in danger, so there'll probably be a police car parked outside at night from now on. Until the killer's caught, anyway.' I pause. 'Did you hear about Jenny Crofter?'

She nods, her expression appalled. 'It was on the local news earlier. The police are appealing for information. Poor Jenny. Though it's so strange, isn't it? I don't understand what she was doing in Eastlyn Woods at all. I wouldn't go near there if you paid me.'

'Neither would I. She should have known better.' I check the time on my phone. 'Look, I'm going out for a while. Are you working again tonight?'

'For my sins, yes.' She looks me up and down, and smiles. I'm in black jeans and a red strappy top that clings rather too tightly, but is the only clean item of clothing I could find today that didn't need ironing. 'Meeting Tris for a date? You two looked good together yesterday.'

I hesitate, a little embarrassed. How much did she hear before leaving for work last night? There would probably have been a tremendous thud on the ceiling when we fell out of bed ...

'Just going to the pub.' I don't mention Connor. She would only leap to the wrong conclusion.

'Well, have a nice time. I'm off to the vicarage garden party soon with my rock cakes. Will you be taking that policeman with you too?'

I stare. 'I'd forgotten about him. How annoying. I bet he'll want to follow me to the pub.'

'So give him the slip,' she says, shrugging. 'You can always go out the back door.'

I laugh, but go back downstairs more slowly than I went up, thinking hard. That is not such a bad idea.

I hit Connor's number on my favourites list. He answers on the second ring, like he's been waiting for me to call. 'You're late,' he says.

'Yeah, sorry, I overslept.' I stand in the narrow hallway, looking out at the police car still parked in the turning area of the cottage. 'Look, can we skip lunch at the Green Man? Maybe go somewhere else instead?'

'But I've reserved a table.'

'I'm sorry,' I say again, trying to placate him. He sounds annoyed, and small wonder. I hate it when people switch plans on me last minute. 'The place will be packed with locals for Sunday lunch, and I'm not in the mood for meeting villagers. Everyone will want to ask me about the body in the cemetery, and what the police think … I just can't face all the questions, I'm really sorry.'

He pauses a beat. 'Of course you can't. Stupid of me not to think of that before. I'll come and pick you up. We can drive over to Blisland. They do good Sunday lunches there. Or up to Jamaica Inn. It'll do you good to get away from the village for a few hours, anyway.'

'Don't come to the house.' I grin, a little self-conscious. 'I have a shadow I'm trying to shake.'

'The police?'

'You're quick. Yes, the police are staking out the cottage. It's driving me mad. I feel like a beetle in a jar.'

'Tris told me. And about Jenny too. I'm very sorry, I know she's a close friend of yours. But I'm sure she'll turn up safe and sound. You shouldn't worry.'

'I'm trying not to,' I agree, watching as the police officer gets out of his car. What is he doing? 'Hang on a tick.'

But the policeman merely performs some stretching exercises, linking his hands behind his back and yawning copiously, before climbing back into the car.

'Trouble?' Connor asks in my ear.

'No, false alarm.'

I try not to consider what, 'Tris told me,' means, but it nags at me. Told him what, exactly? That we slept together last night? Part of me is worried that it's the stupidest thing I've ever done. Sleeping with the enemy. Or a potential killer. And I already know that Connor will not approve of that development. I'm not right in the head, he said so himself, and will only cause trouble for his little brother.

Which is no doubt what he wants to talk to me about.

'Can you pick me up on the lane to the village? I'll be waiting where the path comes out between the ford and the sharp right-hand bend.'

'No problem. How long?'

'Fifteen minutes?'

'I'll be there in ten.' Connor sounds amused by the subterfuge. 'Don't get caught.'

I enjoy my hurried jog across the back fields to avoid having to explain my outing to the police officer, and find Connor's clapped-out old car waiting for me when I drop down from the fields onto the lane.

Connor leans over to open the door for me. I climb in, and glance at his face. I'm not sure what I expected. Tension, perhaps. Hostility. But his easy smile reassures me.

'I take it the cops aren't five minutes behind you?'

'I doubt my guardian even knows I've left.'

Connor looks at me sideways, his expression curious. 'Not worried to be out on your own and unprotected? From what Tris told me, you seem to be his main target.'

'Whoever the killer is, if he had wanted to kill me, he would have done it that first day in the woods. Right where he killed my mother. Besides, I can't stand being watched twenty-four seven. It's like being in prison.'

He stares. 'You think it's the same man who killed your mother? But that was years ago. He would be an old man by now.'

'Or he could have been a young man when he killed my mother, and middle-aged now.'

Connor nods slowly. 'Yes. I hadn't thought of that.'

'So where are you taking me?'

He laughs, and starts the engine. We splash through the

ford at the bottom of the hill, then climb steeply up the other side towards the A30. It's another warm day, but rain is never far away on the moors and I can already see dark clouds moving in from the east. Everything looks damp after yesterday's rain, the hedgerows washed clean and sparkling, the lane damp with puddles and tyre tracks.

'I thought Jamaica Inn,' he says comfortably.

'Okay.'

He glances at me. 'You don't sound keen.'

'Bad memories of a childhood visit, that's all. It won't stop me enjoying their steak and kidney pudding and chips. I'm starving.'

'My dad used to take us there all the time when we were lads,' Connor admits, looking ahead as the road narrows towards the summit. 'My mum hated it too, funnily enough. They had a museum of curiosities. We would go in to look at the exhibits while she sat outside in the courtyard and had a coffee.'

I think of the hidden room in the farmhouse. The stuffed animals I saw. The weasel with its bared teeth.

'Yeah, I remember that place. I never liked it either.'

Connor makes a face. 'Each to their own, I guess.' He hesitates, and his hands tighten on the wheel. 'The police came round early this morning to speak to us. They took Tris to the police station.'

I'm stunned, and do not know what to say at first. Then I manage, 'But why?'

'The woman whose body you found in the cemetery,' he tells me, 'it turns out she was a dental assistant in town. Tris knew her. In fact, he'd been to that dentist's surgery a few times and spoken to her.'

'*Spoken* to her?'

'Chatted her up. You know what he's like.'

No, I don't.

I fold my hands in my lap and digest that information. Dawn Trevian: that was what the inspector had called her. And Tristan knew her. I think back to the moment he saw her, remember his stiffness, the appalled shock on his face. Had it been more than shock, though? Had it been recognition?

So why had he not said something?

Because he killed her, a little voice whispers in my head, and it's hard to dismiss it as nonsense. Yet what other reason could there be to lie?

I am unsure what I feel in response to this revelation. Cold. Numb. Disillusioned, perhaps. But not surprised.

Connor studies my expression, then says reassuringly, 'Look, I had a call from DS Carrick while I was waiting for you at the pub. He told me Tris isn't under arrest. They're just waiting for DI Powell to get a chance to question him. Apparently the inspector was over at the mortuary in Truro most of this morning.'

I shudder, but am relieved to know Tris is not under arrest. The police cannot have any evidence against him, or I feel sure they would have charged him by now. I know how much pressure the inspector must be under to get a quick result on these killings at Eastlyn.

'And Sarah McGellan?' I ask abruptly. 'The other victim. The one buried in the woods.'

He stares. 'You think Tris knew her too?'

'Is that possible?'

The A30 is not too busy, considering that the summer season is nearly here. Connor glances automatically in his mirror before overtaking the car ahead of us. Rain is starting to fall now, drenching the hedgerows, pattering loudly on the car roof and the broken side window covered in plastic.

'Strictly between friends, yes, it is *possible*,' he admits, reluctance in his voice. 'I didn't tell the police this, so please don't repeat it or you'll get me into trouble. But we went surfing up at Widemouth Bay a few times the week Sarah McGellan disappeared, to catch the last big tides of the spring. I wasn't with him the whole time. How could I be? You know how Tris likes to go clubbing after a day on the beach. I dropped him off at Newquay several times, and once at least he didn't come home until late the next morning. Maybe more than once, I can't recall.'

What is Connor suggesting? That his brother spent that night in someone's bed? Maybe even the dead woman's bed?

It doesn't sound like Tris. But then, how well do I really know him?

I went out clubbing with Tris and Connor when I came back from university last summer, and with Hannah too. I remember Tris liked to dance with the holidaymakers as well as the local girls, and even scored a few times at the end of the night. Connor tended to hang back more those nights, talk to me and Hannah, dance with us. It was always Tris who was on the prowl, never his brother.

And I recall how annoyed he was that Connor wanted to go home that night I met up with them in the club in Newquay. Furious, actually.

'Tris could have met Sarah McGellan when he was surfing. The woman was a surf instructor, she was always on the beaches. Or at Newquay, in one of the night clubs there.' He glances at me as though he can read my mind. 'Hey, I know what you're thinking because I've thought it myself, many times since this started. But Tris claims he didn't know Sarah and I'd rather believe that. He's my kid brother.'

I know what you're thinking because I've thought it myself.

I feel cold. My brain is working slowly, struggling to keep up with what he's saying about the man who made love to me last night.

'But whoever killed those women has access to a car or a van. They must have done.'

'True.'

'So it couldn't be Tris. He doesn't drive. He doesn't even have a licence.'

'Also true. Though that's never stopped him.' Connor grins. 'He rides that bloody quad bike all over the farm, and up and down lanes like a maniac. You know that as well as anyone. And of course he's taken the van out without permission a few times.'

'The van?'

'My dad's van. It's untaxed, and a rusting old heap, frankly. But I've not had the heart to get it scrapped yet.' He stares out at the dark clouds. 'It's as though, while the van's still here, so is Dad.'

I remember his dad's ancient van. But when I visited Connor's farm, there was no sign of a van in the yard, and the only mechanical thing in that cobweb-festooned garage was a lawnmower.

'I've not seen that van in over a year.'

'I keep it parked down at the mill. You don't have to tax a vehicle that's not kept on a public road.'

'Dick Laney mentioned that place to me. He says you're thinking of renovating it?'

'Oh, the house is totally derelict. Most of it is boarded up. But I'm hoping to make a start on the renovations, at least, then maybe sell it to some rich Londoner looking for a second home in Cornwall. Make my fortune.'

'Sounds like a good idea.'

Connor glances at me. 'Perhaps you could come down and see it one day, help out with the renovations. There used to be a rose garden at the back. It could do with a make-over.'

'I'm not very green-fingered.'

'Well, you could just visit. Watch me work.'

I hear something behind his words, some kind of emotional resonance that lingers in the silence like the after-echo of a guitar string vibrating. I realise he means more than just a quick visit from a friend. Alarm bells ring. He's already asked me out a few times, and I know he's hoping for more than a kiss at the end of the night.

I like Connor. He's attractive and charming, and he reminds me of Tris. We have history too. There are no secrets between us. But ...

'Yeah, maybe. When this term ends,' I agree, hoping he will not read too much into my acceptance, 'I'll bring some gardening gloves and a trowel, dig up your weeds.'

'That would be great.'

Connor smiles across at me, and I can see he's really happy with that. His fingers tap on the top of the wheel.

'And you're right,' he adds. 'It's ridiculous to think Tris might have anything to do with these dead women. He gets upset when the lambs are taken to the abattoir, for God's sake. No, if you ask me, the police are looking in completely the wrong place.'

'So who do you think killed those women?'

CHAPTER THIRTY-TWO

'I'm not a detective,' Connor says sharply, seeming surprised by my question. 'I don't have a clue who killed them. Do you?'

'Not really.'

'You see? It could be anyone.'

I think of Reverend Clemo watching me and Tris out of the vicarage window, and his strange looks whenever he sees me lately. 'Even the vicar?'

He laughs humourlessly. 'Why not? Yes, it could be the vicar for all we know. Though I suppose we can't blame the poor sod for having a dead body in his cemetery. More's the pity.'

He signals to turn off the road and up the hill towards the remote, grey stone village of Bolventor and Jamaica Inn. The rain lets up long enough for us to cross the cobbled yard from the car park into the quaint, old-fashioned bar area.

The place is busy but not packed. The clouds have kept most people on the A30 perhaps, in hope of better weather further into Cornwall. After we have each enjoyed a plate of roast beef in gravy and all the trimmings from the Sunday carvery, Connor goes to the bar to order two coffees and I wander about the old inn, studying the pictures and posters on the wall. It's an eighteen century coaching inn, made famous by the novelist Daphne du Maurier, who set her story about Cornish smugglers here and named the novel after the inn.

I stop, staring down at the brass plaque set into the floor of the bar. *On this spot Joss Merlyn was murdered.* One of the fictional characters from du Maurier's novel. I think of my mother, strangled in Eastlyn Woods, and walk back to our table.

'Your coffee, my lady.' Connor puts my cup and saucer down, then slides into the seat opposite. He checks his phone, and frowns. 'Still nothing from Tris. Those bastards. They can't have finished talking to him yet.'

'Taking their time,' I agree.

'Hey, don't worry, everything's going to be all right,' he insists, laying his hand briefly over mine, and his smile almost convinces me.

I taste the coffee. It's delicious, just the right blend of the smooth with the rich. 'So,' I say, setting the cup back into the saucer, 'what did you want to talk to me about? Something about Tris, I presume, since you wanted to see me alone.'

'Yes, I can't dodge the bullet any longer, can I?' He laughs uneasily. 'Here's the thing. I want you to back off from Tris.'

I stare. 'I'm sorry?'

'I know you two spent the night together. But even before that, I could see him getting close to you. I mean, he and you have always been best friends, even when we were at school. But now, it's becoming something else. Something deeper.' He shrugs, looking up at me from his coffee. 'I don't want to see him hurt, Ellie.'

'And I'm going to hurt him how?'

'By losing interest. By dropping him after a few dates. By going away.' He holds my astonished gaze. 'That's what you do, Ellie. You hook people in, you make them care, and then you just … fuck off.'

'I've never *fucked off*,' I repeat angrily.

'Keep it down.' He glances round at the other people in the bar, but no one is looking our way. He lowers his own voice. 'You went to university.'

'Don't most people?'

'Not me. I didn't go to university. Neither did Tris. I know he wanted to go, yes, but it was you who put that idea in his head. Before you went away to get a degree, he was happy to be a farmer his whole life, like our dad. But after you went away, it was always, *I could go to college too, I could get a degree.*' He shakes his head. 'But of course it was impossible. There was always the farm to think about, and then Dad got sick. We couldn't spare the money, and I certainly couldn't spare Tris. In the end, we had to have a serious talk about it, and I showed him our accounts. Then he stopped talking about university. But I could see that it was eating away at him. The resentment of having to stay behind. Of losing you.'

'Tris hasn't lost me,' I say, bewildered. 'I've come back to Eastlyn, haven't I?'

'But for how long?'

'Maybe forever, I don't know. My dad's here – '

'And when he dies?'

I shake my head in disbelief. 'Seriously, what kind of question is that? This is out of order, Connor.' I stand up. 'I think you should drive me back home.'

'Sit down, I haven't finished.'

I hate the tension in his voice. But people are staring openly now, and that makes me uncomfortable. I've had people stare at me most of my life, and it never gets easier.

Besides, I don't think he's said what he came here to say yet.

I sit down again. But I'm not happy, and I don't care if he knows it. My tone is aggressive. 'So you want me to stop seeing Tris?'

Connor nods, leaning back in his seat, his gaze steady

on my face. 'I know you probably think me a monster for asking this, but that's only because you don't know Tris like I do. He's not the man you think he is.'

'In what way?'

'You think he's strong. Hardy. Like one of these plants that will grow anywhere, however cold the wind blows.' He shakes his head. 'He's not. He's fragile. He's damaged goods, Ellie, and this game you're playing is going to break him. I know the signs, I can see where this is leading.'

'I'm not playing any game.'

'He told me about the photograph.' He leans forward abruptly. 'About you breaking into our house.'

Fuck.

I can feel heat in my cheeks. 'I'm sorry about that. I can explain.'

'You don't need to. You fancy yourself as a detective. Looking for clues, the girl in the deerstalker, one step ahead of the police. They searched the farm this morning, did I mention that? The whole house, attic to cellar, and all the outbuildings and fields. Yes, you may well stare. But that's the price of being friends with Eleanor Blackwood.'

'That's hardly fair,' I exclaim, shocked by what I'm hearing, but he is no longer listening.

'They didn't find anything, of course, because there is nothing to find there. But you are going to back off now. No more lying and trying to get close to Tris. Because I know what your agenda is with him. And it's not a relationship.' He pushes his coffee cup away, his voice sinking to a whisper. 'When he was in the hospice, dying of cancer, I promised my dad that I would look after Tris when he had gone. And I plan on keeping that promise, whatever it takes.'

I meet his gaze, struggling to understand what this warning is about. 'You … you think Tris killed those women, don't you?'

'Christ.' Connor sits back, closing his eyes. His hand on the table top clenches slowly into a fist. There's agony in the lines of his face, yet he looks to me like a man on the verge of violence. 'I can't believe you said that. To me, his brother. Please, just let it go, would you?'

I don't know what to say. But I feel awful.

Unsteadily, I push back my chair and stand up. 'I have to visit the ladies,' I tell him. 'Then we're going back to Eastlyn. This conversation is over.'

Connor does not reply.

I walk to the ladies and stand there, staring at myself in the mirror. My cheeks are flushed, my eyes over-bright. It looks like I may have betrayed myself with Tris, and that possibility makes me angry. I thought what I said to him was private, just between the two of us. But he told Connor about the photograph. He told his brother about me breaking into their house.

Perhaps Connor is right. Perhaps I don't know Tris as well as he does.

Though in actual fact, if I track this back, things started going wrong as soon as I started listening to my body instead of my head.

I managed to persuade myself that Tristan Taylor had nothing to do with the murders; I even went to bed with him on the strength of that belief, for God's sake. But now I don't know what to think. If his own brother suspects him …

I go to the loo, then splash my face with cold water. I tell myself, *I can do this, I can do this.* And I have to think about Jenny. She's still missing, and she needs someone to be looking for her, to believe that she can be found before the worst happens. Even if I have to ask tough questions of my friends to achieve that.

When I walk back out to join Connor, I find him looming in the dark pub entrance, looking out at the rain.

He smiles when he sees me, his face lighting up with relief. 'Ellie, good.' Maybe he thought I had slipped away on my own without telling him. 'I just spoke to Tris.

They've finished with him. Look, I'm sorry about what I said before, I went too far. I'll drop you at the cottage, then head on over to the station to pick him up.'

'Of course.'

I know then that Connor is not my enemy, that he has never been my enemy. He just wants to protect his little brother from me. Even if he suspects his brother may be guilty of murder.

There's something nagging at me though, like one of those cryptic clues in a crossword puzzle. Something Connor said in the car on the way here. *It could be the vicar for all I know. Though I suppose we can't blame the poor sod for having a dead body in his cemetery.*

My brain keeps returning to what he said, examining it, then pushing it away again as unsolvable, too tired and stressed to unravel the tangle of ideas. So I shelve it and trust the answer will come to me eventually. Maybe tomorrow, when my head is clearer.

I only hope it won't come too late.

CHAPTER THIRTY-THREE

We're back to glorious weather the next morning, though the Cornish fields are still sodden from last night's rain, the air fresh and damp. It's Monday morning and I'm going back into work, even though my head is still screwed up over what Connor told me. There's been no news about Jenny, and it's hard to enjoy this beautiful morning and not wonder if she is still breathing. It feels like my fault she has disappeared, and guilt is making it hard for me to focus on work.

I'm standing beside my scooter, keys in hand, when another police car arrives.

It's a few minutes after eight o'clock.

PC Helen Flynn, who's on bodyguard duty today and was already waiting in her car, ready to follow me to work, climbs out and stares in surprise at the approaching car.

'It's Detective Inspector Powell,' she says. 'And that's DS Carrick with him. I did hear something on my radio earlier, but ... ' She tails off as the inspector gets out of the car, perhaps deciding it is better to let Powell do the explaining.

But what is he here to explain?

I turn, leaning against the car, half expecting to be hit

by the worst news imaginable. That Jenny has been found and is dead. But DI Powell is smiling.

'On your way to the school, Eleanor? I hope PC Flynn was planning to accompany you.'

'Of course, sir,' she says, standing to attention beside her vehicle, hands clasped behind her back.

'Well, I don't think that will be necessary.' DI Powell pushes his hands into his trouser pockets, pleased with himself. 'You'll be glad to hear we've got him.'

I stare. 'Got him? You've caught the killer?'

'We picked him up yesterday for questioning, kept him overnight, and charged him first thing this morning.' The inspector glances at his watch. 'Nearly two hours ago, actually, after he confessed.'

'To what?'

'To double murder.' The inspector has an air of grim satisfaction. 'He's confessed to the murders of both Sarah McGellan and Dawn Trevian.'

My hands clench into fists. It's hard to keep my voice level. 'Is it Tris Taylor?'

'I'm afraid I can't discuss his identity. That's a police matter.'

'This affects me. I've got a right to know.'

'It'll be made public soon enough,' he says soothingly. 'Meanwhile, you're safe, Eleanor. Think about that. The murderer is in custody.'

'Please, Inspector.'

He sighs, then shakes his head. 'Strictly between the two of us, it's *not* your friend Tristan.'

I feel myself sag with relief. It's not Tris. Not Tris.

'Is it the vicar, then?'

'The vicar?' Now it's his turn to stare. 'You mean, Reverend Clemo?'

'I've suspected him all along. He was there on the anniversary of my mum's death, the morning I found the first body in the woods. I could swear he's been watching the cottage too, creeping around at night. Hannah even heard noises in the walls once; I think he's got some way of getting into the house unseen.' I press on urgently, though DI Powell is shaking his head. 'No, listen, Inspector, he knew my mother back in school. Knew her well. Even went to my parents' wedding, he admitted it himself. And he's been acting so suspiciously – '

'It's not him.'

'But the way he looks at me, he seems so angry. And I saw a police car parked outside the vicarage a while ago. So I thought maybe – '

His brow clears. 'I see what this is about. Reverend Clemo's mother-in-law has come to live at the vicarage with him and his wife. Unfortunately the old lady has Alzheimer's. Apparently she's been getting very upset about all the disturbances in the village, becoming confused and believing the police are there to arrest her. I don't think it would be indiscreet to say there was an incident recently where she went missing for hours. Some officers came out to search the village and woods for her. So I imagine the vicar isn't feeling too happy with you at the moment.' He pauses a beat, watching me. 'Not your fault, of course. But perhaps he associates you with his mother-in-law becoming upset and difficult to manage, which is why he's been less than friendly.'

I'm shocked to find that I've been basing my conclusions on a totally false premise. So much for having an analytical mind. 'I didn't know.'

'How could you?'

'But I still want to know who you've arrested,' I insist.

Powell hesitates, looking from me to PC Flynn. Then he makes a small, fatalistic gesture. 'The man's confessed and we've formally charged him. It looks pretty watertight. I expect we'll be making a formal announcement to the press soon, so it can't do any harm to tell you first.'

'Thank you.'

'The man we've arrested is Richard Laney.'

I stare, too stunned to react.

'Dick Laney? From the Woods Valley Garden Centre? I don't believe it.'

'Trust me, he's our man. We have his confession. Once he realised we had strong forensic evidence, Laney crumbled. Told us everything.'

'The sacking used to wrap the body in the cemetery,' I say, thinking rapidly. I remember helping Dick with his delivery up at Hill Farm. 'Is that the forensic evidence? You mean it came from his garden centre? But of course it would have his fingerprints on it. He and Jago deliver those sacks all over north and mid-Cornwall.'

The inspector looks at me, frowning, and does not comment.

'What about Jenny?' I ask. 'Did Dick Laney tell you where to find her? Has he hurt her? Is she safe?'

'Unfortunately, Miss Crofter's disappearance is still unresolved,' Powell admits.

DS Carrick, who has been leaning against the police car, listening to us, now straightens up. 'So far, Mr Laney is denying any involvement in Jenny Crofter's disappearance. But there is a possibility that her case isn't connected to these killings, so we're pursuing that at the moment.'

'In other words, you don't have a clue where she is?'

Carrick glares at me. 'One step at a time. That's how the police have to move. Mistakes get made when people try to rush things. And this has been a good result for us.'

'Why would Dick Laney do it though? Kill those women and taunt me with their bodies?'

'We're not certain yet,' Powell admits. 'He may have been harbouring some kind of grievance against you and your family. In particular, there was an old photograph – '

'From when he was at school with my mum,' I say abruptly. 'Dick Laney had a crush on her once, when they were teenagers. But I don't think she was ever interested in him.'

Powell looks at me sharply. 'You knew about this but didn't tell us?'

'I didn't think it was important.'

'Everything is important in a murder enquiry, Eleanor. If there's anything else you can tell us, anything that might illuminate Mr Laney's motives, let's hear it now. '

'I saw an old photo on the wall in his office. That's it.'

Powell nods. 'Okay, leave it with us.' He nods to PC Flynn. 'You had better go back to the station, constable. Miss Blackwood no longer needs round-the-clock protection.'

'Yes, sir,' Helen Flynn says, smiling, unable to disguise her relief, and climbs back into her car.

'You will keep looking for Jenny Crofter though,' I say as the two detectives turn back to their car, 'won't you?'

'Of course,' DI Powell agrees smoothly, opening his car door. 'She's our number one priority.'

I don't think he grasps the irony of what he's just said.

Down by the water, the sandy, half-moon bay at Widemouth dazzles us with afternoon sunshine, the beach busier than it looked from the car park. The narrow stretch of water between the yellow and red-striped flags – the area deemed safe by the lifeguards for swimming and body-boarding – is thronging with body-boarders, come, like me, straight from a day job in search of big rollers. Despite the sunshine, even the innocent-looking shallows will be freezing after the recent rain. But I've been coming here since I was a small child, and I know the sea in summer only feels icy for the first few minutes. After that the body adjusts. Besides, a properly-fitted wet suit protects surfers from the worst of it.

'Here, can you zip me up?' I ask Hannah, and she puts her car keys between her teeth, then zips up my wetsuit while I hold my hair up out of the way.

'You've lost weight,' she comments, eyeing me disapprovingly.

'I'll gain it back.'

Hannah faces away from me. 'My turn.'

I fasten her wetsuit at the back, fixing the Velcro strip across the top of the zip.

'Done.'

As always, we head straight for the surfing zone marked by black and white flags to one side of the main sweep of the bay. The surf board feels long and awkward under my arm, but that's only because it's been months since I last went surfing. Muscle memory will kick in soon, and I'll feel at home here again. I look to our left, the wind whipping at my hair. There's a line of jagged rocks there, exposed by the receding tide and jutting out of the sand, where we used to go netting for crabs and sea anemones when we were younger. Me and Hannah and Tris and Connor, with our dads looking on. That seems an awfully long time ago now, we have all changed so much since those days.

Guilt nags at me. 'You don't think this is disrespectful? Coming out to the beach, going surfing while Jenny is still missing?'

'You came here to speak to Denzil too though, didn't you?'

'True.'

'So this isn't just for leisure. Well, it is for me. But you need to learn to relax, Ellie, enjoy the moment.' Hannah looks at me sternly. 'You're always taking responsibility for things that go wrong, even when it's nothing to do with you. It doesn't always have to be your fault, you know.'

Perhaps I do often think it's my fault when things don't go to plan. But where Jenny's concerned, I'm probably justified in thinking her continuing disappearance is down to me.

I was in work today, and there were worried looks and questions from staff and students alike. She's a popular teacher and her absence is deeply felt. *Where's Miss Crofter? What's happened to her? When will she come back?* As if I magically know the answers to such questions. As though I'm the one who's to blame, the one who's spirited her away from them.

'I just hope Denzil can help,' I mutter.

There's a surf school in training on the sand: new surfers lying face-down on their boards on dry land, pretending to paddle with their arms. The surf instructor is a fit-looking young man with fair hair flopping into his eyes as he demonstrates the correct arm movement for the newbies. His wetsuit is folded down to his waist and his bare chest is smooth and tanned.

He looks up and grins as we pass. 'Hey, Hannah, how are you?'

She squints at him, unsure for a moment without her glasses, then smiles. 'I'm good, Alex,' she says warmly, as though she knows him well. She glances at his students. 'Surf school still keeping you busy, I see.'

'Damn newbies,' he agrees, and they both laugh.

I look at her sideways as we reach the water. 'Okay, who was that?'

'Oh, just Alex. We learned to surf together when we were kids. Now he teaches surf. We still hook up now and then for a drink.'

'Only a drink?' I glance back over my shoulder at Alex. 'He looks very … athletic.'

'You have a filthy mind, Miss Blackwood,' she says, but laughs. 'Don't judge me by your own standards.'

I laugh too, but only mechanically. I'm sure Hannah means nothing by it, but it's obvious she was thinking about Tris spending the night when she said that.

A sliver of fear works its way under my skin, despite the sunshine and the pleasure of being in the open air like this. I haven't spoken to Tris since that night, and his silence is beginning to worry me. He must know about Dick Laney's arrest. Why hasn't he been in touch?

Perhaps Connor is putting pressure on him to stay away from me. A two-pronged approach to keep us apart. It would not surprise me. But if Tris genuinely wants to see me again, even to come over for the night, I have no intention of saying no. I'm sorry for Connor, he's a good friend and I know he only wants to protect his brother. But I don't believe Tris is as 'damaged' as Connor seems to think. Or if he is, I have yet to see how and why.

Because his mother walked out on them when Tris was still very young, perhaps.

I guess that would mess up most people's heads, to know their mum loved them so little she chose to leave them behind after a family split. But Tristan has always struck me as someone who copes with the blows, and keeps going.

Is it possible I have been wrong about him all these years?

Hannah drops her towel and keys a safe distance from the water's edge, then splashes out ahead of me, thigh-deep now, surprisingly keen on surfing given her total lack of sportiness at school. Though of course her father has been bringing her here every summer since she was six, so she's a surfing expert compared to me. Today she's left her glasses in the car to avoid losing or breaking them, which means I have to wave to get her attention once we're more than a few feet apart.

'Look,' she shouts back at me, pointing out to sea. 'Is that Denzil?'

My surf board still tucked under my arm, I shield my eyes and stare in that direction. It's Denzil, all right. I would know that mop of tawny hair anywhere. But it won't be easy to reach him. He is already far out past the body boarders, lying face-down on an electric-blue surfboard, paddling hard to reach the bigger breakers beyond the shelf.

'I'll get him for you,' Hannah shouts.

'No, it's fine. I can wait.'

But she can't hear me over the noise of the tide.

'What?'

She turns, waist-high in the rolling waves, shielding her eyes and grimacing myopically at the shadowy figures of other surfers between us. It's clear she can't see me.

'Ellie, where are you?' she shouts.

'Over here.'

I wave, and she grins, finally spotting me. She waves back, but keeps stubbornly pushing out, holding her board under one arm. 'Come on, you wuss. It's not that cold.'

I follow, wading slowly into deeper water, my board an awkward weight under my arm that keeps dancing to be free, to swim on the waves.

Staring out across the ocean, I try to envisage America somewhere out there beyond the hazy blue line of the horizon. How far away is the US from this exact point on the Cornish coast? Three thousand miles? Maybe more? I imagine a woman standing on an Atlantic beach in the United States, surfboard in hand, looking out to sea and wondering ...

I can't see Denzil anymore. I can't see anyone nearby, actually. The water is very deep now, and the waves are hitting me side-on as I keep swimming out to sea. Hannah surfs past me with a triumphant shout, half-crouched on her board, an absolute natural in the water.

I turn to face the ocean, pulling myself up onto the slippery board.

The first really big wave takes me by surprise. It always does, even when I've been steeling myself for it. I make a complete mess of it, slide off the board and dip down under the salty water.

The next wave, I'm ready for it.

I manage a few exhilarating seconds of wobbling ride, feet planted maybe not quite far enough apart, knees slightly bent, arms spread wide, before the wave gets the better of me.

The board tips, and I overbalance with it, fail to regain an upright stance, and end up falling ...

I survive the cold plunge, but the feeling is horribly familiar. Like being in deep over your head, and not being able to do a damn thing about it.

A hand grabs at my shoulder and helps me back to the surface.

'Thanks,' I splutter.

It's Denzil, treading water next to me, his own board floating beside us. 'No problem,' he says, but his eyes are wary. He slicks wet hair back from his forehead. 'How are you, Ellie?'

'Still alive.'

He does not smile. 'I heard about Dick Laney's arrest. It's bullshit.'

'The police seem to think he did it.'

'What do they know?' The sun is bouncing off the choppy water all around us, making it hard to look him in the face. But I can feel the hostility coming off him in waves. 'When you rang, you said you wanted to talk to me.'

'Not in the ocean though.'

Reluctantly, Denzil glances back at the shore. We are both treading water now, just out of our depth. 'So, what, you want to go up the beach? Dry off and grab a coffee?'

'Later,' I say. 'Let's surf first.'

He smiles then, looking relieved. Like he's had a stay of execution. 'Yeah, let's surf.'

It's roughly an hour later when I hear Hannah calling my name. The water is rocking me gently, and the sun still feels warm through my wetsuit, even though the time must be heading towards half past five. I look round, lying face-down on my surf board as I wait for a bigger wave, and see her standing in the shallows, chatting to her friend Alex.

She waves, and points significantly up the beach.

Turning my head lazily, I see two familiar figures heading down the beach from the car park.

Tris and Connor.

CHAPTER THIRTY-FOUR

I push up on my elbows, swearing under my breath. What the hell are they doing here?

Both men are wearing wetsuits – Connor's flopping down from the waist – and carrying surfboards. I am shocked by the way my body responds to the sight of the two brothers. It's a visceral reaction: all my muscles instinctively constrict, my nipples stiffening against the wet board, a disturbing cross between fear and intense desire. Both men look sexy in wetsuits, Tris dark and powerfully muscular, Connor tall and lithe. Dr Quick would have a field-day with this physical response, I think. Meanwhile my face is burning, and I have to get it under control.

The tide is out, and it's a long walk over pebbles and wet sand from the car park to the water's edge, so I have a few minutes before they arrive.

Denzil, surfing a little way from me, has seen them too. He meets my gaze but says nothing, then strikes further out to sea.

I catch the flash of his electric-blue board, then he disappears between surging wave crests.

I can't blame him for swimming in the opposite direction. Last time he saw Tris, Denzil got knocked to the ground and taken away by the police. I only hope this won't stop him from talking to me. Being on the beach has been wonderfully relaxing after the traumatic events of the past few weeks, but the real reason I came all the way out to Widemouth Bay is to speak to Denzil.

I turn slowly and paddle for shore, letting the waves carry me forward every few yards. By the time I get there, the two men have almost reached the water.

Hannah says goodbye to Alex, then splashes out of the shallows towards the brothers, dropping her board a few metres short of the incoming tide. Hair dripping down her neck where it's escaped from her ponytail, she embraces Tris affectionately. 'How are you? I suppose you know about Dick Laney? Such a surprise, but I'm pleased they don't suspect you anymore.' She turns and hugs Connor as well. 'You must be relieved that it's all over too.'

Connor does not reply to that. He studies me grimly as I wade out of the sea towards them, dragging my surf board after me. 'Well, well, this is a surprise. I didn't know you two would be here.' He glances round at his brother. 'Did you?'

'Of course not,' Tris says, and half turns away, shielding his eyes as he looks out to sea.

He's lying, and we both know it. I sent Tris a text after work, telling him we were going to Widemouth to catch the afternoon sun. But I'm not going to admit that any more than he is.

'Denzil is here too,' Hannah comments innocently, then squints before pointing out his distant figure on the rolling waves. 'See?'

Tris stiffens, and Connor turns to stare out to sea, his feet rooted in the sand, legs far apart, the surf board leaning against his hip. I can practically smell the testosterone in the air, like hot tar. Both men are tense, giving little away.

Hannah asks eagerly, 'So, are you two coming in? I was just about to head out again. We could go together. It's not bad today. The waves could be a little higher, but I'm not complaining. This is the first time I've had a chance to surf in ages.' She smiles at me. 'It was Ellie's idea, of course.'

I tense, worried she is about to tell them how I arranged to meet Denzil here for a chat. But my friend is smarter than that, of course.

'I'm celebrating the end of my night shifts,' Hannah tells them blithely, 'and Ellie's celebrating the end of this horrible business with the killings. And then we bumped into Denzil. Now you're both here. If anyone happened to bring a barbecue and some sausages, we could stay after sunset and make a beach party of it.' She grins at them both. 'A beach barbecue. Now I know summer's finally here.'

'We won't be staying long,' Connor says flatly.

'Oh.'

I pull Tris aside while Hannah is trying valiantly to engage Connor in conversation. He's looking withdrawn, though that's hardly a surprise. 'I'm sorry the police questioned you. Again.'

He shrugs. 'They treated me quite well, actually. They were just being thorough. If it was you who was missing, I'd want to see everyone in the village questioned like that.'

'But they still haven't found Jenny,' I tell him.

'Not yet.'

Something in his voice makes me think he knows more than he's telling. 'You have an idea where she might be?'

'Christ, no,' He looks shocked.

'Sorry.' I hesitate. 'Perhaps they'll be able to get something out of Dick Laney. I hope so. He must be keeping her somewhere, don't you think? In some building they haven't thought to search yet.'

At the same time, I can't believe that Dick Laney, however annoying he's been at times, is a serial killer. The police might as well have arrested my own dad.

For the first time, I wonder if my dad was ever on their

list of suspects. But of course he was. Ben Blackwood must have been at the top of their list. Most women who are murdered are killed by someone who knows them intimately, usually their husband or partner. And this whole business started with my mother's murder.

Could my father have killed his own wife?

I don't want to consider that question, though of course I must. If only to be able to dismiss it as a possibility. Perhaps my parents had fallen out of love. Perhaps she had started seeing someone else, and he wanted revenge. I remember how hard he hit me that day in the caravan, his sudden anger taking me by surprise. Yet he has always had a temper.

Tris is staring out to sea. I get the feeling he's avoiding my gaze too. But I can feel the heat from his body. We are as bad as each other.

'I expect you're right. I hope the police are out there now, looking for her. They need to find her soon. Unless ...' He tails off into silence.

'Unless she's already dead.'

'Exactly.' His tone is clipped, terse. 'Do you think Dick Laney's the right man? The killer?'

'No.'

'Neither do I.'

'Who is, then?'

His dark eyes come back to mine, his brows drawn sharply together, and again I feel that sense of unease. 'I don't know,' he says automatically, but his voice is empty and I don't believe him. 'That's up to the police to find out.'

I nod, then say quietly, 'Why did you tell Connor that I broke into the farm? That I found the photograph and asked you about it?'

He stares at me.

Hannah has grabbed Connor by the hand and is dragging him into the sea with her usual exuberance. 'Come on, we're missing the big waves.'

'Hang on.' Connor glances back at us, his expression unreadable, then stops to draw his wetsuit up over his shoulders.

Expertly, Hannah fixes the zip for him, then the two stride out together, carrying their surf boards under their arms, soon reaching the point where the beach shelf becomes pebbly and steep, then dips abruptly, the water suddenly so deep you are forced to swim or drown.

'Well?' I ask Tris, still waiting for an answer.

'I didn't want to tell him,' he says, watching his brother with Hannah. 'But he made me distrust you.'

'How?'

'Connor said you were sick in the head. That you had told the police to arrest me because I was the one who killed both those women.'

'And you believed him?'

He struggles for a moment. 'Yes.'

'I see,' I say. 'And if the police don't manage to work out who the real killer is?'

'Then I guess Jenny's body is going to be the next one they find.' His voice is so low, I almost miss the last few words.

Tris turns away and splashes out into the water.

Shocked, I stumble after him through the warm shallows, forgetting to watch my footing on the stones hidden under the creamy, churning water, and nearly fall several times.

I try not to let it affect me, but I'm both horrified and deeply hurt by what I just heard. I know Connor thinks I'm losing my mind. But how the hell could Tris believe I would ever do such a thing to him, ever behave in such a way?

Perhaps he thinks I'm mad too.

Or is Tris lying to put me off the scent? There was something in his face. Something he's not telling me. He made that conversation with Connor sound so plausible, and yet ...

What does he know?

'Hey, hurry up, you lazy lot,' Hannah is shouting, beckoning us to join them. It's hard to hear her over the incoming rush and spray of the tide. She's pointing out to sea. 'Look.'

The wind is up, stronger than before, and gigantic rollers are starting to rise majestically out of the distant grey-blue haze.

Tris stops, waist-high in the water, buffeted by the waves. He turns, unsmiling, and holds out his hand. 'Coming?'

We ride the waves as a group for the next half hour, our line staggered, surfing a few metres away from each other for safety. Smashing into another surfer on the way in is not only embarrassing, it's also dangerous. People are injured or die every year because of accidents like that. We rise up on the surge, then hang onto each roller for as long as we can, riding in on the white crests and paddling into the shallows afterwards, or falling under the wave to resurface as soon as the swell has passed.

I keep an eye on Denzil, surfing alone to my left, his resentment almost palpable, and swim over to him as soon as I get the chance.

'Denzil?'

He turns to stare at me, clinging onto his board. 'You didn't tell me you were bringing the Taylors.'

'I'm sorry about that. I didn't know they would show up.' Or not both of them, anyway. 'Can we talk?'

Denzil does not look very friendly now, the welcome gone out of his face. But he does not tell me to get lost either. 'What about?'

'Jenny Crofter, for starters.'

'I don't know anything about the woman. Except that she's missing.'

'When I spoke to her about you, she remembered you from school.' I hate how easily I've slipped into referring to Jenny in the past tense. Like her death is a *fait accompli*, a done deal.

He shrugs. 'So what?'

I tread water, using my board to keep afloat, looking at him steadily. Dangerous though it is, I want to test a theory.

'I haven't forgotten how you came at me after the memorial service,' I say softly. 'You wanted to do me some damage that day. I could see it in your eyes. Is that how you felt about being arrested? Murderous?'

'No,' he says angrily.

'Though of course the police were always there, keeping tabs on me. So you couldn't get anywhere near me. But Jenny wasn't being watched. She was an easier target, wasn't she?'

We bob up and down on the water for a moment as he digests that.

'Yeah, all right,' he begins reluctantly, 'I was out of order at the church. I was high, I wasn't thinking straight. But don't try and twist that shit into making me out to be some kind of sick psycho. I've never hurt a woman in my life, and I wouldn't have started with you.'

'You would never have got the chance,' I tell him.

Denzil looks suddenly uneasy. Frowning, he gazes past me to where the others are catching a late wave. 'Look, I don't know anything about Jenny Crofter. Perhaps you're asking the wrong man.'

'Meaning?'

He says nothing for a moment, a muscle working in his jaw. Then he shakes his head and turns his back on me, beginning a measured front crawl out to sea.

'Forget it, Ellie,' he says over his shoulder. 'And don't ever fucking call me again. We're done.'

I swim slowly back over to the others. By the time I reach them, they have returned from the shallows and are waiting for another big roller. Hannah is shouting something, waving her arm, but over the noise of the water I can't hear what she's saying. She's on the far left of our line, near the body boarders' section, just where the flagged area ends. Tris is closest to me, his wet hair slicked back, staring out to sea. Connor is close too, a few yards further on, lying flat and well-balanced on his board, head turned in my direction as though to shield his eyes from the sun glare.

The waves grow higher as we paddle slowly forward, waiting for the next promising big roller. The water is choppy out here near the protective edge of the bay, but we stay in formation. Then a vicious side wind hits our line, and I watch as their bobbing heads disappear, then reappear, then disappear again, the sunlight dazzling.

These sets of smaller waves are surprisingly powerful. I have to turtle roll several times to avoid being swept back to shore, holding tight to the board under the rush of white water, then rolling back on top as soon as the wave has passed.

Coming up out of one of these slow rolls, I find an immense roller bearing down on me. It's a giant Daddy of a wave, rising high above us with a pale white lip just beginning to curl on the underside.

'Looks like it's going to be a big one,' I shout, turning my board to catch it, but nobody answers.

I stare west, directly into the sun, but can no longer see the others. But then I'm down in a dip here, and the water is so choppy, white waves are churning and surging all about me.

I paddle as slowly and deliberately as I can, long arm-strokes to keep me centred on the board, waiting for the huge wave to catch up with me.

Where is Tris? He was nearest to me before, now I can't see even the top of his head above the water. And Connor was on my other side last time I looked, yet he's also out of sight. Possibly he's behind me now. I dare not look back over my shoulder, or I'll risk losing my balance.

Here in the surge zone, I can see nothing but bobbing water on either side and the distant matchstick figures of people on the beach.

Are we really that far out?

For a few seconds I feel totally alone on a massive ocean, light bouncing off the waves, a late sun beating down on my head. Which is ridiculous, given that I know the others must be out there too, on their boards either beside or behind me, hidden momentarily by the swell.

Yet I can't seem to shake this feeling of isolation.

Perhaps you're asking the wrong man.

The wave's almost upon me. No time to see if the others are going too. With a long-practised move, I move my hands flat onto the wet board. Suddenly the water begins to swell and rise around me. In the deafening roar from the unseen wave, I jackknife my feet out of the water and onto the central line in one smooth movement, straightening to a standing position.

Only my surf board doesn't respond as it should. Something is dragging it down at the back. Down and sideways.

What the hell?

The wave hits as I flail sideways, taken unawares, slipping off the board like a novice.

I try to right myself, scrabbling wildly for the board before it can be jerked away from me by the next wave. But before my fingers even touch it, I'm struck from behind by an immense and irresistible wall of water. The sky abruptly tilts, then disappears as I tumble under the sheer white fall of the wave.

The huge wave drags me with it, my body rolling over and over in the dizzying surge of bubbles under its surface. My board is still attached to my ankle by a thin black leash; I can feel it tugging at me from beneath. It should be a buoyancy aid, helping me to spring back to the surface. But it's no help at the moment. If anything, it seems to be dragging me further down, as though anchored to something on the bottom of the ocean.

I struggle to rise, lashing out for the surface. Or where I imagine the surface should be.

But the world has shifted.

My clawing hands meet only more water, not air, and my eyes fly open on grey-green darkness, dirtied by the churning filth of bubbles and sand in the wake of a big roller.

I can't breathe.

I had no time to take even a quick gasp of air before being dragged under the wave, and now my lungs are running out. I have maybe a few more seconds before my desperate lungs try to take in fresh air and I drown, breathing water instead.

My mind panics. I close my eyes against the sting of salt water. I don't understand. Where are the others? Did no one see me slip from my board and under the wave? I'm struggling, flailing my arms and reaching up for air, but I'm going nowhere.

Something seems to be tugging me down and down.

I force my eyes open and peer downwards through the dark churning. The leash on my ankle is still attached to the board, which is beneath me. How is that possible?

I stare back along the thin black line of the leash. There's a vague shadow below me. The surf board? It must have got attached to something deep under the water. Maybe a rock. They are a few out here, hidden away in odd dips where the bay shelves steeply, but they don't usually pose a problem to surfers.

Then suddenly I see it. A flash of white below me.

I blink, staring at the moving shadows. It's so dark and cold this deep, my ears are popping, my lungs burning. My vision is starting to blur as my body is starved of oxygen.

Thrashing about in panic, I see the shadow move again. It's a blackness that shifts with me, like someone in a wet suit holding my surf board down under the water, with me attached to it.

Which is insane and impossible.

I catch a flicker of light above me. The sun is shining up there, dazzling and glinting off the waves. It feels like I'm fathoms deep, but I'm probably only a few metres from the surface. I'm going to drown within a few hundred feet of my friends, lost and invisible to them under the rolling Atlantic waves.

I have to undo the leash or I'm going to die. I bend double, fumbling for the leash on my ankle, but my fingers slip uselessly over the fastening as I lose strength and sensation.

My lungs are a black pit of pain. My mouth opens, an instinct I can't hold back a second longer, and cold salt water floods my lungs.

My whole body jerks backwards in shock and suddenly I'm convulsing, my lungs full of water. The pain is sharp and intense, focused in my chest at first, in those fluid-filled sacs that are my lungs and are designed to carry only air, not brine. Then it explodes like a series of grenades through the rest of my body.

I am drowning.

The ocean shifts around me, shadowy and echoing, a dark ballroom of bubbles with a high ceiling, the grey-green gloom punctuated by thin shafts of sunlight filtered by water. I feel my brain function rapidly disintegrate, my mind awash with blurred and confused memories.

And as I thrash against the inevitability of death, I stare down through the murky depths and see that odd flash of white again. And the shadowy outline of a man floating above it.

A man whose face I recognise only as darkness begins to close in.

CHAPTER THIRTY-FIVE

I'm six years old again, standing with my cheek pressed to the gnarled bark of an old oak, both hands clutching the enormous trunk. My cheek is wet because I've been crying. I'm sobbing now, but silently, biting my lip until it bleeds, too scared to make a sound now that I've seen him.

The man in white trainers.

He was bending over Mummy when I crept back through the tangle of brambles and ferns. I came slowly at first, slipping from tree to tree, careful not to make a sound, half scared, half wondering if it was a game. But Mummy shouted, 'Run!' and I knew from the high, angry note in her voice that I'd be in trouble if she saw me coming back.

But when I got back to the path, she was lying still on the ground and he was bending over her.

Is Mummy hurt? Did he hurt her?

My skin is scratched and bleeding from where I fell among the brambles. My hands are dirty. Nasty and dirty. A bramble has ripped the sleeve on my coat. My tears fall faster. Mummy is going to be so cross with me.

I risk a quick glance round the tree. Just a peek to see if he's still there.

The man is crouching beside Mummy now. He's wearing a black tracksuit and clean white trainers, and brown gloves. I don't see his face. His head is bent, looking down at her, and he's talking under his breath.

'You made me do this, Angela. It's your fault. If you had kept your mouth shut … But oh no, you couldn't just put up and shut up. You thought you knew best.'

He slaps my mum's face, and her head flops limply towards me. Her eyes are open and her throat is red and swollen, but she's not in there. Not anymore.

'Now see what you've done. I won't be blamed for this, Angela. This is your fault. You hear me?'

Suddenly he turns.

I gasp and duck out of sight behind the tree again.

It's Mr Taylor.

Mr Taylor. I see him at the school gate sometimes. He's Connor and Tristan's dad. He often stops to talk to Mummy after school. She calls him Pete. Sometimes she sends me to play in the field with the boys while they sit in the car and talk.

But Mr Taylor likes Mummy. Why would he want to hurt her?

I hear him crash away through the trees a moment later, and wait until the sound has faded, still not daring to move in case he sees me.

I step out quietly, trembling and unsteady, deliberately not looking at the body on the path. Instead I'm staring up at the wooded slope all the way, watching for the white flash of trainers through the trees.

When the trainers have finally gone, I kneel down beside my mummy and take her hand. She's warm, and I try to remember what you have to do in an emergency. Call an ambulance. But Mum doesn't have a phone with her. Pump their chests so they can keep breathing. But I don't know how. And she's so still.

'Mummy?'

She does not reply, lying like a rag doll on the path, knees drawn up to one side. Her lovely hair is fanned out across the dirt, a tiny piece of green fern caught amongst the fine strands. Her throat looks so swollen, and there's a smudge of mud on her cheek. I wish I could put something under her head to stop her from getting dirty.

I stare at her, rubbing my eyes. I'm starting to sob again and can't stop myself. Everything is so confused in my head. It's jumbled up with odd dreams I've had, noises in the night, then getting up for a glass of water and finding Mummy downstairs with a man. With Mr Taylor.

'You won't tell Daddy that Mr Taylor came to visit me while he was away, will you? Daddy wouldn't understand.' I remember her hand squeezing mine, her voice urgent. 'You must promise, Ellie. Promise Mummy you won't ever tell anyone you saw Mr Taylor with me.'

'Mummy, Mummy.' Tears are running down my cheeks and everything becomes misty. I can't see her face properly anymore. I wipe my nose on the back of my coat sleeve. 'Tell me what to do, Mummy.'

Her voice is still in my head. 'Daddy wouldn't understand. Promise me you won't ever tell.'

I'm shelving it all away behind the dark line of trees, packing the unwanted memories into a box with a lid under my bed. They can stay there for a while. Until I'm sure what to do with them. They'll be safe enough, so long as I never forget. Never forgive.

I know she's dead. But I have to check before I run to the village for help. You always have to check, right?

'I promise, Mummy.' Cross my heart and hope to die. 'I promise, I promise.'

The birds are singing overhead. In a minute, I will drop her hand and start to run.

With one last violent effort, my body convulses. I'm flailing backwards with the last of my strength, acting on some final message to the brain that translates as *escape*. I jerk my foot, snapping the leash on my ankle, then I'm kicking upwards to freedom and salt air. To the promise of sunlight.

I burst the surface, choking and spewing water from my lungs. But it's too late, I have no strength left for swimming. The water is so heavy now it feels like thick velvet curtains, wrapping around me, hampering my attempts to stay afloat. A strong wave crashes over my head, knocking me under the water again, and the world rolls above me through a thin layer of white foam, dazzling and cold. The ocean feels so warm, a good place to rest a while, to sleep.

I begin to sink again, my head tilted to one side, arms limp, letting the water take me where it will.

'Eleanor ...'

It's Tristan's voice but I don't have the energy to listen. His hands hook under my arms, pulling me up again, out of the comfortable green depths. He's tilting my head back cruelly, forcing his body under mine, his legs kicking against the relentless rush of the tide.

'I've got her, she's over here.'

My eyes close.

Four hours later, I'm sitting up on a bed in a cubicle of the Accident and Emergency Department at Truro Hospital, Treliske, feeling very weak and foolish. My head is throbbing like I hit it on a rock, and I have a severely bruised ankle where I fought to get the leash free. But at least I'm alive. Which still feels like a miracle. I can't remember much about how I got here – there's a vague memory of sirens and the bright interior of an ambulance, an oxygen mask over my face – but I am glad I'm not so much flotsam in the Atlantic Ocean.

The nurses are very sympathetic and concerned, but a little wary of leaving me alone. It's as though they think I tried to kill myself.

The curtain rattles open, and the smiling nurse with braces on her teeth pops her head back in. 'Feeling better?'

'Much, thank you.'

'Cup of tea?'

'I was wondering when I could go home.'

'That depends on what the doctor says. You may be kept in overnight if she thinks you need a few more hours' observation.' The nurse busies herself with tidying away some empty packets on the trolley next to my bed, then meticulously washes her hands at the sink. 'You may be feeling right as rain, my love, but you did have a good gargle of sea water. Not good for the lungs, you know.' She smiles. 'Now, are you sure I can't get you a cup of tea?'

'No, thanks.'

She shrugs and slips out again, drawing the curtain shut behind her.

I lean back and close my eyes, then snap them open them again. Whenever I shut my eyes, I see *him* again. Pete Taylor. Connor and Tristan's dad. Bending over my mum in the woods.

I pick a point on the wall and stare at it, willing myself to stay awake until the doctor pronounces me fit to leave. Jenny is still out there, dead or alive, and she needs to be found. I have things to do. People to see.

But my fatigue wins in the end. I close my eyes, unable to keep them open any longer, and dream.

When I wake up again, it's dark outside and my father is beside the bed. I struggle to sit up. 'Dad, what are you doing here?'

'Someone needs to take you home,' he tells me. 'No, stay still for now. I'm waiting for the doctor to check you over again.'

I stare up at him, uncertain. He's clean-shaven, and looks sober. He even appears to have changed his clothes recently. 'You look good, Dad. You look … better.'

'You look awful,' he says bluntly.

'Thanks.'

'What on earth happened? They told me you went surfing at Widemouth and nearly drowned.'

'I did, yes. But I can't remember much. Who pulled me out?'

'Some lifeguards,' he says, then adds reluctantly, 'and Tristan Taylor helped too, I believe.'

'You don't like Tris much, do you?'

He looks away, his face shuttered. 'I didn't like his

father much either, to be honest. Pete was a difficult character. Always saying one thing and meaning another. Maybe that's the problem. I've never been able to see past my dislike for Pete where the Taylor boys are concerned.'

'Men,' I correct him. 'They haven't been boys for a long time.'

'I still remember when they were teenagers. Always hanging round the farm, sniffing after you, making a bloody nuisance of themselves. Especially that Connor. He was very keen on you as a lad.' He looks at me closely. 'Is he still keen on you?'

I change the subject, nodding to the coat on the back of his chair. 'Whose coat is that?'

He stands and lifts it up, frowning. It's a black mid-thigh length coat, looking a little damp and rumpled, with deep pockets on either side. 'I don't know. Why?'

'I think I was wearing it in the ambulance.'

'It's a man's coat.'

'Someone must have put it on me at the beach.'

An image flashes through my head. Someone draping foil over my wet shoulders. A paramedic, perhaps. Tris in the car park at Widemouth Bay, a strange look in his face, bending over me with a coat in his hands. *Here, put this on.* Then the ambulance doors shutting out the light.

'I'll ask Hannah,' I say, leaning back on the pillows. 'She'll know who it belongs to.'

My father hesitates, then drapes the long coat over the chair again. 'We'll take it home with us,' he says, then glances at his watch. There's something in his voice, some quiver of emotion, but I can't pinpoint what it is. 'I'm sorry for the way I spoke to you in the caravan. I should never have hit you. It was unforgivable.'

I say nothing.

'Where's that bloody doctor?' he demands irascibly, not looking at me. 'You try to rest. Let me call one of those nurses back. See if we can't get them to release you.'

While he is gone, I flex my arms and legs, wiggle my

fingers and toes, and shift carefully about in the bed, trying to ascertain whether I've damaged myself, and where. But apart from a dull pain in my chest, and the lingering headache I've had since waking up, I seem to be miraculously intact.

My mind is another matter though. I haven't mentioned to anyone that I saw a face in the water when I was drowning. Nor whose face it was. They will only think I need further psychiatric help if I tell them what exactly I saw. Or thought I saw.

I saw a man in the water who's been dead for months. I think he may have strangled my mother when I was a child. Oh, and he just tried to drown me, too.

My father rustles back through the curtains a short while later, closely followed by a harassed-looking nurse who picks up my chart and examines it without even glancing in my direction. I watch my dad thoughtfully. He is still avoiding my gaze.

I study his face. 'Dad, what is it you're not telling me?'

He swallows, then shakes his head.

'Tell me,' I insist.

My father looks stricken then. His face just crumples. 'It's Hannah,' he admits, tears in his eyes. He takes my hand and squeezes it. 'I'm sorry, Ellie. I'm so, so sorry.'

CHAPTER THIRTY-SIX

I wake at home the next morning with a series of unanswerable questions burning a hole in my head, horribly aware that time is running out. Not just for me but for Jenny, who is still out there somewhere. There are so many things that need to be done. And I have done none of them. The worst has happened, and I feel trapped in my own bed by that truth, my arms and legs weighed down by these heavy, too hot bedclothes, by the knowledge that I have failed.

'Ellie?'

Someone is tapping quietly at my bedroom door and repeating my name. Like a deathwatch beetle. Tap-tap-tap.

Go away.

I know who it is, because there is only one person it can be.

Mentally, I turn away from the grief waiting for me on the end of that thought, circle the terrible dark pit in my head, pushing away the reality I can't yet accept. That Hannah is gone.

Dad puts his head round the door without asking permission.

'Sorry, Ellie, were you asleep?'

If only I could have persuaded my father to go home last night. Instead I feel awkward, needing him gone but equally not wanting to hurt his feelings. He's my flesh-and-blood, my only remaining close family, and I can't push him away just because I desperately need to be alone.

'Not anymore,' I say wearily, and turn my head on the pillows to look at him. 'What is it?'

'Tris is here to see you,' he says apologetically. 'This is the third time he's knocked at the door today. I told him you didn't want any visitors, that he wasn't welcome, but I have to give it to him, he is nothing if not persistent. I think he's been standing outside for the past hour, in fact, just waiting. Should I tell him to go home?'

My sleepy brain grapples with those concepts. *Tris. Here. Now.*

I groan, throwing back the bedclothes. I'm in pyjamas. Baby-pink. Hannah gave them to me as a present last birthday.

'No, I'll get dressed. What time is it?'

'Just after twelve. I thought you might like a lie-in.'

'It's midday already?'

I swing my legs urgently out of bed and sit up. My head throbs like someone's hit it with a hammer and I have to wait a moment, head bent, eyes closed, before moving again.

I have to call the police and tell the inspector what I know. Yet how can I, when I'm not even sure of my own memories? How to explain a vision seen while drowning? How to put a hunch about a recurring nightmare into coherent words?

It all feels a bit tenuous and unlikely.

I can't just walk into police headquarters and say, *the shadow man did it.* Not with my history of psychosis. They'll lock me up and throw away the key.

I open my eyes and try to focus on the problem. 'Has DI Powell been in touch?'

'He rang last night to see how you were.'

'Nothing since?'

My father shakes his head.

'So the police haven't found Jenny Crofter yet?'

'I have no idea.'

I'm still groggy, but reach into my drawer for a clean pair of jeans. 'Send Tris up, would you?'

He stares. 'But you're not dressed yet.'

'I will be in a few minutes,' I say. 'And I need to do my teeth. Count to, I don't know, fifty, then let him in.'

As soon as the door closes on my father, I pull my PJ top over my head and finish dressing. Jeans first. Then a black vest top, in need of a little ironing. It's the first thing to hand, so on it goes.

In the bathroom, I use the toilet, then brush my teeth and rinse out. I don't bother with earrings or make-up. I've been signed off work for a week, and besides, it's not going to be that sort of day. But I drag a brush through my hair, since this is Tris, glad that I took ten minutes to shower when I finally got home last night, and am just beginning to feel awake when he knocks at the door.

'Ellie?'

I throw open the bathroom door.

Tris is standing outside on the landing, looking haggard, his hands in his jeans pockets. I see the pain and loss and fear in his eyes, and understand what he's feeling because I'm feeling it too. Except that I've pushed it aside for now so I can deal with what's next. There just isn't time to break down. There will be time later, but I can't let any of that pain happen yet or it will rip me apart.

'Hannah,' I whisper.

He gives a jerk of his head. 'I still can't believe it.'

'How did it happen?'

'You don't know?'

'I was told she swam over to help me, and must have been caught by the riptide.'

'There was so much going on. We realised you had

311

disappeared, so we all swam back. Connor was there. Denzil too, at one point. Everyone was shouting and diving down to see if they could find you. Then the lifeguards came out on their dinghy. It was chaotic.' He shakes his head. 'I didn't notice she wasn't there until we followed the dinghy back to shore. Then Connor said, where's Hannah? And I couldn't even remember where I had last seen her.'

I touch his face. He's trembling. 'It wasn't your fault.'

'Whose then?'

'No one's fault. You know that.' I touch his forehead. 'You know that here.'

'She was such an experienced swimmer.'

'It happens even to the best. The currents round the north coast are treacherous. We all know that.'

'But Hannah ... ' His voice chokes. 'Why?'

I lean against his broad chest, listening to the muffled beat of his heart. I loved Hannah too. Fiercely and forever. But I'm thinking, *not now, not this.* We have to move on, and come back to Hannah later. I decide to let him have the moment though. It will comfort both of us.

He takes an unsteady breath. 'And I almost lost you too.'

'Except you didn't. I'm still here.'

He makes an abrupt noise under his breath, then seeks my mouth. I let him kiss me. My hands cup his face as we kiss. I feel stubble along his jaw, and imagine him pacing about outside the cottage since first light, probably.

'Did you come on the quad bike? With the trailer?'

'Yes.'

'Good, you can give me a lift.'

He draws back, frowning. 'Where to? Shouldn't you be resting?'

'I can rest later. There's something I need to do first.' I head into my room to grab a jacket, and see the long dark coat hanging over the open wardrobe door. 'Whose is this, do you know? I came home in it last night.'

He looks at it hesitantly. 'That's mine.'

'*Yours?*'

Again Tris hesitates. Then he nods, and says, 'Yeah, it used to belong to my dad. It's usually kept in the back of the car. When they brought you up the beach to the lifeguard's hut, you were shivering. I ran to the car for a blanket to wrap around you, and found that instead. Not that you needed a coat. The lifeguards had foil and blankets in the dinghy, and then the paramedics arrived. But I left it with you, just in case.'

'Thanks,' I say softly.

'You're welcome. It was the least I could do.' He takes the coat from me, running a hand over the black wool mix, shiny where the fabric is worn, and then lays it carefully over his arm. 'I'll take it home with me later.'

'No,' I say, holding out my hand for it, 'let me wear the coat, it will save you carrying it. I want to go home with you anyway.'

He hands the coat back blankly. 'You want to come to our place?'

'That okay?'

'Sure,' he agrees. 'I was just wondering why.'

Because I want to look round your farm to see if Jenny is being held there by your late father, who may have risen from the grave as a zombie killer.

'I want to talk to Connor. To thank him for helping to save my life yesterday.'

I shrug into the long dark coat, loving the way the sleeves are slightly too long for my arms, and it falls almost to my knees. A bit too heavy for a summer's day, but maybe I'm in need of a little warmth today. I think of Hannah, and hold back the brimming grief with difficulty.

'Come on,' I say huskily, 'let's go.'

We head down the stairs, and as we descend, I glance up at the closed door of Hannah's room. I can still smell her perfume on the air.

'Shit,' I mutter.

He turns at the bottom of the stairs. 'What?'

'My phone.' I make a face. 'I left it in my room. Go on, turn the bike round. I'll tell my dad I'm going out, and join you outside in a minute.'

He says nothing, but carries on outside while I run back upstairs.

To my surprise, I can't take the stairs two-at-a-time as usual, and find myself breathless at the top. But the doctor did say I might find my strength and lung capacity would take a few days to return to normal. I did almost drown, after all, and should probably still be in hospital.

My phone is still on the bedside cabinet. I check it. No messages. No emails. No notifications. That has to be a first. But Patricia did promise the school would leave me to recover until I was ready to come back.

I slide my phone into the deep pocket of his old coat, enjoying the padded comfort and faint scent of his body still lingering on the dark wool. Then my fingers close around something hard and cold at the bottom of the pocket.

Frowning, I pull the object out of his coat pocket. It's a school ID badge, precisely like my own, except this one is minus its blue-and-white striped lanyard.

Miss J. D. Crofter. Head of P.E. And there's her miniature photograph. Smiling up at me, next to a barcode.

It's sunny again, only a few soft clouds in the blue-chintz sky over the valley. A glorious day Hannah will never see. I take a deep breath, then pull the cottage door shut behind me. I've told my dad to go home to his caravan and get some sleep, that I don't know when I'll be back. I had to stop myself from saying, 'if I'll be back.' What happens now is something I have to do alone. To alert the police would be to risk Jenny's life, assuming she is still alive. This is my fault, has been my fault all along, and it's up to me alone to finish it.

I look up, try to enjoy the sun on my face; there's a

dark irony to the way the weather has blessed us recently. The coat feels heavy on my shoulders now, too hot for the sunshine. But I keep it on. Like a penance for not seeing the pattern clearly until this moment.

Tris is waiting for me on the quad bike, the engine running, his right hand keeping the throttle open. 'Hop in,' he says, nodding to the small trailer behind.

I climb in easily, and grip the sides of the trailer as he accelerates down the lane. Sheep wool is snagged on the metal surround, and it smells of animals. I'm jolted up and down as he turns down towards the ford, clipping the verge on the sharp bend, but cling on stubbornly.

When we get to the battered old sign for Hill Farm, I shout, 'Not here,' over the noise of the engine, and he shifts in his seat to stare back at me. 'Take me to the old mill.'

He stalls the engine, but does not restart it. 'The old mill?'

'Yes, I want to see it.'

'I don't think that's such a good idea.'

'Take me to the old mill, Tris,' I tell him. 'Or let me off here and I'll walk the rest of the way.'

He hesitates. 'Ellie, there's something I need to tell you.'

'Don't bother. It's over between us. It was over the minute Hannah died. Now take me to the old mill.'

He stares at me for a long moment, his eyes very dark. Then he faces front again. Pulls in the clutch, kicks down into first, and gets the bike going. We jolt off again like before. But the atmosphere between us has changed.

We head down past sloping fields in full sunlight. The grass in the lower meadows is ankle-high, dotted with patches of fresh green nettles and thistles, but will soon be cropped once the sheep are moved down from the hills. There is barely a breath of wind, and the mature oaks and beech trees that grow along the stream are hanging heavy with new foliage. It is an idyllic scene, and on any other day I would be enjoying it, admiring the beauty of the Cornish countryside.

But today is different.

I put my hand in the coat pocket, trace the rectangular plastic block of Jenny's ID badge. I think of her talking to me in the gym, whistle dangling from a ribbon in her hand, her ID badge hanging round her neck on its lanyard.

Why did she go running in the woods again?

Was Jenny lured there by someone she knew and trusted? Someone she never thought would hurt her? Maybe two someones.

But surely she would not have worn her ID while out running, even if she had gone to the woods straight after work; she would have removed it in the car, perhaps, and put it where? On the passenger seat of her Renault? In the glove box? Either of those seems likely.

So how did it find its way into Tris's pocket?

The track to the old mill is bumpy and overgrown with rough grass and brambles, but I can see where it has been used recently by a van, probably carrying a heavy load. The mud ruts are higher in places than others, fresh tyre marks carved out on the edge of some indents.

Tris stops the bike at one point and jumps down, leaving the engine running, to move aside a thick wire fence blocking the track. The roll of wire fencing delivered to the farm by Dick Laney, and that I helped him carry out of his van.

Tris climbs back into his seat, not looking at me, and kicks the quad bike into gear again.

Through thick undergrowth I catch a glimpse of high grey stone walls ahead. Then we round the bend in the track, the rhododendron bushes give way, and I see the whole house. It's a disused mill house with water course running alongside, a lichened stone channel diverting water from the nearby stream, and a broken-down wheel still attached to the far wall, the wood cracked and rotten, spokes missing.

Like many Cornish buildings of its age, the mill was built hard against the slopes behind, providing some shelter from the winds that tear down off the moors in winter. That did not help the house escape decades of neglect though. The slate roof is sagging in several places, slates missing, and the walls are overgrown with greenery, nature attempting to take it over. Two narrow, ivy-thick window frames without any glass left yawn into a gloomy interior.

And there's his dad's old van, rusting near the front entrance. I see him glance at it before stopping the bike a few feet away.

The silence is deafening after he turns off the engine. Tris gets off the bike and stands there, watching me climb out of the trailer.

'Dad had big plans to renovate this place,' he says, turning to look up at the old building through narrowed eyes. 'But he ran out of money. So it just sat here and rotted away. Like him.'

The place is perfect for a psycho killer's lair, ruined and remote. It even has its own witch's familiar. There's a shabby black crow perched on the roof as we approach. It cocks its head, watching us with one ironic eye, then caws loudly and flies away into the trees.

'You sure you want to do this, Ellie?' he asks, looking back at me with an expression I don't recognise.

'No, but I'm going to anyway.'

He takes a deep breath, rather like I did on leaving the cottage, then walks round to the front of the old mill and stands there a moment, scanning the ivy-covered walls and broken windows. There is not a sound.

He cups his hands to his mouth. 'Connor? Are you here, Connor?' He waits, listening to the silence that follows his call, then rubs a hand across his forehead, closing his eyes.

'Looks like we're alone,' I say.

He nods.

'What now?' I ask him.

Tris opens his eyes again, considers me in silence, then nods his head towards the back of the old mill.

'Come on,' he says heavily, 'you want to see it, I'll show you. But don't say I didn't give you a chance to turn back.'

His voice is bitter now too, like he hates me. Which perhaps he does. I remember us in bed together, and fight to block out that memory. The whole thing was an act, designed to draw me in. A honey trap, with him as the bait.

My head is a mess but I'm looking down on it from above, keeping a safe distance from the emotion. I let this man touch me, kiss me, even make love to me. I believed him, let him work his way into my heart. And he's a stone-cold killer.

'Lead on,' I say.

We walk round the back of the old mill. It's a large building and mostly in serious disrepair, though I can see where small efforts have been made to renovate parts of it. The traditional Cornish gardens are badly overgrown once we move away from the front of the house, all sprawling rhododendrons and palms and vast-leaved gunnera blocking out the sky, but there's a path through wild, tangled shrubbery that Tris takes, hesitantly, looking back at me occasionally as though he expects me to change my mind at any moment.

Past the mill wheel, hidden away in the shadowy green light of the overgrown shrubs, there's a crumbling flight of steps down to a trapdoor into a basement or cellar. The area must have flooded badly several times over the years. It's boggy, pitted with marshy tracts bulging with reeds, almost more water than dry land. But either Tris or Connor has been hard at work, keeping the stream at bay with the sacks of soil and sand dutifully delivered by Dick Laney.

Tris leads me along an uneven pathway made of damp sandbags, and pauses just before the open trapdoor, staring down at the dark space of the cellar.

'What's down there?' I demand.

He shakes his head.

'What, you don't know?' My voice is bitter, laced with contempt. I'm burningly angry, and it's showing. I pull the ID badge out of the coat pocket and hold it up, showing him. 'I suppose you don't know anything about this, either?'

He stares blankly. 'What is that?'

I fight the urge to choke him to death with Jenny's ID badge. 'You should get a bloody Oscar. This is your coat, Tris. So explain to me how my friend's ID badge got into your pocket, and use short words because I'm in a hurry.'

'I don't know what you're talking about.'

'Dick Laney didn't murder those two women, did he? Or abduct Jenny. I have no idea why he confessed, though I have my suspicions. But the killer is someone completely different, isn't he?' I face him, my heart beating a tattoo in my chest, hard and fast. 'Or perhaps I should say, *aren't they?*'

His eyes fix on mine as though trying to gauge how serious I am, how much of a threat. Then he turns abruptly away, saying, 'Okay, this has gone far enough. I'm taking you home.'

Coming behind him, I thrust my knee into the back of his, catching him in the vulnerable spot just below and to the outer side of his kneecap. Tris gives a gasp of pain, and his knee starts to fold. As he collapses, I dance away, grabbing his right arm, then use the momentum of his body as he crumples sideways to drag it behind his back, rendering him helpless.

The coat hampers me, which gives me a split-second of doubt. But he goes down anyway. It's a textbook move I've demonstrated hundreds of times on a mat in a gym. It's only now, kneeling above him, my knee set into his back, holding him immobilised by twisting his arm, that I realise how deeply satisfying it is.

Tris grunts, heaves, struggles against the painful joint lock, then gives it up, breathing with heavy resentment beneath me.

'Very wise of you,' I say into his ear, leaning forward over his back.

He says nothing.

I can smell his aftershave, spicy, lingering on the air. Below the razored cut of his hair, the skin on the back of his neck is tinged faintly red. I feel a crazy impulse to kiss his neck but resist it. Any show of weakness now could be fatal.

I'm tall for a woman at five foot eight. Muscular too, what some people might call an athletic build. But Tris is easily six foot one, maybe two, and broad with it, a big man. So he has at least thirteen stone on my nine stone, eleven pounds. Possibly more. And I've brought him down with a basic Jujutsu grapple and joint lock.

Suddenly there's a noise from somewhere inside the millhouse, and we both look round. A muffled echo, like a door banging shut. Or something heavy and metallic falling to the ground.

I look down at him, suddenly very still. 'Now what was that, would you say?'

'A rat,' he says harshly.

'Let's find out, shall we?'

'Ellie, don't.'

But I drag him up, and he does not resist, his face darkly flushed. With anger or shame, though?

'Come on,' I insist, 'time to go rat-catching.'

I push him forward, foot by shuffling foot, towards the yawning black hole of the trapdoor, careful to keep his right arm twisted hard behind his back. I don't intend to break it, but the pain and stress of that position should control him, keeping resistance to a minimum.

Once we're standing on the lip, I see a flight of steps leading down into darkness. There's a strange mechanical hum from below. Tris stiffens, listening to it too.

I nudge him forward until he's standing on the top step.

'You first, darling.'

CHAPTER THIRTY-SEVEN

I watch him take the first few steps gingerly down into darkness. I follow, still attached to him, so close I can feel his body warmth, keeping his arm twisted behind his back like an umbilical between us.

'Easy,' I warn him when he nearly slips. 'Watch your step. Take it slowly.'

We reach the bottom step and pause, letting our eyes adjust. There's just enough light filtering down from the trapdoor above to see a few feet in front of me. But further into the cellar there is nothing to see but shadow. I try to assess the size of the place. Maybe twenty-five feet wide, the ceiling about eight foot high, but how far back does this pitch darkness go? Impossible to tell without speaking to test the acoustics.

I smell oil and dust and mildew, just as you would expect in any cellar, any general utility room. But something more pungent on top of those. The stink of acrid sweat, of unwashed flesh. I half close my eyes, concentrating on my other senses. There's a low hum somewhere in the deepest shadows at the back. Something continuous and mechanical. The sound I heard from above.

'What is that?'

'I don't know,' he whispers.

A voice speaks from the shadowy interior of the cellar. 'It's a generator. It used to be powered by the wheel, now it runs on oil.'

A shaft of blinding light bounces off damp stone walls, feels its way towards the steps, seeking us out. Tris takes a hurried step back, colliding with me. I tighten my hold on his wrist and he stops, rigid.

Connor steps out of the darkness, a torch in his hand, wearing a grey hoody, the hood pulled up to partially obscure his face. 'Hello, Eleanor.' He shines the powerful torch beam directly into his brother's face, temporarily blinding us both. 'Did you bring her here, Tristan? That wasn't very clever, was it?'

'Connor,' he begins urgently, and I twist his arm higher up his back.

Tris yelps, then mutters, 'Fuck,' under his breath. I can hear the pain in his voice. He's not going anywhere, not while I have him trussed up like this.

'What do you need a generator for?' I demand. Like the torch beam, my voice bounces off stone, echoing everywhere, distorted. 'I thought the mill was disused.'

'Do the police know you're here?' Connor counters with a question of his own, interrogating me with that bloody torch beam. 'Are they on their way? Tris?'

His brother says nothing, standing passively in my grip now. I duck my head behind Tris's shoulder, blinking, knowing my eyes will retain the after-image of the light for several minutes if I let him dazzle me.

'Well, I don't suppose it matters much,' Connor says, surprisingly calm. 'Not now you're here at last.'

He switches off the torch and we are plunged into darkness again, this time all the more complete because our eyes have no longer adjusted to it. I stiffen, fearing an attack. But the dark shadow that is Connor merely turns and gropes his way along the wall, then another light comes on above us. It's an unshaded bulb, one of the old-fashioned types, hanging from the roof on a thin electric wire, and its illumination of the room is harsh but patchy.

When I stop blinking at the sudden light, I realise that I'm looking directly at Jenny.

She's hanging opposite us on the far wall, attached by her wrists and ankles to some kind of metal frame. The frame looks rusty, but strong enough to hold her weight. I remember Sarah McGellan in the shallow grave, the fading bruises on her wrists. I thought she must have been manacled somewhere before death. Presumably here.

'Oh my God, Jenny,' I say.

Jenny is pale but clearly still alive. There's silver tape across her mouth, though I don't imagine many people would ever come close enough to this wilderness to hear someone shouting for help. Above the tape, her wide eyes stare back at me in apparent horror. No doubt she thinks I'm about to become their next victim. And perhaps she's right, but I intend to get her out of this place first if I possibly can. One of us has to survive.

Her clothes have gone, but she is wearing knickers and bra, and, to my relief, does not appear to be marked or cut anywhere. Dawn Trevian and Sarah McGellan were both found naked, with signs of bruising, and I had worried that the brothers' tastes as torturers might be extreme. She's filthy and unkempt though, hair hanging greasily about her face. The place stinks of stale urine, and I can guess the reason. The stone floor is clean though and looks damp in places, like it's been washed down recently. There's a hose on a reel against the wall, attached to an ancient green-crusted tap that must connect to the water course outside.

I shudder to think why he would need a hose down here.

'Oh Tris,' I mutter, 'what have you done?'

Connor turns to put the torch away on a low table at the back, pushing down the hood of his grey hoody. I squint round the cellar while he's bending, and spot a narrow shelf near the metal frame, bracketed into the walls at an angle across a corner. It's dusty but holds a useful selection of tools: screwdriver, pliers, saw, hammer, a few glass jars of nails and screws. Connor the workman, with his tools. I can readily imagine him making this sturdy metal frame. To keep women like Sarah McGellan and Jenny Crofter prisoner.

When Connor turns back, he has a shotgun in his hand. I remember seeing it in the farmhouse, chained and locked up for safety. Now it's levelled towards me, and he's smiling.

'Welcome to the old mill,' he says, apparently without irony. 'It's good to have you here at last, Ellie. I've been waiting for you.'

I remember the face I saw in the dark waters when I was drowning, the man holding down the board, trying to prevent me from rising. The eyes that watched as I fought and struggled to be free. Not their dead father, as I'd thought at the time, my head muddled with lack of oxygen and vile, repressed memories. Not Pete Taylor, my mother's secret admirer. Maybe her lover too, I don't know.

No, it was his son, Connor Taylor, that tried to drown me in the ocean. And his dark figure I have been seeing at the foot of my bed, watching me while I sleep.

Shadow man, shadow man.

My grip on Tris's arm must have slackened, because suddenly he twists away and I am knocked sideways, taken off guard.

I am back on my feet in seconds and crouched, ready to fight. But Tris is shaking his head, staring at me as he backs towards Connor and the shotgun.

'Run, Ellie,' he says urgently. 'And don't stop running until you're clear of this place.'

Run, Ellie, run!

I stare at him, struck by his wording. Almost exactly the

same words my mother used eighteen years ago in Eastlyn Woods. I hear her voice in my head again. *Run, Ellie, run!* I ran that day, ran for my life, ran like the devil was after me. But then I could not run any further. Not without Mummy. So I came creeping back through the crowded trees, and saw the face of her killer.

I straighten out of my defensive crouch.

I refuse to run this time.

As I should have refused to run in the woods.

Though I probably would have died too if I had stayed with her. So perhaps Mum was right. She saved my life, and not just by telling me to run. She saved my life when she made me promise never to tell anyone about the man I saw in the woods that day, when she buried those memories deep in my subconscious. Because it was my silence that has kept me safe all these years.

'It was your father,' I say clearly, 'Pete Taylor, who killed my mother in Eastlyn Woods eighteen years ago.'

Tris makes a strangled noise, shaking his head.

Connor sidesteps his brother, pointing the shotgun directly towards me. 'Yes,' he agrees, looking almost relieved that he can finally admit the truth.

'Pete Taylor strangled her because she refused to keep seeing him and he couldn't bear it. Or maybe she wouldn't go to bed with him and was threatening to tell my dad that he wouldn't leave her alone. I suppose we'll never know. But it was Pete Taylor who killed her. I remember everything now. How he followed us into the woods, how he strangled my mother, the flash of his trainers as he ran away ...'

'I knew you would remember eventually,' Connor says. 'But when did you guess about me, and this place?'

'I only knew for sure today when I found Jenny's ID badge in the pocket of Tris's coat.' I put my hand in the pocket of the coat I'm still wearing, and produce her ID badge. 'See? He lent this to me yesterday after you tried to drown me.'

Tris turns to stare at his brother. 'That was you? You tried to drown her?'

Connor shrugs.

'I don't understand.' Tris sounds distraught. 'Why would you want to kill Ellie? I thought you wanted her for yourself, that you loved her.'

I stare at the two brothers, bewildered. 'What are you saying, Tris? That you had nothing to do with this?'

'Eleanor was always going to be my Number One,' Connor tells him coolly, ignoring me. 'I just didn't know how it was going to happen until yesterday when you told me she was surfing out at Widemouth Bay.' He looks across at me, his eyes intent. 'Drowning is so easily seen as an unfortunate accident. I wasn't happy about it though. I had wanted to talk to you first. Talk properly, like we're doing now. Only you were making too much of a nuisance of yourself. It wasn't fun anymore. I knew I had to end you, and quickly.'

'Okay,' I say, glancing at Tris in apology. I pause to adjust my thinking: Tris not guilty of anything; Connor guilty. It takes some doing. 'So you were never involved in any of this?'

'I tried to tell you,' Tris says flatly. 'You wouldn't listen.'

'It wasn't your coat.'

'Connor's,' he agrees. 'Though it used to belong to Dad.'

'Sorry, my mistake.' I stare at Connor, hating him more than ever. 'But why did you have to kill Hannah? And I want the truth. She was my friend.'

'I didn't want to. But she saw me. In the water. I couldn't let her live.' Connor looks regretful. 'A pity too. I liked Hannah.'

I dig my fingernails into my palms, resisting the urge to spring at him. The double-barrelled shotgun between us would make any attack suicidal. 'Hannah wasn't wearing her glasses in the water. She probably didn't even recognise you. Didn't have a clue who you were. You could have let her live.'

He stares, a flicker of emotion in his face.

I press him. 'You wanted to kill Dawn Trevian and Sarah McGellan though.'

'I didn't mean to kill Dawn. It was an accident.'

'So you panicked and tried to hide what you'd done by storing her body in a freezer.' I tilt my head, listen to the mechanical hum in the background. That was why he brought a generator down here, to run the freezer and the light. At last I begin to understand his twisted logic. 'But then you remembered how close it was to the anniversary of my mother's death. Tris and I were getting too friendly, weren't we? And you didn't like that. So you decided to play a little trick on me, see how fragile my mind really is.'

Connor nods slowly, his gaze on me. 'I enjoyed watching you suffer.'

'But why?' Tris exclaims, moving towards him.

The shotgun, which has been wavering, comes up at once, aimed at my heart. 'Get back, or I'll shoot her. You don't understand. How could you?'

I can see that Connor is beyond reason. Worried he will shoot one or both of us, I try to distract him, to keep him talking.

'You must have moved quickly to shift her body before the police arrived, then get home before Tris missed you.'

'It was a close call,' he agrees. 'I nearly made my first mistake then. Tris walked in while I was scraping mud off those white trainers, telling me he'd had a phone call and we had to get up to your place immediately. But he's so obsessed with you, he didn't even notice what I was doing.'

'And then you killed Sarah, I'm not sure why.' I frown. 'But you couldn't stand seeing me dancing with Tris in Newquay, so you spiked my drink, then stole my anklet. You left that note on Denzil's windscreen.'

Connor is unable to stop himself smiling. He's proud

of what he has done. 'Very good,' he agrees. 'That's pretty much how it happened.'

'But if I'm your Number One,' I say sharply, 'then why is Jenny here? If this is supposed to be a serial killer's countdown, you've fucked it up. You started your countdown at three. If I'm number one, what number is Jenny? Or isn't maths your strong point?'

Connor looks at me with distaste. 'Have I killed her yet? Have I? No, and for that very reason. Jenny was never part of my plan. But she had to be got rid of.'

'Why?'

'Because she called me on Friday. Mentioned the old mill. She knew the police were searching empty properties in the area and wanted to know if they had searched here. Well, I couldn't risk her going to the police with that suggestion. They might have found this cellar, checked it for DNA. Then I would have been screwed.' He shrugs. 'So I told her to meet me in the woods.'

'You think I never suspected you, Connor?' Tris demands angrily. 'I did, trust me. I just didn't want to believe it. But I couldn't keep my eyes closed forever. Your constant disappearances, the way you kept warning me off Ellie, and that photograph I found here … '

He is breathing heavily, staring at his brother. 'I mean, shit, Connor. Two women are dead. You've got Jenny tied up. What the fuck is *wrong* with you?'

'I could ask you the same question. How can you choose Eleanor Blackwood over me? Your own brother?'

Tris is beginning to look dangerous. His big hands clench into fists, and he starts towards his brother. 'You're not my *real* brother. You never have been.'

'Not another step.' Connor swivels, pointing the shotgun directly at his brother's stomach. 'She's not worth your life.'

Tris laughs wildly. 'You going to shoot me, Con?'

'I don't *want* to shoot you. I promised Dad I'd look after you when he was gone. And I've always tried to do that. Kept you at home on the farm where you couldn't get involved in the kind of drinks and drugs scene that messed up Denzil. Stopped you from making a fool of yourself over Eleanor when she came back from university.' He glances at me, a sudden hatred in his face, then looks back at his brother. 'But you know she'll never love you, right? Never marry you, never settle down, never have kids. She's too restless. She won't stay in Cornwall either. And I couldn't bear it if she took you away with her.'

'I'm going to break you in half, you sick bastard.'

'You don't want to do that. Anymore than I want to hurt you. Think what you're doing. It's not too late to be on my side.'

Tris lunges wildly for the shotgun. But Connor is ready for him. He turns, smashing the butt end down on his brother's forearm, then runs towards me, his face intent, straightening the barrel. He's planning to shoot me, I realise too late. Only Tris staggers after him and kicks him in the back of the knee, just as I did with him.

Connor overbalances, grimacing with pain, and drops the shotgun almost in front of me. 'Fuck.'

I run forward and kick the shotgun away as he tries reaching for it. It's heavy, heavier than I am expecting, but goes skidding away across the stone floor.

Connor turns. 'You bitch.'

I charge forward and tackle him, but he grabs at Tris, bring all three of us down at the same time. My head smacks into the stone floor, and for a few seconds I'm dazed, the world a dark blur. Beside me I feel Connor stir, groaning. Then he staggers to his feet and thuds across the cellar.

Tris bends hurriedly over me. 'Ellie? Are you okay?'

'My head ... ' I mutter.

'Leave her,' Connor shouts from across the room. He sounds half out of his mind. 'Get away from her.'

I look up through Tris's legs to see Connor standing directly under the naked light bulb. He's staring at us both with madness in his eyes. In his hands is the double-barrelled shotgun.

'Look, it's over,' Tris tells him flatly. 'You're never going to stop me leaving home. Not with that,' he says, gesturing to the shotgun, 'or with anymore of your lies. So you might as well put the gun down and let Jenny go.'

'No,' Connor says, shaking his head. 'I'm not going to prison. And you're not going to get the Blackwood girl.'

Someone has to stop him, I realise. He won't stop on his own. But even as I scramble up onto my knees, there's a deafening explosion. I hear Jenny jerk against the metal frame, the whole thing jangling, and for an awful moment I think Connor has shot her.

I look through the acrid drift of gunpowder filling the cellar. Tris is lying on the stone floor a few feet away, clutching his leg. There's blood already spreading out like a dark halo around him.

Connor levels the gun at me as I stumble towards Tris, but to my surprise he does not fire. If both barrels were loaded, he has one shot remaining. But perhaps he's hoping to hang me up beside Jenny and have some fun with me before he kills me.

Like Tris said, a sick bastard.

I kneel beside Tris. I expect to find his whole leg shattered, maybe even blown away. A shotgun makes a hell of a mess of a wild animal at close quarters, and I dread to think what it does to a human being. But it looks as though Tris has been lucky. Connor appears to have only nicked the front of his right thigh, both men standing far enough apart for the lead to have dispersed a little before impact.

I feel my way along the bloodied leg, and Tris watches me, speechless, clearly in agony. Miraculously, it looks like only one or more pieces of lead shot have passed through the front of his leg. But perhaps Connor unconsciously aimed to miss his brother, despite his worst intentions.

'I don't think the leg's broken. He needs an ambulance

though,' I say, 'or he's going to bleed out.'

'No ambulance,' Connor says raggedly, coming towards me with the shotgun. 'No police.'

Tris makes a rough noise under his breath. I meet his eyes, and see him shake his head. He doesn't want me to push Connor. He's white with shock though and needs medical attention urgently.

I stand up, blood smeared on my hands, and walk past Connor to where Jenny is bound to the wall. Close up, the structure she's attached to looks like part of an old metal bed frame. She stares at me, wide-eyed behind her gag, while I tidy the greasy strands of hair obscuring her face. 'Sorry, Jenny. This is going to hurt.'

'Get away from her,' Connor warns me.

I ignore him. He won't shoot me. Not yet. He hasn't told me everything yet, and it's obvious he needs to.

I unpeel one end of the silver tape and rip it off her face, apologising again. There's no way to do it gently. The skin beneath is red-raw. I guess she's had to suffer the tape being unpeeled numerous times since being brought here.

'Water, please,' she whispers.

There's a plastic water bottle on the floor next to the metal frame. I tilt the bottle to her lips, and wait while she takes a few greedy sips. Then I put it down and start unfastening the thick wire ties Connor has used to secure her to the frame.

'Thanks,' she says through dry lips.

'Can you walk?'

Free of her prison, Jenny takes a few wobbling steps, then sinks to the stone floor and shakes her head. 'N ... not yet,' she manages to say, and starts rubbing her legs and feet as though trying to get her circulation back. 'Pins and needles. Give me a few minutes.'

I glance at Connor. 'Take off that hoody. I need it.' He hesitates, then steps back ten paces and puts the gun down momentarily. He strips off the hoody and throws it across at me, then picks up the shotgun again. He's wearing a plain tee-shirt underneath. I stretch the hoody round the top of Tris's thigh as a tourniquet. 'He still needs an ambulance.'

Jenny says faintly, 'Put pressure on it, Eleanor. As much as you can. And keep the leg elevated.'

'I know.'

I spot a cardboard box about two foot high. Turning it on its side, I lift his ankle until his foot is resting on the box. He gives a muffled cry, yet somehow manages not to pass out.

'You have to let Jenny go,' I tell Connor.

'If I do that, she'll go straight to the nearest house and call the police.'

'That's a long walk and she's barefoot.'

'She's a PE teacher. She could probably jog to the village in ten minutes, barefoot or not.'

'She's also been chained to a cellar wall for the past five days. How fast do you think she's going to be moving? You could let her go now and still be out of here before the police arrive.'

'You think I'm afraid of that idiot Powell? He couldn't even work out why Dick Laney confessed to the killings. Shall I tell you why? Because I put a few doubts in the man's head about his son Jago. The police knew that the sacking had come from the garden centre; it was only a matter of time before they traced all the recent deliveries. So I dropped by, spoke to Dick, laid a trail of breadcrumbs that would have led him to his son as chief suspect ... and next thing, he's down the police station, claiming to have murdered those women.'

I hesitate, still pressing down on Tris's leg, trying to slow the bleeding. It's not looking good though. His skin is cold and clammy, and his eyes look unfocused.

'Now let me tell you what I think,' I say in response. 'I think you want to give me your reasons for killing those women before you're arrested. I think you want your voice to be heard.'

333

'Who says I'm not going to kill you too? Then myself?'

'I don't think you've got it in you to kill me. We've been friends too long.'

He bares his teeth. 'Friends? I don't think so.'

'Let her go and we'll talk.'

'We can talk with Jenny here. I like an audience.'

I ignore him, gambling on my instincts being right. 'Jenny,' I say clearly, 'can you manage to walk yet?'

Her voice is only a whisper. 'I think so.'

'Then go. He won't stop you.'

Jenny looks uncertainly at Connor, then pushes herself up into an ungainly crouch and grabs at the leg of the table to pull herself to a standing position. It takes her about ten unsteady steps to reach the stairs, then she begins to crawl up the slippery steps like a crab trying to climb out of a bucket.

It's painful to watch.

As I predicted, Connor makes no attempt to stop her, his gaze fixed on me instead. If he had intended to kill her, she would have been dead already.

'Okay, Jenny can go. But no tricks,' he warns me.

'She's almost naked. She needs a coat.'

'No,' he insists angrily.

I turn my hands up, palms empty. 'No tricks.' I shrug out of the coat, and hurry to the steps, avoiding Connor's furious hand as he tries to grab me. 'Just give me three seconds.'

I run up the steps, hand Jenny the coat, then rush back down, losing my footing and sliding the last three steps.

Straight into Connor's waiting arms.

'I told you, no tricks,' he snarls, pressing the cold double barrels of the shotgun against my temple, then thrusts me back towards Tris.

'I only gave her a coat. She's got no fucking clothes on, for God's sake.'

I check over my shoulder. Jenny has gone.

And she has my phone now.

GIRL NUMBER ONE

CHAPTER THIRTY-EIGHT

Connor pushes me away. 'Over there, bitch,' he says, pointing to the metal bed frame with his shotgun.

'You going to tie me up and play with me?' But I walk slowly backwards, hands in the air, as he threatens me with the shotgun. 'In front of Tris? That's not your kind of thing, is it?'

I'm not sure if there's a mobile signal right down here in the bottom of the valley, especially in such a heavily wooded area. But it was worth giving her the coat with her ID badge and my phone in the pocket. Now there's a possibility that Tris may make it out of here alive.

My own odds are less encouraging.

I stop walking, only halfway to his self-styled torture area, but Connor does not push the point. Maybe I'm right and he doesn't like having Tris as an audience for his sick games.

'I know your mum left when you were both kids,' I say, trying to defuse the tension in the air. 'That she walked out on you and your dad. Never came back. Not even for his funeral. But that's not entirely true,' I add gently. 'Is it, Connor?'

There's silence. Then Connor gives a soft little laugh.

'You hear that?' he asks, tilting his head.

There's a mild vibration that permeates everything in the cellar, like it's coming up through the floor.

'The freezer. Where you kept Dawn's body.'

He walks across to the shadows at the back of the room. 'That's right. It's a chest freezer. Good capacity.' Connor clicks on an overhead bulb. The white chest freezer looks surprisingly clean. He lifts the lid, then glances back over his shoulder at us, the shotgun cradled in the crook of his arm. 'Empty now, of course.'

'Did you keep both bodies in there?'

'It's not what you said before,' he tells me. 'Leaving them for you to find, that was an afterthought. I froze them because I didn't want them to decay before they could be properly buried. The dead are disgusting when they decay. Though,' he adds, frowning, 'they also take a very long time to defrost, I discovered.'

Tris looks horrified. 'For God's sake, Connor. Why would you do something so sick?'

'Well, you're adopted. How could you expect to understand? It was a family thing, only between me and Dad. Our little secret.' Connor drops the lid with a hollow thud. He snaps off the overhead light. 'You won't believe me but the first girl was a genuine accident. Dawn Trevian.'

'The dental assistant from Bodmin,' I say.

'I was feeling low after Dad had died, wishing I could speak to someone about it. I met her coming out of Bodmin Library one day. She recognised me and stopped to talk. Then she asked after Tris. That annoyed me.'

Tris whispers, 'You killed Dawn because she liked me?'

'I didn't mean to. I took her phone number, said I'd call her. But I still don't think I would have gone out with her, except for the date.'

'What date?' I ask.

'The anniversary of your mum's death. I overheard Tris talking to Hannah about it. How you two had to look out for Eleanor, make sure she got through the day okay.'

'And you didn't like that.'

'Her death didn't just affect you,' Connor points out coldly. 'People think it's all about the victim and her family. They forget there are always other people involved in a murder. Other *children*.'

I wait, silent.

'I rang Dawn the week before the anniversary,' he continues. 'Agreed to meet her after work. We never got to the pub though. It was obvious what she wanted.' He's sneering again. 'It was nearly dusk. I pulled up in the woods' car park. There was no one about. She was up for it, letting me touch her, kissing me back. Then suddenly Dawn started fighting. Said I was trying to rape her, that she was going to tell the police.'

'You lost your temper.'

'I just wanted her to stop screaming,' he says. 'It all happened so quickly. One minute she was clawing at my face, spitting at me like a cat, the next she was lying still and quiet on my lap. Like she'd fallen asleep.'

I feel a creeping sense of horror, imagining those large hands about my own throat.

'I sat there for ages. The body was getting cold. I didn't know what to do. I knew it would mean prison. Perhaps half my life behind bars.' He pauses. 'Then I remembered what Dad had shown me.'

'The perfect hiding place.'

'That's right.'

Tris is watching us, lying white and still. He says thinly, 'I ... I don't understand.'

'I'm really sorry,' I tell Tris gently, and hope my guesswork isn't wildly inaccurate. 'I think your dad killed your mum, then told everyone in the village that she'd left him for another man. Only she hadn't gone far. I think he kept her in a chest freezer at the farm.'

Tris stares at me in horror.

Connor interrupts his protests, talking to me. 'No, Dad

wasn't that much of a monster, he never meant to leave her in the freezer. We buried her together after he showed me her body. Up there in the rose garden. I can show you the exact spot where we buried her if you like.'

Tris looks like he's going to be sick. There's agony and disbelief in every word. 'But why? Why would he kill Mum?'

'Because he killed Angela Blackwood first,' Connor tells him.

My body goes ice-cold at his words. It is exactly as I suspected. But hearing those words out loud is very different from considering them in the dark spaces of my head.

But what he says next is even more sickening.

'She was going to tell her husband he tried to rape her. Just like Dawn did with me. And if Dad had kept quiet about what he'd done, none of this would have happened. But you know how he liked his beer.'

'He got drunk and admitted to his wife what he'd done,' I whisper.

Connor nods. 'It was awful. Mum stood up to him for once. She said he had to go to the police, confess everything. He strangled her in the kitchen. A few days before my fourteenth birthday.'

Tris is shaking his head. 'But Dad said … He told us she ran off with another man.'

'To protect you, Tris.'

'But he told you the truth.'

'I was older, and his own son. Not adopted like you. He took me out to the garage in the middle of the night, about six months after she'd vanished. He was very drunk. There was a chest freezer in the garage, just like this one. Mum was inside, frozen solid. Her eyelashes were stuck together with frost. I could still see the black mascara on them. He said we had to bury her. Together. We took spades, dug a hole under the rose bushes here at the old mill, and put her in.' He pauses, remembering. 'I said a prayer for her. Then we closed the hole and replanted the roses over her body.'

I remember the butterflies under glass that I saw in their house. The stuffed dead animals, staring back at me with glass eyes. Pete Taylor liked to kill. But he also liked to preserve his trophies.

In the silence that follows, I ask quietly, 'Is that when he told you about killing my mum?'

Connor looks round at me, his eyes hostile. 'Your mum led him on, then said she was going to tell her husband about him. Dad decided to teach her a lesson she wouldn't forget, to scare her into keeping quiet. He followed her into the woods when she was out walking with you. And crept up from behind.'

For a second I'm right back there in the dappled sunshine, smelling the spring flowers, hearing the crow in the tree overhead ...

'He only intended to play-strangle your mum. Show her would might happen if she made him *really* angry.'

'It doesn't take much, you know. The slightest pressure on the windpipe, and they start to choke, then lose consciousness. The easiest thing in the world.'

I make a noise under my breath, then put a hand to my eyes. My fingers come away wet. It feels like a wound has opened in my heart and blood is gushing out of it. The truth is so raw and cruel, I don't know how I'm going to survive it.

Tris is silent too, dark eyes wide and luminous under the bare bulb. He looks stunned. Like he'll never recover either.

Connor touches the lid of the freezer. 'So I bought a new chest freezer and put Dawn inside, like Dad did with Mum, and kept it down here where Tris would never find it. I thought I was safe. That it was over. Then I met Sarah McGellan one night in Newquay.' His voice becomes bitter. 'I liked Sarah. I brought her back here to show her the house. Only she didn't want to stay, said it was too creepy. When I refused to take her home, she got hysterical.'

'So you hit her.'

He nods. 'After that, I knew I couldn't let her go. I couldn't risk the police coming here. They would have searched the place, found Dawn's body in the freezer.'

I look at the metal frame on the wall where Jenny had been restrained, and remember the marks on Sarah's wrists.

'Tying her up felt easier for you. It meant you didn't have to kill her immediately.'

'There was an old metal bedstead up in the mill. I cut it down to size, fixed it to the wall there,' he agrees. 'Sarah was smart, she understood what I was going through. She had a nice smile too. I liked having her around. I knew I'd have to kill her eventually, of course. But I wanted to make her death significant. That's when I came up with the plan.'

'Three, two, one,' I whisper.

'Exactly,' he says. 'A simple countdown. First Dawn Trevian. Then Sarah McGellan. And then you, Eleanor Blackwood. My number one.'

I look at Connor, hating him. 'And the shadow man?'

'What?'

'You used to watch me from a distance. Come into my room while I was sleeping. Steal things.'

'Even when I was a boy,' he admits. 'I was obsessed with you. I hated that everyone was so fucking sorry for you. Poor little Ellie Blackwood. Nobody cared about me and Tris, yet our mum had been murdered too. And we were still living with the murderer.'

Tris says, 'He was sick, Connor. Just like you.'

I can see Connor getting angry again, and try to divert his attention. 'How ... how did you do it? Get Dawn down to the woods, I mean?'

'I covered the inside of dad's van with plastic sheeting, put Dawn in the back. I parked near the bridge, out of sight of the road. Then carried Dawn over my shoulder through the stream.'

'And positioned her exactly where my mum died.'

He nods.

'And the number three?'

'There was a black permanent marker in the glove box.'

I listen to the silence above us and wonder how long it will take for the police to arrive. Surely Jenny must have managed to call them by now? By the look of his face, Tris can't hang on much longer.

'But where did you get the forestry sign for the diversion? That looked so realistic.'

'They stack the signs behind the toilets in the car park. I changed the wording, then set it up it where the path divides. That was the tricky bit. You might have ignored the sign and stayed on the upper paths. Or someone else might have come along first.'

'But why move Dawn's body afterwards? That's the part I don't understand. Why not leave her for the police to find?'

'What, and have you treated like a celebrity again?' His voice grows cold. 'Poor Eleanor, her mum was strangled right in front of her, and now she's found *another* dead woman in the woods.'

'And Sarah?'

'I didn't want Sarah to end up frozen for months like my mum. She deserved better. I washed her body to remove any traces of my DNA before taking it to the cemetery though. I needed to make sure there was nothing to link her death to me.'

I look at my enemy, seeing Connor properly for the first time. He's a killer, like his father before him. Maybe he was driven insane by the horror he witnessed. But my mum was strangled in front of me, and I didn't grow up to be a murderer.

I can remember the day she died now. I remember everything. What Connor has told me is slowly piecing together those odd gaps in my knowledge that had always felt so huge and gaping that they could never be filled. But how small the truth feels now. So small and hard, I could put it in my pocket.

'I'll make it easy,' he promises, advancing. 'I don't want to blow a hole in you with this bloody great gun. That would be too ugly. A little pinch round the throat, and it will be like falling asleep. I won't make it painful like it was for our mothers.'

'Kill me, but let her go.' Tris's voice is a mere thread of sound. 'You have to let her go, Connor. She's ... done nothing ... to you.'

'Done nothing?'

Connor swings violently back towards him, tightening his grip on the shotgun. I can see the last shreds of reason slipping away as he glares down at his brother.

'You haven't listened to a single word I've said. It was because of that whore Angela Blackwood that Mum had to die. It was because of Ellie that you and I started drifting apart. All our lives, she got the love, the attention, the pity. What did we get for losing our mother? Nothing, bloody nothing. She has to be made to suffer. Can't you see that?' His face twists in anguish. 'If you're not on my side, Tris, then you're against me.'

I remember the shelf across the alcove near the metal bed frame. The tools I saw there. A workman's tools.

'I'm your brother. Have you forgotten that?'

'You were never my brother. That's obvious to me now. You don't have the same tainted blood. That's obvious to me now.'

'Connor, for pity's sake ... '

'Sorry, Tristan.'

Connor takes deliberate aim at his brother's head. He's planning to blow his brains out, I realise. Destroy the last thing in his life that's still good. And then he'll turn the gun on me.

'You had your chance. You chose Eleanor Blackwood

over me.' His voice cracks. 'You've broken my heart. This is the hardest thing I'll ever ...'

He has no chance to finish.

I hoist the long-handled hammer above my head in a two-handed grasp, and smash it down across the base of Connor's skull as hard as I can.

There's a nauseating crack as metal meets bone, and metal wins.

Connor crumples without a sound, the shotgun clattering across the stone floor. I drop the hammer, which is stained with blood, and crouch down, fumbling for the pulse at his neck.

There isn't one.

Cars are approaching along the road from the village. Two or three vehicles, by my guess, coming as fast as it's possible to drive on these narrow Cornish lanes. I hear sirens too, that eerie wail bouncing through the trees.

I look down at Tris, but his eyes have closed.

'Hang on, Tris,' I tell him urgently, and then kneel, lifting his head into my lap. I remember how he ran for a coat to wrap around me after I nearly drowned at Widemouth. Connor's coat, as it turns out, not his as I thought. Now it's my turn to keep him alive until help arrives. 'You need to hang on. The police have arrived. You'll be in hospital soon. We're going to get you fixed up, do you hear me?'

The cars screech to a halt a short distance away, probably outside the front of the old mill. I hear car doors slam, the sound of voices.

The police, at last.

'I'm sorry I thought it was you,' I whisper.

Tris does not stir. His head falls back into my lap, his mouth slack, one hand trailing in his own blood.

EPILOGUE

The church service is quiet and subdued, only a few locals turning out for the funeral. I asked DI Powell to discourage journalists from attending, promising them a press statement tomorrow if they stay clear. And it seems they have listened to his warning, because I don't see a single photographer at the church. After the simple ceremony, the coffin is driven slowly up the hill in the undertaker's black hearse, followed by the congregation on foot, with the Reverend Clemo at their head in his black robe.

It's a windy morning after several days of rain and heavy cloud over the moors, but at least the sun is shining now. Up ahead, the wind whips at the vicar's robes, flapping them about his ankles; I catch flashes of the green wellington boots he's wearing underneath.

DI Powell is there to pay his respects. He shakes hands with me at the gate, and we talk for a few minutes before walking up to the grave. The inspector is wearing a black suit with black tie, very smart, very sombre.

'I pushed you too hard during the investigation,' he admits. 'I should have been more understanding. Listened to your instincts more.'

'You wanted a result.'

'I'm just sorry about the outcome. Not our finest hour, I'm afraid.'

I know he's talking about the first investigation too, when the police failed to find my mother's killer. But there was never any evidence to link Connor's dad to her murder. And I had been programmed never to mention his name, so deeply and traumatically that it took me eighteen years even to remember the details of that day.

DI Powell sees my father coming, nods to me again, then continues on ahead.

'Here, you'll want these.' Dad hands me the bouquet of long-stemmed white lilies we've brought to lay on the headstone. He studies my face, then bends to kiss me on the forehead. 'You okay, love? You look pale. You don't have to do this if you don't want to.'

'I'm fine.'

'I still wish they hadn't agreed to let Connor Taylor's service take place up at the crematorium. His ashes shouldn't be buried locally. Not after what he did.'

'He's dead. What does it matter?'

'It matters because he strangled two women and shot his brother. Kidnapped Jenny Crofter, did God knows what to the poor woman. He nearly killed you too.'

'I know.' I pat his arm.

I am feeling quite emotional, I realise. The lilies are all open, the perfume from their white throats so sweet and intense, it makes me almost light-headed.

Jenny appears from behind us in a floral dress and pumps for once instead of her tracksuit. The long sleeves carefully hide any marks still lingering from her imprisonment. I am surprised to see her, considering what she went through. But I guess she is trying to be supportive.

She kisses me on the cheek. 'Come on, everyone's waiting for us. You first, Eleanor.'

Reverend Clemo actually smiles at me as I walk up to the burial plot, flanked by Jenny and my dad, a bouquet of lilies fragrant in my arms. Unlikely as it seems, he appears to have forgiven me for bringing so much unrest to his parish.

But then, so much has happened since that day at the mill. Soon after the police arrived and set up camp there, a fluttering crisscross of Police Do Not Cross tapes were wound between the tree trunks, sealing off the whole area from the public. The buildings were thoroughly searched and items tagged and removed as evidence. Then, with the vicar in solemn attendance, Mrs Beverley Taylor's body was exhumed from the overgrown rose garden.

Acknowledged at last as a murder victim, just like my own mother, Mrs Taylor was given a full postmortem, kept at the morgue while the investigation was still ongoing, and finally released for burial once the police had closed the case.

We buried Hannah last week. It was traumatic. I don't think I will ever get over the loss of my best friend, nor the guilt I feel over the manner of her death. Her absence in my life is an aching space that no one else can never fill.

Tris is waiting for us at the graveside, leaning on crutches, his leg still bandaged. He only recently left hospital; thankfully the lead shot that grazed his thigh was not as serious as the loss of blood he had suffered. An emergency transfusion saved his life.

There's a sheet of handwritten paper, much creased, clenched in his fist. He wants to say a few words as his mother's coffin is lowered into the grave.

Wordlessly, I reach out and touch his hand. I know what it's like to stand at a grave and mourn a mother.

Hill Farm will be sold, he has told me. And the old mill too. 'Too many bad memories,' Tris told me when I showed surprise at this decision. 'I'll use the proceeds to pay my way through university. Better late than never. Then I'll get a job somewhere far away from here. London, perhaps.'

I hope he won't go away forever.

Reverend Clemo begins to speak. Tris turns his gaze towards the vicar, straining to hear every word. There's desolation in his face. We watch in silence as his mother's coffin is lowered slowly and solemnly into the grave.

Everyone falls silent, listening as Tris reads from his sheet of paper. His voice is strong, carrying right across the village cemetery in the sunshine.

He stumbles over his brother's name, but ends more firmly, 'If you can hear me, Mum, I'm sorry you lay undiscovered for so long. I love you and I wish I'd known you better. God bless.'

Afterwards, as the mourners slowly depart down the slope, I tell Dad I'll meet him at The Green Man, where a few of us are gathering for drinks and a buffet lunch. Tris is still at the graveside on his crutches, hunched over, staring down at the earth.

'Tris.'

When he turns, I lean forward and kiss him on the lips, taking my time. He tastes great. 'I'm glad you've decided to go to university,' I tell him. 'But I'll miss you, you know.'

'Come with me, then.'

'I like my job too much. And I'm still settling into it.' I meet his intense gaze. 'Maybe later.'

'I love you,' he says. 'Going away won't make any difference to that.'

'You say that now, but – '

'Tell me not to go, and I won't. I could get a job here.' His gaze holds mine, and I see no bitterness in it. We've never spoken about Connor's death, and we probably never will. What is there to say, after all? 'Haunt your every move.'

'I want you to be free, Tris, and to get out from under the shadow of this place.' I turn my face into the sun, enjoying its warmth. It reminds me that I am alive, that I survived. 'Besides, we're both still coming to terms with what's happened. It's like any kind of shock. We need plenty of space around us or we'll end up doing things wrong, suffocating each other.'

Tristan nods.

'We can stay in touch.' I hold up my mobile. 'Being apart doesn't have to mean we never speak to each other again.'

He looks at me through long lashes. 'True.'

'We really should get to the pub. They'll be waiting for you.' I hesitate, my voice becoming husky. 'Though you could always come back to my place afterwards. Would you like that?'

Tris smiles slowly. 'I would.'

ABOUT THE AUTHOR

Born in Essex, the middle daughter of romance legend Charlotte Lamb, Jane Holland is a poet, novelist and critic who has published six books of poetry and nearly thirty novels to date, plus numerous novellas and short stories. As a novelist, she writes as Jane Holland, Victoria Lamb, Elizabeth Moss and Beth Good.

She currently lives in the South-West of England with her husband and young family. A keen home schooler, she educates her children during the day and writes in the evenings. When she's not messing about on social media.

You can find her on Twitter as @janeholland1

Printed in Poland
by Amazon Fulfillment
Poland Sp. z o.o., Wrocław